CW01496766

IT'S ALL GREEK TO ME

HAVE YOU EVER WONDERED HOW BOOKS ARE MADE?

UCLan Publishing is an award-winning independent publisher. Based at The University of Central Lancashire, this Preston-based publisher teaches MA Publishing students how to become industry professionals using the content and resources from its business; students are included at every stage of the publishing process and credited for the work that they contribute.

The business doesn't just help publishing students though. UCLan Publishing has supported the employability and real-life work skills for the University's Illustration, Acting, Translation, Animation, Photography, Film & TV students and many more. This is the beauty of books and stories; they fuel many other creative industries! The MA Publishing students are able to get involved from day one with the business and they acquire a behind-the-scenes experience of what it is like to work for a such a reputable independent.

The MA course was awarded a Times Higher Award (2018) for Innovation in the Arts and the business, UCLan Publishing, was awarded Best Newcomer at the Independent Publishing Guild (2019) for the ethos of teaching publishing using a commercial publishing house. As the business continues to grow, so too does the student experience upon entering this dynamic Master's course.

www.uclanpublishing.com
www.uclanpublishing.com/courses/
uclanpublishing@uclan.ac.uk

*To Paul, for believing I could from the very beginning,
when I didn't believe it myself.*

It's All Greek to Me is a uclanpublishing book

First published in Great Britain in 2025 by
uclanpublishing
University of Central Lancashire
Preston, PR1 2HE, UK

Text copyright © Andrea Christodoulou, 2025
Cover illustrations copyright © istock.com
Cover design by Holly Macdonald

978-1-916747-51-7

1 3 5 7 9 10 8 6 4 2

The right of Andrea Christodoulou to be identified as the author
of this work has been asserted in accordance with the
Copyright, Designs and Patents Act 1988.

All rights reserved. No part of this publication may be reproduced,
stored in a retrieval system, or transmitted in any form or by any means,
electronic, mechanical, photocopying, recording or otherwise;
or be used to train any AI technologies without the prior permission
of the publishers. UCLan Publishing expressly reserves this work from
the text and data mining exception subject to EU law.

Set in Kingfisher by Becky Chilcott.

A CIP catalogue record for this book is available from the British Library.

Printed and bound in Great Britain by Clays Ltd, Elcograf S.p.A.

Andrea Christodoulou

IT'S ALL GREEK TO ME

uclanpublishing

PART ONE

My life, the Greek
tragedy . . .

Ismeena Eliades' New Year's Life Resolutions

1. Cut down on the booze. It either makes me cry like a banshee or inhibits my ability to see (or both), resulting in some questionable end-of-the-night snog choices.

2. Go to Greek Church with Mum more so she stops renouncing the Devil every time she sees me due to my 'unorthodox' lifestyle.

3. Learn how to make moussaka (or anything else from the recipe book of my ancestors).

4. Confess to Mum and Dad that I failed my corporate solicitor exams and have been demoted to administration assistant ever since. Which leads me to . . .

5. Overcome my baker's block and have another go at turning it into a viable business.

6. Pretend to shack up with Anthony so Mum thinks I'm settled with a Good Greek Boy.

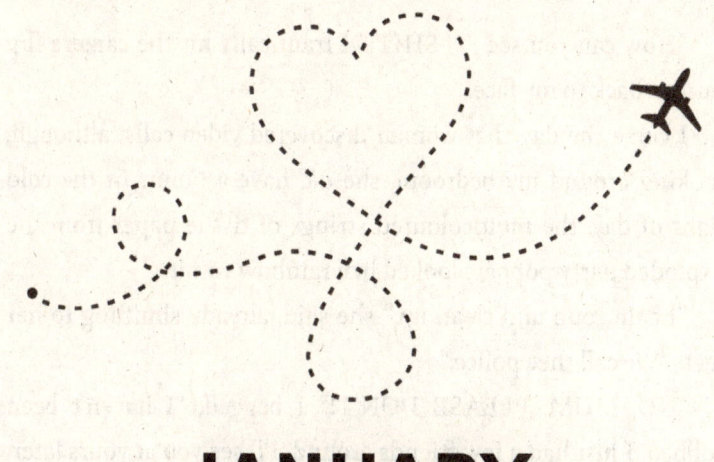

JANUARY

NEW YEAR'S DAY. A DAY TO REFLECT FONDLY ON THE achievements of the last year, and to start making some achievable resolutions for the year ahead. Or, in my case, reflecting on the fact that another year of pissing away my thirties has passed, and my only achievement: reaching a PB on my 'Words with Friends' record.

Then there's the gobshite of a hangover. You know the one, where you make a genuine pledge never to drink again, only to find yourself with a glass of pinot in your hand days later.

To make matters even worse, Mum FaceTimed me the second I peeled my weary eyes open. I swear the woman has bugged the flat so she can purposefully ring me at *the* worst times.

"*O thee mou*, Isme, what has happen to thee flat? You bin robbed?"

"How can you see . . . SHIT!" I frantically hit the camera flip button back to my face.

I curse the day that woman discovered video calls, although, looking around my bedroom, she *did* have a point. In the cold light of day, the multicoloured strings of tissue paper from the exploded party poppers looked like rainbow vomit.

"I cam roun and clean up," she said, already shuffling to her feet. "We call thee police."

"NO, MUM, PLEASE DON'T!" I begged. "I haven't been robbed. I just had a few friends around. I'll see you at yours later. OK?"

"But, Isme, I—"

I hit 'end call' before she caught sight of any other post-party debris, including the life-size cardboard cutout of Bradley Walsh in the corner of the living room. I still wasn't *entirely* sure how he'd ended up there, but I couldn't deny that it was quite nice having a man around the place. Especially one that wouldn't judge me when, five minutes after the call ended, I unashamedly scoffed down four pieces of stone-cold pizza.

*

My ultimate aid to post New Year's Eve recovery is going to Mum's and stuffing my face with as many home-cooked Greek delights as my stomach can handle. She always makes enough food to feed a small country and insists no one goes home until it's all eaten.

It seems that most Greek women (me aside) are born with the ability to cook. I imagine they pop out of the womb, recipe book in one hand, potato peeler in the other, whilst I seemed to have been born with a microwave ready meal and a bottle of pinot.

Mum and Dad live in a four-bedroom semi-detached house in the leafy suburbs of South Liverpool, about a twenty-minute drive from my flat; not too close where Mum can come knocking round whenever she pleases, but not too far away for me to call round unannounced when I can't be bothered 'cooking' i.e. throwing a pizza in the oven.

The comforting smell of Mum's *afelia* – a pork-based Greek dish made with red wine and coriander – greeted me as I opened the door, making my stomach growl like an animal in the wild.

"Isme, *agape mou*, how is your love life?" asked Mum before my coat was off. She was frantically peeling a mound of potatoes on the kitchen counter, which resembled a pyramid of past-their-best Ferrero Rocher.

I took a seat on one of the dining room chairs and observed in amazement the sheer speed at which she worked.

Her short black hair was tied back, although some rogue pieces had escaped and were sticking to her perspiring face. She was wearing a cooking apron, with a picture of the Greek Cypriot flag on and the phrase, 'Everything's better with a little feta', that was a little snug around the chest and waist area.

I inherited Mum's curves, along with some of Dad's six-foot height, giving it more room to spread out.

"You know our girl is too busy with all those big important cases in the city to have time for a fella," said Dad, appearing from the living room and planting a kiss on my cheek.

I shifted awkwardly in my seat.

"What abou Carlos?" Mum continued, ignoring Dad's attempt to get me off the hook. "He is a Good Greek Boy, and his family very wealthy!" She emphasised the wealthy bit by rubbing her thumb and two forefingers together.

I rolled my eyes. Carlos and his family owned a chain of fish and chip shops and were part of the same Greek community here in Liverpool. Mum would love nothing more than to see me married off to Carlos, despite the fact he reeks of chip fat and dresses like a 1970s pimp.

"I jus wan you to be more like your sista," said Mum with a sigh, wiping her forehead with the back of her hand.

"What, demented?"

Right on cue, Maria burst into the kitchen with her three-year-old twins, Theo and Tomaso, in tow, who seemed to be riding the crest of a major sugar wave, chasing each other round the kitchen, almost knocking Mum's potato pyramid over in the process.

If you're not sure whether you're ready to have kids, just mind the twins for the afternoon and you'll have your answer. I only have to spend five minutes with them and my ovaries shrivel up.

I love them really, but they're just at that age where their energy levels don't seem to deplete, no matter how long you leave them to run riot around the park or how many games of 'hide the pound' you play with them (SPOILER ALERT – there is no pound).

"Will you two calm down!" shouted Maria in her most authoritative voice, which even made me cower a bit, but the twins carried on regardless.

Maria took a seat on one of the dining room chairs, stretching out her tired legs to reveal yellow stained toenails peeking out of her sandals that looked like something out of biblical times.

"Wow, Maria. When did they last see any nail varnish? Also, you do know it's winter and you're at risk of frost bite?"

"It's called having three-year-old twins and a lazy-arse husband, Isme," she retorted. "If you must know, we were in a rush and these were the only things I could find."

"Where did you look, 100 years B.C?"

"Oh piss off, you." She ran her fingers through her dishevelled hair, which looked like it hadn't seen a brush in weeks, while dark circles sat underneath her eyes.

Growing up, I had always looked up to Maria, the Greek goddess with the shiny brown hair and deep olive skin. I had train-track braces, an untamed fringe and a freckly face, with the kids at school aptly changing my surname from Eliades to Freckiades – a nickname which unfortunately stuck throughout my academic years.

These days, however, Maria was more Greek economic crisis than Greek goddess, while I . . . well, I mean, I hadn't exactly transformed into Kendall Jenner, but I was an improved version of my younger self.

The moral of the story here is, don't miss your pill and have a one-night stand with someone you just met at a family wedding. It could result in tiredness, twins and neglected feet.

*

Back at the flat, I (begrudgingly) decided to tidy up after the party to get it back to a more livable and less crack-den standard.

Anthony called in just as I'd finished to fill me in on my memory gaps from the party.

"You know you came on to me, Freckiades?"

We were laying on either side of my too-large black leather corner sofa. I failed to check the size before I bought it, so it dominated most of the space in my tiny living room, leaving me with just enough room for a small black shaggy rug and glass coffee table.

"Pah! As if!" I replied in disgust, hitting him with a cushion. "I know I was drunk, like, but I still had my wits about me . . . I think."

I'd known Anthony most of my life, our families having lived in the same road since moving over to the UK from Cyprus after the Greek Cypriot diaspora, or, as Mum calls it, the 'invasion of the Turkish *bastardos*.'

Whilst he's not bad-looking, with his dark hair, olive skin and chestnut-brown eyes, I couldn't go there. When you've known someone for that long they almost feel like family, and the borderline between exogamy and incest becomes a little foggy. Also, the lad had seen me piss my knickers. Granted, I was four, but it hardly set the foundations for a healthy, lustrous relationship.

"Nah, you were fairly well-behaved." I breathed a sigh of relief. "Apart from when you tried to convince us to move the sofa out of the living room so we could do a full *sirtaki*," he added.

I buried my crimson face in my hands.

I'm not known for my dancing skills, but I often get these mad ideas in my head about my own abilities. Take our last office

Christmas party, where I harassed the DJ to play 'Cry of the Celts', convinced that I could re-enact the Stavros Flatley dance, and everyone would follow my lead like the last scene from *Dirty Dancing*. I envisaged them all coming up to me afterwards, like, "Where did you learn to dance like that?" and I'd for ever be known as the cool Administration Assistant who lit the dancefloor alight at Mulligan Solicitor's best Christmas party EVER.

It's fair to say though, that is *not* how it turned out. I ended up looking like I'd been tasered, and someone scurried off the dancefloor to get the first-aid kit.

*

I'd only been off work ten days, but waking up to the familiar (and dreaded) jingle of my alarm clock, and realising that all the fun of the Christmas and New Year festivities were over, was like a slap in the face with a stale pitta bread.

I stumbled round the flat like an extra from *The Walking Dead*, trying to get ready, my mind swirling with any plausible excuses not to go in and struggling to find suitable clothes. I opted for a plain black baggy tunic dress and black tights that I only ever wear at funerals.

Mulligan's is a small solicitors and law firm based in an old three-storey building near the centre of Liverpool's commercial district, and where I've 'worked' (I use the term loosely) as an administration assistant for the last two years. This basically involves anything from taking minutes at partner-and-client meetings to photocopying and filing endless mounds of legal papers.

As I stepped out of the rickety lift and shuffled my way through the office, mumbling the odd 'morning' here and there, I thought I heard sniggering and had to check I hadn't tucked my dress into my tights (again). But then I heard someone playing the Stavros Flatley video from YouTube, and the penny dropped.

*

One of the (few) perks of working at Mulligan's solicitors was that every other Friday, they put some money behind the bar at our local pub, The Pig's Ear – a small, traditional pub just a stone's throw from the office, and the general jump-off for after-work drinks for most firms in the area, largely because you can get a pint and bowl of chips for a fiver. You just have to overlook the fact that it smells of bleach and sweaty feet. Friday night is also karaoke night, so we all inevitably ended up singing our arses off by the end of the night.

I hadn't planned on going last night, and instead was looking forward to a cosy night in with Christian Grey and a bottle of blush. But when Zara heard, she told me to get my Greek arse to the pub or she was going to tell everyone I waxed my muzzy. Cue me breaking *most* of my New Year's resolutions by 11 p.m.

I arrived a little later than everyone else due to a hold up at the cash machine – the hold up being that I didn't have any cash in my bank *to* withdraw, so it would be straight home once the bar tab ran dry.

I would have asked Zara for some cash, but she was a bit funny about lending me money, ever since I forgot to give her a fiver back that she put in for me for someone's birthday collection.

I wouldn't mind but she was part of one of the most affluent families in the Greek community, her mum and dad both being retired lawyers who previously owned Mulligan's, or Baros & Co. as it was previously called, before they sold out to the Mulligan family. Word on the street was it was a seven-figure deal.

"Finally!" said Zara when I arrived, shoving a glass of white wine into my hands. "I am sooooo BORED!" She'd been cornered by a few from residential conveyancing, who stared down into their wine glasses gloomily. Granted, they had about as much charisma as a dead fish, but that still didn't warrant Zara's *Mean Girls* outburst.

Zara looked every inch the stylish city girl, in her grey fitted Karen Millen dress, black Louboutin stilettos and French twist hairstyle, that wasn't a strand out of place despite it being the end of the working day. Quite a contrast to me, looking like I'd had a fight with a bush with my frazzled hair, and white Primark shirt that was about as creased as Mick Jagger's face.

"Where's all your commercial law buddies?" I asked, as Zara ushered me away in the direction of the bar.

"Still at the office, the gang of bores."

The bar was already heaving with office workers, who were loosening their ties and downing their glasses of prosecco and bottles of beer to commemorate the end of the working week. The music coming from the sound system could hardly be heard over the noise of chatter, beer bottles being opened and chest-rattling guffaws.

We found two empty seats at the bar, and it wasn't long before

Luke from criminal law came sliding over, along with a couple of his cronies. They looked like a corporate version of the T-Birds, in their matching black suits and slicked back hair, but way less cool (and fit). I didn't recognise one of them so he couldn't have worked at Mulligan's long, although with his baby face he could have passed for Luke's son.

"Hi, gorgeous," said Luke, sliding in between us and leaning against the bar, facing Zara. I may as well have had a sign on my head that said 'Inferior acquaintance. Please ignore'. "When are you going to return my calls?"

"Cheating bastard," I muttered loud enough for him to hear, which made the T-Birds snigger. Luke scowled at them, and they stopped.

Luke and Zara had been sleeping together on and off for about a year, and if he had it his way, he'd leave his wife for her in a heartbeat. She wasn't interested in settling though, and was just happy to get her fix from him as and when she needed it.

With Zara occupied with Luke, I wasn't in the mood to stick around so finished my wine and was just about to leave when juvenile T-Bird, who I later found out was called Alan, shuffled over to me and said, "Can I get you a drink?"

My immediate thought was to politely decline, but there was something about the way he was looking at me with his puppy-dog blue eyes.

By the end of the night, I was cooped up in the corner playing tonsil tennis with Alan, who I vaguely remember kept telling me how amazing the kiss was. Almost like it was his first time.

Anthony: Freckiades, when were you going to tell me you had a thing for sixth-formers?

Isme: What you on about?

Anthony: *Photo of Isme kissing Alan*
I believe this was you last night in
The Pig's Ear??

Isme: I AM GOING TO KILL ZARA 😡😡😡

Anthony: It's not Zara you need to be worried about, it's Child Protection 😂

Isme: 🖕

I was hardly surprised Zara took the picture. She was always looking for opportunities to make a show of me, especially to Anthony – she's never exactly hidden the fact she fancies him and has always been resentful of our close friendship.

Me and Anthony grew up with Zara in the Greek Orthodox community. She was popular and pretty and always had a swarm of lads in Greek school wanting to snog her, while I was the one they all wanted to knock a footy about with. She had no interest in Anthony back then, probably because of his gappy teeth and thick-lensed glasses that made his eyes look huge. She soon changed her tune though after he discovered braces and contact lenses.

After Greek school finished I hardly saw Zara, apart from at the occasional Sunday mass when our parents would get chatting afterwards and we'd have no choice but to make small talk – and by small talk I mean Zara bragging about her high-flying career as a trainee corporate solicitor.

"Isme wants to be a solicitor too!" said Mum one week when she'd overheard our conversation. "She is going to be thee next Judge Rinder!"

"Well, that's not exactly true, Mum. I think I said once that his job looked cushy." The truth was I was in a post-university career lull, and my intention of having a gap year to figure out my next move had somehow turned into ten.

Zara tilted her head at me. "Oh, I thought you were just working on the rotisserie counter at Tesco?"

"Yeah, I am," I replied defensively, "but it's only a stopgap."

"Why didn't you say?" said Zara's mum, pulling her phone out of her handbag. "We're currently in the process of recruiting for trainees, so give me your number and we'll arrange for you to come into the office and see what we can do."

Two weeks later I was thrown into a career I never intended on being in, and which I very quickly learnt was not for me. The whole 'corporate' world felt fake and stuffy, all black suits and loud guffaws, with everyone scrambling to be the best, no matter what the cost. It also didn't help that I couldn't seem to grasp any knowledge of the legal world, probably because I found it boring as fuck, so every day felt like I was just blagging my way through. But with no other prospects and bills to pay, I felt I had no other choice but to stick it out.

From my first day at Mulligan's Zara couldn't have been nicer, inviting me out to lunches and after-work drinks and generally showing me the ropes. I didn't know whether she was just being nice or whether her mum had put her up to it, but either way I was grateful. It was only when she insisted that I bring Anthony to one of our work nights out and she honed in on him like a moth to a light that I realised her ulterior motive.

It worked for me, though. Zara was more than capable of sabotaging my job if things ever turned sour between us, especially considering her dad was still a silent partner in the firm. So, if using me to get closer to Anthony kept her sweet, then who was I to complain?

*

EMAIL
From: Jeffrey Mulligan
To: Ismeena Eliades
Subject: Professional conduct outside of the office

Isme,

Please can you come into my office after lunch. There is something we need to discuss.

Regards,
Jeff

The subject line of his email sent a shudder of dread through me.

Jeff is the senior partner at Mulligan's and it's not an unusual occurrence for him to ask me into his office; I'm always being summoned to make him a cuppa or photocopy something. He *has* got his own Personal Assistant, Derek, but he's about ninety and hard of hearing so by the time he understands what Jeff's asked him to do the day is nearly over.

"Take a seat, Isme," he said as I entered his office, which smelt like a combination of old varnished wood and sour body odour.

Jeff is in his early sixties, about ten foot nothing and has a balding head, which he tries to disguise by combing the sad little wisps of grey hair he has left across it. He's married to Sue, the administration manager and (unfortunately) my boss.

I smiled politely and took a seat in the worn-down brown leather chair opposite his desk.

"OK, I'll get right to the point," he said, leaning back in his chair. "It's come to my attention that you were seen, how do I put it . . . canoodling with our young work experience fellow on Friday."

I felt a flush sweep across my cheeks, the words 'work experience' flashing red in my head like a warning sign. Exactly how old *was* Alan?

"Now, don't get me wrong, Isme, whatever you get up to outside the office is up to you. God knows I like a good canoodle myself . . . with Sue, of course!" My stomach quivered at the thought. "However, Alan is here on work experience from sixth-form college, and we don't want to be giving him the wrong impression of the firm and what a professional career entails."

I blushed and sank lower into my seat.

"While I've got you here, Isme, I want to mention your position here at the firm. It's been two years since your training contract was terminated and you started working in the administration department, is that right?"

I nodded.

"And have you given any thought on where you'd like to see your professional career going, here at Mulligan's?"

I squirmed in my seat. I knew it was only a matter of time before my cushy job in the admin department would be challenged. I just wasn't quite ready for it.

"You know, there are lots of opportunities here to climb up the financial ladder," he continued after several painful seconds of me staring helplessly around the room, trying to drum up a suitable answer. "Why don't you go away and have a think, and we'll reconvene in a few weeks?"

I nodded and smiled. *He* didn't need to know that the only reconvening I planned on doing was with the tub of Ben and Jerry's ice cream I'd half eaten the night before.

*

I saw Carlos on my drive home from work, which was the last thing I needed after my bollocking from Jeff. He pulled up beside me at the lights, the sound of Shabba Ranks's 'Mr Loverman' booming from the speakers. I recognised the car – a 1995 red Ford Fiesta which, from its black alloys, oversized spoiler and silver stripe along the body, looked like it'd been on a UK version of 'Pimp My Ride', 80's style, hosted by Pat Sharp.

"Hey, *agape mou*," he shouted over the noise, with a sly grin and a wink. "When are you going to marry me? You know it would make our mamas so happy." Luckily, the lights changed to green before I had to drum up a sarcastic response.

Mum would have me married off to him tomorrow if I gave the nod. In fact, the woman would have no qualms in seeing me married off to the head honcho of the bloody Mafia, so long as he had the Greek blood flowing through his veins. Oh, and preferably a nice healthy bank balance – her obsession with seeing me marrying into money being one of her (many) flaws.

Take my big sister, for example, the lovely innocent Maria who, according to Mum, is the shining example of a 'Good Greek Orthodox Woman'. This is despite the fact she was pretty reckless growing up, regularly getting suspended from school and getting caught smoking weed in her bedroom.

Yes, all of that was forgotten on the day she married George Cypriana.

*

"You know your mum just wants the best for you, love," said Dad, plonking his six-foot frame into my two-seater and resting his size twelves on the coffee table. "But you can do far better than that Carlos bloke. I mean, what does he use on that hair of his, Lurpak?"

"Ha, I know. I can't stand men with long hair, it gives me the proper ick."

"It's not the hair you need to worry about, love, it's those leather pants and silky shirts. Where does he shop, 1975?"

I almost spat out my mouthful of tea.

Dad had called round to fix my toilet, which hadn't been working properly since the New Year's Eve party, which *will* happen when people are using it every five seconds to empty their alcohol-filled bladders.

When it came to Mum and her never-ending ploy to marry me off, I could always rely on Dad to have my back. Like me, he didn't understand the Greeks and their need to get involved in their children's love lives. In fact, there are a lot of the Greek ways that can sometimes seem a bit baffling.

Don't get me wrong, I'm proud of my Greek heritage and always get a tinge of smugness when people ask about it. But it's harder for Dad, having been adopted at a very young age by one of the most British, tea-drinking, weather-discussing, Royal-family-loving couples you can imagine.

Nan and Grandad (God rest their souls) adopted Dad when he was a baby, having struggled for a long time to have a child themselves. They insisted that Dad stay connected to his Greek roots in some of the more traditional ways, so they had him baptised Greek Orthodox and took him regularly to mass. It's thanks to them that him and Mum ever met. But, other than his connection to the church, Dad was pretty much brought up following the English way of life, hence his bewilderment when it came to Greek culture.

Dad finished his tea and hoisted himself up from the chair. In his words, he's 'built like a brick shithouse'.

We often joke that his biological dad is Richard Kiel, who

played Jaws in the old Bond films. Dad laughs along, but I can't help but think he must be intrigued sometimes as to who his parents were. As far as *I'm* aware, though, he's never tried to find out.

"Another tea?" I asked, but Dad wasn't listening – he was distracted by someone ringing his phone. "Dad, tea?"

"What, sorry? Oh, no thanks love. I, er, better go." He fumbled inside his pockets for his car keys, a flush sweeping across his cheeks.

"Everything OK?"

"Oh yeah, it's just your mum wondering where I am, you know what she gets like!"

I nodded – the poor fella couldn't take a piss in peace these days without Mum banging on the door making sure he wasn't going into cardiac arrest again.

I'll never forget getting the phone call from Mum three years ago that Dad had suffered a heart attack. Seeing him lying in the hospital bed, his face drained of any colour, dark purple bruises all over his arms where the doctors had taken numerous blood samples.

When he turned his head slowly towards me, placed a fragile hand over mine and croaked, "Bleedin'ell, Iz, you look like shite," I'd never been so happy (and slightly offended) before in my life.

*

Isme: I'm here. What drink do you want?
Got us a bottle of pinot 🍷
You best hurry up, I've almost drunk half
the bottle already 😬

Where the hell are you, Zara? I'm worried now

Zara: Sorry, something's come up 😵

Isme: Something or someone?
You know you should really put that lad out of his
misery and tell him to stay with his wife

Zara: Just one more bite of the apple first

I slammed my phone down on the table and poured myself another wine. I wouldn't mind, but *she* was the one who'd invited *me* to come for a drink. I'd hoped she wanted to apologise for sending that picture to Anthony – even booking us a table at her favourite city centre wine bar, that's well known for its overpriced wine tasting packages and la-di-da sommeliers, who were just missing sticks up their arses.

So there I was, on my own, on a Saturday afternoon in mid-January, in a bar I didn't like. I thought about messaging Anthony, but then remembered he had some family thing, so decided to call Agnes, an old friend from university, on the off-chance she was in Liverpool. She was a loud, burly Scot who was always up for a laugh, and the reason I spent many lectures embraced in the foetal position trying not to spew.

We lost touch a bit after uni. She was forced to move back to Glasgow after her parents split up, but would still show up in Liverpool every now and again without warning, usually sending

19

me a scrambled text which, although I can never read it, generally translates to the fact she's in Liverpool and wants to meet up.

Agnes: "OK, Iz. I'm not back in Liverpool for a few months."

Me: "Aw that's a shame, Ag. Feel like I haven't seen you in ages!"

Agnes: "Aye, I know. How's ya ma? I always loved that Maddie!"

Me: "Yep, still as mad as ever. Still trying to marry me off like it's *Pride and Prejudice*."

Agnes: "Ha! OK. So, I'll see you in a few months then lassie, yeah?"

Me: "Deffo. Can't wait!"

With no more viable options, I downed my wine, settled the overpriced bill and headed home.

It was a brisk winter's day, but that didn't seem to stop the many groups of girls and lads that stumbled past me, most of them on a hen or stag do, from roaming the streets in their skimpy outfits and T-shirts. Who needs a coat when you've got vodka?

Watching them, all carefree, I couldn't help but feel a pang of jealousy. There was only one thing for it.

I walked into the nearest newsagents and headed straight to the booze fridges, but something en route caught my eye – a shelf full of all the necessary essentials to bake a cake. Coincidence? Or some invisible power steering me towards a more productive afternoon than getting pissed?

I used to bake regularly when I was living at home, mainly basic Greek sponge cakes, traditional honey cookies and, one of my favourites, baklava – a layered pastry dessert made of filo pastry and filled with honey-sweetened chopped nuts. Ask me to knock up a lamb moussaka and I'd crumble on the spot, but the dessert side of Greek cooking always felt like second nature, probably due to my unquenchable sweet tooth.

I'd even tried making a business out of it at after finishing university, setting up a stall at local trade markets and taking cake orders for special occasions. My *ultimate* goal was to have a shop, but the harsh reality was that, with no savings to my name and banks unwilling to lend due to my reckless teenage years maxing out store credit cards, what I thought could be a feasible goal soon turned into a distant pipe dream.

I'd intended on keeping the baking business ticking along after getting the trainee solicitor job. That was until I was handed those hefty study books and realised I would be lucky to even have time to go the shop to *buy* cake.

The study books were long gone now though, yet I still felt hesitant. What if I'd forgotten all my baking skills and had to learn everything again from scratch? Worse still, what if I ended up with a soggy bottom?

*

Unknown number: Hey agape mou, I can't stop thinking about you 😊

Isme: Sorry, who is this please?
Were you in Revolution last week?

Unknown number: It's Carlos, the love of your life! 😜

Isme: How did you get my number?

Unknown number: Your mama gave me it!
When are you going to let me take you out?
How about Friday? 🙏

Isme: Sounds great, can't wakjkfdjkfjkjds

"ANTHONY, GIVE ME THAT BACK!" I grabbed the phone just as he hit send, and sent another one, blaming predictive text and making it quite clear that I wasn't free on Friday, or any other day this *year*.

"Imagine if you ended up marrying him," laughed Anthony, taking a sip of his pint. "At least you'd have free chippy meals for life."

I shuddered, taking a handful of (ironically) chips – we were in The Pig's Ear, making the most of the 'chips and pint for a fiver' deal, which we quite often did. "Yeah, and bottles of Crisp 'N Dry for babies. Now do something useful, will you, and go to the bar."

I watched as Anthony strode up to the bar in his smart black suit, catching the attention of a couple of girls on a nearby table, one of them whispering something to the other and giggling. Anthony was too busy looking at something on his phone to notice.

I'd always found it quite funny when Anthony got attention from women (and sometimes men) when we were out. I suppose if we're talking types, he was your typical 'tall, dark and handsome', but to me he was still the muddy-faced dinosaur-obsessed kid who loved re-enacting scenes from *Jurassic Park* and digging up holes in the garden in the hope of finding fossils.

"Is that him again?" said Anthony, returning from the bar with our drinks and catching me staring at my phone.

"No, thank god. It's a message from Zara asking me to remind you about her birthday drinks on Friday."

"Is she desperate for numbers or something? She's already messaged me twice about it."

"I don't know why you're surprised. You know she won't give up until she has your babies."

Anthony took a sip of his pint. "Yeah, well, she's going to be waiting a long time. Speaking of kids, whatever happened to that lad you snogged from work?"

*

I called Mum to pull her up on giving Carlos my number, who hadn't stopped popping up on my phone like a persistent spot ever since. Dad answered, reminding me that Mum was at her beloved Zumba class – how could I forget that Wednesday was geriatric rave night.

Dad: "I didn't know anything about it, love. Maybe it was a mistake?"

Me: "You don't pass on somebody's number 'by mistake', Dad. Come on, I'm not soft."

Dad: "All right, I'll have a word with her when she gets in, OK? Right, I best be off."

Me: "Thanks, and while you're at it tell her there's absolutely no way I'm ever gonna agree to go on a date with him, so she might as well give up the ghost now."

Dad: "OK, love, will do. Right, I'd better go—"

Me: "Oh my god, can you imagine someone ever willing to marry the lad? They'd have to be void of all their major senses, not to mention completely . . . Dad, who's that? Is Mum back? Put her on, will you?"

Dad: "No, it's, er, just the telly, love. Right, I've got to go. I'll call you tomorrow, OK?"

*

EMAIL

From: Jeff Mulligan

To: Ismeena Eliades

Re: Career progression

Isme,

Following our chat a couple of weeks ago, I wanted to make you aware that some new vacancies have become available, which will be a step up from your current role, both in terms of daily responsibilities and pay.

We are still in the process of finalising the details, which will be announced in the coming weeks, and I would urge you when they do to consider putting yourself forward.

Jeff

I replied with 'Will do, Jeff, thanks' although I had zero intention of putting myself forward. I had to play the game though, if I wanted to keep my job and still afford my rent. In the meantime, I needed to give some serious thought to my next career move.

Aside from my cake shop dream that never came to fruition, I'd never had a strong desire for a particular career. I did help out at the family restaurant after school for a bit when I was fifteen, but it's fair to say my calling was not in waitressing – I smashed more plates than at a Greek wedding, and in the end, Mum demoted me to glass collector.

The restaurant, or 'The Fat Greek' as it was aptly called, was a small, traditional Greek restaurant which Mum inherited from her parents. Like most long-standing Greek restaurants, the décor was dated – white stone-washed walls, blue-and-white checked tablecloths, random artefacts related in some way to Greece splattered all over the walls and on the ceiling.

It didn't seem to bother the customers, though. The place was always busy, which was hardly surprising with the delicious homely Greek meals they served up. Me and Anthony would often sneak into the kitchen to pick at whatever was cooking on the stove, only to be chased out by Mum.

Unfortunately, once the credit crunch hit, the number of customers started to dwindle, and in the end Mum and Dad couldn't afford to keep it open and were forced to sell up. Now all we had was our fond memories and a fake, stuffed donkey with a Greek flag and saddle that Mum could never seem to part with.

*

Isme: Is it wine o'clock yet? 😫
What and how many bottles do you want
me to buy?

Maria: Not coming. George is pissed as a fart
and has just passed out on the bed 😠😠😠

Isme: Do you want me to come to yours instead?

Maria: Not worth it with the twins still bouncing
off the walls. Maybe I'll get them to bounce
on his head instead.

"CBA George strikes again," I muttered to myself as I clicked my phone off. I threw my head back on the sofa and sighed, wondering, yet again, why Maria put up with his shit.

I actually didn't mind George back at the start, when Maria first met him. He was like the brother I never had and we got on well, mainly taking the piss out of each other. He was a bit cock-sure of himself, like, but he had reason to be. He was like a rugged gentleman with his dark features, slim frame and designer stubble. When Maria told him the news about the twins, we all thought he'd do a runner, but he was surprisingly overjoyed.

They seemed happy for a while, about six months to be exact, which was when they moved in together and Maria started to see George for the typical mummy's boy that he was. So used to everything being done for him at home his whole life, George expected nothing less from Maria, who tried convincing herself that he'd change once the twins came along and he became a dad. Yeah, he changed all right – into an inattentive, bone-idle version of his former self.

Say hello to Can't-Be-Arsed George, and these days he was more like the brother I never wanted rather than the brother I never had.

I considered what to do with my unexpected free night. Maybe it wasn't such a bad thing, giving my liver a rest for the night and waking up with a clear head. I thought back to my deliberation in the newsagents after seeing the cake ingredients. I'd chosen wine that night, and had been unable to shake off the pang of regret ever since. I knew my hesitation was down to lack of confidence, but surely the longer I put it off the harder it was going to be to get going again?

I decided to leave it to the fate gods. If I could drum up some ingredients from the kitchen to knock something together, then baking it was, otherwise I'd be hitting the bottle.

As I scrambled through the kitchen cupboards, something shiny and familiar at the back of one of them caught my eye. Slowly and carefully I pulled the cake mixer out of the cupboard, placed it on the worktop and stood back to admire its beauty.

Mum had bought me it for Christmas one year, and that same excitement I'd felt as I tore off the wrapping paper and first laid eyes on it came flooding back, like a kid getting their first bike or game console.

I stroked a hand over its chrome surface, wiping away cobwebs as I did, recalling the many delightful bakes it had helped me make over the years, and that real sense of achievement I always got from pulling something golden and delicious out of the oven hours later.

The fate gods had spoken, I found the ingredients and started baking.

Two hours later, I was stood in the kitchen with a cuppa, admiring the vanilla sponge cake that was slowly rising in the oven, filling the flat with a delicious, sugary aroma.

It was a basic recipe, and one that wouldn't get me a Paul Hollywood handshake, but it felt good to be at it again. I'd made a start, so even if it tasted like cardboard, that in itself felt like an achievement.

But it actually didn't taste half bad. The sponge was light and fluffy and melted in the mouth, and the sweetness of the caster sugar mixed with the vanilla was delightful.

"A bit too basic for me, but a good bake" is what I reckon Paul would say, and I'd happily take that.

*

I got to The Pig's Ear a little earlier than everyone else to put up some balloons and banners for Zara's birthday, which took me all of five minutes. I gave up after blowing up four balloons when I started seeing dots but was hopeful that she'd still appreciate the effort.

"These are for you." I turned round to find Alan standing there holding a card and some chocolates. He looked even younger than

I remembered, which made me want to crawl into a pit and die of shame.

"Oh, er, h-hi Alan," I stuttered, my face burning red. I hadn't seen him since I ate his face off, mainly because every time I spotted him around the office I'd duck under the nearest table.

"It was my last day of work experience today, and I just wanted to say thank you for making my experience so special. I really will never forget it. Or you." He handed me the card and chocolates, and I couldn't help feeling a little flattered, inappropriate age difference aside. It was the most romantic gesture I'd ever had from a man-child, or any man for that matter.

"Ah that's so kind of you, Alan, thank you."

"You know, if you want to, you can give me your numb—"

"Isme, you could have at least got me matching balloons and banners, for fuck's sake." Phew. Saved by Zara and her unsurprising lack of appreciation for my handiwork. "Are these for me?" she added, snatching the chocolates out my hand.

"No, they're from Alan—"

"Isme, you know I only like Lindt." She slammed the box down on the table and dragged me up to the bar. I looked back to apologise to Alan for Zara's impoliteness but he'd scarpered, like a mouse scurrying back to its hole to escape a wild cat.

People started to filter through in their drones, and it wasn't long before the place was heaving, the karaoke underway. First up was Pete from Private Law, or Pongy Pete as I called him (not to his face of course) due to his daily diet of cheesy Doritos and hummus which made his farts smell nuclear.

"Freckiades, what have I missed?" Anthony appeared, sliding into the seat opposite that Zara had been occupying for all of five minutes before she went to 'work the room'.

"Pongy Pete's about to do 'Candy Shop' on the karaoke."

"Amazing." I slid Anthony's pint across the table. "Where's the birthday girl?"

I nodded in the direction of the bar, where Zara appeared to be in a heated discussion with Luke. Clearly, he wasn't taking the 'break-up' too well. She caught my gaze and came striding over when she spotted Anthony.

"You came!" Zara plonked herself right onto Anthony's lap and wrapped her arms around his neck. From over her shoulder, I could see Luke staring with pursed lips.

Anthony shifted awkwardly in his seat. "You know there's a seat right there, Zara—"

"Are you going to take me to the bar and get me a birthday drink or what?"

"Isn't there a bar tab? Can't you just get it yourself?"

"Come on, Anthony. I'm thirsty!" Zara dragged Anthony up from his seat and, reluctantly, he walked her over to the bar, turning around and mouthing 'sorry' to me as he did. I shrugged my shoulders – it was hardly the first time on a night out that Zara had steered him away and left me flying solo.

I watched as she sidled up to him at the bar, thrusting her chest towards him and laughing exaggeratedly. She was persistent, I'd give her that, but I knew Anthony and there was no way he'd ever go there.

31st January marked the last day of the most depressing month of the year and I, along with everyone else, would be glad to see the back of it. And what better way to see it out than with a binge watch of *Ru Paul's Drag Race* and a sharer bag of Sensations to sort my throbbing head.

"I quite like January," said Anthony, grabbing a handful of crisps and shoving them into his mouth. "It's a clean slate, where you can forget about everything you did wrong last year and start again." He'd stayed the night on the sofa after Zara's birthday drinks, which had ended in disaster after she caught Luke snogging one of the trainee girls outside.

"I'm going to need a concrete slab, never mind a slate," I scoffed. "Also, can you please stop eating with your gob open, it's making me feel sick."

Anthony opened his mouth wide to reveal the contents of his chewed-up crisps, and I hit him in the arm.

"I really don't know what Zara sees in you."

"Ha! You know she's called me twice today already; keeps asking me to meet up."

I rolled my eyes, although I was hardly surprised. She'd no doubt be on the lookout for a rebound one-nighter after catching Luke with another girl, and Anthony would be first on her target list.

"Would you ever be, like, tempted? To go there with her, like? I mean, you can't tell me you don't think she's attractive?"

Anthony hesitated before answering. "Yeah, she is, I'm not

gonna lie, but she's far too vain for me, not to mention high maintenance. You know I can't be arsed with girls like that. Remember that girl I was seeing who expected me to drive her round everywhere, and got a cob on when I'd say no?"

"How could I forget! You made me ring her and tell her you'd been deported."

"Ha! Yeah, I did. And she bought it, the stupid cow." Anthony held the bag of crisps up to his mouth and downed the remaining contents.

"Just do me a favour, will you? If you do ever decide to take Zara out or anything, promise me you'll tell me first so I can prepare myself for any fallout if things go wrong between you."

Anthony held out his little finger. "Pinky."

I linked my little finger with his and we shook on it. It was something we'd done ever since we were kids, and which set the foundations for the trust in our friendship. And Anthony knew just as well as I did that you could *never* go back on a pinky promise.

"Honestly though, Anthony, you may want to meet up with her and let her down gently to nip it in the bud."

"Yeah, you're probably right. What about you, anyway, any fellas on the horizon?"

"God, you sound like me mum." I sighed. "But no, my love life is as dry as a bone. I mean, who wouldn't want this?" I indicated to my messy hair and baggy pyjamas, which were housing some questionable stains.

Anthony jumped up from the sofa and, with one hand on his hip and in his best American voice, said, "If you can't love yourself, how in the hell are you going to love somebody else? Now, can I get an amen up in here?"

"AMEN!" I cried. With that, he clicked his fingers and sashayed off to the kitchen.

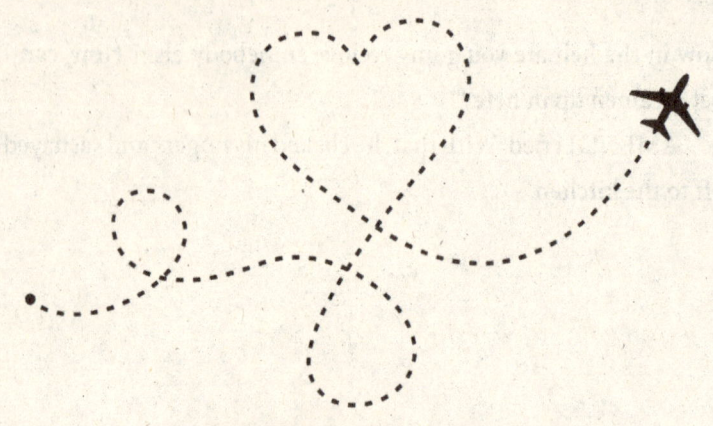

FEBRUARY

I **WAS WATCHING THAT EPISODE OF** *FRIENDS* **WHERE**
Rachel, fed up with her mundane job at Central Perk, spontaneously decides to quit and pursue her dream job in fashion, and
it gave me an epiphany. I picked up the phone and called Maria.

Me: "I'm quitting my job at Mulligan's to pursue a career in . . .
er, fashion. And stuff."

Maria: "Since when have you been into fashion, Isme, other
than when you used to put on those cringy fashion shows for us
all when you were a kid?"

Me: "OK, maybe not fashion. But something, *anything*, to get
me out of that place and which will earn me the same money."

Maria: "Why don't you stop pissing about and either have
another go at the exams or find something else, like baking.
Wasn't that your dream?"

Me: "It was, but it's not that easy, Maria."

Maria: "Oh, and suddenly deciding to become the next Anna Wintour is? Anyway, why isn't the baking thing that easy? It's not like you've got two little humans depending on you or a husband who can't even work the dishwasher."

Me: "True. I wish I'd found my calling from a young age, like you."

Maria: "I would hardly call hairdressing my calling, like, and although I do love it, I still had to work hard to get where I am now. Nothing gets handed to you on a plate, Isme."

Me: "Sorry, Mum, I must have called you by mistake."

Maria: "Oh haha. Anyway, piss off now, it's five minutes past my bedtime."

Me: "Maria, it's nine o'clock."

Maria: "Yeah, and? Bye."

After Maria hung up, I thought some more about her suggestion of having another go at the exams. I couldn't say it hadn't crossed my mind from time to time – it'd do wonders for my bank balance if I passed, and I'd never have to tell Mum I'd failed them in the first place.

I could already feel my anxiety levels rising at the sheer thought of picking up those stodgy textbooks again and devoting my evenings to reading about 'affidavits' and 'arbitration'. So that left the baking, although the reality of quitting my job and starting up the business again from scratch when I had rent and bills to pay felt way beyond my reach.

The enjoyment of making the sponge cake was still fresh in

my mind though, so I decided there was no harm in making it a hobby. Next on my agenda was a scrummy loaf.

I remember the first time Mum showed me how to make bread. She used to make a load every week for the offertory at Sunday mass, until they started outsourcing it to one of the locals who'd opened up a bakery and could make twice as much than Mum in her average-sized kitchen. She was livid – if there's one thing Elana Eliades does not take well, it's rejection. And if it involves her cooking . . . well, the person rejecting her may as well have a death wish.

I sat and watched her many a time with my elbows propped up on the worktop, my face so close, the flour would get up my nose and make me sneeze. She would expertly knead the dough for each loaf, pushing into it with the palm of her hands, and then pounding it on the worktop with so much force it vibrated under my arms.

"Don forget, Isme," she would say, as she pulled the dough out and then folded it back in again, "stickia dough is lighta bread." I had jotted this down in my little notebook, much to Mum's annoyance. "*Ochi*, Isme, no writing! You work with your senses, your instincts." This was something she swore by in all her cooking and which, after a disastrous attempt at a Gary Rhodes bread recipe from one of his books, left me with a loaf that had more holes than a sponge and completely fell apart when I cut into it – I'd swore by myself ever since.

After leaving the dough to prove for an hour, by which time it had swelled up to double its size, I placed it on the flour-dusted worktop and got to work on the kneading, making sure to follow Mum's foolproof push and pound technique. The silky-smooth softness of the dough felt soothing against my hands.

By the time the loaf was in the oven and I'd tidied up the kitchen, my arms felt like they'd been lifting weights and my eyes stung where I'd rubbed my floury hands to get some stray hairs out my face. But inside I felt elated, and as the savoury aroma of the bread, rising in the oven and turning a golden brown, filled the flat, I couldn't help but feel a teeny tiny bit smug.

*

Zara: Will you come to a gym class with
me this morning? 🧘

Isme: Absolutely not

Zara: Oh, come on, Isme. It's ariel yoga.
You'll love it
It'll do wonders for your bingo wings you're
always moaning about
And I need to use up my 'bring a friend and
get a month free' voucher before it runs out

Isme: You owe me

I pictured a calm serene room full of scented candles and the soundtrack to *The Little Mermaid* playing in the background as we slowly contorted our bodies into various yoga positions.

"It's *aerial* yoga, Isme, not *Ariel*," said Zara impatiently as I waltzed into the room singing 'Under The Sea'. It reminded me of a scene from *Fifty Shades of Grey* – strips of red silk material hung from the ceiling like hammocks, some of which were already occupied by twenty-somethings with about as much fat on their whole bodies as on my big toe. They were elegantly suspended in the air like trapeze artists, not a bead of sweat in sight.

"Please can we go to the back?" I pleaded, but Zara was already setting up camp at the front, carefully removing her designer yoga mat out of its leather carry case and placing it on the floor. I hadn't even brought a towel.

"Just chill out, Isme," said Zara, as she caught me nervously peering around the room. "It'll be a laugh." The smirk on her face told me that by 'it' she meant 'me'.

Zara, along with everyone else, was able to carry out every move with ease and elegance, while I was about as graceful as a three-legged elephant on roller skates. The instructor had to unravel me several times as I kept getting caught up in the material.

In the end, I was ordered by the instructor to sit on the mat for 'health and safety reasons', much to my relief – of all the ways I'd ever thought I might go, 'death by chiffon' wasn't on the list.

I watched as Zara contorted her slender frame around the material, wrapping her long legs tightly around it like a snake constricting its victim. An unexpected thought suddenly popped into my head of her legs being wrapped around Anthony in the same way. Luckily, the class finished before any more disturbing thoughts of my best friend having sex entered my head.

"Maybe step aerobics would be more suited to you," Zara suggested once the class finished. She swept her Versace towel across her forehead, despite there not being any visible signs of exertion.

As we made our way outside to the car park, Zara insisted on telling me all about an upcoming case she was working on, despite me not asking – which she quite often did. I think it was her way of reminding me that whilst I'd been left behind in the mundane confinement of administration, she was out there in the 'thrilling' legal world, strutting her stuff like Ally McBeal.

"So I take it you've finally finished things with Luke after all that at your birthday drinks?" I asked once she'd taken a breath.

"Oh god yeah, I am SO done with wasting my time on stupid boys. I need a man." Zara clicked open the boot of her white Audi TT and threw in her yoga mat. "Speaking of men, is Anthony seeing anyone at the moment?"

"Not that I know of. Why?" Although I think I already knew the answer to that one.

"No reason," said Zara with a sly grin, before speeding off.

*

I called to Maria's after work for my quarterly root touch-up. One of the many advantages to having a hairdresser for a sister is not having to sit in a stuffy salon for four hours while they insist on applying all kinds of lotions and potions to your hair, convincing you that it'll fall out otherwise, then charge you a small fortune at the end for the privilege.

The only downside was the twins, who make the whole thing

about as relaxing as plucking your pubic hairs out with a tweezer, and tonight was no exception.

"Why is Mum putting that on your hair?" asked Theo, who was sat cross-legged on the floor in front of me, watching intently while Maria brushed the dark brown hair dye over my roots.

"To hide my grey hairs."

"Why?"

"Because they make me look old."

Tomaso, who had been sat quietly colouring at the dining table, jumped down and assumed the same seated position next to Theo, clearly wanting a piece of the question-time action. "Why don't you just use a pen?"

"Because they won't work."

"Why?"

"Because pens are for drawing, not for colouring your hair."

"What about chalk?"

"GEORGE, WILL YOU COME AND TAKE THESE TWO!" cried Maria, running a hand through her dishevelled hair and rubbing at her red-rimmed eyes. She looked like she could do with a lie down, never mind tackle my grey-infested mane.

Once Maria had finished putting the colour on my hair, I tried freeing up space on the worktops to make us some tea and toast from the bread I'd made a few days earlier.

"Sorry Isme, I know it's a mess," sighed Maria, as she caught me playing Jenga with the dirty dishes sprawled next to the sink. "I just haven't had time to clean up since I got home from work."

"Why couldn't lazy arse do it?"

"Er, I think the clue is in the title. OH MY GOD this is INSANE!"

"Do you like it?"

"Like it? Isme, this is amazing! You're so bloody talented." Maria took another bite of the toast and closed her eyes up at the ceiling.

"Bloody hell, Maria, you'll be banging the table and moaning next!"

"Well, it'll be the closest I've had to one in about, er, let me think, how long have I been with George?"

"Did someone shout me?" George's head peered round the door of the kitchen and we both burst into hysterics.

*

There were times when I really wished I hadn't bunked off in Greek school with Anthony and learnt the language properly – every time I go to Greek church with Mum being those times. I could hardly make out what the priest, Father Demetrious, was saying, and had no clear means of escape for the whole three hours the service droned on for. To make matters worse, Father sang throughout the service, and let's just say *The Voice* wouldn't be knocking on his door any time soon.

The church itself *was* quite impressive, both inside and out – red and white brickwork, geometric arched windows, a tri-domed roof with the same geometric style. Inside, beautiful marbled archways ran through the centre with pews either side, and an altar comprising a special wall of holy icons – images of saints in gilded frames that have some form of significance. What significance that was, I didn't know.

"Isme, will you stop fidgeting, *parakalo*," whispered Mum angrily halfway through the service, slapping my twitchy leg.

"But I'm sooooo booooored."

"Shush!" This from a geriatric in the row behind who, with her creased face and white hair poking out of her black headdress, looked like she'd just come off the Olivio advert.

The upside of today's mass was that it was some special service where you had to kiss the priest's hand at the end to bag a loaf of bread. Slightly weird and inappropriate? Yes, but it can come in handy when you've eaten your last piece that morning and won't make the shops for the four o'clock Sunday closing time.

Tea and cake were also being served up in a little side room afterwards, which, if you can ignore the dreary beige décor and lack of natural light, makes the last three hours of boring hell a teeny tiny bit worthwhile. I headed over there as soon as the three-hour holy sing-a-thon had finished.

I'd just stuffed a piece of baklava into my gob, whilst making a mental note to find out who made it to get the recipe off them, when a waft of stale cigarette smoke hit me from behind, and a deep, hoarse voice said, "Isme, how lavely to see you."

It was Carlos's mother Theoulla who, like my own mum, was always on the prowl for a suitable suitor for her offspring. She resembled something from Roald Dahl's *The Twits*, with her wiry, short black hair, long nose and rounded frame.

"I hear you and Carlos have been getting closer?"

"If by closer you mean him stalking me, then yeah," I wanted to say, but I was still battling with the baklava, that was so chewy it was making my jaw ache.

"Good, good." She took a long, loud slurp of her tea, which was as grating as nails on a chalkboard. "We look forward to thee dinner on Tuesday."

"Oh, where are you going?"

Theoulla roared so loud I thought I saw smoke coming out of her nose.

"Oh, Isme, you so fanny!" With that she was gone.

*

"Isme, look! Carlos and Theoulla have come to join us for dinna, isn't that lovely?"

"Yes, lovely," I said through gritted teeth, as I arrived at Mum's a few days later and spotted our special guests.

I considered making a swift exit, blaming a sudden case of the squirts, but the meaty, cinnamon smell of Mum's moussaka was like a dangling carrot, and there was no point trying to resist.

Theoulla insisted I sit next to Carlos for dinner, who kept 'unintentionally' brushing his hand against mine by reaching for dishes at the same time. I tried to enjoy my moussaka, but it was difficult with Theoulla's judgmental eyes boring into me, and her probing questions about my lifestyle.

Theoulla: "Isme, do you cook?"

Me: "Erm, not really."

Theoulla: "Hmmm."

Awkward silence.

Theoulla: "I don't always see you at Greek church?"

Me: "I try and go when I can."

Awkward cough from Mum.

Theoulla: "Do you drink much alcohol?"

Me: "Yeah, a bit at the weekends."

Theoulla: "Hmmm."

"Do you have a generous supply of eggs in your ovaries?" she might as well have asked. I tried catching Mum's attention over the dinner table to give her a 'what the fuck?' look, but she was doing her utmost to avoid my gaze. Normally this would be where I could rely on Dad to step in and have my back, but he'd abandoned me to do some computer course (I'll process that one another day).

"I just say you were single and looking for a nice Greek hasband, Isme," Mum confessed once they'd gone, and we were tidying up.

I slammed a plate into the dishwasher. "Even if I *was* looking for a husband, which I'm not, Carlos would be at the bottom of the pile. No, he wouldn't even be *on* the pile. The lad wears leather trousers and crocodile shoes, for God's sake!"

"You have to think about settling down soon, Isme, you not getting any younger. Everything will start to seize up if you not careful." She nodded in the direction of my lady bits, and I rolled my eyes up at the ceiling.

The woman was impossible. She later confessed that she'd even told Theoulla I'd go on a date with Carlos. I told her there was absolutely no chance I'd go on a date with him, not even if he was the last man walking this Earth.

*

I agreed to go on a date with Carlos. Absolutely nothing to do with the kind offer from Mum of cooking for my tea for a month. Nope, totally doing it out of my own goodwill.

*

I had low expectations of where Carlos would take me for the date. But there's low, and then there's ten feet under.

"Your family chippy? Really?" I said, looking up at the familiar blue and white signage. Thankfully, I hadn't dressed up for the occasion – black jeans, baggy jumper and Converse trainers – although unfortunately the same couldn't be said for Carlos who, in his black leather trousers and purple silk shirt, looked like a poor effort for a Prince tribute act.

"Yes! Surprise! Now come, I will show you where all the magic happens!"

Suddenly I was being ushered through the chip shop doors and round the back, where Carlos began talking me through the process of making chips, which I actually would have found mildly interesting if it wasn't for his hyped enthusiasm.

"Can you believe it, Isme! The machine actually peels the chips for you *and* cuts them! Isn't it just amazing!" Carlos stroked the top of the machine, and for a second I thought he might actually start humping the thing.

"So, Isme, what do you think? It is good, yes?" asked Carlos, once the 'tour' had finished and we were sat at the plastic table, on plastic chairs, at the front of the shop, tucking into some chips.

"Hmmm, yeah, lovely," I said, which wasn't a lie. Soft and salty, with just the right amount of grease.

Carlos banged his hand on the table in delight, which made me jump. "See! I told you." His outburst caught the attention of some customers waiting for their food, and I wanted the ground to swallow me whole.

"Bloody hell, Carlos, calm down. They're only chips," I muttered, whilst smiling apologetically at the customers.

"Ha, sorry Isme. I'm just so excited to have you here! You know, you are the first girl I have ever brought."

I almost choked on a chip. "As if! I bet you've got a new girl in here every week, showing them 'where the magic happens'."

"It is true, Isme. You are very special to me." He placed a hand over mine and, before you could say 'battered sausage', he was leaning in for a kiss. Luckily I managed to dodge it at the very last minute with a well-timed head turn. He did still get my cheek though, which left a stench of chip fat that I could still smell despite washing my face three times after I got home.

The things I will do for food . . . I mean, family.

*

"Anyone who says they enjoy being single on Valentine's Day is lying out of their arse. If I see one more soppy Facebook status or staged Instagram photo of a bunch of red roses, I'm gonna poke my own eyes out."

"What's got into you?" laughed Anthony, opening the boxes from our Chinese takeaway. "Is it something to do with your dad not getting you a card?"

"No," I mumbled, but there was no hiding my disappointment. Dad had given me a Valentine's card every year since I can remember, and it never failed to cheer me up. He'd always swear blind they weren't from him, even though I can always tell his tiny, neat handwriting a mile off. He got Mum to write it one year to throw me off the scent, but there's no denying her big, clumsy longhand.

So when I arrived home to find a measly leaflet about some new takeaway place that had opened nearby, I couldn't help but feel disheartened.

"Do you think maybe he's finally decided you're a bit old for getting a card off him?"

I sighed. "Yeah, maybe." It still didn't stop the heavy feeling in my chest.

"Ooooooh *Fifty Shades of Grey*, eh!" jeered Anthony, after we'd eaten and were settled on the sofa ready for a film. "Isn't Jamie Dornan like twenty years too old for you?"

I quickly snatched the remote control off him. "I don't know how that got there," I said, frantically trying to delete it from my Sky recordings, heat rushing through my cheeks.

"Woah, hang on a minute, Freckiades. Can't we watch it? I've been dying to see what all the fuss is about."

"Piss off, Anthony. It'd be like watching a porno with me mum."

"Oh come on, pleeeeaassee?! We can turn it into a drinking game. Every time Dakota Johnson shows her tits you have to have a sip of your wine, and every time Jamie reveals his knob, I'll have a sip."

He had me at drinking game. I soon regretted my decision though when, forty minutes in, Christian and Anastasia have their first 'encounter' and the screen was overtaken by tits and bums. Luckily the drinking game made it feel slightly less awkward, and by the time it had finished I was feeling a bit wavy.

"Right, I'm off. I'll leave you to do some bean flick – WOAH!" The cushion missed Anthony's face by an inch.

*

"What are you doing here, Christian?" I opened my eyes to find him hovering over my bed, a smouldering look etched across his face. The room was dark, but I could just make out the silhouette of his chiselled face.

"I can't stop thinking about you, Anastasia," he said in a low, gravelly voice.

Slowly, he lowered himself on top of me, pinning me down with his hips. He hovered there for an intense moment, our lips almost touching, his hot breath in my face.

I groaned as he kissed my neck and then slowly began working his way down to my chest.

A strip of moonlight peeked through the curtains, highlighting the room, and as I opened my eyes and looked down I suddenly realised that his face had changed.

"ANTHONY?!"

I woke with a start, my body hot and a throbbing sensation down below.

"No more drinking games and soft porn for me," I mumbled to myself, before drifting back off to sleep.

*

Maria: "HEEEELLLLOOOOO!!!"

Me: "Hello? Maria?"

Maria: "YOU STINKY POO HEAD!!!"

Me: "Oi you little sh—"

Maria: "Tomaso give me that phone, NOW."

Me: "Hello, you there?"

Maria: "Hi, sorry. What's up?"

Me: "Not much, just wondering if you've ever had a sexy dream about someone you'd never thought of in that way before, except it's not really them in the dream, but like a version of them. Do you know what I mean?"

Maria: "I once had a dream about Bradley Walsh. Does that count?"

Me: "Er, kind of. I suppose."

Maria: "So, who was it in the dream? Or who was it supposed to be?"

Me: "It was supposed to be Jamie Dornan, but then he, like, morphed into Anthony. We *had* been watching *Fifty Shades of Grey*, like. And I haven't had sex in yonks."

Maria: "Well, there you go then. TOMASO, WHAT HAVE I TOLD YOU ABOUT CLIMBING INTO THE WASHING MACHINE! I'm going to have to go, sorry Isme. I feel like running away some days, I really do. I'll text you tomorrow."

Me: "OK, bye."

*

"*Toso poly chaos*, Isme!"

"Nice to see you too, Mother." I sighed, closing the door to the flat behind her. "And to what do I owe the pleasure?"

"I was jus in town looking for a new . . . coat and thought I'd come and see my *agape mou*." She squeezed my face in between her hands and kissed me on both cheeks. I didn't question the week's supply of moussaka and keftedes I'd spotted in her handbag.

I was used to these monthly unannounced 'spot checks', which she no doubt carried out to satisfy herself that I hadn't burnt down the flat, or turned into a druggie. I never complained though, as it always meant I had something other than ready meals for tea the following week.

"Isme, what is that smell?" She sniffed up at the air, not giving any clues as to whether she liked the smell or was disgusted by it.

"Oh, it might be the bin, I *was* just about to empty it."

"*Ochi*, it smell like, like honey? And almonds?"

"Ah, it'll be the baklava I tried to make the other day. It was as dry as a bone."

"You remember to butter each layer of the pastry like I always taught you?"

"No I, er, ran out of butter." Truth was, I'd spilt the entire contents of my pan of butter all over the floor, and couldn't be arsed going to the shop for more.

"Ah, well, there you go. Now, Isme, why you dry your knickers on the radiator? Is not very like a lady! *O thee mou.*"

Mum continued scurrying around the flat, cleaning up any mess and chastising me in the process. The way she carried on, you'd think I was living in squalor, but I left her to it, like I always did. She secretly loved the fact that (in her eyes) I still needed looking after.

"I've been meaning to ask, who was in the house with Dad when you were at Zumba a few weeks ago?" The inspection was over, and we were sat down with a Greek coffee. It's like English coffee only way stronger and made using a special type of coffee pot called a *briki*. I've never liked the stuff, it tastes chalky and leaves a bitter taste in my mouth for hours after, but Mum refuses to accept it.

Mum frowned. "What you mean?"

"I rang the house when you were out and I could definitely hear a voice in the background, a woman's voice."

Mum took a sip of her coffee, a flush sweeping across her cheeks. "Oh yes, it will have been, er, Doris. She cam to clean thee house."

I stared at her in disbelief – the day Mum trusts someone else to clean her beloved abode is the day I become a size zero.

"Is true, Isme! I'm getting too old to be bending over cleaning thee bath or getting on my hands and knees too scrub thee floors."

"Doris hardly sounds like someone who should be exerting herself in that way either!"

"Yes, well, she very, how you say, agile? Anyway, I mast go to thee bathroom. That coffee has gone right through me." Mum scurried to the bathroom, while I tried to think of anything other than her bodily functions. Suddenly the sound of Ricky Martin's 'Livin La Vida Loca' came bursting from her hand bag.

"MUM, YOUR PHONE'S RINGING . . . MUUUUMMM!!!"

"*OCHI*, ISME, I ON THEE TOILET! WILL YOU GET IT FOR ME, *PARAKALO*."

The ringing stopped before I could answer it. A voicemail notification came through moments later and without thinking, I pressed to listen.

"Hello, Mrs Eliades. This is Julie from the bank. I have been trying to reach you for weeks after you missed our meeting to discuss your finances. You now have three missed credit card payments and we really need to discuss how you plan on getting yourself back on track. Please call me back as soon as possible."

"Who was it, Isme?" Mum had reappeared from the bathroom and I quickly shoved the phone back in her handbag.

"I don't know, it went off before I could answer it."

"Ah well, they will call back. Now, we need to talk about thee mould in your bathroom . . ."

*

I was still living at home when The Fat Greek went under and it was, to say the least, a stressful time in the Eliades' residence. I remember many a night listening to Mum and Dad from my bedroom, arguing about where the next mortgage payment was coming from or how they were going to afford Maria's wedding. I knew things were really bad when Mum only gave me three roasties at Sunday lunch compared to my usual six or eight, which she claimed was due to a shortage of potatoes at the supermarket.

Then, one day, the arguing subsided, my plate was piled high with spuds and plans for Maria's wedding were going full steam ahead, with no expense spared, including hiring Stavros Flatley for the party. I had presumed at the time that they must have come into money from somewhere, and I dared not ask any questions in case it opened up a can of worms.

But it seemed from the call from the bank that maybe that wasn't the case after all.

*

'Clean Monday' marks the start of Greek Orthodox lent and is celebrated with a feast of my favourite Greek delicacies; taramasalata, unleavened flat bread, olives, and, my ultimate favourite, dolma, which are like little parcels of heaven – vine leaves stuffed with juicy mincemeat and succulent rice, that melt in the mouth.

It was also the last day everyone was allowed to eat meat, eggs and dairy products for the forty-day lent period, since it's traditionally forbidden. The only person who truly stuck to it in the Eliades family, though, was Mum, while the rest of us masked our burger breath with mints and covertly added milk to our tea when she wasn't looking.

Given the amount of food Mum knocked up on a normal family gathering, she usually approached Clean Monday like Jesus feeding the five thousand. I purposefully starved myself all day in preparation, but I needn't have bothered.

As soon as I turned up at Mum and Dad's, I knew something wasn't right. For starters, I wasn't greeted with the savoury smell of freshly baked flat bread, or the sound of Mum banging around in the kitchen like she was rehearsing for a band audition. I was about to shout something sarcastic like 'where's the fire?' when I heard hushed voices coming from the kitchen. I popped my head round the door to find Mum sitting on one of the dining chairs with her head buried in her hands, with Dad stood behind her.

"Come on, love," he was saying, rubbing her back, "we'll work something out. We always do, don't we?"

"Is different this time, Stephen," cried Mum, wiping her eyes with the 'feta' part of her apron, "and you don't know because you not been around lately."

Dad sighed. "Not this again, love, come on. You know I've been busy with that computer course."

"Yes, but why Isme say you have somebody in the house when I not here?"

"I told you, love, it was a Jehovah's Witness at the door."

Something in my stomach dropped as it became clear that Mum *had* been lying about a cleaner to protect Dad, although from the sounds of it she didn't know what or who she was protecting him from.

I became aware that I was listening in on a very private conversation and started to backtrack away from the door at the same time that Maria, George and the twins came bursting through the house.

"Ah, you're all here!" said Dad, appearing from the kitchen. "Your mum's just finishing up so let's go and wait at the table, eh."

He ushered us all into the dining room like he was escorting us out of a collapsing building. Maria and George chose seats at opposite ends of the dining table, and it was like a game of two halves – Maria on one end trying to frantically pin the twins down, who were crawling around the floor pretending to be dinosaurs, while George casually played on his phone at the other end.

I would have helped Maria, only I was distracted by the table. Usually so jam-packed with food you could barely fit your plate on, it was, aside from a few small bowls of olives and plates of pitta bread, as bare as my purse after a night out.

I looked over at Maria in bewilderment, but she was too busy trying to stop Theo from sticking an olive up his nose.

"Mum, where's all the food?" I asked politely when Mum came in from the kitchen holding a plate of yet more pitta bread.

"Yes, yes is comin now!"

She scurried into the kitchen and returned with a platter of potatoes, which made my stomach grumble in anticipation. When she plonked a measly three onto my plate, it all made sense. The parents were definitely in trouble.

*

Ways to help Mum and Dad out of shit creek:

1. *Sell the car. But could I really face being a bus wanker? Plus, I doubt I'll get many takers for my 2005 Renault Clio that's had more bumps than a toddler learning to walk.*

2. *Swallow my pride (and dignity) and give Carlos another chance. You never know, there might be a charming and sophisticated side to him that I haven't seen yet . . .*

3. *Go for the promotion at work when they get*

announced, which would mean being tied into the corporate way of life for many more years to come.

4. *Start baking for money again in my spare time, which would probably take up most of my nights and weekends, and remove any joy I've been getting from the leisurely nature of it recently.*

I'd been replaying Mum and Dad's conversation over in my head, which had left me with so many unanswered questions. Like, since when was Dad into computers? He was still trying to figure out the basic workings of his iPhone and he'd had it two years. Then there's the Jehovah's Witness excuse, which sounded like a pile of crap, and Mum agreed by the sound of it, otherwise she wouldn't have lied to me about it being a cleaner.

With the forgotten Valentine's card to add into the mix too, everything seemed to be pointing in one direction. But Dad having an affair? Really? It seemed about as likely as Victoria Beckham being caught breaking a smile. For starters, Dad was like the Olympic torch: he never went out. So where would he even meet someone else?

Plus, I was fully aware that Mum could burn his head out sometimes with her overbearing ways and erratic personality, but I knew he adored her. You could see it in the way he held her hand in church and the occasional kisses he planted on her head.

So, it begged the question, if it wasn't an affair, then what *was* he hiding?

*

Isme: Will you be much longer?
If I'm longer than an hour
Sue will have a fit

Anthony: Sorry! Will be there in 5 🏃

I clicked my phone off and sighed, taking a sip of my wine. The bar, a posh place in the business district, was heaving with the Monday lunchtime traffic, largely consisting of overbearing corporate types in black suits that seemed to be playing a game of 'who can guffaw the loudest'.

My stomach grumbled at the smell of meat sizzling on charcoal that wafted through the air, and I internally cursed Anthony for making me wait.

Suddenly, a loud howl from the front of the restaurant caught my attention. I looked up and saw that it was coming from the hostess, who was greeting a new guest with much more enthusiasm than the one I had got, flicking her hair and pushing her chest out.

I could understand why though. He stood out amongst the sea of black suits, in his blue chinos, crisp white shirt and slim fit grey blazer, which accentuated his toned arms. I found myself wondering what it would be like to stroke them myself ... when he looked over and waved at me.

"Sorry I'm late, Freckiades," said Anthony, taking the seat

opposite me. "I had to sort out some paperwork at the office."

I smiled and took a gulp of my wine, internally willing my flushed cheeks to pipe down. Had I *really* just unknowingly perved on my best mate?

"What's up with you?" said Anthony, eyeing me suspiciously. "You look like you've been on the sunbeds, which I know you haven't since 2004."

"Oh, nothing. I'm fine. I just, erm . . ."

He was looking at me expectantly, waiting for an explanation for my odd behaviour, but all I could think about was how his brown eyes stood out against the white of his shirt, and how I'd never realised before how his caved-in cheeks sharpened his jawline.

As soon as I left, I rang Agnes in a panic.

Me: "First the sex dream, now this. What the hell is going on with me?"

Agnes: "Howay, Izzy lass, you just need to get your end away, and fast."

Me: "Yeah, you're right. You know I got the flutters the other day from watching a clip of Dermot O'Leary trimming a bush on *This Morning*?"

Agnes: "Ha! That is class. What about that Carlos laddie? He's keen for a shag, isn't he?"

Me: "There's desperate, Ag, and then there's Carlos."

Agnes: "He canee be that bad? Look, why don't you just go on a second date with him and see if anything stirs, if you know what I mean? Best case, you get the flutters and he gives you the best night of your life. Worst case, you get a blow-up doll and put Dermot O'Leary's face on it."

Me: "Ha! Now, when you put it like that . . ."

*

Carlos: Hey gorgeous lady,
are you ignoring me? 😍

Isme: Yep

Carlos: 😅
When can I take you out again?

Isme: You took me to your family chippy,
I wouldn't call it 'out'

Carlos: Oh come on, I'll take you somewhere
else next time. Please? 🙏

I hesitated as I contemplated my response. Did I listen to Agnes and give him another chance? After all, with his family's wealth he could be the lifeline I needed if Mum and Dad ended up bankrupt and homeless. Have them move in with me versus spend a lifetime with Carlos? I honestly wasn't sure what would be worse. But, as Agnes said, what was there to lose?

Isme: Go on, then. But only if it doesn't involve
showing me the workings of a chip shop fryer

Carlos: 😎

Will pick you up at eight.

Wear something nice 😝

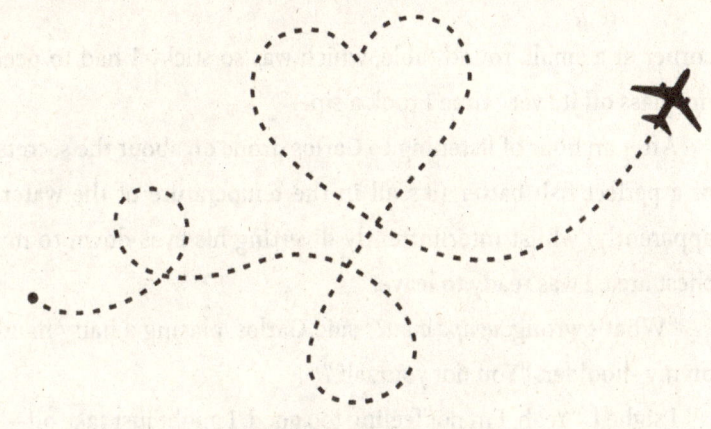

MARCH

I **REGRETTED MY DECISION TO GO FOR A DRINK WITH**
Carlos as soon as I opened the front door. He was leaning
against the door frame holding a bunch of flowers, which had
about as much life in them as Bruce Forsyth (God rest his soul).
Then there was the black leather trousers and animal print shirt.

"Oh, *agape mou*, you look just mmmmm!" He kissed his
fingers and threw them up into the air like one of those Italian
chefs when they're pleased with their creation. It was hardly the
reaction I was expecting since I'd just thrown on some casual
jeans, a baggy grey jumper and ankle boots. The lad would find a
bin bag appealing.

Carlos took me to an Irish bar in town that smelt of eggy farts
and was packed full of hen and stag dos who'd clearly googled
'cheapest places to go in Liverpool for a drink'. We sat in the

corner at a small, round table, which was so sticky I had to peel my glass off it every time I took a sip.

After an hour of listening to Carlos drone on about the secrets of a perfect fish batter (it's all in the temperature of the water, apparently) whilst intermittently diverting his eyes down to my chest area, I was ready to leave.

"What's wrong, *agape mou*?" said Carlos, placing a hairy hand on my shoulder. "You not yourself."

I sighed. "Yeah, I'm not feeling too good. I might just take off—"

"Aha! I know how to cheer you up!" He swaggered up to the bar and returned moments later with two shots of sambuca.

"Oh, I don't know, Carlos. I don't really want a hangover tomorrow and—"

Carlos shoved the shot glass in my hand, and as the smell of the aniseed hit my nostrils, I knew I was a goner.

Two hours and three more shots later, I found myself telling Carlos all about Mum and Dad's financial woes.

"Surely you can help your *mama* and *bampas* out once you become a lawyer?" said Carlos who, five rounds of drinks later, was looking more like John Travolta in *Night Fever*. "You know I've always had a thing for Ally McBeal."

"Weeelllthatsjustthething," I slurred, poking an index finger into his chest. "I'mnoteventaking the examsanymore, I'm justan administrationassistant ha!"

The rest of the night was a blur, but when I woke up in the morning to the familiar smell of chip fat on my cheeks, I had a strong suspicion that this time he hadn't missed my lips.

I knew as soon as I picked the phone up to Mum and heard the cheer in her voice that she'd got wind about me going on another date with Carlos.

Mum: "Oh, Isme, I so happy! I knew you two would get on."

Me: "No, Mum, you see I—"

Mum: "He is such a Good Greek Boy. And you know his family very wealthy!"

Me: "Yeah, you haven't mentioned that before. Anyway, Mum, I—"

Mum: "And with your salary when you qualify you two will have so mach maney! Don't forget your mama, OK?"

Me: "No, Mum, you've got it all wrong, you see—"

Mum: "Oh, Maria is ringing me. She probably heard thee news too! Speak to you later, Mrs Carlos!"

*

Mum: Isme, why you no answer your phone?
What time you pick me up to take me to church?
ISME!!!!! 😠😠😠

Isme: Sorry, just woke up. Why can't Dad take you?

Mum: I tell you he got his computer course!

Isme: Oh, sorry yeah, I forgot you asked
On my way

Computer learning course my arse. What courses take place on God's day of rest? I had more important things to worry about though, like how I was going to mask my wine-fuelled breath from Mum in the car, and finding the location of my one pair of decent black tights that have no visible holes. The answers? Febreze and in the washing basket (lucky I had the Febreze to hand).

"My God, Isme, what's that smell? Is like turps." I should have known that nothing gets past Mum's conk. She shuffled into the front seat of my car and folded down the creases in her black A-line skirt, which she wore with a black cardigan and thick black tights.

"Dad and this computer course, eh. It's a bit mad, isn't it?" I said as we drove off.

"Why is mad? He just want to learn, Isme."

I told her I didn't understand why, after sixty-two years of not so much as looking at a laptop.

"I mean, don't you think it's a bit weird?"

Mum sighed. "*Ochi*, I don no. Isme, I don no."

Mum didn't speak to me throughout the entire mass, which was a blessing since it got me out of any questions about Carlos. I could only hope that him and his stifling wench of a mother weren't around which, from a quick scan of the church, they didn't seem to be.

She did break her silence briefly at one point to berate me for crossing my legs, which was considered 'improper' in Greek church and likely to gain you some disdainful looks. I was tempted to do a Sharon Stone in *Basic Instinct* style leg display for my own entertainment, but instead did as I was told. I didn't need Mum being more annoyed with me than she already was.

After the mass finished, Mum scurried off to the side room for a chin wag with the other Greek Wives and Girlfriends, or GWAGS as I liked to call them. I lagged behind – normally I'd love nothing more than to listen to some local juicy gossip but feared that after my recent dealings with Carlos, I'd be the source of today's hearsay.

I headed to the cake table, but given it was Lent and dairy was off limits, the only thing on offer were some digestive biscuits and a vegan-friendly karidopita cake that looked as dry as my mouth after a heavy night on the booze. It was shaped like a curly turd and covered with a very fitting dark brown chocolate glaze, so didn't exactly scream out 'eat me, I'm delicious'.

I opted for the safe bet of a few digestives and a brew, and sought refuge in a quiet corner. It wasn't long before my presence was detected. Thankfully, it was only Stavros.

"I see you've given the cake a swerve. I don't blame you, girl, it looks about as appealing as my trotters after a twelve-hour shift in the restaurant!" Stavros smelt of Old Spice aftershave, which tickled my nose. He reminded me of Omid Djalili, with his short broad frame and bald head. Close your eyes and listen to him talk, though, and you'd think he was a born and bred scouser.

Stavros owned a Greek restaurant in town which was renowned for its lively entertainment, consisting of plate smashing and belly dancing. I'd spent many a drunken night there thanks to Stavros and his generosity with the ouzo. He also owned a villa in Cyprus, which he'd kindly allowed the Eliades family to use from time to time. If it wasn't for Stavros, we probably would've never been able to afford to go on holiday at all.

"What's all this about you having a fella then, eh?"

I gave him an incredulous stare. "Who told you that?"

"Never mind that. Now, come on, tell your Uncle Stavros."

I took a long, drawn-out drink of my tea. "I honestly don't know what you're talking about. I'm as single as a Pringle!"

I made my excuses before Stavros could probe any further and went in search of Mum to stop her spouting her mouth off to anyone else about my love life. My plan was to tell her on the drive home from church that I had no interest in taking things further with Carlos, but she'd already been offered a lift home by one of the other regulars who owns a Range Rover, and there was no way she was going to miss an opportunity of being seen in a big, shiny, expensive four-by-four.

*

"I just can't believe you went on a second date with him, Isme," laughed Anthony, as we tucked into a pizza at the flat, which was greasy and delicious all at the same time. "You've been out with some muppets in the past, like, but Carlos has to be the worst. He's like Glenn Quagmire off *Family Guy* . . . giggity, giggity, giggity."

I couldn't help but chuckle at Anthony's impersonation, which *was* quite apt. It also wasn't the first time he'd taken the piss out of my choice of men. Like Tom, for example, who I met at college. He was a nice lad, quiet and unassuming until he'd blow his nose and morph into a trumpet. The amount of times I almost had a coronary when he'd do an unexpected blow. Anthony even went as far as buying a toy trumpet to imitate his nose blowing.

But piss-taking aside, I'd always appreciated his honesty.

"I think I was completely blind-sided by the need to get laid . . . which I absolutely didn't do, by the way. We just kissed," I quickly added. "I do have *some* standards." I wiped my greasy hands with a tissue. "You know, I even had a dream about you!"

Anthony's eyes widened. "Is that why you were all weird with me at lunch the other week?"

'What?! No, that was just, er, time of the month." I grabbed my can of Coke and took a long sip, willing my flushed cheeks to go down. Thankfully, Anthony didn't seem to notice.

"Well if it makes you feel any better, I've had loads of sex dreams about you."

"Woah, what?! How come you've never told me?"

Anthony shrugged his shoulders. "What's there to tell? They're just dreams. I've had one about Maria too, and—"

"Oh my God, please don't say my mum, or I might throw my pizza back up."

"Ha! No. I was going to say Liz Truss."

I wasn't sure what was worse.

*

Carlos: Hey sexy lady, I can't stop thinking about you and that kiss . . . 🍆🍆🍆
Can we do it again soon? 🙏
I'm free next weekend?

I wondered how long I could ignore his texts until he gave up and preyed on some other poor, unsuspecting female. Something told me it'd be a while. I was probably the only hope he'd had for intimate contact with an actual real-life female in ages.

With Mum and Dad's bleak finances weighing on my mind like big concrete blocks, maybe I needed to stop being so picky. But surely I could find another lad out there who was a bit more marriage material than Liverpool's answer to Austin Powers?

*

EMAIL
From: Jeffrey Mulligan
To: All Staff
Subject: New Job Opportunities

Dear all,
Here at Mulligan's, we strive to help our staff reach their potential. With that in mind, there are a number of new roles that have opened up that I would like to make you aware of:

• Finance Apprentice
• Legal Typist
• Case Administrator

We will be advertising these roles to the general public, but current staff are also able to apply should they so wish. All candidates, internal and external,

will be treated equally and will go through the same
interview procedure.

If you are interested in applying, please contact Sue
before the deadline of **Thursday 28th March**.

Regards,
Jeffrey Mulligan

I'd been dreading the email coming through, knowing it was only
a matter of time before Jeff would be on my case about putting
myself forwards. I almost had to do a double-take when I saw the
list of roles, though. Having helped out in the payroll department
from time to time, I knew that the pay grades for these roles would
be much higher than *my* current measly salary.

I still didn't want to stay at Mulligan's in the long term, but
this promotion seemed like the quickest way of getting a decent
amount of (guaranteed) extra income, and helping out Mum and
Dad.

I needed to think, so took myself out for a stroll at lunch.
It was a cool, sunny spring day and people were taking advantage,
enjoying lunchtime beverages in the sun, or eating their homemade butties on a bench. There was a sense of hope in the air that,
although a jacket was still a must to take the edge off the cool
breeze, summer was most definitely on the horizon.

I wandered aimlessly through the centre of town, lost in a cloud
of thoughts about whether I could stomach another year or so at

Mulligan's, when a poster in the window of Costa Coffee for their new mini eggs hot chocolate caught my attention. It seemed like just the pick me up I needed to get me through the rest of the day.

I peered through the window to assess the queue damage, not wanting to risk going over my one hour lunch quota and dealing with the wrath of Sue, who was like a Sergeant Major when it came to timekeeping. That's when I spotted them.

They were too engrossed in conversation over their drinks to notice me, although it seemed from where I was standing that Zara was doing most of the talking. Anthony sat protectively cupping his mug with both hands.

Anthony must have said something funny because Zara threw her head back and laughed with so much exaggeration, I was surprised she didn't give herself whiplash. A wave of irritation rushed through me as I thought about the promise Anthony had made at the flat after Zara's birthday drinks, and how he'd assured me he had no interest in pursuing anything with her.

But there was another feeling niggling away at me as I sulked back to the office, a feeling that was surprising and unfamiliar when it came to Anthony.

Jealousy? Really?

*

It seemed that Mum was speaking to me again after I annoyed her by questioning Dad's newfound love of IT, although she didn't have much of a choice. Their car was in the garage and she needed a lift home from her Clubercise class. Unfortunately, I had no other plans.

As I waited in the car park, my mind slowly wandered to Zara and Anthony and their cosy little coffee shop date, which it had been doing for the past two days since I saw them. I'd been wracking my brain wondering why, after all this time, Anthony had suddenly changed his mind about her – and why did it bother me so much?

I was hopeful that the reason for their meet up was purely innocent, but my stomach still lurched at the thought of the pair of them staring longingly into each other's eyes over candle-lit dinners, and spending lazy days embroiled under the sheets. Anthony's strong arms wrapped around her as she lay on his chest . . .

KNOCK, KNOCK!

I jolted at the sound of Mum banging on the car window with her glow sticks, but the sight of her was far more frightening. She looked like she'd just been to a 1970s roller disco, in her black leotard, pink headband and matching sweat bands.

I was so tempted to drive off for a laugh but thought I'd best not, considering I needed to get back into her good books before telling her that Carlos was off the wedding table.

The whole drive, I had to listen to Mum reciting every detail from the class like an excitable puppy, including the full set list. Please kill me before my highlight of the week becomes a choreographed dance session in a dark room with a load of blue rinses waving their glow sticks in the air like they just don't care.

I wasn't complaining, though – anything to distract her from mentioning the 'C' word. As we pulled up outside the house,

I felt cautiously optimistic that maybe Mum had realised for herself that me and Carlos were no more suited than beans on Weetabix.

KNOCK, KNOCK!

Another bang on the car window, only this time it was Anthony's mum Sandra with, thankfully, no neon lycra in sight. She was out walking their dog – a Frenchie called Bella.

They say owners unintentionally choose dogs that resemble them, and never has a truer word been spoken than when it came to Sandra and Bella, with their small features and gentle temperaments. I reckon if Mum had a canine, it would be a bulldog.

"You look great, Isme!" said Sandra, as I wound the window down. I didn't, unless by great she meant unwashed hair that had been tied up in a messy bun and a pasty make-up free complexion, but I smiled gratefully at the compliment. "Anthony tells me you've started baking again? I used to love eating your lemon drizzle, although my hips didn't appreciate it!"

I'd always had a soft spot for Sandra. She exuded gentle and calm, with her soft-spoken voice and inoffensive demeanour. She also made *the* best karidopita cake (don't tell Mum, she'd string me up), a deliciously moist walnut cake covered in a honey lemon syrup that tingles your taste buds and leaves you with a satisfied pallet. The amount of times me and Anthony would sneak a piece of a freshly made batch from the kitchen after school, burning our mouths in the process.

"Did you hear about Isme's new boyfriend?" Mum had unlocked her seatbelt and was leaning her busty chest over me.

Sandra smiled at me weakly. "A boyfriend, eh? So, who's the lucky man?"

"There is no lucky man, Mum's just—"

"Don lie, Isme, you seeing—"

"WOOF WOOF WOOF WOOF!"

The dog went into an uncontrollable fit of barks, jumping up at the car window and snapping at Mum, causing Sandra to make her excuses and head home.

At least someone had my back, even if it did have four legs and did its business in public.

*

I'd been photocopying some papers for Sue when Zara came totting over in her four-inch stilettos, a smug look etched across her face.

"So, when should I buy my hat?"

I frowned. "What are you on about?"

"For the wedding, Isme! I hear Carlos is buying the ring as we speak."

"Pah! Don't be daft. You know as well as I do that it's like Chinese whispers in our community."

I scooped up my photocopying and headed back to my desk, willing Zara to give up the ghost and do the same, but she followed behind me in close pursuit. I felt my face boiling up with rage with every *click clack* of her heels against the wooden floor.

"Bloody hell, Isme, first Alan, now Carlos. You really know how to pick them, don't you?"

"FUCK YOU, ZARA!" I surprised myself with my loud outburst,

never mind Zara and the rest of the office, most of whom were now peering over their computer screens like meerkats on the lookout for a predator.

Zara stared at me in disbelief. "That was a bit uncalled for, wasn't it?"

"No, I'll tell you what's uncalled for: commenting on *my* choice of men when you've been going around sleeping with married ones!"

Zara laughed awkwardly, her cheeks flushing pink. "Keep your voice down, will you—"

"AND SPEAKING OF WHICH, HAS LUKE TOLD HIS WIFE ABOUT YOUR LITTLE SORDID AFFAIR YET?"

A chorus of gasps filtered across the room, followed by an exaggerated cough from close behind me. I turned round to find Jeff standing there with his arms crossed and a look of disapproval on his face.

"Zara, can I see you in my office, please."

"Jeff, I can explain—"

"Now, please." He signalled his arm in the direction of his office and Zara stomped off in a huff like a moody teenager, muttering 'you bitch' to me as she walked past.

With a zero-tolerance policy for inter-marital affairs within the office, I knew things wouldn't look good for Zara, as confirmed by an email that came through from Jeff later that day.

EMAIL
From: Jeff Mulligan

To: All Staff

Re: Staff update

Dear all,

I would like to make you all aware that, due to
personal reasons, Zara Baros will be away from the
office for the next two weeks with immediate effect.

Jeff Mulligan

*

"I can't believe you got her suspended!" laughed Anthony, taking
a sip of his pint. "I would have paid money to see the look on her
face." In desperate need of a wine after the Zara incident, I'd asked
him to meet me in The Pig's Ear after work.

I eyed Anthony suspiciously, still unsure of the regularity of
their contact and whether he already knew about the incident at
work. But from the way his eyes bulged and he shook his head, he
seemed genuinely surprised.

"I honestly feel really bad about it," I said, and I wasn't lying.

Isme Eliades did *not* grovel. If I'd said something to piss you off,
then you'd probably done something to piss me off, so whatever
I'd said would be perfectly justified with no need for a redress.
But this 'incident' with Zara, and her subsequent suspension/
sabbatical/involuntary holiday, had left me with a ball of anxiety
in the pit of my stomach. I'd only intended on shaming her a bit
when I blurted out about Luke for the whole office to hear. The

last thing I wanted was to put a black mark against her squeaky-clean employment record.

We sat in silence for a bit. Our silences were usually easy and comfortable, but today it felt deafening amongst the general chatter of other pub goers – not that Anthony seemed to notice. He was engrossed in some silly YouTube video on his phone.

"Can I ask you something?" I said, circling the stem of my wine glass. "And I need complete and utter honesty."

Anthony looked up from his phone, a sincere expression etched across his face. "Of course, you know I'm always honest with you."

I took a deep breath. "Are you starting something up with Zara?"

"What? No, why do you ask that?"

"I saw you the other day, in town, in the coffee shop with her."

Anthony leant back in his chair. "Oh, that. Yeah, I'd asked her to meet me so I could put an end to this whole situation of her trying it on with me. It *was* your suggestion, remember? To let her down gently?"

I suddenly remembered our conversation at the flat when we were having pizza, and the penny dropped. "God, yeah, I did. I completely forgot."

"Come on, you know me better than anyone, and I would *never* go back on a pinky promise."

Whilst I still hadn't quite made sense of the jealousy I'd felt seeing them together, I couldn't help feeling relieved that nothing was going on between them. We'd never let something or someone come between us in our whole thirty years of friendship, and I wasn't ready to let it happen now. Especially when that something and someone was Zara Baros.

*

I called round to Mum and Dad's after work to find them shuffling around in the garage.

"What's going on?" I asked, as I spotted the pile of bin bags and boxes.

"We having a clear out!" declared Mum, cheerily. "Isme, do you still want this signed poster of Peter Andre?"

"Pah! No way. Isn't he, like, fifty now?" I scoffed, taking the poster from her and holding it up admiringly as I reminisced about my obsessive 'Mysterious Girl' phase. "Actually, on second thoughts. Which one is the 'to keep' pile?"

Dad laughed, pointing to a box containing some old CDs and DVDs.

"You do realise that these things are practically obsolete now, don't you?"

"Yeah, but Barry down the pub said there's a website where you can sell them. I think he said it was called Apple Pie?"

I smiled. "It's Magpie, Dad. But seriously, Mum, you haven't thrown anything away since 1985, so why the clear out now?"

Mum and Dad exchanged a glance before Dad exclaimed, "We're turning it into a gym!"

"Yes, yes, that's right. A gym!" confirmed Mum.

I eyed them suspiciously. "Yeah, right. Oh my god, you're selling the rotisserie machine?!" I cried, as I spotted the familiar silver grill that had provided years of delicious homemade souvlaki.

"Yes, I don't really use it any more," said Mum, avoiding my glare.

"Mum, you use it more than the toilet."

"Yes, well. We need the mon— SPACE! We need the space. Now, make yourself useful, Isme, and start shredding those letters."

I sighed and did as I was told. I didn't need to delve more into the sudden desire to create a home gym from the two people who hadn't so much as picked up a weight in my thirty-three years of living. I already knew the cause.

*

EMAIL

From: Sue Wright

To: Ismeena Eliades

Subject: Promotion opportunities

Hi Isme,

Thank you for registering your interest in the case administrator role, as per Jeff's email on 7th March.

I am delighted to inform you that you have been accepted for an interview, which will take place on 11th April. We will inform you shortly of the format that the interview will take so you can suitably prepare.

Sue

I closed down my laptop and rubbed at my temples, trying to convince myself that it was the right decision.

It didn't stop the sinking feeling in the pit of my stomach.

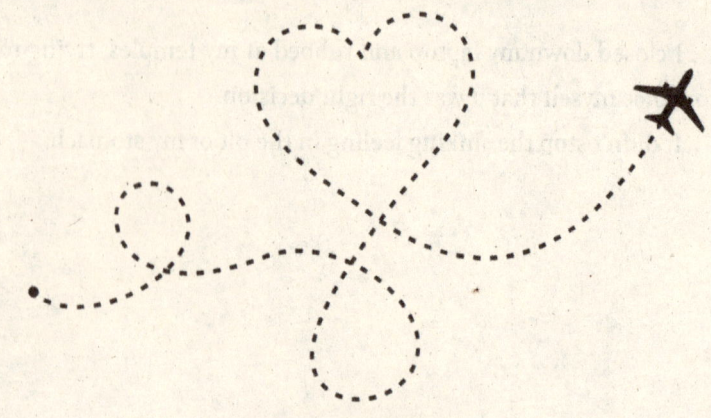

APRIL

Isme: Happy birthday, Dad! 🎉 🎂

Dad: Hi Isme, it's your dad. Thanks. Love Dad xxx
😎 🤍 👽

Isme: I know it's you, Dad, I sent you the message!
I've told you before, you don't need to sign off
your messages like it's an email!

Dad: Sorry, love. I still can't get used to these
message thingies. 🙈 🤍 👽

Isme: 😄 See you later in The Fig Tree
for your birthday meal

*

The Fig Tree was Dad's favourite English restaurant, mainly because of their generous-sized portions of fish and chips, and it being only a short walk from their house.

The savoury smell of freshly baked bread and meat searing on a stove wafted past as I opened the door to the restaurant, making my stomach growl.

I was late, as per, landing me the unfortunate seat sandwiched between Theo and Tomaso, who already had Maria up the wall.

"Mummy, where's our food?"

"Mummy, can I have some ice cream?"

"Mummy, I'm hungry. Where's our food?"

"Mummy, mummy, mummy, mummy!"

George's lazy arse was nowhere to be seen – my guess was that, in true Mandy Jordache style, Maria had put a spade to his head and buried him under the patio. I could just picture her on the next episode of *Killer Women* with Piers Morgan.

"Why did you murder your husband in such a brutal way?" Piers would ask. And, after a long, thoughtful pause, Maria would say, "To tell you the truth, Piers, he was getting on me nerves."

"He's at home," said Maria, bursting my fantasy bubble.

I was shortly followed by Anthony, much to the twins delight, who shouted "ANTHONY! ANTHONY!" as they jumped out of their seats, hurling themselves at him and almost winding him in the process. They squealed with delight as he rubbed his knuckles on their heads and tickled their tummies.

"Right, Anthony, you're playing Dad for the rest of the night," said Maria, pouring herself a large glass of wine. Anthony laughed, but she looked deadly serious.

"How's work going, Izzy, love?" asked Dad after the waiter took our order, and Theo and Tomaso were sat quietly on their iPads getting lost in the YouTube rabbit hole.

"Yeah, good. I'm going for a promotion, actually."

"I thought you hated it there?" said Maria, eyeing me suspiciously over her wine glass.

"I do . . . I mean, it's OK. I just need— WANT some extra cash, you know?" I took a sip of water to clear my dry throat.

"I think you should give the baking business another go," said Anthony, taking a sip of his beer. "Especially now you've started making some stuff again."

"Yeah, well, it's not as easy as that, plus—"

"Oh my god, Anthony, you should have tasted the toast she did with the bread she made the other week. It was ri-di-cu-lous."

"Well of course it was, Maria, she was taught by thee best."

"My ever so humble wife, everybody," laughed Dad, wrapping his arms around Mum's shoulders and giving them a squeeze. "Seriously though, Isme, love, I thought you hated it at work. Why would you want to tie yourself in?"

Because I'm trying to get you some extra cash as quickly as possible to relieve some of your financial stress, which means putting my baking business dream to the side (again).

Instead of saying this, I fumbled with some crumbs on the table.

"Well, if you ask me, I think you should follow your drea—"

"Well I didn't ask you, Anthony. I never asked *any* of you. Now can we just drop it, please."

Silence descended around the table. Glances were exchanged, awkward sips of drinks were taken, bums were shuffled. Eventually, Mum, who'd looked deep in thought, said, "So this promotion, is more money, yes?"

*

Carlos: Hey sexy lady, when are you going to stop ignoring me and let me take you out again? 😎

Isme: Didn't you hear? I'm becoming a nun

Carlos: Mmmmm, I bet you would look sexy in a habit 😎
Well at least I get to see you next Sunday when you and your family come to my house for dinner 😁

I immediately called Mum.

Me: "Mum, have you told Carlos and his mother that we'll go to their house for dinner next week?"

Mum: "Yes, Isme, she asked us roun and so I say yes."

Me: "Well, you could have at least asked me first!"

Mum: "Why? We all family now. And don speak abou your mother-in-law like tha. Is rude."

Once my initial anger had subsided and I had time to reflect, I decided that it might not be a bad thing having everyone in the same room. I could put an end to the whole ridiculous situation.

All that was needed now was to buy some protective gear for when Mum started hurling keftedes and pitta bread at me.

*

We all descended on the Loukas residence after Sunday mass – 'we' being Mum, Maria, George and the twins. Dad was at his computer course again, which I was considering enquiring about myself if it got me out of church and awkward meals.

Given their supposed wealth, you'd expect the house to be some gated mansion set beyond a long and winding stone path, with a butler waiting by the front door to take our coats and hand us a glass of fizz. However, much like Carlos's dress sense, it was quite a disappointment.

It wasn't a bad size – a five-bedroom detached off the main road that connects North and South Liverpool – but it was about as well kept as my lady bush which was currently in hibernation. Speaking of bushes, I could hardly make out the front path from all the overgrown shrubbery sprawled across it, the cat wee-like smell of pollen making my eyes water. Either that or it *was* cat wee.

"This is what happens when you haven't got a man around to look after the place," muttered George, referring to Theoulla's late husband, who sadly passed away several years ago. I'll never forget his funeral, mainly because it's the only Greek one I've ever been to and it was quite an eye-opener. Especially at the burial when someone whipped out a trestle table by the grave and placed a load of halloumi, crusty bread and olives on it for everyone to tuck into, like some kind of graveyard picnic.

"Oh yeah, like you'd know anything about that," I retorted.

I pressed the bell and the front door burst open, causing a waft of roast chicken to escape. It was a pleasant change from animal urine.

"Welcome, everyone! Come in! Come."

Theoulla directed us through the hallway and into the living room, which was in dire need of a modern revamp – brown and beige floral couches, a burnt-orange carpet and retro lampshade. Carlos was waiting like a lion ready to pounce, and I had to hold back the laughter when I caught sight of him. He looked like he'd just walked in from the 1970s in a crocodile-skin print shirt and black PVC trousers.

I was about to pull him aside for 'the chat', keen to get it over with before any talk of wedding plans from our mothers inevitably started, but Theoulla announced that dinner was ready, leaving me no choice but to wait.

We took our places at the big, oak dining table, which was packed full of culinary delights, perfuming the room like a savoury candle – kalamata olives, tzatziki, pitta wedges, avgolemono soup, dolmades, keftedes. As much as I disliked Theoulla, there was no denying her ability to put on a good spread. I subtly checked my chin for drool.

"Wow, Theoulla, this all looks amazing!" said Maria, followed by a chorus of compliments and appreciation around the table. Apart from Mum, who was casting a judgemental eye over the feast.

"Yes, very nice, Theoulla," she said, smiling through her teeth. "This, homemade?" She was pointing to the tzatziki, which is about the only thing Mum won't make herself because grating the cucumber hurts her arms.

"Of course, Elana! Everything is homemade."

Mum sank into her seat like a deflated balloon. She hadn't seemed herself all day and had even passed on tea and cake after mass, which I knew was to avoid any questions about Dad's absence. But there was no getting away from Theoulla and her scrutinising ways.

"Computer course, you say?" she asked once the feeding frenzy had begun, and plates were being passed in every direction like a motorway junction.

Mum nodded weakly.

"How strange that they have them on a Sunday."

"Theoulla, these keftedes are delicious!" I interjected, in a bid to change the subject. "How do you get them so soft?" If there was one way to distract a Greek woman, it was getting them to talk about their beloved cooking. As Theoulla started reeling off her step-by-step guide to meatball making, I took the opportunity to snaffle Carlos for a chat. I had to prize his fork out of his hand and managed to poke him in the eye in the process.

"Everything OK over there?" I hadn't noticed that the cookery lesson had finished, and now all eyes were on us.

"Sorry, yeah, I just wanted to talk to Carlos about something, in private."

"Well, you can speak to him here." Theoulla grinned. "We are all family now, remember."

The whole table was looking at me expectantly, and for a split second I considered telling them all I just needed the loo, but I *had* to put an end to this farce. I took a huge breath and hoped for the best . . .

*

"How dare you treat my son like this!" scorned Theoulla once I'd laid my cards on the table, who had shuffled out of her seat to wrap her arms around Carlos, who looked like he was about to cry.

"I'm sorry, honestly I am." I was doing my best to sound sincere, but the way she was cuddling his head into her bosom like a baby was pure comical. I had visions of her whipping one out and letting him have a toot. "We're just not very well suited, that's all."

"Then why the kiss?" asked Carlos, looking up at me like a sad dog.

Bugger. This was not shedding me in the best light.

"Well, it's a lucky escape anyway, Carlos," scorned Theoulla, before I could respond. "I'm sure we can find you someone better than an administration assistant anyway."

"What you mean, Theoulla?" said Mum, with a puzzled look on her face. "My Isme, she a lawyer."

"Are you sure about that, Elana? I think you need to ask your daughter what happened with those exams she took."

Mum was looking at me, waiting for an explanation, but I was finding it hard to speak with the ball of rage that was building up in my stomach, ready to explode out of me like a meteor.

Before I knew what I was doing, I grabbed my coat and made

for the door – but not before my parting shot of "YOUR FOOD TASTES BLAND!" which was one way to really enrage a Greek woman.

*

Mum: Isme, we need to talk about yesterday

Isme: I'm sorry, Mum, really I am. I'll explain everything, I promise. Just not right now

Mum: You come round after work. I have to show you something

Isme: Is it the back of your hand?

Mum: Just come round, Isme

*

This is the last will and testament of Christina Eliades.

I appoint Elana Eliades to be the Executor of this Will.

I give the following legacies absolutely with any tax due to be paid by my estate:

1. My land in Cyprus as per the attached title plan to my daughter, Elana Eliades.

2. £25,000 cash to my surviving grandchildren,

conditional upon them marrying a man of Greek heritage. The trustees are instructed to release the cash after the marriage has taken place.

If this condition is not satisfied by the time they reach the age of 35, the trustees are instructed to gift the money to a charity of their choosing.

If the marriage is dissolved within ten years of taking place, the money has to be paid over to the Greek Orthodox Church.

3. I give the remainder of my estate, both real and personal, to my trustees to hold on trust, either to sell or if they think fit to retain all or any part of it and to pay my debts, testamentary expenses and inheritance tax payable on or by reason of my death.

Elana Eliades
Signed and dated
14 August 1974

I stared at the piece of paper. My eyes were seeing the words, but my brain was struggling to process their meaning.

"Is this a joke?".

"No, Isme, this is your *Yiayia's* handwriting. Is what she wanted."

"What, to bribe us all into marriage with a Greek fella rather than allowing us to find someone we're happy with, whatever their ethnic background?"

"She was very . . . how you say it, traditional woman, Isme, and keen to keep Eliades bloodline going, especially after we had to flee Cyprus. She worry that we would all meet English men and, eventually, the Greek bloodline would be lost. So she change thee Will just before we left."

I didn't remember my Greek nan, she passed away when I was a baby, but she sounded like a right bitch if the Will was anything to go by. It was bad enough being forced into a Greek marriage, never mind my money being given away to charity if I failed.

"Why are you just showing me this now? *Yiayia* died ages ago, so you and Dad have known this all that time and didn't think to tell me?"

Mum looked at me sheepishly. "Your father, he not know about the Will."

"What do you mean, he doesn't know?"

"I, I never tell him. When your *Yiayia* died, he very stressed with the restaurant and I worry he have another heart attack. I tell him she left all her money to thee church."

I slumped back into the sofa, trying to digest her words. I could understand her wanting to protect him, but I wasn't convinced it was the *sole* reason she didn't tell him. My guess was that she knew that by telling Dad the truth about the Will, he'd realise that her keenness to see me married off went beyond tradition – just like I realised that now.

"I suppose it makes perfect sense now why you've been so eager to see me married off to Carlos."

"*Ochi*, Isme, thee Will has nothing to do with that. Carlos, he is a Good Greek Boy, that's all. Also, that money, when you get it, is yours."

"I bet it would come in handy now though, you know with your little debt problem and that?" I said with a frown.

Mum's eyes widened, like a rabbit caught in the headlights. Before she had a chance to think up an excuse, I told her all about the voicemail message I'd listened to on her phone, and the conversation I'd overheard her and Dad having in the kitchen.

"OK, Isme. Me and your papa, we have some money problems," she said, holding her hands up. "But that's got nothing to do with me wanting you to settle down and get married."

"Sorry, Mum, but I don't believe you. You'd have me married off to Carlos tomorrow and sign me up to a lifetime of unhappiness just so you can get your hands on that money."

"Is not true, Isme! Is not true!" cried Mum, shaking her head. "I tell you, Carlos is very nice boy and he make you very happy, I'm sure. You know his family very wealthy and—"

"OH MY GOD, MOTHER, YOU ARE UNBELIEVABLE!" And with that I stormed out of the house, but not before grabbing a tub of pastitsio from the fridge en route. Anger made me oddly ravenous.

I called Maria as soon as I turned on the engine.

Maria: "She's always been like this, Isme. Remember before I met George and she made me go on that date with Kostas from church with the bog eye? I spent the whole date trying to figure out whether he was looking at me or the table of girls behind us. It was very confusing."

Me: "I know she's always been keen for us to marry Greek, Maria, and I've always put it down to a traditional thing. But after hearing about the Will it all just feels very *Indecent Proposal*."

Maria: "Oh my god, I'd sleep with Carlos if he looked like Robert Redford."

Me: "It's not the point, Maria! I feel very exposed, and used! Also, I'm guessing from your lack of surprise that you already knew about the Will?"

Maria: "Yeah, well, Mum obviously told me after I married George so I could get my share, but she swore me to secrecy. And no offence, Isme, but you're not worth suffering her wrath for. No one is. I would have told you if it got close to the deadline though, and there was no wedding on the cards."

Me: "Great, thanks."

Maria: "Look, just speak to Mum and tell her how you feel. I'm sure she'll understand."

Me: "No chance. I'm not speaking to her until she apologises."

Maria: "Ha, good luck with that one. The woman hasn't apologised for anything since 1995."

*

Having a barny with your mum the night before a big interview was hardly good prep. I spent the whole night tossing and turning, going over and over the Will and the realisation that my own mother was trying to sell me off, that same flush of anger

I'd felt when I'd first realised it rushing through me every time I did.

My heart wasn't in the interview – it never *had* been, but I'd been doing it for them. Now all I wanted to do was tell Mulligan's to stick their promotion where the sun doesn't shine, and leave Mum to sort her debt shit out on her own. But it all felt a little too late, and if I backed out now who knows where it would leave my job? Mulligan's had got rid of 'dead wood' before, and I was sure they could do it again, so I had to at least give the promotion a fighting chance. After all, a job (no matter how much I disliked it) was better than no job at all.

As I walked into the office and smelt the overpowering scent of Chanel No. 5, I knew that Zara was back. She was sat in Jeff's office and it seemed from the loud laughter that was coming from the room that all was forgiven. I slipped into my seat and waited patiently for her to come out so I could play out my well-rehearsed apology.

"Zara, can we talk?"

"Yeah sure, what's up?" she said without halting.

"Look, I just wanted to say sorry for—"

"You don't need to apologise. I'm over it." Zara sat down at her desk and started shuffling some papers around.

"Really?" Either I'd dodged a massive bullet, or Zara's cool, calm demeanour was all a front, and behind the scenes she was drumming up a cunning plan to get her revenge.

"Absolutely. Having the time off has done me the world of good. I even managed to get away to the Maldives, which was just fabulous." Zara swished her hair back, sending a waft of fruity shampoo my way.

"Oh, that's great, Zara. I'm so pleased for you. I just still feel really bad and—"

"I think Sue is looking for you." Zara smirked, nodding in the direction of Sue, who was storming across the office in my direction.

"Jeff and Trudie are waiting for you in the boardroom."

I looked at my watch. "But my interview isn't for another few hours?"

"Just leave your coat on and go."

Trudie was the Managing Partner and was well known in the office for her no-bullshit style and vibrant dress sense, which today consisted of a multicoloured striped top that she wore under a royal blue suit with matching-coloured glasses.

She was usually out schmoozing with clients or closing big deals so was rarely seen around the office – that is, unless there's an important staff matter to attend to. So, if you were getting called into a meeting with her, you were either getting a promotion or getting fired.

"Isme, take a seat," said Jeff, who was sat at the top end of the large oak boardroom table. Trudie was positioned on the edge of the table next to him typing furiously on her Blackberry.

"So, Isme, how are you?" asked Jeff, in the way a therapist would ask a client.

"I'm fine, thanks, looking forward to the interview later—"

"Right, let's cut to the chase," Trudie interjected, placing her phone down on the table and removing her glasses. "Isme, we know about your drinking problem."

I sat motionless as I tried to digest Trudie's words. I looked over at Jeff for more clarification, but he refused to meet my gaze. "I'm sorry, what?"

Trudie sighed impatiently. "Right, OK, this is going to be more difficult than we thought. Jeff, the bag." Like an obedient dog, Jeff reached under the table and pulled out a plastic bag and emptied the contents onto the table. "Are these familiar?"

I stared at the empty bottles of miniature wine bottles and spirits. "They're not mine, if that's what you mean. For starters, I don't drink spirits – well, not those ones anyway. And that wine is far too sweet." Jeff and Trudie exchanged a pitiful look.

"OK, so if they're not yours then why were they found in the drawer of *your* desk?"

I shrugged my shoulders. "I've no idea – maybe someone confused my desk with theirs. Either that or someone put them in there intentionally."

Trudie rolled her eyes, clearly bored by this menial staff matter. "And why would someone do that, Isme?"

"To get me into trouble, to sabotage my promotion, to, to . . ." I suddenly thought about Zara and the smirk on her face, and a light bulb went off in my head. "ZARA! It was Zara, she put them there!"

"Isme, you can't go round making accusations without any proof."

"But I can get you proof, I know it was her, I—"

"We're putting you on an involuntary leave of absence," said Trudie, opening the door and declaring the meeting over. "When you come back, we expect you to have cleaned up your act, and maybe then we can start to consider your promotion again."

With that, she slammed the door in my face, and I stood frozen to the spot, my heart racing at a thousand knots. I wanted to storm back in there and plead my innocence, to demand a thorough investigation of the mystery bag of alcohol. But I knew Trudie, and once her mind was made up, there was no getting her to back down.

I sulked back to my desk to grab a few belongings (mainly my framed picture of Jason Mamoa and a packet of Quavers). I could feel the many eyes of the office on me as I made my way over to the lift and tapped furiously on the down button in the hope that, for once, the old piece of tin would do me a solid and not take an age.

"Going somewhere nice?" I looked up to find Zara's smug face coming out the lift.

"It was you, wasn't it?" I said through gritted teeth.

"I have no idea what you're talking about," she said with a smirk, before brushing past me and sashaying back to her desk.

*

"You really think it was Zara who planted all that booze in your desk?"

"Well, who else could it have been, Maria? The girl has never liked me, she's always just tolerated me coz I'm mates with Anthony. Getting her suspended was just the fuel she needed to get one over on me."

"Yeah, makes sense, I suppose. What a bitch, eh?"

"Amen to that." We clinked our wine glasses together in unison.

We were sat eating dinner on my tiny balcony, making the most of a warm mid-spring day. It was my favourite season, when the birds start chirping and the smell of fresh-cut grass fills the air. And the sun, with its energetic glow, but not yet warm enough to be reaching for the factor thirty, which was great news for my pasty complexion.

"What did you do with *your* dosh then?" I asked Maria, referring to the inheritance money. "Did Mum make you donate it to the Eliades failed restaurant fund, which no doubt she'll make me do once I get mine? That's if I ever speak to her again, like."

It had been a week since our spat over the Will and still no apology had been forthcoming, or *any* communication for that matter. It had been like a breath of fresh air for the first few days, not getting inundated with daily messages asking me if I'd eaten enough, or calling me to tell me the latest scandal on *Eastenders*. But annoyingly, as the week went on, I'd found myself checking my phone more than normal in the hope that she'd decided to cave, and feeling a little deflated every time I'd see my blank screen.

"Oh, don't be like that, Isme. She's really upset about it, you know. Dad said she didn't even go to Zumba this week." Mum missing her beloved fitness class for the fossils spoke volumes, and I couldn't help but feel a little pang of guilt.

"Anyway, luckily I got my money before the restaurant went under," said Maria, shoving a forkful of the crispy spinach and feta pie I'd made into her gob. One of the positives of being temporarily unemployed was having time to cook some proper food rather than the frozen stuff. There was also an orange ravani cake still baking in the oven for afters, filling the flat with a glorious, sweet citrus aroma. "Remember that bright pink Mini Cooper I had with the soft top and diamante-encrusted alloys?"

"How could I forget? You used to drive round L18 thinking you were in a Britney Spears music video."

"Yeah, we had some great times, me and Barbie." Maria stared off into the distance, as if watching a 'best bits' clip of her and the car. "Such a shame I crashed it into Mum's front garden wall and had to write it off."

I laughed to myself at the memory, scooping up the left-over flakes of pastry from the pie on my plate which, I had to admit, wasn't half bad. The pastry was golden and crispy and complemented the salty taste of the filling of feta cheese, sundried tomatoes and spinach nicely.

"I didn't waste *all* of it on the car. The rest has been used as a makeshift savings account since George lost his job. My income alone hasn't been enough for us to live off." Maria prodded mindlessly at a rogue piece of feta on her plate.

Their finance situation was clearly weighing her down. I was suddenly grateful my money was still locked away, safe from any frivolous purchases or husbands bumming off it. Although, with the promotion now on the back burner and the cake business more out of reach than ever (I mean, what bank was going to lend to a temporarily unemployed thirty-something with zero savings to her name?), I may end up needing the key.

"No matter how many times I've watched it, I still crap meself at the T-rex scene."

"Hmmm, yeah. I know what you mean." I fumbled with the drawstring on my hoodie. We were sat in Anthony's bedroom on his leather sofa bed watching *Jurassic Park*, something we'd done a million times before. But today my mind was elsewhere.

Sensing my distraction, Anthony pressed pause on the film and said, "Are you OK? You don't seem yourself."

I sighed. "Yeah, just got a lot on my plate."

"Is this about the whole Zara thing again?" He rolled his eyes up at the ceiling, which made my blood boil.

"Well, yeah, it is actually. I may not have a job because of her, and that was my quickest route to trying to help Mum and Dad out. The whole bloody family will be homeless at this rate."

"Oh don't be so dramatic, Isme," laughed Anthony. "You've always got Carlos to fall back on."

I glared at him. If he was trying to lighten the mood, it was having the opposite effect. "Why are you being such an arse?"

"I'm not! All I'm saying is I really don't think it was Zara that planted that alcohol in your desk, and that maybe you need to move past it or you'll drive yourself crazy."

I folded my arms across my chest. "Fine. I just don't see why you're suddenly all Team Zara."

"I'm not 'Team Zara'. I just think you should get your facts straight before you go round accusing people." Anthony jumped up from the sofa. "I'll go and get some drinks, give you a chance to calm down."

After he left, I rested my head on the back of the sofa and closed my eyes. I knew I was behaving like a spoilt brat, but I couldn't help it. I just didn't see why he was so adamant it wasn't Zara.

It was then that I noticed his phone, that he'd left on the sofa beside me, which had come to life with some message notifications. I peered over absent-mindedly but immediately regretted it as I caught sight of the messages.

> **Zara:** It was great seeing you.
> When can we do it again so we can
> finish what we started?

I stared at the phone in disbelief. Anthony had made me believe he'd quashed Zara's persistent chasing when he met up with her in the coffee shop, but it was clear from the messages that something had happened between them since. It hurt that he felt she was worth breaking our trust for, but it hurt more that he was continuing to lie.

*

Agnes: "Iz, are youuuu gunna come out or what? It's buzzin here!"

Me: "Shit, sorry, Ag. I completely forgot you were in town."

Agnes: "Don't worry, just get your arse here now!"

Me: "Where are you?"

Agnes: "Pogue Mahone's. I'll get the Guinness in."

Me: "Oh, er, I don't think I can, Ag. I'm busy with, er . . ."

I looked down at my sad Saturday-night-in-for-one essentials (bottle of wine – check, packet of Walkers Sensations – check,

Superdrug face mask promising to give me a 'renewed radiance' which I read to mean 'make me look fifteen again' – check), and the paused opening credits of *Power* on the telly. Spend the night alone perving on James St Patrick or go and down pints of Guinness until my poo turned black?

Agnes: "Isme, you still there? You coming or what?"

I suddenly heard the dulcet tones of 'Irish Rover' in the background, and before I knew it, I was changing out of my pyjamas into some black jeans, a loose green T-shirt and a shamrock headband and heading out the door.

*

I woke up this morning with the Big Mac of all hangovers, an actual Big Mac, half-eaten on the pillow beside me, and a major case of 'the fear'. You know, when you wake up with a dreaded feeling in the pit of your stomach that you did something really silly.

In a panic, I picked up my phone and dialled Agnes's number.

Agnes: "Don't worry, Izzy lass, you didn't do anything silly."

Me: "Phew!"

Agnes: "Belter night, though. I canee believe how blootered we were!"

Me: "Ha, I know, but what did we expect having sambuca chasers with every round? My tongue feels like a burnt carpet!"

Agnes: "Aye! So, did Anthony message you back?"

Me: "What do you mean?"

Agnes: "You said something in Maccies about messaging him about Zara."

Frantically, I ended the call and opened up my messages.

My heart sank as I realised the cause of my 'fear'.

Isme: *Anthony! Is me, Isme. I JUS want yout know tha IMhapy for youuuuuuu* 😬
ActuallyIm not. Imabit jealous
Goingtbed now. Wanna joinme? 🍆 *xx*

Carlos: 🍆🍆🍆 *Am I too late? xx*

*

I'd been imagining over and over in my head how Anthony would have reacted if I *had* sent those messages to him. What if he'd turned up at the door ready to get my clothes off? The thought filled me with a mixture of overwhelming anxiety and unnerving excitement.

Whilst occasional thoughts had shifted to what it might be like to be intimate with Anthony lately, I'd been imagining it in more of a fantasy world where he resembles Mr Darcy and I'm Elizabeth Bennet, and we're in a barn rolling around in the hay, his stiffy poking out of his jodhpurs and rubbing against my petticoat. All very nineteenth century saucy stuff.

What I *hadn't* really considered was the reality of being fully naked in front of him and, like, doing 'bits'. I mean, I would be touching Anthony's *actual* willy, and not the tiny worm I used to look at inquisitively when our parents made us get baths together at sleepovers. No, we're talking about his proper veiny, grown-up man's schlong. Was I really ready for such a three-hundred-and-sixty-degree turn in our friendship? Also, what if the sex was absolutely crap and then we could never look each other in the eye again? It's fair to say that our friendship, as we currently knew it, would be over.

Then there was another scenario I've played out, if I had sent the messages to Anthony, where he never acknowledges my text messages, and I'm too embarrassed to bring it up, and the whole thing becomes this big awkward unspoken elephant in the room. Anthony stops getting in touch, and I don't want to look desperate so do the same, and then, before you know it, we're only seeing each other at family gatherings, exchanging small talk about the weather.

Either way, our thirty-year-old friendship would have been at risk, and the last thing I wanted was to lose Anthony as a friend. I needed to turn my attention elsewhere, starting with revisiting some of the New Year's resolutions I'd made at the start of the year that seemed to have fallen by the wayside. First on the list: cutting down on the alcohol to avoid any further drunken mishaps.

*

Three days and not so much as a drop of alcohol had crossed my lips, *and* I hadn't really found it that difficult – Phil Mitchell, eat your heart out.

I even managed to swerve the welcome drinks at a recent networking lunch, opting for a glass of buck's fizz instead of prosecco, and needed to call someone to tell them my good news.

Anthony: "Isme, you do know that buck's fizz has alcohol in it, don't you?"

Me: "Sod off, Anthony. It's just fizzy orange juice."

Anthony: "I'm not messing, Google it."

Me: "Right, hang on a second . . . AAARRRRGGGGHHHH!!!"

*

Maria: The Pig's Ear, 6 p.m. ⚓

Isme: Yeah, OK. I'm not sure they'll
allow the twins in though

Maria: Don't worry, they'll be with Mum
Don't be late 😁

"Ibiza!!!" Maria was waving a brochure of some sort in the air as I fought through the throngs of business folk, clearly in high spirits after the end of the working week from the high-pitched chatter and clinking of glasses that were making my head throb.

"What are you on about?"

Maria's eyes were wide and animated. She slammed the brochure down on the table in front of me and eagerly awaited my reaction.

"Where did you get this from, the nineties? You *do* know that everything is online now, don't you?"

"Just shut up and look at it, will you."

On closer inspection, the brochure was for a company that specialised in holidays for the eighteen to thirties age bracket. There was a picture on the front of some young skinny minnies laughing and dancing on the beach, and my first thought was that I hoped they were wearing suitable levels of SPF.

"OK, before you say anything, I was watching that Ibiza weekender last night and they all looked like they were having an absolute ball. So, I was thinking we could go! I'll ask George to—"

"Er, aren't you missing something, Maria? Like the fact we're both quite a few years too late?"

"Come on, Isme! You're young, free and single – you should be jumping at the chance to go away!"

I sighed and took a sip of my wine as I contemplated her proposal. Did I have the spare cash to just throw about on a spur-of-the-moment holiday, where I would probably be ridiculed for wearing a costume rather than a barely-there two-piece and come back riddled with crabs (and that would just be off the bed sheets)? Absolutely not. Could I do with a break at the moment to help my no-more-thoughts-about-Anthony-and-Zara cause, and Mum and Dad's financial situation? Absolutely.

"I'll pay for you! Or George will, rather. I've got his credit card and the stupid fucker probably won't even notice."

I swallowed down the ball of unease at the thought of another member of the family racking up unnecessary debt.

"Will you at least think about it, Isme, pleeeeeeeeease? I NEED a break." Maria stared into her wine glass and fiddled with the stem of the glass. "I need it for the sake of my marriage."

I felt a pull on my sisterly heartstrings, and before I knew it, I was saying, "OK, but instead let's see if Stavros will let us use his villa in Cyprus. That way we'll only have to pay for our flights."

Maria jumped out of her seat and gave me a tight squeeze. "Thank you! You really don't know what this means."

*

Dad: Isme, it's your dad. Are you coming round for Easter dinner on Sunday? Your mum wants to know. Love, Dad 🐣🐰👻

Isme: Still not got the hang of the 'message thingies' Dad, no?! Why doesn't she just ask me herself?

Dad: Sorry, love. What am I like! 😆 Because she said you're not speaking to her, although I don't know why

Isme: Yeah that's right. I'm not not speaking to her. Well, not really

Dad: Bleedin' hell. I bet the *Krypton Factor* wasn't this hard. Are you coming round or not?

Isme: I suppose so, yeah, but only if we're not on spud rations

Dad: Maria and her riff-raff are spending it with George's mum and dad, so there'll be plenty.
Love, Dad
Ooops 😂

*

Mum was in the kitchen preparing the food when I arrived, shuffling pots and pans around like she was conducting an orchestra. I stood watching her for a moment as she manoeuvred round the kitchen, stirring this, chopping that.

"Hi, Mum."

She turned round, her face flushed and sweaty from the heat coming off the pans. She smiled, and opened out her arms. The still-mad-at-her part of me hesitated for a moment, but the family tug in my chest was stronger. I walked into her arms, taking in her familiar scent of cinnamon and rose water perfume.

"Ah, I've missed my *koumera*," she said, squeezing my cheeks between her fingers and giving them a little shake.

"Oh, come on, Mum, leave it out. It's only been a week!"

"Yes, well, it feel longer. Now cam, sit." Mum signalled to one of the dining room chairs and I did as I was told. She said, "I want to say I am sorry for not telling you about thee Will sooner. It was wrong of me, but I didn't want you to feel pressure to get married."

"Yes, but I do feel pressure, Mum. From *you*. All you ever seem to be interested in is whether I've got a fella, and then there's Carlos, who you've been thrusting in my face since I was barely out the womb."

Mum sighed. "I just want you to be happy, Isme, like your sis—"

"Sister, yes, I know, Mum. But I *am* happy." Or at least I thought I was, job suspension and confusing feelings for Anthony aside.

"OK, Isme, I promise no more talk of Carlos. Now, tell me. Why you lie about thee exams?! Is very bad, lying to your mama. And then you embarrass me at Theoulla's house, saying her food is no good. I do agree, her tarama is too salty and she uses too many vine leaves for her dolmades, but you never disrespect another woman in her own home. Now, what you have to say for yourself?"

Sheepishly, I muttered, "I'm sorry, I should have told you that I failed the exams. I just didn't want you to be disappointed in me."

Mum placed a hand over mine. "Oh, *Koumera*, I would never be disappointed in you, and I'm sorry that you felt like you couldn't tell us. Just promise me, no more lies, OK?"

I nodded.

Mum got to her feet, declaring our reconciliation meeting over. "OK, good. So, now we are friends again, I have a surprise for you!"

My stomach did a flip. The last time Mum landed a surprise on me, it didn't end well. What was it going to be now, my Greek hubby also has to be able to do the *sirtaki* with his eyes closed whilst eating a plate full of dolmades?

"Maria tell me about your holiday. So I speak to Stavros and he agree to let us use the villa for the summer! He say it is special gift for his favourite Greek family."

I stared at her in disbelief. "Woah, hang on. I can't just up sticks and leave for the whole summer! What about work? What about *Maria's* work?"

"Isme, you tell me your office was closed for refurbishment, remember, because of the fire? And Maria's salon too. How funny that they both have accidental fires around the same time." I smiled awkwardly.

"It's going to be great spending so much time together, and

it's been so long since we all went away." Mum averted her gaze to the floor, and clutched at the cross on her necklace. "Me and your papa, we are not getting any younger. Who knows, this might be our last chance to all go away together before we, how you say, pass on."

And there it was, like a mic drop.

PART TWO

**You don't need magic to disappear,
all you need is a destination . . .**

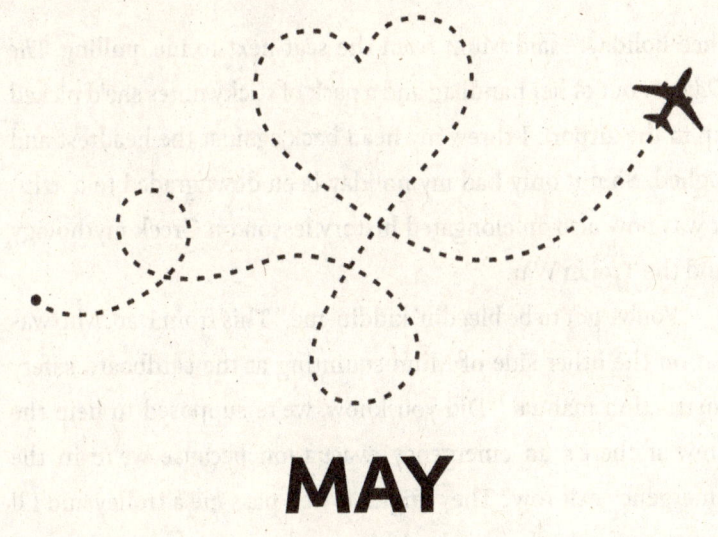

MAY

UNLESS THAT DESTINATION IS WITH *MY* FAMILY AND then you'll need some form of sorcery to make *them* disappear. And some Valium, if it's to hand.

"I did tell you, Isme, it's not called a holiday when you go away with kids, just a trip," came Maria from the row behind me on the stuffy 7.47 a.m. flight out from Liverpool to Cyprus, while the twins consistently bashed their tiny, but unusually powerful, feet against the back of my seat. The plane hadn't even taken off and I was already eyeing up the nearest emergency exits.

"More like an endurance test," I scoffed under my breath.

"It's not like I didn't warn you."

"I don't remember any warning about spending the whole holiday in a neck brace from whiplash."

"Oh, Isme, leave thee boys alone, they are jus excited about thee holiday!" said Mum from the seat next to me, pulling *The Odyssey* out of her handbag and a pack of sticky notes she'd picked up in the airport. I threw my head back against the headrest and sighed. So not only had my holiday been downgraded to a 'trip', it was now also an elongated history lesson on Greek mythology and the Trojan War.

"You've got to be bleedin' kiddin' me." This from Dad, who was sat on the other side of Mum squinting at the cardboard safety instruction manual. "Did you know, we're supposed to help the crew if there's an emergency evacuation because we're in the emergency exit row? They might as well pass me a trolley and I'll start serving drinks, the cheeky buggers."

"Stephen, stop thee moaning, you know I need thee extra leg room or my ankles swell. You remember what happen when we wen to Corfu."

"How could I forget, woman, I thought we were going to be charged an extra seat for them— OUCH!"

Dad rubbed at his arm where Mum had given him a dig.

"Excuse me, Miss, will this seat be remaining empty?" One of the air hostesses smiled while pointing to the empty seat on the end of the row next to Maria, revealing her magnificent white, almost translucent, teeth. Her thickly applied make-up reminded me I needed to sort a plasterer out when I got home to fill the hole in my kitchen ceiling.

Maria sighed. "Yep, unless by some miracle my lazy arse husband comes to his senses and realises that leaving his wife to travel alone with our two young children so he could go and watch the opening matches of the Cricket World Cup was one of his most selfish acts in our four years of marriage."

There was an awkward pause as the air hostess stood frozen to the spot, unsure whether to laugh or offer her condolences.

"The answer is yes," I said, putting her out of her awkward misery. With that, she scurried off, leaving a waft of over-powering Jo Malone perfume in her wake, making my throat tickle.

When Maria first told me George wouldn't be joining us for the first week of the holiday, I'd let out an uncontrollable 'whoop!'. I was determined to enjoy it, despite it turning from 'Girls' Trip' to 'Holiday with The Clampetts', and I didn't need him killing my positive holiday vibes. Now the slow realisation was sinking in that it was one less adult to keep Theo and Tomaso in check. And alive.

Finally, the plane started to manoeuvre before taking off, and I watched out the window as the city below us became smaller and smaller, the countryside resembling a patchwork blanket.

This was it. The beginning of my summer and, hopefully, the beginning of a new chapter for me. A chapter that didn't involve any more conflicting feelings for my best friend, or daydreaming of a life where I'd never met Zara. Yes, all that crap was getting left behind, and as the city below me faded into the distance, for the first time in a while I felt almost at peace, maybe even content.

That was, until a kick of almighty strength hit me in the back, almost knocking the breath out of me, and my contentment abruptly manifested into contempt.

*

Stavros's villa was in a small residential village in Larnaca called Maroni, about a twenty-minute drive from the airport, and looked a lot smaller than I remembered, but still just as visually impressive – dated but traditional with its cobalt blue window shutters and doors, which stood out against the bright white-stonewashed walls. Two Corinthian style pillars stood tall on either side of the wooden front door, like guards on watch, above them, an architrave embellished with the Greek key.

We unloaded ourselves and our luggage from the taxi, before making our way inside to the familiar open-plan kitchen and dining room, with its stone floors, pine wood furniture and low wood-beamed ceilings. Then there was the shared outdoor area, with its table and chairs if we fancied some *al fresco* dining, decent sized rectangular swimming pool and surrounding sunbeds.

It's going to be a good summer, I thought to myself, as I closed my eyes up at the Mediterranean sun. I could feel the stress of the last few months oozing out of me like lava as I pictured myself sunbathing on one of the beds, glass of something cold and refreshing (preferably alcoholic) in one hand, the latest Marian Keyes novel in the other.

I clocked some easy-on-the-eye Greek fellas scattered around the poolside, some in small mixed-sex groups, or *pareas* as they're better known in Greek culture – a mix of childhood friends, university pals and/or colleagues. Oddly though, most were seemingly in the company of their mothers, or cougar mistresses (I couldn't decide which was worse).

*

"Isme, you have to be careful in this heat, you are not like Maria. You have thee skin of an albino."

"Jesus, nice one, Mum." I sat up, wiping the slobber from the side of my chin. I hadn't realised I'd fallen asleep until I felt Mum's heavy hands rubbing sun lotion onto my back like she was marinading her lamb.

"She is right you know, love, you take after me. I only have to *look* at the sun and I go pink." Fittingly, Dad was sitting under an umbrella, squinting hard at what appeared to be a map he was holding. Despite the thirty-degree heat, he was fully dressed in a pale blue shirt and long beige trousers, like he was about to raid the lost ark.

"UNCLE ISME, UNCLE ISME. WATCH THIS!"

"GO ON THEN, THEO," I shouted back, before mumbling, "Let's see you jump in the pool again for the one hundredth time today while I act impressed, even though every jump has been exactly the same."

"Oi, don't be a sly arse, they're just excited," said Maria, as she plonked herself down on the end of my sunbed, "and it's the one hundredth and eleventh time, to be exact. I should know, I've had to watch every single bloody one."

"Aw Maria, they so clever! You should be proud! They going to be thee next Tim Daley."

"It's Tom, Mum, and I'm not sure dive-bombing into the pool when you're three-and-a-half is a sure sign you're going to be an Olympic diver."

"They've all got to start somewhere, love." This from Dad, who had put down his map and was now squinting at something on his phone.

"*Efcharisto*, Stephen." Mum did a hallelujah type gesture with her hands. "So, Isme, what are your plans?"

"What, like, in life?"

"No, silly, I mean while you here over summer."

I rolled my eyes up at the cloudless blue sky. "Er, what does it look like?"

"*Ochi*, Isme, you can't lay around thee pool every day. You mast do something!"

"There's a nice new hotel down the road, you should go and check it out. I reckon it'll be prime for some Greek fitties." Maria licked her lips. She had clearly already been giving it some thought. Maybe a little *too* much thought.

"Nah, I can't be arsed, Maria. Plus I've come here to—"

"Please don't say 'find yourself' or I'll have to slap you."

"I wonder what's going on over there?" I nodded in the direction of a man in overalls, who was pinning a colourful poster up on the back wall. The *parea* I'd spotted the day before stood close by talking in high-pitched voices, clearly excited by the contents of the poster. I craned my neck to try and get a better look, but before I could make it out, Mum stood in front of me, completely blocking my view.

"Ah, is nothing. Probably a lost cat or samthing. Now stop changing thee subject, Isme. You know I seen a leaflet on thee notice-board in the kitchen about a bakery course in thee local hotel."

I rested my head on the back of the sunbed and sighed. She was as persistent as the stray hair on my chin that keeps regrowing no matter how many times I pluck it. Anthony calls it my 'Caerus', the Greek god of hair who's bald except for one lonely lock of hair.

"Bloody hell. Why can't I just enjoy my holiday in peace!"

"I just saying, Isme, you should make use of your time here."

"Oh, I intend to," I said, making a point of slurping noisily on the dregs of the mojito I'd been drinking before I dozed off, desperately trying to maintain a neutral expression despite it tasting like warm minty water.

"Which is why I pay for you to do the course. It starts in a few days. Now, I mast go and start preparations for tea." She scurried off inside, leaving me to catch flies with my gawping mouth. The woman's idea of a holiday and mine were about as different as chalk and feta.

I looked over at Dad, in search of some solace, but in the midst of it all, he'd sloped off, taking the map with him, making me wonder whether he *was* going in search of a lost ancient ruin after all.

*

It'd been three whole days, and I hadn't even got to chapter two of *Watermelon* thanks to the two hyperactive juveniles splashing and thrashing about in the water.

Admittedly, it *had* been quite cute at first, seeing Theo and Tomaso come trotting out of the villa in their little matching Spiderman UV suits and dinosaur-shaped rubber rings, the positioning of their goggles making their eyes droop and ears stick out like two adorable puppies.

But after one splash of epic proportion sent a tidal wave of water over me, causing me to hot foot it off the sunbed and sending my beloved book flying into the pool, the cuteness abruptly dissipated.

"OH, FOR FU— FUDGE SAKE!"

Angrily, I tried scooping the book out of the pool with the cleaning net, but it was useless. The pages had already come apart and were drifting around the pool like paper lily pads.

"Do these belong to you?" came a voice from behind me, with that familiar northern twang I'd recognise anywhere. I turned round to find a light-haired lad with piercing blue eyes and pleasant cheekbones holding my sunglasses, which must have flung off me when I jumped up from the sunbed.

"Oh, er, thanks." I took the sunglasses from him gratefully, our hands briefly touching. I wasn't sure if it was the unexpected human contact or the manliness of his hands, but I felt myself blushing. I noticed he was on his own, which was a pleasant change from the rest of the fellas around the complex.

"Are you staying here too?" I asked, with an unintended keenness to my voice which I was hoping he hadn't noticed.

"No, I'm staying in Hotel Adonis down the road, but I run group training sessions here. You should come along to one." He handed me a flyer, which had a picture on the front of him wearing a tight vest and shorts, and 'Train With Neil' written in big bold letters above it. "The hotel also runs weekly cookery courses, if you're interested."

"Oh yeah, I'm already booked on to that." *By my mum because, even at the age of thirty-three, she still likes to exert some level of control over my life*, I was hastened to add.

"Great! I'll see you there."

I gazed dreamily as he walked off, copping a good look at his toned arms, which would give the Hulk a run for his money, and backside that was as perfectly pert as a ripe peach. I was completely oblivious to the commotion going on in the pool below until Maria shouted, "ISME, CAN YOU PASS ME THAT POOL SCOOPER. THEO'S DROPPED A LOG."

*

Are you a lover of Greek cuisine but wouldn't know your dolmades from your keftedes?

Or perhaps you're already an avid cook looking to improve your skill set?

Well, look no further! Come along to The Adonis Hotel for our weekly Greek cookery classes, where you'll learn about the history of our wonderful culinary culture, as well as getting to make some food of your own!

Come on, what are you waiting for?

WOOPAH!

I stared at the leaflet pinned up on the noticeboard in the

kitchen. Was I *really* contemplating wasting some of my holiday sweating my tits off in a stuffy kitchen, just so I could escape the villa and perve on some lad?

I think we all knew the answer to that one.

*

Hotel Adonis was situated by the marina, about a mile down the road from the villa. I decided to take a leisurely stroll and enjoy the picturesque views of Maroni village. My thoughts would intermittently turn to Neil every time I spotted a man in shorts, and my stomach bubbled at the prospect of seeing him again.

The sky was a perfect blue, highlighting the white of the buildings along the narrow, cobbled roads, and the colourful flowers that spilt out of window boxes. I waved and shouted "Yassas!" to a petite older Greek lady, who was sitting on the doorstep of one of the houses. She nodded with a gummy smile that lit up her warm brown eyes.

I came to a small *platia* in the centre of the village, lined with shops, cafes, and a traditional Greek taverna, with a few locals enjoying a midday Keo under the vine-decorated wooden pergola. Taking centre stage was a beautiful Orthodox church, with its pristine white walls, cobalt blue dome and white cross topper. It made the Greek church at home seem like a poor relative.

"I'm-so-sorry-I'm-late," I panted as I burst through the doors half an hour late, thanks to the steep path of cobbled steps leading up to the hotel. I made my way across the brightly lit room, to the only available high stool on the far right of the demonstration kitchen. As I went to sit down, I was distracted at the sight of Neil on the opposite side, who smiled in my direction and looked just as fit as I remembered, causing me to completely miss the seat and fall arse over tit. No one laughed, including Neil, which made the situation all the more awkward.

"*Yassas!* Welcome," said a woman in a white chef jacket from behind the kitchen, which was made of shiny steel and marble work tops. "I am Andrea, thee course instructor. Welcome to my kitchen!" Despite my sore backside and bruised ego, I relaxed.

Andrea continued her demonstration of a karidopita cake, a Greek walnut sponge. I listened intently, jotting down some of Andrea's handy tips and advice in the notepad I'd nicked from the villa, whilst trying not to look over at Neil.

Easier said than done when he's right in your eyeline, and his toned, tanned arms are calling out like homing beacons.

"OK, now is your turn!" declared Andrea, once her cake was in the oven. "Please, go and find yourself a workstation, where there's an instruction sheet and all the ingredients you need."

"Nice to see you again. Isme, isn't it?" I looked up from my workstation to find Neil standing in front of me, those bulky arms now within touching distance.

"You know those things are absolutely riddled with sugar," he said, pointing to the Tracker bar that was poking out my bag. "You'd be better off with a protein shake or superfood smoothie, or, better still, both – balance out the macros."

Superfood? Macros? What language was he speaking?

"This is looking good, Isme." Andrea appeared, scooping some of my cake mixture with a teaspoon and putting it to her mouth.

"Hmmm, maybe a little more brandy. But, other than that, *teleios*!" She gave me a gentle pat on the back, which made me feel like I was on *Bake Off* getting a Paul Hollywood handshake.

"Have you baked before, then?" asked Neil, as I whisked some more brandy into the mixture, trying to disguise the fact that my arm felt like it might fall off.

"Yeah, kind of." I didn't get into the whole 'baking is my passion but I got sucked into a job I hate so I could pay the bills instead' thing. I'd only know the lad five minutes.

"So, are you planning on doing it more while you're here? You're clearly good at it." I felt myself blushing at the unexpected compliment.

"I mean, I wasn't planning on it. It's not *really* the reason I'm here."

"Oh, are you here for something in particular? Except for a holiday, of course."

To escape my life back home? To drink my body weight in ouzo?

"To get myself healthy, I suppose, both mentally and physically." Well, I had to say something.

*

"Isme, tell me, how was thee cooking course."

My thoughts immediately shifted to Neil, and something fluttered in my tummy. Or perhaps that was from the jerky movements of the minibus as it tackled the many bumps and turns of the dusty roads leading us to an old fortress on the outskirts of Larnaca. It was Mum's idea to go, insisting it would be 'quality family bondage time', despite the fact that Dad couldn't make it – something to do with a local fish market he'd been dying to visit.

I certainly smelt something fishy, that was for sure.

Without wanting to divulge any information about Neil to Mum, and be questioned the rest of the journey about his heritage, I just shrugged my shoulders and said, "Yeah, it was all right."

"What was, the course or that hunk from the pool?" Maria gave a wink in my direction from the adjacent seat. "I mean, *phwoar*! You could cook eggs on those abs!"

"Bloody hell, calm down, Maria. You have a husband, remember? Goes by the name of George; black hair, brown eyes, impressive moobs?"

Maria gave a distasteful look. "Yeah, don't I know it. THEO, FOR THE HUNDREDTH TIME WILL YOU PLEASE STOP WAVING THAT TOY STICK AROUND!"

"*Ochi*, Maria, don't shout at him like that," tutted Mum. She patted the empty seat beside her. "Theo, *ela*, sit with your *Yiayia*. I give you sweets." Theo bounced over, as Mum showered him with kisses and squeezed his tiny shoulders.

"They could literally chop her hand off and she'd still insist they were innocent," huffed Maria.

I nodded in agreement, although I was glad of the turn of attention. The last thing I needed was Mum questioning Neil's blood type, or his pay package. There was only one package of his I was interested in, and it had nothing to do with money.

*

We lasted half an hour in the fort before heading back to the bus. Between Mum complaining about her swollen ankles, and Maria berating the twins every five minutes for something or other, who gave zero fucks to the (many) unfenced gaps between the stony walls, it was a miracle we'd even lasted that long (or hadn't ended up splatted on the cobbled streets below).

I *did* manage to round up the troops for a selfie at the top though, with the impressive view behind – clusters of colourful stone-built buildings tightly packed together, and in the far distance, an impressive dome-shaped church housed on a rocky peninsula. Unfortunately for Mum, a gust of wind had swept her black hair across her face, although you could still make out her eyes, and Theo's toy samurai sword that she was holding could have been mistaken for a whip.

I couldn't help myself and immediately posted it to Instagram with the caption: 'Nothing like a bit of special family bondage time!'

A comment notification pinged moments later.

> **Anthony:** Haha! Has she been watching
> *Fifty Shades of Grey* too?!
> Hope you're having a nice holiday

I then spent the whole drive back to the villa stalking his Instagram for any hints that he'd been with Zara. There was none, which hopefully meant their little rendezvous was over, maybe because he'd found out she had some weird deformity, like three nipples, or a fanny the size of a small continent.

*

> **Unknown number:** Hi Isme, it's Neil,
> from the cookery course!

I got your number off Andrea,
I hope you don't mind 😌

Isme: No, not at all!
So long as you're not a stalker, or have some
weird foot fetish or something! 😂

Hercules: 😄 Do you fancy grabbing some
tofu or something after the next class?
We can discuss your training for your mental
and physical health

Isme: Tofu? 🙈 Don't you just hate predictive text!

Hercules: ???

Isme: There's a little coffee shop round the
corner from the hotel?

Hercules: They probably won't have tofu
but I'll take a coffee instead 👍
See you then x

*

The cafe was situated along the marina, which was buzzing with
Cyprus life – mopeds whizzing past frantically, locals sat outside
waterfront tavernas chatting loudly in their native tongue, kids
playing a game of football on a small stretch of sand.

The hustle and bustle of it all reminded me of the Albert Dock back home on a Saturday afternoon, minus the hen parties and Beatles tourists. I felt a sense of longing for home, which I shook off. Home = Anthony, and now was *not* the time to be thinking about *him*.

"Well, that was a bit of a disaster!" I said, referring to my failed attempt at making puff pastry, missing the crucial part where Andrea said to keep your butter *out* of the fridge. "Thank God for Jus-rol, eh."

"Don't beat yourself up, it was your first go."

I smiled appreciatively and took a sip of my coffee, while trying to catch a sly glimpse of his toned pecks that were pushing against his tight fitted sports vest. He caught my gaze and I quickly looked away.

Clearing my dry throat, I said, "So, have you always been into baking?"

"Only over the last year or so, really. Needed something to occupy the mind."

I nodded in agreement as I thought about how much the classes had taken *my* mind off thinking about everything that had been going on at home before I abandoned ship.

I waited for Neil to divulge the cause of *his* need for a distraction, but he just sat running a finger around the rim of his cup. I couldn't tell whether his composed, almost standoffish demeanour was a self-preservation thing or down to boredom. He was more difficult to read than *The Da Vinci Code*.

We sat in silence for what felt like several painful minutes. I took a long, drawn-out sip of my coffee as I tried to think of something to say, but my mind was a complete blank. The intensity of the silence against the loudness of our surroundings was too much to bear, and before I knew it words were spilling out of my mouth. I found myself telling Neil all about my heritage, from Dad being adopted, to Mum and her never-ending ploy to marry me off.

"Wow, and I thought my family was bonkers," laughed Neil, baring his perfectly aligned gnashers. It was the first time I'd properly seen him smile.

"We're not bonkers per se, we're just Greek."

Neil leant back in his chair and ran a hand through his blonde locks. He seemed to be more relaxed than when we'd first arrived, although there was a still an air of mystery to him that I couldn't quite put my finger on.

"Another coffee?" As I watched Neil stride inside to the counter, I found myself wondering whether maybe we were just too different, and this 'date' wasn't such a good idea after all.

I'd never really had a type, but if you put a gun to my head I'd say tall, dark and unconventionally handsome, like Adam Driver or Benedict Cumberbatch (there's just something about men in capes), and a good sense of humour. Neil, with his light features and serious composure, was the complete opposite. Yeah, I was attracted to him physically, but was it enough?

"What's with all these men hanging around with older women?" I asked once he was back with our drinks, nodding in the direction of a 'couple' walking along the beach, the woman at least ten years the man's senior. "I've seen a few around the villa complex as well, and I can't make out whether it's mums with their sons or a cougar-type set up."

"It's probably to do with the singles—"

"Excuse me, sir, this yours?" interrupted the cafe owner, handing Neil his wallet that he must have left at the counter.

"*Efcharisto,*" said Neil, taking the wallet from him gratefully. "That's what happens when you're too busy checking your work emails."

"Is that why you're over here? For work?"

"Yeah. The hotel is looking to expand and I'm advising on the feasibility of it all. The training stuff is just an added bonus." Neil continued to tell me about his job as a quantity surveyor, and I'd be a liar if I said my eyes didn't glaze over just a teeny tiny bit.

"Other than that, there's not a lot to say really. I'm pretty boring." He downed his coffee, again in one gulp – the man drank his coffee like I drank my ouzo. "Other than work and the baking, I go to the gym, like, five times a week. Oh, and I'm a bit of an animal rights nerd."

"Oh, come on," I probed, "there's got to be some ghosts in that closet of yours! An estranged wife? Kids scattered all over the country? A gambling addiction?"

Neil shifted awkwardly in his seat. Unfortunately, I'd always been terrible at reading the signs for when you should shut your cake hole.

"My guess, from the way you down your coffee and how often you go the gym, is that you're substituting exercise and coffee for something else. Ah I know, it's sex! You're a reformed nymphomaniac, aren't you?"

"You know what, I've got a really early shift tomorrow," said Neil, getting up out of his seat. "It's been nice, Isme. Thanks."

With that he patted me on the back, like I was one of the lads, and walked out.

*

They say when you dream something it usually means the opposite. Like, if you dream about dying, it means a new chapter or beginning in your life. Or if you dream about getting married, it's symbolic of growth in the different aspects of your life, or some other shite like that. So what about a dream were you're being chased through town by a giant jar of Douwe Egberts, and the lad you've just met comes to your rescue wearing nothing but his cooking apron? Maybe that I prefer tea and fully clothed women?

Whatever the psychoanalysis of my dream, it made me wake up in a bit of a sweat, keen to see Neil again despite my doubts at the coffee shop – which was a shame considering I seemed to have completely messed things up. Although I still wasn't *entirely* sure what I did wrong.

"I mean, calling him a nymphomaniac just because he likes going the gym and drinking coffee *is* a bit weird, Isme," scoffed Maria, after I filled her in on Neil's hasty exit from the coffee shop the day before. We were sat by the pool, enjoying a rare moment of quiet and calm while Mum and Dad occupied the twins inside.

"It was only meant as a joke, like, and what's wrong with being a sex addict anyway? That Russell Brand made a book out of it!"

"Yeah, but I just don't see why you needed to probe. Sometimes leaving an air of mystery between you is good, exciting almost! I know everything about George, even down to what time he takes his dumps, and trust me, it's shit. Pardon the pun, ha!"

I almost choked on my mouthful of Coke, causing some of it to drip out my nose. The pair of us burst into a fit of hysterics, much to the disgust of one of the 'mums' sitting close by, next to her sleeping 'son'. She pressed her index finger against her lips and pointed to him with the other.

"Aren't naps supposed to stop when you're about four?" muttered Maria, which made me giggle even more.

It was the first time since we arrived that we'd had a good laugh together, like we did before she got married and her life turned into one big ball of stress, and it felt nice. Unfortunately, it would probably be the only time – George was due to fly over soon which meant that the stress ball was probably going to inflate to the size of a hot air balloon.

"Oh shit, angry cougar mum incoming." We lowered our positions on the sunbeds, as if it would somehow make us invisible, but before she made it over to us, Mum's bulky frame appeared from nowhere, blocking the woman's path. Thankfully, she retreated back to her seat.

"*Ela*, you two, is time for dinna. I shout you lots of times! Cam!" Mum stood wafting her arms in the air from side-to-side, like an American road traffic controller, whilst side-eyeing the woman. I felt like a prisoner being guarded from an angry mob.

"Seriously though, Isme, have you thought that maybe Neil just doesn't fancy you?" said Maria, as we made our way into the villa.

I sighed. "Of course I have, but then why would he ask me on a date?"

"I would hardly call downing Ibriki amongst the locals at midday a date, Isme."

I sighed. I knew she was right, but that still didn't stop the uneasy feeling of rejection that was rising up from my belly and threatening to burst out. Or was that just the bubbles from the Coke?

A text message came through on my phone, making me jump. Was it . . . ? Could it just be . . . ?

> **Hercules:** The hotel are putting on a mini
> Olympic games. Shall I put your name down?
> Also, check out this Netflix programme
> about battery hen farms
> www.youtube.com/battery-hen-farms

"Yeah, he definitely doesn't fancy you," said Maria, peering over my phone.

*

Was there a possibility I'd got it wrong with Neil and maybe he *was* going to come to my rescue like in the dream, preferably half naked? Most probably not. Was I currently loitering around Hotel Adonis to try and catch a glimpse of that muscly bod just one more time anyway? Absolutely. It was a risky business though – I still hadn't responded to his message from a few days earlier about the mini Olympics, nor had I thought up an excuse to get out of it yet.

I also needed to escape the villa. George's arrival was imminent, and I wasn't in the mood for his sly comments about my poor effort at a sun tan, although it *was* quite pathetic: blotches of red amongst patches of brown where my freckles had lumped together.

I ordered a margarita and perched up on a sunbed by the pool. I was wearing a head scarf and sunglasses in an attempt to look inconspicuous, but the effect was quite the opposite. I noticed a few people in the pool peering over, and a voice from the bed next to me as I sat down said, "Babe, are you OK? You look like you're on the run from the feds." It was a nasally drawn-out accent I'd recognise anywhere. I whipped off my sunglasses and sat bolt upright.

"OH MY GOD, MADDY!"

"OH MY GOD, ISME!"

I threw my arms around her, so happy to see a familiar face.

Maddy had been an office junior at Baros & Co. when I first started. She was your typical Scouse princess with her enhanced pout and excessive eyebrows, and one of the smartest yet doziest girls I knew. As the saying goes, what she lacked in common sense she made up for in intelligence. When she plonked herself in the chair next to me on her first day and said, "Babe, what's with the two computer screens? Is it in case I lose the other one?" I knew we'd get on.

Maddy left Mulligan's about six months ago to grow her own aesthetics business. From the looks of her puffed-up lips and creaseless forehead, she'd spent that time practicing on herself.

"I'd seen on Insta that you were in Cyprus looking for a potential shop for your new business, but I didn't expect to see you here!"

"Yep, still looking, like, but there's potential. I've got a mate who does those Turkey teeth and he's got a spare room in his clinic so that's always an option! You know, like Tic Tac teeth that are super-white and super-square?" added Maddy for the benefit of my confused expression.

"So, are you staying in this hotel, then?"

"Pah! I wish. Far too pricey for me, babe. I've got an Airbnb about half an hour away. Bit of a mish to get here, like, but I seen on Insta that the margaritas are on point so had to come and try them for meself!" Maddy downed the contents of her cocktail glass, and signalled to a waiter to bring two more. "Who are *you* with anyway, babe? How did you manage to get Jeff to sign off your holidays?"

I rolled my eyes up at the perfectly blue sky. "It's a long story, Mad."

"Babe, I'm on me holidays! I've got all the time in the world. Now, let's have a bevvy."

*

"*You* need a blow out," said Maddy, two hours and six margaritas later once I'd finished filling her in on the events prior to the holiday, from finding out about the Will to getting suspended from work. "And *I* need to get away from the weird Joan Collins vibe in this place. I mean, what's all that about, please?" Maddy nodded in the direction of the pool bar, where a couple of older men were sitting having a drink in the company of their (much) older acquaintances. "So, what are you doing tonight?"

"Not much. Why?"

"There's a bar down the road putting on a belly dancing night tonight and you're coming with!"

"Oh, I don't know, Mad, I'm trying to lay off the booze a bit." We both looked at the collection of empty cocktail glasses on the table and laughed. "No, honestly, the last time I drank too much I almost sent some provocative text messages to Anthony."

"Oh, babe, don't be such a bore!" Maddy interjected before I could explain. "Come on, we'll have the locals slut dropping round their jars of olives by the end of the night!"

I sighed. "OK, but only if we can get them to dab to Zorba's Dance as well."

"Deal!" We sealed our plan with a high five, although I had to be cautious not to get sliced by her false talons, which were pointed and half the size of her actual fingers.

*

Hercules: Are you up to anything today?

Isme: Just trying not to drown my brother-in-law
if he makes one more sarky comment about my tan
And avoiding Mum, who wants to know the whys
and wherefores of my night out last night. You?

Hercules: I've got a great strength and
endurance exercise in mind 😊
Will pick you up in an hour

Something tingled down below as I read the words 'strength and endurance'. Could he possibly mean what I thought (and hoped) he meant?

*

Three words: Wall. Fucking. Climbing. Without the fucking. I thought Neil was having a laugh when I caught sight of the old run-down church, which had been turned into an indoor climbing centre. We'd driven past it on the way from the airport to the villa, and it had made me wonder what type of people would choose to waste their precious holiday time there rather than sunbathing and drinking retsina wine.

"So, what do you think?" said Neil enthusiastically as we stood outside, looking like he was about to take part in the Tour de France in his cyclies.

"Erm, yeah, great." I found it hard to hide the disappointment in my voice, and had to swallow down the bile that was rising up from my stomach from the many drinks I'd had the night before thanks to Maddy, the devious cow. She had a plan all along to get me pissed, starting with going the bar to get me a lemonade and coming back with a G&T.

I could have just not drank it, but once I recognised the citrusy burn of the gin as I swallowed, I knew I was a goner. Pandora's box had been well and truly opened, and even Zeus himself wouldn't have been able to close it back over. The last thing I remembered was attempting to copy the moves of the belly dancer with Maddy in the middle of the dancefloor.

"It's a great way to clear the mind, and get rid of all those nasty alcohol toxins," he said, taking a big intake of breath to emphasise his point. "You know, it wouldn't do you any harm to stay off the booze, especially if you're trying to get yourself fit."

"My mind is pretty clear to be honest, Neil," I huffed. It was like being on a date with Gillian McKeith. Next thing, he'd be asking me for a stool sample.

Neil trotted inside whilst I lagged behind, contemplating the distance back to the villa and whether it was runnable, but concluded that I had no chance in sliders.

I was grateful I'd chosen my black shorts and oversized T-shirt, until I got inside and realised that everyone else was wearing lycra. I was half expecting Mr Motivator to jump out shouting "Everybody say yeah!" and make us all do star jumps.

We were greeted by a lycra-wearing enthusiast with long black hair which he wore in a low pony, and a tattoo of the Troodos mountains on his right arm. After taking us through a short health and safety briefing, he fitted us with some harnesses that were a little tight around the groin area. Luckily, my T-shirt just about covered my camel toe but the same, unfortunately, couldn't be said for Neil, who looked like he'd stuffed some socks down his undies.

"Don't be nervous, Isme!" laughed Neil, once we were strapped in and I was stood staring up at the wall with a look of sheer terror. "Just stay by me, and you'll be fine. Promise." He squeezed one of my hands, and I smiled gratefully. I took a deep breath and we started to ascend.

A few minutes in and Neil was already halfway up the wall.

He seemed to be able to tackle each foothold with complete ease, never losing his grip, whilst I felt like Bambi on ice. I had to concentrate hard on co-ordinating my next move, and then pluck up the courage to actually do it, which became increasingly difficult the higher up the wall I got. It's also hard to concentrate when you're surrounded by a sea of willy bulges and camel toes. If Anthony could have seen me, I would have never heard the end of it.

"Are you OK down there, Isme?" shouted Neil, who was almost at the top.

"All good!" I shouted back, with as much enthusiasm as I could muster.

"You're doing great, not far to go now."

I closed my eyes and took a deep intake of breath. "Come on, Isme. You can do this," I muttered to myself. Determined not to be a complete failure, I regained my composure and started to clamber up with more momentum, getting myself into a good rhythm. My hands started to burn against the grip of the hand holds, which felt like they were made out of sandpaper, and I could feel sweat start to trickle down my back. But there was no going back.

By the time I was almost at the top, I was panting like a dog on a hot day and had lost most of my nails, but, despite all that, I felt good – like for the first time in a while I'd actually achieved something.

"Troodos mountains, eat your heart out," I shouted to Neil, who was now almost within reaching distance.

"Well done, Isme! Just one more last push."

I reached my leg over to place it on the last foothold but as I did, a willy bulge of epic proportions whizzed past me and caught my attention, causing me to misjudge the distance. I completely lost contact with the wall and was left suspended halfway down with a red face and camel toe the size of a baboon's arse.

Wall wankers. *That's* the type of people that choose to spend their holiday suspended up a pretend rockface, and I wouldn't be becoming part of their gang any time soon.

*

Hercules: How are the knees? 😬

Isme: Bruised, but not as much as my ego

Hercules: I thought you did great!
Especially with it being your first time.
Fancy doing something again tomorrow?

Isme: Yeah OK, but only if it doesn't involve climbing any walls 🧗

Hercules: It won't, promise 😂
Meet me in the platia at 7 p.m.

"Everything all right, love?" said Dad, peering over his copy of *The Larnaca Post.*

I put my phone down on the arm of the couch and sighed. "Yeah, fine. Just stupid boy stuff."

"Anthony?"

"What?! No, why . . . why would you think that?" I cleared my dry throat. I proceeded to tell Dad all about my dates with Neil, and how I'd convinced myself that he wasn't interested in me in a romantic way. "And then I get these messages about meeting up again and my head is well and truly battered."

Dad, who had been listening intently, closed his newspaper over and rubbed at his tired eyes. "You know, back in my day, all you needed was a bit of chasing and a peck on the cheek to know where you stood with a girl. Now it's all mind games and playing hard to get. It must be hard work, Iz."

I sighed. "Yeah, you could say that."

"Well, if you want my advice, he sounds like a bit of a plonker."

I gave him a playful nudge. "I actually think he's a decent lad to be honest, Dad. I just get the impression he's a bit clueless when it comes to women."

"Ah well, I wouldn't know anything about that." He winked. "Just ask your mother."

The words 'eugh' and 'vile' came to mind.

*

Maddy offered to take me into town for a 'Scouseover' ready for my date with Neil. I hadn't really given it much thought until I realised there was a teeny tiny possibility that I could be getting intimate with an actual real-life man, and my pre-holiday bikini line shave was beginning to wear off. Then there was my neglected feet that could get a cameo in *The Hobbit* films, and don't even get me started on my roots.

We discovered, after wandering around for over an hour, that beauty salons seemed to be the exception rather than the norm in rural Cyprus, unlike in Liverpool where you can't walk ten feet without being offered the latest brow craze or lip filler treatment.

We found one eventually, hidden down a side street and only discoverable because of a faded old sign at the top of the road with 'Aphrodite' written on it, who I knew from a history lesson from Mum earlier in the day was the Greek goddess of beauty.

"Hiya, babe, what brow treatments have you got?" asked Maddy to the beauty therapist, who looked petrified at the prospect of customers, never mind loud Scouse ones.

"I sorry, I no understand English."

"E-Y-E-B-R-O-W-S?" Maddy said repeatedly in a slow, drawn-out voice, as if doing so would give the woman the ability to understand the English language.

"Er, *frimia*?" I added, whilst running a finger along my eyebrows. "*Fribia?* Er, *frilia*?"

The therapist's eyes lit up. "Ah *fridia!*" she exclaimed, which was a relief because I'd ran out of guesses. "*Ela.*"

She pointed to the chair, and I sat down reluctantly. I should have left five minutes earlier, but it was like when you get so far down the ride queue at Alton Towers and you know there's no going back.

Things went from bad to worse when Maddy had to intervene mid-treatment becuase the beauty therapist started filling the space in between my eyebrows with her brow ink, which she must have thought I'd wanted when I'd given the eyebrow demonstration earlier. Apparently, unibrows *were* quite the rage in ancient Greek times – and I must stress the word *ancient*.

*

By the time I got back to the villa it was dark and I was exhausted, both emotionally and physically – a mixture of almost ending up spending the rest of my holiday looking like Helga from *Hey Arnold* and the repercussions from the wall climbing.

So I could have cried when I tried to open the front door to the villa and realised it was locked and I didn't have a key – Mum didn't trust me with such responsibilities after I stumbled in drunk after a night out at home once, completely forgetting that I didn't live there any more, and ate most of the moussaka she'd premade for lunch for the following day.

"What took you so long?!" I cried once she finally opened the door. Two smartly dressed men followed behind, holding clipboards with some kind of property logo on the front that I couldn't make out.

"We'll be in touch soon, Mrs Eliades," said the tallest of the two, with an air of arrogance I didn't like.

"Who was that?" I asked, following her into the villa.

Mum dabbed at the beads of sweat that were trickling down her forehead. "Bloody Jehovahs!"

I laughed. "Since when were Jehovahs a thing in Cyprus? And more importantly, since when do you let them in the door?"

"I feel sorry for them, Isme, walking roun' in the heat." I didn't believe her, but the tantalising smell of beef and pasta from the Makaronia tou fournou wafting through from the kitchen was making my stomach growl, and I couldn't wait much longer.

We sat down to eat once Dad, who'd been to the supermarket, came back – Maria and George had taken the twins into Larnaca for a McDonalds – but just as I was about to take my first mouthful, Dad's phone started to ring from inside his pocket.

"STEPHEN!" Mum looked like she might explode with rage. Eliades' house rule number one: no phones at the dining table, or you won't be eating your dinner, you'll be wearing it.

"Sorry, love, my bad. I'll just, er, turn it off." He retrieved his phone clumsily from his pocket and started frantically pressing at the screen to try and turn it off, but inadvertently answered the call and put it on loudspeaker.

"Hello, Stephen? You there?" came a female voice from the phone, that had a foreign twang to it that I couldn't quite distinguish. By this time, Mum's face was purple. Dad, by contrast, looked like he'd seen a ghost.

Luckily, I was sitting next to him and managed to grab the phone and press the red button to end the call.

"Bloody PPI callers using my name now! The barefaced cheek of them."

"That's weird, they don't usually—"

"Yes, it happened to me too the otha day," Mum interjected. They are unbelievable."

We continued eating our food in silence, my head swirling in a sea of lies and mistruths, from the Jehovah's witnesses to the PPI call. The Makaronia tasted delicious, but I couldn't eat much of it. I was already full from the lies I'd just been fed.

"Sorry, I didn't tell you to wear your gym gear, did I?" exclaimed Neil when I arrived at the *platia* for our 'date', and he spotted my outfit – a white floaty summer dress and tan wedges – and he saw the sheer look of confusion on my face when *I* spotted *his* blue shorts and blue and white striped vest top.

It was like that scene from the first *Bridget Jones* film where Bridget turns up to a tarts and vicars fancy dress themed party dressed as a Playboy Bunny, only to find out when she gets there that it's not fancy dress any more.

Neil was accompanied by about ten other people, an equal mix of both men and women, wearing the exact same top. They were huddled together in little groups doing some leg stretches and lunges on the pavement. It was like some terrible skit of the 118 advert, except no one was laughing, and only one of them had a muzzy.

"Don't worry, I've got a spare vest in the car." As Neil sprinted over to retrieve the vest, I found myself looking longingly into a local taverna, taking in the familiar sound of glasses clinking and people laughing (probably at us) and wishing that this was all some terrible nightmare that I was going to wake up from soon. Someone opened the door, and the enticing smell of charcoaled meat and wood-barrelled beer wafted past, making me want to cry out in frustration.

"So, this your first time at running club?" I jolted at the sound of a small voice beside me, which was coming from a little old grey-haired fella that should have been at home watching *Clash of the Titans*, never mind roaming the streets of Maroni in nothing but a pair of flimsy shorts and vest on this breezy May evening.

"Yeah, you could say that."

"Ah, don worry," he said, patting me on the back with surprising force from such a little human, making me feel like a baby being winded. "We look after you."

Somehow, some shorts and trainers were found for me, and before I knew it, I was jogging through the windy, narrow streets of Maroni village hoping for some kind of time vortex to appear in the floor for me to fall into and take me to better times.

It was the poor tourists I felt sorry for, trying to take a picture outside the picturesque village church with me unintentionally photo bombing in the background, leaning on a wall looking like I was about to keel over. Then there was the middle-aged local women, who had been loitering at every corner, watching intently and talking in hushed tones to each other, as if sizing their meat up for the local trade fair.

"Wasn't that great!" exclaimed Neil afterwards. He was hardly out of breath, whilst I was sat on the church steps with my head in between my legs feeling like my chest might explode.

"A bit of a heads up that we were going to be running would have been nice, Neil," I scoffed. He sat down on the step next to me.

"I wanted it to be a surprise. After all, you did say you wanted to get yourself fitter."

I looked up at him in disbelief. "If you want to surprise a girl, Neil, get her some flowers or take her out for a nice meal. Don't force her into exercise and make her feel like Ten-Ton Tess."

Neil stared down at his feet. "Sorry, I didn't realise. I—"

"I'm gonna head off. I'll see you around, maybe."

As soon as he was out of earshot, I dialled Maddy's number.

Me: "I'm fully aware that I live an unhealthy lifestyle, but it's up to me if I want to do something about it. I don't need some fella I barely know shoving green juices and various forms of exercise down my throat like I'm on an episode of *How to Lose Weight Well*."

Maddy: "Give me his Insta address, I'm gonna send him some abusive DMs."

Me: "Seriously though, Maddy, shall I just stop wasting my time?"

Maddy: "I dunno, babe. I reckon he does like you. Otherwise he wouldn't have asked to see you again after the coffee shop. It just sounds like he's got zero game when it comes to girls, which is mad because he's fit as fuck."

Me: "Yep, that's the problem. I think I would have told him to do one by now if he didn't have abs for days. And don't even get me started on those arms, mmmm mmmmm."

Maddy: "How long did you say you hadn't had sex for again?!"

*

It had been three whole weeks since arriving in Cyprus for my 'life affirming' holiday, yet all I seemed to have affirmed in that time was that HD brows were not (and will never be) my thing, and that I've still got shit taste in men.

I decided not to go to the third and final cookery lesson. As much as I wouldn't have minded copping another look at Neil's bod, he clearly didn't fancy me and I wanted to spare myself the embarrassment of him saying it.

I took a leisurely stroll to the beachfront to try and clear my head, sitting on one of the benches that faced out towards the water, the sun reflecting on it like glitter. I smiled as I listened to the cheery sound of kids playing on the sand, and the distinct sound of *bazouki* music playing in the distance. I followed the direction of the noise, coming from a nearby hotel, where chairs and tables were being set up on the beach along with a makeshift bar area.

Suddenly my phone pinged, and my stomach flipped when I caught sight of the sender.

> **Anthony:** Yo, Freckiades, how are the hols going? 😎
> Me and the family are flying out in a few days
> for the Limassol food and drink festival
> Hopefully see you there? 😊

My insides fluttered at the prospect of seeing him, and I immediately started typing back.

> **Isme:** Hols been OK. Pretty uneventful tbh 😉

Apart from meeting some absolute hottie who's treating me like his little weight loss project and has got my head well and truly battered, I was hastened to add.

Anthony: Really? I assumed from the lack of contact over the last three weeks that you've been busy finding your 'Good Greek Boy'?! 😂

Isme: 😂 😂 😂 I'd need to get past the overprotective mas first
How are things back home? Any goss?

And by 'things', I meant Zara.

Anthony: Yeah, pretty uneventful here as well

Was he lying? In the same way that I was . . . ?

So see you at the festival? That's unless you've got other plans with some Greek hunk! 😂

Isme: Greek, no. Hunk, yes! 😬
See you there

It was meant as a joke, but I'd be a liar if I said I wasn't trying to make him jealous just a teeny tiny bit.

Anthony: ☹ Sounds like we've got a lot to catch up on then . . .
Look forward to seeing you

I couldn't help but smile to myself at the last message and, despite what he may (or hopefully may not) have been getting up to with Zara back home, I suddenly couldn't wait to see him too.

*

Hercules: I saw you on the beach earlier.
You looked great 😊
Will you meet me at the church in the platia later?
I think I owe you an explanation

I almost didn't recognise Neil sitting on the church steps wearing a khaki T-shirt and black jeans with rips on the knees as I arrived at the *platia* – a refreshing change from his sports gear.

I'd opted for the 'not arsed' look in denim shorts and a T-shirt, although they *were* my best ones, and I'd spent over an hour trying to perfect my 'natural look' make-up after a FaceTime tutorial with Maddy. I'd been unsure whether to even go after the lack of any signs that he fancied me. But the 'I think I owe you an explanation' filled me with intrigue, and curiosity got the better of me. And if he *was* planning on letting me down gently, I wanted to at least look good while he did.

"I want to start by saying sorry," he said once I'd sat down next to him, and all initial small talk had dried up – all we had left was the Greek economic crisis of 2009, and we didn't have all night. "I've been a complete idiot."

He hesitated for a moment, as if waiting for me to disagree, but I didn't.

He took a sharp intake of breath. "Look, I like you. I should have told you that in the coffee shop, but when you started asking me about my personal life, I panicked because I've never told anyone before about my, ahem, past."

The way he said 'past' had me wondering all sorts. Had I been right from the start when I'd probed him at the coffee shop about him having an estranged wife, loads of kids or a gambling addition? I scoured the *platia* for an easy escape route if things turned sour.

"You see, I'm in remission. From alcohol. That's why I took the job over here, after having a bit of a relapse a few months ago."

I sat, stunned into silence. It was the last thing I'd expected him to say.

"I've been off it for about two years now, aside from the relapse," he went on. He then told me how it had started at university, and how he realised he had a problem when he found himself still drinking a bottle of vodka a day months after graduating.

"I've pretty much spent the last two years trying to exert my energy into other things, like exercising and baking, basically anything where alcohol isn't. But, as you can imagine, it's hard to meet women anywhere other than bars." He hesitated for a moment. "That was until I saw you by the pool."

I felt myself blush. "Well, that explains why you took me wall climbing and running for our first dates then!" I let out a laugh. "And there's me thinking you were trying to get me to lose some weight."

Neil stared down at his hands. "It's just I haven't been to a bar or restaurant in so long and wasn't sure how I'd be. Plus, you did say you had come on holiday to get healthier."

Neil shuffled himself along the step until our bodies were touching, the heat from his making my heart quicken. Was this it? Could it be my first proper snog of the year? (Not counting the one with juvenile Alan as I was drunk and could hardly remember it.)

The setting was perfect – the hazy Mediterranean sun setting in the distance, the sound of the *bazouki* music playing from the local taverna, swallows flying overhead across the *platia*. But as Neil leant his head towards me, and I closed my eyes ready for those sparks I'd been waiting for since we met to blow my head off, an image of Anthony unexpectedly popped into my head, catching me completely off-guard. I turned my head at the completely wrong time, so instead it was my nose that ended up taking a blow.

"SHIT! I'm so sorry, Isme," cried Neil, rubbing at his nose where we'd collided. "It's fair to say, I'm a bit rusty."

I laughed awkwardly. "It's my nose you need to apologise to, ha!" A drunken snog with a lad half my age suddenly didn't seem quite so bad. At least I'd had the alcohol in me to numb the embarrassment.

He leant in again, only slower this time. His lips felt nice, smooth and soft with a hint of mint. But as pleasant as the kiss was, all I could think about was Anthony and his imminent arrival. Plus, the spicy-sweet smell of Neil's Lynx was making my stomach bubble.

After I left, I immediately called Maddy to fill her in on the disappointing lack of fanny tingles.

"The Acropolis wasn't built in a day, babe, sometimes these things take time."

"Yeah, you are right, Maddy. I mean, it also didn't help that imaginary Anthony decided to butt in."

"Ha, exactly, babe. What was that all about, like?"

"I dunno, I think with him messaging me yesterday out of the blue it's brought any thoughts of him that I'd been trying to put to the back of my mind now firmly at the front."

"Fair enough. I tell you what though, babe, if Liverpool's answer to Thor can't make you get the flutters, then I'd consider retiring your libido."

*

Hercules: I really enjoyed last night, Isme. Thank you for listening and giving me another chance 😳 I'm sorry about your nose though! 🙈

Isme: Ha, don't worry about it! I'm Greek, our noses are made of strong stuff 😂 I had a really nice time too 😊

Hercules: 😂 I'm busy with work the rest of the week but can I take you out again after that? Don't worry, there'll be no exercise involved this time, I promise 😊

"Who is this Hercules?"

"MUM, STOP LOOKING AT MY PHONE!" I shifted my position on the couch so that my screen was no longer visible to her beady eyes.

"I can't help it, Isme, it right there."

"Well it will be 'right there' if you're hovering over me like that!"

"*Ochi*, Isme, why you so angry all the time?" She stomped back to the kitchen to continue making her Greek coffee, which was perfuming the air with an earthy, bitter aroma.

"Isme's got a boyfriend, Isme's got a boyfriend!" chanted George from the other sofa.

"Piss off, George, he's not my boyfri—"

"Ey, boys, Uncle Isme is going to marry a Greek hero!"

Theo and Tomaso, who until then had been sat quietly next to George engrossed in their iPads, sprung to their feet.

"Like, a super hero? Is it Spiderman, Uncle Isme?" said Theo excitedly. "No, wait, is it Iron Man? Oh pleeeease let it be Iron Man!"

"Boys, I'm not marrying anyone, he's not even my boyfrie—"

"Or Superman! Maybe he could teach us how to fly! How cool would that be, Theo!"

"SO cool! We could fly to space, and the moon and—"

"MCDONALDS!"

Whilst the twins carried on hypothesising about my fantasy superhero boyfriend, I opened my phone back up and quickly typed a reply.

Isme: I'd really like that, Neil.

See you then.

Have a good week x

They say absence makes the *heart* grow fonder, but in my case, I hoped it would be more a case of absence makes the *fanny* grow fonder.

JUNE

SINGLES NIGHT!

Are you single and ready to mingle?

Do you dream of your own Big Fat Greek Wedding?
Then why not come along to our annual Maroni Village
singles night on the private beach of Hotel Athena!
Famous for its 'unique' twist on modern speed dating,
where the mamas of the men get to choose their
sons' dates, it really is a night not to be missed!

Don't delay, sign up now!

"Are you having a laugh?" I stared at the piece of paper like it was written in Greek minuscule.

"*Ochi*, Isme, you going to make it all wet!" cried Mum, snatching the leaflet back off me and flapping it in the air. The way she was acting, you'd think it was the original biblical manuscripts.

"Well, you did just drag me out of the pool whilst I was enjoying my mid-morning swim." I grabbed a towel from the back of one of the dining-room chairs and wrapped it around my waist. I didn't tell her that I was glad of the break from the sun, which was already heating the pool up like a jacuzzi.

"So what you think, Isme? You will go, yes?"

"Nope. I'd rather get myself on Tinder and be judged on my looks by some pervy fellas than have a load of overbearing mas turn their nose up at me because I can't knock up a moussaka." I grabbed a piece of cucumber from the salad she was preparing and stuffed it into my mouth. "Also, I'm busy tomorrow." I wasn't, but Greece's answer to Cilla Black over here didn't need to know that.

"Oh, Isme, come on. Is jus a bit of fun!" exclaimed Mum, as she made preparations for lunch, consisting of my favourite – keftedes and Greek salad. I could see what she was trying to do, but I wasn't going to let her 'stomach over matter' jedi mind trick work, despite the irresistible smell of the meatballs frying in hot oil making me drool like Homer Simpson over doughnuts.

"Pah! Fun, my arse. I think I'd have a better time rubbing chillies into my eyes."

"Why would you want to put chilli in your eyes, Isme?" said Dad idly, as he glared at something on his phone.

"I DON'T! It's just, like, a metaphor or something, Dad."

"You know, I rubbed my eyes once after cutting up a chilli, stung for days, it did."

"What is this, metapour?" asked Mum, waving her frying utensil in the air.

"I ended up having to get an eye patch," Dad went on. "Do you remember, Elana?"

"Of course! They still call you *Pappous* Hook!"

As the pair of them carried on their pointless middle-aged conversation, I took myself back outside for another dip, quite forgetting that I hadn't put my flip flops on and the floor was like a hot plate.

"OOOOOO! EEEEEE! AAAAAA!" I hot-footed it back to the shade, just as one of the mamas was strolling past, arm in arm with her son. She smiled whilst muttering something to her son, who nodded in agreement.

That's when I realised – the older women walking around with the younger men, being 'watched' at the running club, Mum's keenness for me to do the cookery course . . . It all linked back to this annual singles night, which so conveniently fell during our time out here.

I needed to vent and dialled Maddy's number.

Maddy: "So, hang on a minute, babe, you're telling me your mum put you up to the cookery course to make you look more appealing to all these Greek mas?"

Me: "Exactly! Can you friggin' believe it, Maddy?!"

Maddy: "She's a legend!"

Me: "No, Whitney Houston was a legend. Elana Eliades is a massive crank."

Maddy: "Babe, don't be mad, but I think this singles night sounds like a bit of a laugh."

Me: "Oh piss off, not you an' all."

Maddy: "No, wait, hear me out! The amount of times I've dated a fella and had to put up with his crank of a ma. At least this way, we get to meet them first and decide if we want to date their beloved sons. And if its shit we'll just bail and go and get a gyros."

After the call ended, I sat on one of the wrought iron patio chairs and sighed. The pool, which had been fairly deserted earlier, was now bustling with families surfacing after their breakfast. I watched as kids rushed about, dive-bombing into the pool over and over whilst shouting, "MUM, DAD, WATCH THIS! WATCH THIS!" every time, whilst the parents looked on showing as much enthusiasm as *I* had when Mum had showed me the leaflet.

I wish I could say I'd put Maddy's idea of going to the singles night to bed, but unfortunately she had me at gyros.

*

I arranged to meet Maddy at the beach bar next door to the hotel for a quick one for Dutch courage before we went into the singles night event. *She'd* wanted to meet me at the villa so she could meet 'the legend' but luckily Mum was out with the locals on some speed-walking class, or at least that's what she'd told me. I wouldn't put it past her to be hiding behind a palm tree outside the hotel like Miss Marple.

I decided to take the beach walk to the bar to meet Maddy

to take advantage of the gentle sea breeze, which was a welcome relief from the humidity of the early evening sun.

I took off my sandals and let the waves wash over my feet, as they gently crashed forwards and backwards. The sound was as soothing as a lullaby to a baby, and I closed my eyes to savour the calming moment. So deep in relaxation, I didn't notice the sound of shuffling feet approaching until I opened my eyes and almost lost my footing against an unruly wave.

"ANTHONY, WHAT THE HELL?!"

"Nice to see you too, Freckiades!"

I stood there for a moment, frozen to the spot, unsure how to react to the unexpected meet. We'd never been the huggy type, but I suddenly felt an urge to wrap my arms around him. So I did, taking in the familiar spicy-sweet undertones of his aftershave, and the warmth of his sun-kissed olive skin.

"I was just on my way to the villa to say hello. Didn't you get my message?"

"Shit, no, I never— sorry. Been enjoying the walk. When did you get here, anyway?"

"Only a couple of hours ago. I see you're living up to your name!" Anthony gently touched the cluster of freckles that had set up home on my nose. His touch was like a bolt of electricity which caught me off guard, along with another wave. Luckily, Anthony grabbed my arm before I fell arse over tit into the water.

"So, where are you off to?" he asked, as we started walking in the direction of Hotel Athena. The sun was now setting in the distance, marbling the sky with pink and lilac.

"Nowhere really, just fancied a walk." I could only hope that my blushed cheeks blended in with my tan, but I could feel Anthony's suspicious eyes burning into me.

"Since when does Ismena Eliades just 'fancy a walk'? You always said people who went on walks with no real end goal, like a pub or restaurant, were gobshites."

"Yeah, well, I can change my mind, can't I?"

Anthony chuckled and I couldn't help but laugh.

We continued walking along the beach in silence, the only sound coming from the gentle crashing of the waves. A young couple walked past us holding hands and deep in conversation, which made the silence between us even more deafening. This was my best friend who I hadn't seen in weeks, so why couldn't I think of a single thing to say to him? I knew Anthony felt uncomfortable too, especially when he cleared his throat and made a comment about the weather.

A wave came crashing against the tide, splashing us both up to our waists, the unexpected coldness of it making us hot-foot it onto dry sand. We looked at each other's dripping wet clothes and burst into a fit of laughter, the type of laughter that makes your eyes stream and your belly hurt.

And, just like that, we were Anthony and Isme again.

*

"What do you think's going on over there?" asked Anthony, as we reached Hotel Athena and he spotted the makeshift bar area on the beach, with a tiki-style wooden bar and matching benches and tables, where throngs of men and women were gathered in small groups, mostly in twos. With the canopy of warm, stringed bulb lights overhead and surrounding palm trees, all that was missing was Maya Jama and a fire pit. I'd been enjoying the Anthony 'reunion' so much I hadn't noticed we'd reached the hotel.

"Oh, er, I'm not sure. Maybe some beach party or something," I said, as blasé as I could muster, but the heat was already rushing through my cheeks. With the safety of the beach bar in my sights, I picked up pace, hoping Anthony would do the same, but it was too late. He'd already spotted the huge banner on the outside wall of the hotel.

"Singles night eh, Freckiades!" he said, nudging me in the side. "I thought you hated the whole dating scene after that lad off Plenty of Fish brought his cat on the date?"

"What do you mean? I was just out for a walk, I didn't even know this was going on!" But it was useless – Anthony knew me better than anyone, as confirmed by the smirk that spread across his face.

I wanted to murder Maddy for putting me up to it. I looked around to see if I could spot her, but there was no botoxed-up blonde in sight. Then my phone pinged with a message.

> **Maddy:** Babe I'm so sorry, my stomach is in bulk.
> Think I've eaten something dodge
> Go and find us a hubby 😊

"OK, so if you're *not* going to this singles night, do you fancy coming for a drink with me?"

I hesitated for a moment. Being in Cyprus and away from Anthony had helped me take my mind off my inexplainable feelings towards him, and my hope was that by the time I was back home they would be completely extinguished. Now he was here I could feel them bubbling back to the surface, ready to turn my head into a scrambled mess of 'what if's and 'maybe's. Was it easier to keep my distance?

But this was Anthony. My best friend of over thirty years. And I'd missed him. So I soon found myself saying, "Yeah, go on then."

*

Neil: Are you still free for lunch?
I know a great little vegan place 😌

Thankfully, another message came through from Neil shortly after to say that the vegan place was closed – the last thing I needed after a night on the sauce was a plate of vegetables or, worse still, tofu. I tried it once and it was like eating fresh air, and I needed much more than that to quench my hangover stomach, preferably something meaty and riddled in grease. I remembered Anthony telling me about an English bar in the centre of Larnaca that served up *the* best fry-ups, which was just the cure I needed, so arranged to meet Neil there instead.

What I *didn't* need was to be sat on a stuffy bus for almost an hour with minimal ventilation, making my hangover stomach bubble as it trudged its way down the long and winding roads leading from Maroni village to the centre of Larnaca.

It *should* have only taken half an hour if it wasn't for the herds of goats monopolising parts of the road, who were not a bit put out by the oncoming traffic and prospect of being flattened. The driver waited patiently until they were out of harm's way before driving off, which was quite a contrast to back home where they'd likely be met with lots of horn beeping and angry expletives.

One plus side of the journey was the spectacular scenery en route; rolling hills covered with an abundance of colourful plants and flowers, acting as a backdrop to the clusters of village houses, the morning rays highlighting their whitewashed walls and orange-bricked roofs. It was like stepping into an oil painting, only brighter and more vivid.

The bus came to an abrupt halt, indicating that we had reached our destination, which was a welcome relief – any longer and they'd have to mop me off the floor.

"*Efkharisto*," I said to the driver as I stepped off the bus, and started heading down the main road that ran through the centre of Larnaca, which was lined either side with various bars, restaurants and shops. Wafts of stale beer hit me as I plodded past, and I had to swallow down the bile that was threatening to surface.

I knew I should have said no when Anthony came back from the bar with our drinks and two ouzo chasers. I'd been on my best behaviour since the drunken night with Maddy, but what harm could a few shots from the spirit book of my ancestors do? Quite a lot, it turned out, especially when you have three more. But despite my fuzz-riddled head and queasiness, I'd enjoyed seeing Anthony again. It felt familiar, like spotting an English bar when you're abroad and getting that warm sense of home.

I arrived at the bar and plonked myself down on one of the wicker chairs by the open floor-to-ceiling bi-fold windows, which felt cool against my hot skin. The bar itself was as Anthony had described; pine wood walls throughout with various British-themed pictures and plaques, including a bulldog wearing a Union Jack coat and smoking a cigar, and a portrait of the king.

Neil was running late, so I took the liberty of ordering a fry up for him too, quite forgetting that he doesn't have a physique like his by eating food that's so high in saturated fat it should carry a heart attack warning.

"Sorry, don't you like it?" I asked after the waitress had brought our food over, and Neil stared down at his like he'd been served a plate of turd.

"I'm a vegan. I thought I told you."

I grimaced. "Shit, sorry, you did. I didn't even think. I'll order you something else."

"No, it's OK. I'll just eat the beans and mushrooms." He picked up his fork and started carefully moving the animal elements to one side of the plate. It was like watching a baby tackle solids for the first time. "So, what have you been up to?"

I shrugged my shoulders. "Erm, not much, really. Just been, er, chillin'. Like a villain, ha!"

I let out a nervous laugh whilst fidgeting with a strand of hair that had loosened itself from my pony tail. I would be shit on *The Traitors*.

It was then that I spotted Anthony striding along the road heading in the direction of the bar. In a panic, I grabbed the drinks menu and attempted to hide my face behind it. Unfortunately, it wasn't quite big enough to cover my recognisable curly Greek mop head.

"So, you found it then, Freckiades!" I slowly lowered the menu down from my face and attempted my best surprised face, but I imagine it looked more like I was constipated.

"Anthony, what are you . . . fancy seeing, I mean, what are you doing over here? Wow, what a complete shock it is to see you!"

Now it was Anthony's turn to look surprised. "What do you mean, I seen you last night?"

It was then that Anthony spotted Neil. They caught each other's gaze, and for a moment I contemplated hiding behind my menu again until the whole exchange was over.

"Hi, I'm Anthony, Isme's boyfriend," Anthony said, breaking the silence. He reached out to shake Neil's hand, but he was too busy glaring at me to notice.

"He's not my boyfriend," I clarified to Neil, although he still didn't look convinced.

"I am. I'm a boy that's your friend, ha! Come on, lighten up, people!"

"Ah, I see," said Neil, smiling wearily. "I'm Neil, Isme's, erm, acquaintance."

"Acquaintance, eh." Anthony gave an exaggerated wink at Neil. "She's had a few of them in her time, if you know what I mean!"

"No, I'm not sure I do—"

"I bet you need that, Freckiades, after all that ouzo we got through last night!" Anthony laughed, nodding in the direction of my half-eaten plate of full English. "I might come and have one myself, mind if I join you?"

I opened my mouth to speak, but it was like my voice box had been temporarily switched off.

"Nah, only messing, I'm on my way to meet a friend." I let out a sigh of relief and slunk back into my chair. "It was nice to meet you, Isme's acquaintance Neil." Anthony grabbed a slice of toast off my plate and took a huge bite. "I'll see *you* at the festival." With that, he was gone, leaving a grey cloud of unanswered questions in his wake, along with a sprinkling of toast crumbs.

"What's the story between you two?" asked Neil, wiping some rogue crumbs off his shoulder with the expression of someone who had been shat on by a bird.

"Oh nothing, we're just old mates," I muttered while poking at my food, having lost my appetite after suffering one of the most awkward encounters of non-exes anyone has ever had.

*

Isme: What was all that about? 😠

Anthony: What do you mean?!

Isme: Errr the boyfriend comment? Calling me out on going for a drink with you last night?

Anthony: 😄 It was just banter!
And what's the big deal about us going for a drink?
We've been doing it for the last fifteen years

Isme: Yeah, but it didn't go down well after the boyfriend comment

Anthony: Hang on, you're not telling me you're gonna carry on seeing him, are you?! 🐙

Isme: Maybe. Why?

Anthony: Isme, I've seen more charisma on a dead fish

Isme: 👆

*

I remember the first time Mum and Dad took me to the Limassol food and drink festival when I was a kid. I'd felt like Charlie when he first visited the chocolate factory; the middle-aged Greek fellas in their traditional *foustanea*, standing bare foot in a huge wooden barrel filled with red grapes, dancing the *Sirtaki* to the music of the Limassol Folklore group whilst people watched on and clapped.

The throngs of locals sat around amongst the variety of plants and cypress trees of the Municipal Gardens, laughing and joking whilst sipping from their plastic cups of wine handcrafted by local vineyards. The succulent smell of souvlaki being cooked over coal barbecues wafted in the air.

I was too young to drink back then, but you didn't need it. The atmosphere alone was enough to get you feeling giddy and warm inside. I didn't exactly *need* the wine now either, but it would be rude not to. Plus, I was going to need it to get through an afternoon with the full Eliades clan.

It was another intensely hot sunny day, so we'd set up camp under the shady branches of a large eucalyptus tree. People were already arriving to the festival in droves, a mixture of *parea's*, both young and old, and families keen to sample what wines the local vineyards had to offer. Or, in Maria and George's case, keen to neck as much as they could until the twins got bored and asked them every five seconds when they were leaving until they caved.

"God, this is bliss," said Maria, sinking further down into her camping chair and closing her eyes up at the sky. "If only Mum and Dad would keep the twins in the play area all day— OH FOR FUCK'S SAKE, GEORGE!" Maria began furiously wiping down her maxi dress where he'd clumsily splashed some of his wine onto her.

"Oh, calm down will you, woman, it's only wine— BURP!" If looks could kill, George would have been ten feet under.

"Love's young dream," I laughed as I lay on the picnic blanket next to them, propped up on my elbows. "If this is what's waiting for me behind the marriage door, I think I'd rather die alone surrounded by cats."

"Pah! Rats, more like. I've seen that shit hole of a flat of yours."

"Piss off, George. You've been to the flat once and it was only a mess because your feral kids had stayed the night."

"There was more than one night's worth of dishes in that sink—"

"Will you two shut the fuck up! You're ruining my precious

'I'm-pretending-I-haven't-got-any-kids' time!"

"Yeah, well he started it," I muttered, shifting my position on the blanket so I was lying flat. I closed my eyes and took a slow, deep breath, in and out, in an attempt to tune George out, and instead channel the upbeat and jovial atmosphere of the festival.

As I took in the smell of chargrilled meat coming from a nearby gyros stall, and the dull tones of the local folklore group playing traditional *bouzouki* music, I could feel my whole body start to relax. I could have been at Glastonbury, minus the mud and general stench of piss.

"I hope you've got factor fifty on that pasty skin of yours, Freckiades." I jolted at the sight of Anthony towering over me in his navy tailored shorts and a white polo T-shirt, which complemented his tanned skin.

"I'm in the shade, arsehole," I said, propping myself up onto my bum and crossing my legs, my chilled-out vibes sweeping away with the breeze.

"Means nothing with your skin. Haven't you been here for like six weeks now? I've seen more tan on a polar bear. Now shift over, will you." Anthony plonked himself down next to me, our legs slightly touching, and I became very aware of my overgrown hairs. There was that unexpected spark again from his touch that I'd felt on the beach, and I took a gulp of my sauvignon to wash it down.

"Have you heard about Isme's new fella, Anthony?" smirked George.

"He's not my fella, sarky arse, and if you must know, he's an engineer."

"An engineer of what, flour?" George and Anthony burst into laughter, like two childish teenagers, and I could feel my face begin to redden.

"Oi, leave the poor girl alone, you two." Sandra appeared from the crowd like my very own *Soteria*, God of protection. She gave my arms a gentle squeeze. "He's just jealous because his love life is as dead as that pig over there." Sandra nodded in the direction of a hog roast nearby.

I chuckled, and tried side-eyeing Anthony to try and get a read of his reaction, for any indication as to how he was feeling about things seemingly ending with Zara. Did he look sad? Relieved? Non-plussed? But unless I had eyes in the side of my head, it was impossible.

"How's the baking going, Isme?" asked Sandra, taking one of the spare camping chairs. "You know I've got this local fair I'm doing for the Maroni village school in a few days, and we're desperate for someone to make the cupcakes for it."

I ran my hands along my crossed legs and stretched out my back. "Mmmmmm, I dunno, Sandra. That's quite short notice. Plus I'm quite rusty at the moment."

"Nonsense! I bet it's like riding a bike. And I'll pay you, of course! Now, I need fifty Peppa Pig themed cakes. What do you reckon, are you up to the challenge?"

I hesitated, staring into my cup of wine like it was a magic eight ball that was going to give me the answer. Could I really do it? Or more so, did I *want* to do it? This *was* supposed to be a holiday after all. "*You can't sit around thee pool all day, you mast do something!"* came Mum's voice from inside my head.

"Well, you can't do any worse than the Teletubbies ones you did for Tomaso that year," said Maria, breaking me away from the cup of destiny. "Dipsy looked like he had a giant cock on his head!"

"Ha, yeah! He still shouts 'penis head' when they come on the telly!" Maria and George burst into laughter, and I couldn't help but join in. They *were* pretty shocking.

I needed a chance to redeem myself, so before I knew it, I found myself saying yes.

*

"Why did no one tell me Peppa Pig has a questionably shaped snout? No matter how hard I try, it just looks like a flaccid willy!"

I fiddled with the pink fondant icing, which was becoming wet and sticky against the granite worktops in the thirty-degree heat. It didn't help that Mum had dominated most of the space in the rustic white kitchen with various bowls and pans containing marinading meats and chopped vegetables for the day's meals, leaving me minimal room to manoeuvre. The smell of the oregano and rosemary *was* quite delicious, though.

I suddenly longed for my tiny kitchen back home, where I could bake without anyone peering over my shoulder and had less humid conditions. The heat *did* have some advantages though, like softening the butter without needing to microwave it and risking overheating, making the process of creaming the milk and sugar together much easier. I'd also quite enjoyed using a good old whisk in the absence of a cake-making machine, the motion of swirling the mixture around the bowl and watching it soften beneath my hands almost hypnotising.

Maria peered over my shoulder to inspect the ten cakes I'd attempted so far. "Hmmm, looks familiar." She looked over at George as she said this, who was sat on the beige fabric couch in the living area with his bare feet resting on the wooden coffee table, balancing a large bowl of cheese puffs on his belly. He was too engrossed in some Greek game show playing on the wall-mounted plasma television to notice Maria's sly remark.

"I guess you haven't lost your knack for fondant icing genitalia, Isme, ha!" he shouted without peeling his eyes off the telly.

"Helpful, thanks," I muttered impatiently, whilst wiping sweat off my forehead with the back of my hand. "What am I going to do? Sandra is relying on me to have these done by tomorrow!"

"You should have just said no, love, I'm sure she would have found someone else," said Dad, who was sat at the dining table squinting hard at the twins' iPad screen. "Maria, how do I get those electronic mail thingies up on here?"

"You mean email, Dad?"

"Yeah, yeah, whatever." He seemed agitated and had been since him and Mum had come back from a trip into Larnaca town a few hours earlier. No doubt she'd spent the whole time moaning about her cankles, which had doubled in size since we got here.

"What's so urgent that you need to check your emails while you're on holiday?"

"Why you ask all thee questions, Maria! Jus show him how to get thee messages, please." Mum came bursting into the kitchen, fanning herself with a copy of *The Larnaca Post*. She looked just as agitated as Dad, sheens of sweat occupying her cheeks and forehead.

"Are you two OK?" I couldn't help but ask. "I know it's hot like, but you both seem particularly flustered today."

"Isme, what are these?" Mum had sidled up beside me in the kitchen and was inspecting my poor cake efforts with the look of someone who had caught the back draft of a fart.

"I know, they're awful. I'm just going to ring Sandra and tell her she'll have to get someone else to do them." I reached for my phone, but Mum blocked it with her hand.

"My mama always say, taste comes first before looks. If you get that right, then you are halfway there." She picked up one of the bare cakes and put it to her mouth. I waited with baited breath for her feedback, my palms sweating under the grip of the rolling pin.

After what felt like for ever, she said, "Is good, fluffy and light with jus thee right amount of *zachari*," and I breathed a sigh of relief. "Now, we jus need to sort thee pig. *Ela*, come, I have idea."

*

"Isme, they are perfect!" exclaimed Sandra when I arrived at the playing fields behind the Maroni village school the following day. "The kids are going to love them."

She gave me a hug, releasing a cloud of flour from my hair. I hadn't had time to wash it, but if it wasn't for Mum and her genius idea to visit a local *Zaharoplastio* and ask them if we could use their edible printer, I wouldn't have finished them at all.

"Aw, I hope so, they took me long enough! Turns out I'm a little more than rusty."

"Well if this is what you can come up with when you're rusty, I can't wait to see what you can do once you're fully back in the swing of it!"

I smiled. Despite the stress of pulling them together, which was more down to the icing not playing ball under the heat, the whole process and the praise from Sandra had ignited a little fire in my belly that was telling me this was my calling.

"Here, this is for you," said Sandra, retrieving a small brown envelope from her handbag.

"Sandra, I'm not going to take any money off you—"

"Nonsense. I said I'd pay you and I meant it. Now here, take it." Reluctantly, I took the envelope off her and placed it in the back pocket of my denim shorts.

"That's really kind, thank you."

Sandra smiled and placed an arm around my shoulders. "Now come on, let's get these cakes over to the refreshments table."

I followed Sandra across the field, which seemed a lot smaller than I remembered from all those years ago, when Mum would make me and Maria come to Sunday school during our summer holiday, despite our protests. I smiled to myself as I spotted the old red-bricked outhouse, where we'd chug retsina wine on our lunch break that we'd nicked from Mum's stash at the villa. It was no wonder my Greek vocabulary was nothing short of pathetic.

The school building itself was hardly recognisable following an injection of government funding a number of years ago, allowing them to render the old mud-brick walls, turning them from dull beige to bright stone, which highlighted the red of the new slate-tiled roof beautifully.

"I didn't realise Peppa had broken into the Greek market," I said, nodding in the direction of the *Peppa Pig* themed bouncy castle that was already buckling under the pressure of several excitable kids.

"Oh yeah, you know us Greeks, love a bit of pork!"

"Ha! That is true." I placed the cakes down on the designated refreshments trestle table, which had been covered with a pink wipeable table cover and was bustling with various other home-made delights no doubt contributed by the other local villagers, including one of my favourites, spanakopita, a golden, crispy spinach and feta filo pie.

"I made that myself," said Sandra, who must have noticed my lingering stare. "Anthony said it was your favourite."

"Bloody hell, it's like a zoo out here!" Right on cue, Anthony came striding over holding two crisp cold bottles of Keo, which looked just as appealing as his deep olive skin against his pale blue polo shirt. "I thought you might need one of these." I smiled gratefully, and took a swig to wet my dry throat.

"Aren't they great?" exclaimed Sandra, as Anthony inspected the cakes.

He hesitated for a moment before saying, "I'm disappointed. Where are the willies?"

*

"Do you think you'll have any?" I asked Anthony shortly after. We'd sought refuge from the mayhem of the fair and were sat under an olive tree on the outskirts of the field.

Anthony stared up at the sky pondering my question. "I mean, it looks like hard work, but when I picture my life, like, in the future, I couldn't imagine it without a few little sprogs running about."

I took a swig of my beer. "I only have to take one look at Maria with the twins and my womb closes over."

"Don't be so negative." Anthony grinned, giving me a playful shove. "Maria has got it tougher than most, with the twins and lazy arse. It'll be different for you. You'll have me to babysit for you when you and steg head go climbing mountains, or whatever else it is you get up to."

"Woah, chill out. I've only known the lad five minutes." *Also, unless I'm the Virgin Mary, last time I checked you had to actually have sex to get pregnant.* I didn't say this, of course. I didn't need to give him another reason to take the piss.

We sat in silence for a bit, observing the chaos of the fair, which was akin to a pack of monkeys that had escaped from the zoo, running riot and causing carnage in every direction whilst the exasperated parents chased after them helplessly.

A few of them eyed up our bottles of Keo as they stumbled past, a mixture of disgust that we could have the audacity to drink anything other than fruit juice at a school fair, and sheer envy on their faces.

Anthony's phone pinged with a message, and he chuckled to himself as he read it.

"Zara?" The words spilt out my mouth without any prior thought.

Anthony glanced up from his phone, his eyes wide and eyebrows raised. "No. Why would you ask that?"

I shrugged my shoulders and downed the rest of my beer. Thankfully, the heat of the sun would disguise the cause of my blushed cheeks.

Anthony turned his body to face me. "Look, I'll be honest with you. Me and Zara, we did . . . I mean, it was nothing. But, like, we did, erm . . . we did kiss. A few months ago, like."

And there it was. I stared down at the floor, unable to meet his gaze. I finally had an answer to the question that had been tormenting my brain for months. Did I feel relieved? Yes. Was my stomach bubbling at the thought of them *actually* kissing? Absolutely.

I fiddled with a corner of the label on the beer bottle that was starting to peel. "Why didn't you just tell me when I asked you if something had happened between you after I'd seen you in the coffee shop with her?"

"Because nothing *had* happened at that point. But then a week or so afterwards she rang me, crying. Said that Luke lad from work had been hounding her with calls and messages after she ended things, and she thought she'd seen him loitering around outside her house. I wasn't entirely convinced, you know she can be a drama queen, but she sounded genuinely worried and I didn't want anything on my conscience if anything *did* happen to her."

Anthony took a sharp intake of breath. "Anyway, I went round to check it all out and couldn't see anyone, but she insisted I stayed for a bit longer just to make sure, then pulled out a bottle of wine and two glasses. Before I knew it, she was throwing the lips on me."

I let out a heavy sigh. "OK, so why are you only telling me now?"

"Well, I *was* going to tell you when we were watching *Jurassic Park* at mine but you were so adamant that she was the one who got you suspended, and I thought if I told you we'd kissed you'd think I was a massive traitor."

"Pah! Yeah, you got that right," I scoffed.

"You have a right to be annoyed at me, Isme. I know I promised I'd tell you if anything ever happened. But honestly, it was something and nothing. We kissed, she wanted to take it further, I said no and that was that."

I stared into the familiar deep brown eyes of my best friend for any signs of untruth, but he was still and unblinking. I reached out my little finger. "No more secrets?"

Without hesitation, he linked his little finger with mine. "No more secrets." Anthony jumped up from the bench and stretched out his back. "Phew! I'm glad that's out in the open now. So, another beer?"

As he strode off to get more beers, I closed my eyes and lifted my head up at the sun, letting its rays beam down on me. Despite the madness of the fair, and the knowledge that Anthony and Zara *had* actually kissed, I felt a sense of calmness, the are-they-aren't-they niggle that had been eating away at me for months now blowing away with the gentle early evening breeze.

Hopefully it would take my confused feelings for Anthony with it.

Sandra: Isme, your cakes went down a storm 🎉
A few people were even asking for your details
so you can do some for them
Am I OK to pass them your number?

Isme: Erm, yeah OK! Why not

Sandra: Fab. Just let me know what you want to charge
so I can let them know 👍 Don't forget about your
Auntie Sandra when you're a millionaire from your
big successful cake-making business! 😁

I laughed off Sandra's message about becoming a millionaire. It was hardly realistic to imagine I could make *that* much money from selling cakes, but with the recent cash injection from making the *Peppa Pig* cakes for Sandra for the school fayre, and now the prospect of doing some more paid jobs, it did get me wondering again whether I *could* have another stab at making the cakes a full-time business.

I ran some quick calculations and worked out that to earn the equivalent of what I did at Mulligan's, and based on what I would expect to charge per cupcake, I would need to sell six hundred and twenty-five cupcakes a month. That's about twenty-two a day, not taking into account things like holidays, or sickness.

So, on second thoughts, I decided I'd start writing a saucy book instead about someone with a cupcake fetish, and call it *Fifty*

Shades of Icing.

*

Hercules: Fancy doing something tonight? 😊

Isme: Yeah, you can come round to
the villa if you want?
My lot are going out so we'll have
the place to ourselves

Hercules: Sounds good! 👍
I've got a little surprise for you,
as well . . .

A flurry of butterflies swept through my stomach at the prospect of seeing Neil again. I hadn't seen him since we met up in Larnaca when Anthony gatecrashed, and I'd been worried it had put him off. I also realised it would be the first time we'd be spending time *properly* alone, and not in a public setting where all our previous interactions had taken place. Cue another flurry of butterflies. Was the surprise he mentioned that I was finally going to see what was under those meggings . . . ?

"It's a Nutribullet," said Neil, placing the box that had an image of what looked like a vibrator for giants on the front onto the kitchen counter. "You can make all kinds of healthy shakes and smoothies with it. I use mine all the time."

I regretted investing in some new lacy thongs. "Great, thanks," I said, wondering how much I could get for it on eBay. It was hardly the surprise I'd been hoping for.

"You don't like it?" he said, sensing my disappointment.

"No, it really is great! Honest. Shall we have some coffee?"

Neil smirked and wrapped his arms around my waist, pulling me towards him. "OK, but first, can I do this?" My heart began to quicken as he slowly leant in and pressed his lips on mine. With the Nutribullet opener it took me by surprise, but it was a pleasant one. His lips felt soft and warm, and sent a tingle down my back. I wanted more, but Neil suddenly pulled away. "Right! Coffee," he declared, turning on the kettle and retrieving two mugs from the cupboard. I leant back against the kitchen counter, and ran a finger along my bottom lip where his had been.

As Neil made the drinks, and my heart began beating to a normal rhythm, I filled him in on my recent cupcake success and subsequent orders. He listened intently before saying, "You know you'll have to declare any earnings you make from it to the tax man, don't you?"

"Pah! As if," I scoffed, placing our drinks on the coffee table. "If those MP feckers can get away with putting floating duck islands through their expense claims, then I'm sure I can get away with a few extra bob from baking a few measly cakes."

"Just be careful! That's all I'm saying," he laughed, holding up his hands. "Now, how about that Netflix programme about the poor treatment of Beluga whales in Sea Life centres?"

I smiled weakly. I'd hoped after the kiss earlier that tonight might have been the night after all, but that no longer seemed the case.

I slunk back into the sofa and rested my head on Neil's chest as he wrapped an arm around me. But five minutes in and I was already losing the will, and my new thong was beginning to chafe. I shuffled my position slightly to gain some release, and accidently slipped my hand down to Neil's crotch area.

"Shit, sorry . . . woah!"

Neil's lips were suddenly on mine and, unlike the earlier kiss, there was an urgency to this one, like a caged animal that had been unleashed into the wild.

I tried matching up to his energy, but it was difficult with the background noise of someone talking about being attacked by Free Willy.

As Neil lowered his hands to my chest and started kissing my neck, the tingle that I'd been desperately hoping for finally came. This was it, the end of my dry patch! I almost had to stop myself from texting Maddy mid-flow to tell her the good news.

Then, just as I was getting into a rhythm, Neil pulled away. "I'm sorry, Isme." He sat on the edge of the sofa and buried his face in his hands.

"It's OK," I said, rubbing his back. I wondered whether his reluctance was down to the fact he hadn't been with anyone since rehab. "We can just take it slow."

"I can't, I'm sorry." Neil shifted along the sofa creating a gap between us. "I like you, Isme, honestly I do . . . but I've been brought up a devout Christian. I observe the teachings about no fornication before marriage."

I looked round, half expecting Jeremy Beadle to jump out and shout 'you've been framed!'

"I'm sorry, forni-what now?"

"Fornication. It's from the book of 1 Corinthians, written by Paul."

I slumped back onto the sofa as I felt my libido crawl back into its hibernation cave. "I mean, you could have told me sooner," I said. *Before I bothered shaving my bikini line and wore this skimpy thong*, I wanted to add.

"I haven't been able to find the right time."

"And so you thought, wait until we're passionately kissing? Jes— I mean, flipping heck, Neil."

Neil shuffled back closer and wrapped an arm around me. Reluctantly, I resumed my position on his chest. "I'm sorry, Isme. Really I am."

I sighed. "It's all right." It absolutely wasn't, but how could I make the lad feel bad about his religious beliefs? "Shall we just carry on with the programme." I reached for the remote control, but Neil blocked it with his hand.

"You know, there *is* other stuff we can do . . . if you know what I mean?" he smirked.

My heart started to quicken as Neil slowly lowered his hand to the button on my jeans. I grabbed his neck and pushed his lips onto mine, groaning with pleasure as his hand reached inside.

The whole no sex before marriage thing suddenly didn't seem so bad.

*

Hercules: I can't stop thinking about last night 😁

Isme: Me too 😎

Hercules: Fancy running club tonight?

Isme: Got Mum's birthday meal, sorry
You're welcome to come!

Hercules: It's OK, I wouldn't want to intrude
I could meet you afterwards? 🚀

Isme: Sounds good

Hercules: Great! Will pick you up about 10

My tummy flipped at the thought of seeing him again, and what other 'stuff' he had up his sleeve. I hadn't been able to stop thinking about the unexpected hand action on the couch, and if he was as good with his mouth as he was his hands, then I think I could survive without going all the way. At least for a bit, anyway . . .

I'd be a liar, though, if I hadn't considered the possibility, however slim, of him caving to his manly urges and us taking it all the way.

"You don't hold out for thirty-five years only to throw your celibacy away on some Greek bird you've only just met, Isme," said Maria, as we sat down at the restaurant. "If you were Jennifer Aniston, maybe, but not you . . . no offence."

"None taken, I don't think." I was beginning to regret confiding in Maria about my love life. I could only hope she'd keep her promise and not tell George. I'd never hear the end of it.

The restaurant was like a garden oasis within the heart of the buzzy city centre, with large vine-wrapped wooden beams and string bulb lights that ran along its length, and an abundance of white, yellow and red plants and flowers surrounding it. It was popular with the tourists and one of Mum's favourites, not only because of the beautiful surroundings and delicious food, but their generosity with the ouzo too.

We'd only been there ten minutes and her and Sandra had already downed two, which were having an effect, and they waved their arms in the air to the live *bouzouki* band like they were at one of Mum's Clubercise classes.

Opposite them were Dad and Anthony's dad, Luke, deep in conversation – or rather, Luke was doing the talking and Dad was doing the listening. He looked forlorn, staring into his pint of Keo like he was watching an episode of *EastEnders* through it. He hadn't seemed himself since the whole email emergency a few days earlier, and whatever it had been about was clearly weighing him down. I'd been meaning to ask him about it, but had been preoccupied with making the cakes for Sandra, and tonight was definitely not the right time.

The restaurant was heaving and the smell of succulent meat roasting on charcoal filled the air, making my mouth water. Most tables were taken up by large groups, including a hen party from London all dressed up as The Pink Ladies from *Grease* on the table next to ours.

"Where's your fella tonight, Isme?" asked George, shoving some pitta bread dipped in taramasalata into his gob, leaving a splodge in the corner of his mouth. Maria watched on with disdain, before turning her attention to the young Greek waiter who had come to take our order.

"I think Anthony said he was meeting some old friends." I hadn't realised what I'd said until I noticed that everyone was staring at me, including Sandra who was grinning like a Cheshire Cat.

"You know, I always thought you and Anthony would end up together." Our meals were finished, and Sandra had taken Maria's empty seat who, by now, had integrated herself into the hen party crew, acquiring a large inflatable willy which she hugged with far too much enthusiasm. "I mean, how romantic would it be, falling in love with your best friend?"

I tried to force a laugh, but it came out more like a snort. "I think you've been watching too many romcoms, Sandra!"

"I know, it's silly. I guess I'm just an old hopeless romantic, eh! Anyway, I'm glad you're happy with Neil, although I can't say the same for Anthony."

I strengthened the grip around my wine glass. "What do you mean—"

The lights went out, and the sharp metallic sound of the *bouzouki* belly-dance music came booming from the speakers. The whole restaurant erupted into cheers as the belly dancer came sashaying out in traditional red bedlah.

We all stood to our feet and surrounded the dancer, making a clear path down the middle of the restaurant for her to carry out her routine, which involved plenty of hip shimmying and belly rolls. I was so transfixed by her fluid moves and curves that I hadn't noticed the illuminous ball of yellow on the far side of the restaurant peering over the crowd until Maria whispered in my ear, "Who's that numpty in a high-vis?"

Neil was peering over the crowd with a look of frustration on his face. He waved once he caught sight of me and began pushing his way through the crowd in his bright yellow running jacket. Unfortunately, in his haste, he hadn't noticed that he was heading in the direct path of the belly dancer, who was looking for volunteers.

Before Neil could grasp what was going on, she grabbed his hand and pulled him into the centre of the crowd, wiggling her belly and encouraging him to do the same. His face was crimson, and I didn't know whether to laugh or hide under the nearest table until it was all over.

To everyone's surprise, including my own, Neil whipped off his running jacket and broke into full Greek dance, moving from side to side with his arms out straight, bending one leg behind the other, with the occasional back kick and foot slap. Either he was a quick learner, or he'd done it before.

"Where the hell did you learn that?" I laughed once he'd managed to escape.

"Never mind that, where have you been? I said I was picking you up at ten, remember? I've been waiting outside for like half an hour."

I didn't get a chance to respond. Everyone from our table descended on Neil to praise him for his valiant effort on the dance floor. Everyone apart from Sandra, who watched on quietly from the sidelines.

"So, you mast be Hercules!" said Mum, winking in my direction. "Tell me, what is your ethnic background, Hercules?"

"His name's Neil, Mum, and it's not an immigration interview." Mum wafted a hand dismissively in my direction.

Neil sighed, impatiently. "My mum is English and my dad, well, I didn't really know him, but he was a quarter Greek. So I guess that makes me—"

"It no matter, Hercules, you Greek! *Oh thee mou*, this has made my birthday! *Servitoros*, a round of your best ouzo *efgharisto!*"

I should have told Mum that Neil didn't drink and stopped her from going up to the bar, but I was still reeling from the news that Neil had some Greek bloodline.

"Well, hellooo, sexy lollipop man," slurred Maria, sidling up to Neil and giving him a full eye inspection. "I bet you've got a big—"

"Woah, OK Maria, let's leave the poor lad alone, eh." For once I was grateful to George, who grabbed Maria by the shoulders and ushered her away.

"What?! I was only gonna say 'big house'."

"Sorry about all these, lad," said Dad, putting an arm around Neil's shoulders and steering him in the direction of the bar. "Come on, let's get you a drink. You're going to need it."

"I don't drink, thank you, Mr Eliades," said Neil, removing

himself from Dad's embrace.

Dad burst into laughter. "Ha! Good one. I'll get you a Keo, lad." Dad patted Neil on the back and followed Mum to the bar, laughing and shaking his head as he went.

"Well, I did warn you that my family were a bit bonkers," I laughed, but Neil's face was deadpan.

"I'll meet you outside, Isme. I'm feeling a bit anxious being around all this alcohol."

"He no like ouzo?" said Mum once he was gone, reappearing from the bar holding the tray of shots.

I sighed. If only she knew.

*

Mum: Isme, when will you be back from the market? We need to have family meeting, is very important

Isme: Mum, I've already told you, I don't know what blood type Neil is or whether he knows the main ingredients that go into pastisio

Mum: Ochi, is not that, Isme Just come back soon, please

"Everything is OK?" I stared up from my phone at the sound of the village bakery shop assistant's voice, almost forgetting where I was.

"Oh sorry, er, *signomi*." I placed my three euros on the counter for the flour I was buying for a ravani cake and rushed out of the shop into the bustling *platia*. It was market day and the square was filled with stalls selling anything from fresh fruit and vegetables, to aromatic spices, to handmade jewellery. Normally, I'd love nothing more than to soak up the vibrant market atmosphere and have a mooch around to see what local gems I could find. But not today.

I pushed my way through the throngs of market goers and headed back in the direction of the villa, hoping that the reason for the meeting was trivial, like Mum having another cataracts operation. But when I caught sight of Mum, Dad and Maria congregated at the kitchen table around a pot of tea, as though they were waiting for a magic genie to pop out to grant them some wishes, I knew it was far from meagre.

*

"You're selling the house?"

"We've got no choice, love," said Dad in a calming voice, after delivering the news. There were dark circles underneath his eyes and extra creases across his forehead that seemed to have appeared since we arrived in Cyprus. "Now, why don't you come and sit down, and we'll explain everything."

"I don't want to sit down!" I cried. "I want you to tell me that Mum's just having her cataracts done and the house thing was a cruel joke!"

Mum, who had been staring aimlessly out of the window, turned to look at me. "What you mean, Isme? I had my eyes done last year?"

"Isme, have you been on the sauce?" laughed Maria in an attempt to lighten the mood, but the thought of yet another

Eliades treasured possession suffering at the hands of Mum and Dad's financial burdens filled me with utter rage.

"It's the only option, Isme. We're well and truly up shit creek." Dad rubbed at his tired eyes. "It turns out the land here in Cyprus that we inherited off your *Yiayia* and that we were hoping we could sell, giving us a much-needed cash injection, is worthless."

"But how?"

"Something to do with contamination from an oil leak a few years ago," sighed Maria. "The developers came round a few weeks ago to break the news." I suddenly remembered the suited and booted men Mum was ushering out after my day of pampering with Maddy, and it all started to make sense.

I slumped my body against the kitchen counter and let out a sigh. Looking around the villa kitchen, my thoughts turned to our kitchen back in Liverpool – the heart of our home that held so many fond memories of chaotic family dinners, with the homely smell of Mum's delicious homemade cooking wafting through the air. An image of another family jostling in popped into my head, wiping out our memories like a whiteboard and making their own. My heart ached.

"Where exactly do you plan to live once the house is sold?" I asked, putting aside any thoughts of the three of us fighting for the bathroom every morning in my tiny flat.

"We just get something smaller, maybe a nice cosy apartment!" said Mum. She was doing her best to sound cheery, but inside was no doubt panicking at the thought of knocking up one of her feasts in some poky apartment kitchen. I certainly was.

Mum not being able to fulfil her weekly routine of entertaining and feeding the Eliades clan would be like a Premier League footballer suffering a serious injury and never being able to play in a big league again. It was a big part of her life, and of who she was, and I wasn't sure how she'd cope if it was taken away from her.

Things were bad. Things were very, very bad.

JULY

EMAIL

From: Trudie Evans

To: Ismeena Eliades

Subject: Return to work

Ismeena,

Further to our telephone conversation earlier, I am delighted to welcome you back to Mulligan's Solicitors with effect from 1st August.

I note that you are attending weekly Alcoholics Anonymous sessions, for which you will need an afternoon a week off to attend, and we will fully support this.

I also note that you are keen to re-apply for the promotion, and we will be in touch again shortly to make arrangements for another interview.

In the meantime, please enjoy the rest of your time at The Priory Rehabilitation Centre, and we look forward to welcoming you back in a few weeks.

Regards,
Trudie

"Rehab, Isme? Really? What are you going to say when you turn up on your first day back looking like a burnt lobster?"

I slammed my laptop down. "That they have a really nice garden but were a bit scarce on the sun cream front? Anyway, haven't you got anything better to do than peer over my shoulder like some creepy uncle?"

"Actually, I do. George has taken the twins to the park and *I* am going into the village for a stroll."

"In those wedges?" I glared down at Maria's feet, which were already struggling to withstand the four-inch height of her shoes. I had visions of her stacking it on the cobbled village streets, which were hazardous at the best of times. Then there were the wide steps leading down to the *platia* to contend with, which were just as perilous as they were beautiful, with bright red and yellow flowers spilling out of plant pots on either side.

"All right, *Mum*. Jesus, can't a girl make a little effort without being questioned?"

"Woman, I think you meant to say 'woman'. Girl implies you're young."

"Piss off, Isme." With that, Maria strutted out of the villa, leaving a waft of floral perfume in her wake.

"Ridiculously high wedges and perfume. What *are* you up to, Maria Eliades?" I muttered to myself. But there was no more time for pondering the whereabouts of my elder sibling. I had more pressing matters to attend to.

Like telling Mum and Dad the good news.

*

"So, I need to talk to you."

They were sat outside on the patio area glaring at something on the twins' iPad and jolted at the sound of my voice.

Mum took a sharp intake of breath and looked up at the sky while fanning her top. "*O thee mou*, thank you, Saint Irene, thank you for finding my Isme a hasband! I knew Hercules was a Good Greek Boy didn't I, Stephen, didn't I say?"

"Looking at her face, Elana, I think you may be a bit ahead of yourself," laughed Dad. He was wearing the same white shirt and beige trousers he'd worn on our first day of the holiday, which looked a lot roomier than I remembered.

"Yeah, you could say that," I shot back. "Bloody hell, Mum, it's not the 1800s." Mum slunk back into her chair and folded her arms, like a teenager who'd been told they were grounded.

"Go on, Isme, love, what is it?" said Dad with a concerned look.

I took a huge breath and told them all about my plans to help them out with a promotion at work.

"I thought you went for a promotion months ago? That's what you said at my birthday meal."

"Yeah I did, but I, er, I didn't get it. But they're going to let me have another go, and I really feel I've got a better chance this time."

Mum and Dad exchanged a glance and I knew something wasn't right. Dad stayed seated, looking on with a half-hearted smile. Mum placed a hand over mine, which felt more sympathetic than thankful.

"What is it?" I asked, although I wasn't convinced I wanted to know.

"It wouldn't be enough, love," said Dad, in a low voice. "It's so nice that you want to give us some money with the extra you'll earn from the promotion, but it probably wouldn't even touch the sides."

"How much debt are you *actually* in? And no bullshit this time, I need to hear the truth."

They exchanged glances as if telepathically discussing whether to tell me or not, then Dad spoke. He told me how Stavros had introduced them to a local businessman after selling the restaurant. He'd used him previously to invest money in some foreign bonds, supposedly tripling his initial investment over two years.

"We had no reason to doubt him, Iz, especially when the

recommendation came from Stavros." Dad stared off into the distance, his fists clenching around something – or someone – that wasn't there. "Little did we know the gobshite was fooling us all."

Mum placed a hand over Dad's. "We weren't to know, Stephen. He work for a big important company in town, remember the size of his office? And it was overlooking thee water."

It was hardly surprising, especially from Mum, that they'd invested all their savings in some fella they hardly knew based on the size of his office. But that still didn't stop the ball of anger that was rising up from my stomach at their naïvety.

"Our plan was to sell up after the two years and use the money for the rest of our retirement, maybe buy a nice holiday home for us all," continued Dad. "Then, about six months ago, I tried to get in touch with him. We were keen to get some work done to the house and wanted to know how much the investment had grown. His phone kept ringing out so I left a voicemail, and he sent me a message saying that everything was looking good, and that we should be able to sell up by the end of the year. So, we stupidly decided to take out a whopping big loan so we could crack on with the work, which didn't turn out to be enough, so we had to take out some credit cards as well."

Dad paused and took a deep intake of breath, as if preparing himself for the next part of the story. "We didn't worry because we knew that as soon as our investment came in, we could pay it all off and would still have plenty left for ourselves." Another deep breath. "That was until Stavros rang us in a panic a couple of months ago to tell us that a man had been arrested for conning people into investing in his scheme, and he saw his mugshot on the news. He felt terrible about the whole thing, but we couldn't be angry at him – after all, he'd lost money too, although not as much as us, by the sounds of it."

I thought back to when Mum had first told me about Stavros letting 'his favourite Greek family' use the villa for the whole summer. It had seemed overly generous, but it was clear now that he was trying to make amends for introducing them to the con man.

I held my head in my hands. I wanted to scream at them, to ask them how they could be so naïve, but I could see from their stress-ridden faces that they had already punished themselves enough.

"What about the police? Couldn't they find him and get your money back?"

Dad sighed. "Oh, they found him all right, living in some huge villa in Spain. But the bastard had spent all the money, and because we'd willingly handed over our money without checking if his company was legit, we didn't have a leg to stand on."

"Didn't you think to take out any insurance?" I asked, although based on what I'd heard so far, I already knew the answer.

Dad nodded his head. "We did ask, but he told us we would be covered by the FSA, or something like that."

"We had no reason to doubt him," Mum added.

Maybe if you hadn't been so blind-sided by the 'big' job and the 'big' office you would have noticed that he was full of crap, I wanted to add, but Mum already knew that. I could see it in her tired eyes.

"So now you see, love, we have no other choice but to sell the house, so we can pay off our debts and buy something smaller. It's our only asset. We've already seen a few one-bedroom flats we like."

Dad handed me the iPad, which was open at some website called 'cheap flats to buy'. An unwelcome image of piss-stained hallways and the sound of music blaring at all hours of the day popped into my head.

"I just wish there was more I could do," I said, tears welling up in my eyes. They belonged in their home that they'd owned for so long it was like another member of the family.

"You've already done more than enough," said Dad, wrapping his arms around me.

Mum didn't say a word. She didn't need to; I already knew *exactly* what she was thinking.

*

Was I *really* mildly entertaining the idea of marrying a lad I'd only known for a few months that was only ever intended as a bit of holiday fun? I mean it worked out for Sandy and Danny, but they were madly in love, which I wasn't. Lust maybe, but even that had been questionable at times. It had been more like 'Summer Virgin' than 'Summer Lovin''.

I lay awake most of the night going over everything Mum and Dad told me, reliving every minute detail in search of any other possible resolution, but if anything, it just brought up more questions. Like, why didn't they seek professional advice before signing away all their life savings that they'd worked so tirelessly to build up?

Also, what was the big rush in getting the house extension

done? Though I think I already knew the answer to that one, because it came about around the same time Linda from two doors down started hers, and Mum couldn't possibly let her have one up on her. She still hadn't got over the fact that Linda owned a cordless Dyson first.

*

"So, hang on a minute, babe, let me see if I've got this straight," said Maddy, refilling our wine glasses at a local taverna the next day, which overlooked the harbour, "your nan left you £25k in her will but you can only have it if you marry a Greek fella, and if you get divorced within ten years you have to give the money back and donate it to the Greek church. Your mum and dad are desperate for some cash otherwise they'll have to sell their house. You've met a lad who is a quarter Greek, and if you marry him you would get your hands on the inheritance money and give it to your mum and dad so they don't have to sell the house and can live out a happy retirement?"

Maddy handed me my refilled glass and I downed half the contents in one gulp. "Yep, that's pretty much it."

It was Maddy's last night in Cyprus and we were enjoying a delicious Greek meze, including succulent stuffed vine leaves, a fresh Greek salad, hot bread and a variety of dips. The sun was setting in the distance, casting an orange glow over the skyline, and there was a gentle breeze in the air, which was a welcome relief against my sunburnt skin. I *had* worn factor fifty all day, but we've already established that my skin is practically porous.

"But you've only known this lad a month or so," Maddy went

on, "so marrying him would be absolutely crazy, plus you don't even know if he wants to get married, let alone any time soon. Yeah?"

I nodded. "Yeah, although I gather from his devout Christian upbringing that he wouldn't be *completely* against the idea of marriage." I scooped a piece of pitta bread into the taramasalata dip and popped it into my mouth. It was just like Mum's – silky and smooth and full of fresh sea flavour.

Maddy picked up a piece of cucumber from the Greek salad and put it to her mouth, all the while not taking her eyes off me, her brows furrowed like she was trying to solve the *Countdown* conundrum. "Wow, that is some head fuck that, babe," she finally said, leaning back in her chair. "Surely there's an easier option than signing up to a ten-year prison sentence. What about Maria? Can't she help?"

I let out a gusty sigh. "Doubt it. She's the only one bringing in any money at the moment after George lost his job, so money is tight enough for her as it is."

"But surely your mum and dad living in something a bit smaller wouldn't be as bad as marrying a complete stranger – especially one that lives in the gym. I mean, what's all that about, please? He's as mad as these numpties doing that triathlon in a few weeks."

Maddy nodded in the direction of a group on a small stretch of sand changing into full wetsuits for what was presumably an early evening practice swim.

I nodded in agreement, while hoping and praying one of the numpties wasn't Neil.

"To be fair though, I can't blame them with fifteen thousand euros up for grabs."

My ears suddenly pricked up. "What? You can't be serious?"

"Honest to God, I seen a leaflet at the reception of the hotel. It's some traditional mini triathlon thingy in a few weeks. Apparently it goes back yonks, where you've got to swim to the lighthouse and back, scoff a plate of moussaka and then ride a bike up the hilly streets with a cart full of watermelons attached."

"Oh piss off, Mad."

"Ha, OK, I made up the watermelons bit, but the rest is true! Apparently it's a modern take on chariot racing, although I'm not sure where the eating part fits in." The eating part was the only thing I *knew* I'd be good at. "The first to the finish line gets ten big ones, and five, I think, for second place."

"When did you say it was, exactly?"

Maddy eyed me quizzically. "The 20th babe, and you're off your head if you're thinking about doing it."

The 20th was the day before we were due to fly back home. It was risky – what if I got injured and couldn't fly back? Worse still, what if I ended up going home in a casket?

Afterwards, as I walked back to the villa, my head was swirling, and it wasn't just the wine. Maddy was right: considering marrying Neil was crazy talk.

Maybe this triathlon, if I could survive it, was just the solution I'd been waiting for.

*

MARONI VILLAGE MINI TRIATHLON: ENTRY FORM

Name: Ismeena Eliades

Age: Prefer not to say

Nationality: It's complicated

Will this be your first time competing at a triathlon?:
Does the 1995 sports day at St Margaret Mary's Primary
School count?

ESTIMATED TIMES:

Swim: TBC

Cycle: TBC

Mousakka eating: 60 seconds

The lady behind the desk at the village library peered at me over her bifocals with pursed lips. She wore a tight bun that sat neatly on top of her head, and I felt like a pupil about to get disciplined by Mrs Trunchbull.

She scanned over the form for a second time, and I could feel the heat rising up through my body. Was I about to fail at the first hurdle?

Slowly, her grimace turned into a warm smile. "Sixty seconds, ah, that *is* impressive, Isme." She stamped the form and handed me an information leaflet, which I took from her gratefully. It had a picture on the front of the actual ancient Hercules, and I had to swallow down any opinions on gender equality; I was one step closer to helping out Mum and Dad, and that was all that mattered.

"Thank you, thank you so much!"

"You have two weeks to train, Isme. Is not long. If you like, a group of the competitors are doing a cycle up Troodos mountains tomorrow in preparation. They leave at 9 a.m."

"Great, I'll be there!" I said, before my brain could process what I'd just agreed to.

*

Of course Neil was heading up the practice cycle. I should have expected nothing less. Yet that didn't stop me from doing a double-take when I spotted him at the meeting point wearing a Borat style mankini, better known in the cycling world as bib shorts, that accentuated his manly region beyond belief. I almost had to stop myself from shouting, "Very nice!"

"I didn't know you were coming, Isme," he said, eyeing up the rusted bike I'd dug out of the storage shed at the villa. It was either that or hire one, and I didn't trust that either me or the bike would make it back in one piece, and I couldn't afford to pay for any damages.

"Well, you keep telling me I need to get myself more fit, so here I am!"

"Nice helmet. My son had one just like it," said one of the other cyclists with a smirk, a petite middle-aged woman with a muscular frame, who was also sporting the bib shorts. Clearly I didn't get the Spandex memo.

"Luckily, I've got the same size head as my three-year-old nephews, ha!" I tugged at the strap of my *Spiderman* helmet, which was already beginning to chafe.

"You *do* know that this is for people who are doing the mini triathlon?"

"Yeah, I know, Neil. Duh." I lunged forward with my hands on my hips in an attempt to stretch, but something pinged in my calf and I almost lost my balance.

Lycra lady smirked, and something inside my belly ignited. I'd show her. I'd show EVERYONE.

"Ah, Isme, you remember me?" said a little grey-haired fella who I recognised from the running club.

"Of course! How could I forget. You were meant to be looking after me, but ended up overlapping me several times."

"Ha, yes. Sorry about that. I promise, Nico will take care of you today." He smiled, and I relaxed. What could possibly go wrong?

Quite a lot, it turned out.

For starters, the brakes on my bike were about as ancient as the Acropolis, and every time I tried to engage them, the bike would shudder, making me lose my balance. I almost stacked it several times, only for Nico staying by my side and catching me before I did. Neil, on the other hand, kept well ahead with the more elite, only shouting back to 'keep up!' every so often, which made me want to punch him in the face.

Then there was the intense heat, which was making me sweat profusely and in places I never knew I could (knee caps, anyone?). By the time we were halfway up, I could hardly see from the salty sweat that had crept into my eyes, and I was ready to throw in the towel. I almost collapsed with relief when Neil declared that it was time for a pit stop, and sought refuge on a nearby rock, assuming the faint-prevention pose of head between knees.

"Lovely, isn't it?" said Nico, who had perched up on a rock next to me.

"W-h-a-t-i-s?" I panted, whilst blinking repeatedly in an attempt to regain my sight.

"The view, Isme! *Koita*, look!"

I lifted my head wearily, my eyes still a little misty from the sweat, but I could make out the view, which took my breath away; hundreds of green trees – cypress, olive, oak – rolling downwards into the rocky plains below, and in the far-off distance, a collection of mountains of differing heights, their summits towering above the clouds like picturesque islands of the sky. It really was a sight to behold, speaking of which . . .

"You OK, Isme?" Neil had wandered over, and was resting one of his legs on a nearby rock, his bulge directly in my eyeline. I tried looking away, but it was like when you see people arguing in public – you know you shouldn't look but you just can't help it.

"Yeah, I'm fine – just enjoying the views." I couldn't help but smirk at my own humour.

"Ellie would have loved it up here," sighed Nico, gazing out at the mountainous view.

"Who's Ellie?" I asked, although it was already obvious from the sadness in his eyes.

"My wife, she die three years ago."

"Aw, I'm sorry to hear that, Nico."

"Is OK, she was very sick. She battled cancer for many years."

We sat in silence for a moment, the only sound coming from

the chortle of the crickets in the forage below, and the occasional bursts of laughter from the rest of the cycling crew nearby, who had dispersed into several smaller groups.

"You know, before she die, she say to me, 'Nico, you must not be sad when I am gone, you must live every day as if it is your last'. So that is what I do. She also tell me to remember to feed the cat, but I cannot say I have kept this promise."

I chuckled, thinking it would be the exact same death-bed exchange that I could imagine happening between Mum and Dad, although the cat would probably be me. The thought of them made me wonder whether either of them would have the strength and motivation like Nico to carry on if the other were to perish. Sadly, with Dad's dodgy ticker and the current financial strain they were under, I wasn't convinced that they would.

"OK, everyone ready for the descent?" declared Neil, who had already mounted his bike and was putting on his helmet.

I closed my eyes and took some deep breaths to try and channel my inner Nico. His strength and determination to carry on after losing his wife was admirable, and despite my sore bum cheeks and sweaty knee caps, I had to keep going.

With the triathlon winnings directly in my sight, I hopped back onto the bike and didn't look back.

*

Anthony: Fancy a drink tonight before I head home?

Isme: Can't. I've somehow been roped
into minding the twins

You're welcome to join me

Anthony: Nah, you're all right. I'll catch up with you when you're back home next week

"Bed by eight, read Theo a bedtime story, make sure Tomaso has his comforter and leave the door slightly open," was Maria's parting shot before her and George bailed, leaving the twins gawping up at me with their big brown eyes, like two abandoned puppies.

My plan for the night was simple: bake some Greek butter chocolate-chip cookies, eat said cookies, let them have some screen time and then get them to bed before I opened a bottle of white and parked myself on one of the sunbeds outside for a bit of star gazing.

I'd even gone to the effort of buying them little chef hats and an apron each from a bakery shop I'd stumbled across in town with 'star baker' on the front, and had images of me smiling adoringly as I watched them carefully mixing the ingredients, like an advert for Stork. But the reality was more like *Hell's Kitchen*.

"What are you doing, Uncle Isme?" asked Theo, peering over the bowl. He was sat on the worktop, his little legs dangling over the side, which *would* have been cute if he didn't kick me in the thighs every so often.

"Just mixing everything together."

"Can I taste it, Uncle Isme? Oh, *please* can I taste it?" This from Tomaso, who was sat next to Theo.

"Well, not really, it's raw . . . Right, OK, well your fingers are already in it so you might as well . . ."

"Mmmmm, tastes yummy!" Tomaso rubbed at his tummy and closed his eyes with delight.

"Can I have some chocolate chips?" asked Theo, reaching for the bag.

I sighed, and wiped some stray hairs away from my face with the back of my hand. "Yeah, OK, but only a few because I need them for the cookies."

"Tomaso, look, they look like little poo-poos!" cried Theo, handing one of the chocolate chips over to Tomaso.

"HA! Poo-poo cookies!"

I'm not sure why all kids find the concept of shit so hilariously funny, and Theo and Tomaso were no exception. They spent the next ten minutes running round the kitchen shouting "poo-poo cookies!" at the top of their voices whilst I tried to salvage what was left of the cookie dough.

By the time the cookies were in the oven and the sugary smell had started filling the villa, the kitchen looked like a porridge bomb had gone off and I was ready for a lie down.

The twins, on the other hand, seemed like they had enough energy to do ten rounds with Mike Tyson. So, when I heard a knock on the front door a small, naïve part of me hoped that Maria and George's night had been cut short and I was going to be relieved of my duties.

"ANTHONY! ANTHONY!" The twins sprinted to the door to greet Anthony, who scooped them up for a hug.

"I thought you weren't coming?"

"Yeah, well, I changed my mind. That OK?"

I shrugged my shoulders casually, although inside I was more than relieved for the extra pair of hands.

"We've made poo-poo cookies!" declared Theo proudly.

"Yes, I can see that," said Anthony, as he caught sight of the kitchen. "Why don't you two go and watch your iPads while I help Auntie Isme clean up this mess."

"You mean *Uncle* Isme. Silly, Anthony."

"Still not got their heads round that one, then," laughed Anthony once they were gone. He picked up a brush and began sweeping the floor while I tackled the worktops.

"Nope. I kind of like it now though, to be honest. Gives me a cool edge, don't you think?"

"Not sure about cool, more like *manly* edge."

"HEY!" I threw a blob of wet cookie dough in his direction, which unintentionally hit him square in the face. "Oh shit, sorry. I didn't mean to— WHAH!" I ducked just before Anthony's retaliation dough ball could hit me, but he scooped some more out of the mixing bowl and ran towards me. Before I could escape, he grabbed me from behind and wrapped an arm around my waist, whilst using his free arm to rub the wet sloppy mixture all over my face.

"WHAT THE FUCK, ANTHONY!" I cried, trying to free myself from his grasp, but he was too strong. I managed to twist myself around so our faces were almost touching, but with no more mixture within my grasp, I was helpless.

I became very aware of Anthony's hands resting on the small of my back, and the feel of his hot breath in my face. We caught each other's gaze and stood there for a moment, frozen to the spot.

"Awwwww, wait until I tell Mummy!"

We pushed away from one another at the sound of Theo's voice, as he stood gawping up at us open-mouthed.

"There's nothing to tell, we were just play-fighting! You and Tomaso do it all the time."

"Mummy and Daddy have a play-fight sometimes in their room," said Tomaso, who had also come to see what all the commotion was about. "Usually on a Saturday night, but they never let us join in."

"Yeah, and they close the door so we can't even watch," added Theo.

Me and Anthony looked at each other and burst into laughter, the sore belly and wet eyes kind of laughter, whilst the twins looked on in bewilderment.

Once the tears had subsided and the stomach muscles had stopped aching, we resumed our cleaning positions as if nothing had happened.

Because nothing *had* happened. Had it?

*

"What's with the bike?" asked Anthony, nodding in the direction of the tin on wheels resting against a wall outside. We were propped up on the sunbeds by the pool with a glass of wine each hours later, the twins sound asleep after a fairly drama-free bedtime. "Is George finally doing something about his dad bod?"

"As if. It would take more than a few bike rides to sort *his* moobs out."

Anthony chuckled. "Ha, that is true."

I rested my head against the bed and gazed up at the clear night sky, my heart now beating at a more relaxed pace than earlier in the kitchen. It was a warm, balmy night, the clear night sky sprinkled with scatterings of stars, and the occasional bat flying overhead.

"Actually, the bike is for me. I'm gonna give that triathlon a go."

I didn't take my eyes off the sky, but could feel Anthony's eyes boring into me from the side.

"Let me guess, steg head talked you into it."

"No, it's nothing to do with him. I just fancied the challenge." I avoided telling him the real reason, since I'd promised Mum I'd save her any embarrassment from the GWAGs back home by keeping the severity of their current financial situation to myself.

"Mum said he made quite the impression at your mum's birthday meal." I wasn't sure if he was referring to the dance or Neil's keenness to get away from my family, which wouldn't have got past Sandra. "Quite the snake hips, I hear."

"Ha, yeah, you could say that."

Anthony circled the rim of his wine glass, and I knew more Neil question-time was on the way. "So, do you think you'll see him again, like, once you get home and that?"

I hesitated for a moment before answering. Neil was only ever intended as a little holiday fun, and I hadn't given any thought to seeing him again back home until the whole marry-him-to-unlock-my-inheritance idea was floated. Now the end of the holiday was looming, and I was still no better off in terms of helping Mum and Dad out of their financial mess. Could he still be a viable back-up plan if I didn't place at the triathlon, or if the winnings were not enough?

"I'm honestly not sure," I eventually said, not wanting to divulge my inner thoughts to Anthony, who would no doubt have more questions. "I guess we'll just see what happens."

We lay in silence for a moment, the only sound coming from the chirping of the bats overhead.

"You know, I can't say I would have ever expected you to end up with someone like him, Isme. But as someone once said, the greatest relationships are the ones you never expected to be in."

He meant Neil. Of *course* he meant Neil. Didn't he?

*

Mum: Isme, don't be late for our final family dinner
😢😢😢

Isme: Bloody hell Mum, I bet Jesus wasn't this dramatic at the last supper
We're gonna see Maria, George and the twins again in a few weeks when we fly home

Mum: The villa is going to be so quiet without them

Isme: I know. It's going to be heaven 😄

"Isme, why your face look like a tomato and your body smell like onions?" Mum was in the kitchen unwrapping the boxes from the local (and only) Chinese takeaway which smelt so wonderful, a mixture of garlic and soy sauce, I had to stop myself from throwing my head in one of the boxes and devouring the contents.

"I'd like to see how you looked and smelt after the run I've just done," I scoffed, whilst filling a glass with water from the tap and gulping it down in one. Neil had decided to throw an extra lap on to our 5km run, insisting it was 'essential triathlon stamina-building.' But it had felt more mental than essential, especially with the steep inclines of some of the village streets. At one point, I was overtaken by a little old Greek lady, and *she* had a walking stick.

"You tell her, love," said Dad, giving my shoulders a squeeze. His usually plump hands felt hard against the softness of my shirt. I'd noticed his clothes getting a bit loose, but it was a bad sign if even his hands were getting thin.

"Where are the others?" I asked, taking a seat on one of the dining room chairs and stretching out my sore legs.

"They're upstairs finishing the packing," said Dad, taking a seat opposite me with the same weariness as someone who had also just hiked round the hilly village streets.

Maria had got a call a few days earlier that the salon was going to be ready to re-open two weeks early, and with her holiday pay only lasting until the end of the week, she couldn't afford to miss out on the money. So, her, George and the twins were on an early flight home the following morning. We *were* all supposed to be flying back together, but who was I to complain that I wouldn't have four small feet bashing into the back of my seat all the way home.

"Where's your fella? Has he come to his senses and jibbed you off already?" George appeared in the kitchen wearing a pair of baggy grey jogging bottoms and a white T-shirt that had more creases than Dot Cotton's face. He reached out to grab a chip but was stopped by Mum, who shooed him away like a disobedient dog.

"Where's your wife? Has she realised you're as useless as a concrete parachute and left your arse?"

"*Ochi*, Isme, for one time can you be nice to your brother-in-law, please."

"Woah, hang on a minute, he started it."

"*Hang on a minute, he started it*," mimicked George in a whiney voice – yet somehow that got past Mum's line of hearing.

"If you must know, smart arse, he's got work stuff to do." The truth was the sheer mention of a Chinese takeaway made him break out in a cold sweat.

"Does he like to play fight in the kitchen as well?" he smirked, and the heat rushed to my cheeks. I opened my mouth to retaliate, but for once I was short on comebacks. Damn the twins and their (little) big mouths.

"Isme, will you go and find your papa. We are ready to eat," ordered Mum. I'd been so caught up in my spat with George, I hadn't noticed he'd left.

With no sign of him downstairs, I trudged my weary legs up the stairs and checked the bedrooms, but he was nowhere to be seen. I noticed the bathroom door was slightly ajar and could hear a muffled voice coming from inside, the words becoming clearer the closer I got.

"I'm going to tell her, honestly I am," I heard Dad say in a pleading voice. "It's just not the right time. No, of course I'm not embarrassed by you, it's just with everything that's been going on..."

Despite my curiosity wanting to get the better of me, I stepped away from the door, not noticing that one of the twin's toy monster trucks was directly in my path. Luckily, I managed to catch my fall against the stair rail, but not without making a loud thud in the process.

"Jesus, Isme, you scared the living daylights out of me!" The bathroom door had flung open and Dad jolted at the sight of me, causing the phone to fall out his hand and onto the hard wooden floor, clattering in a way that indicted something had cracked. His already pale face looked translucent against the bathroom light, and he was clutching at his chest.

"Sorry, I didn't mean to. Mum just wanted me to let you know that it's time to eat."

"I'll be down now," he said, picking his phone up off the floor and wiping it down with his hands. The screen had a small crack on it. The caller was gone, and I couldn't see a name.

I wanted to ask who was on the phone, to demand some form of explanation, but as I watched him shuffle back inside the bathroom, his gait weary and shoulders slumped like the weight of the world was resting on him, I couldn't seem to find the words.

*

I was laying on the beach reading my book when a phone call came through from Mum. My first thought was what had she asked me to do that I'd forgotten about? But I knew as soon as I answered and heard the panic in her voice that she wasn't ringing about my inability to take orders.

"ISME! ISME!"

"Mum, what's up? Are you OK?" I could hear her faint sobs, and my heart sank.

"Is your Papa, Isme. He collapsed. They think he has had a heart attack. We on our way to thee hospital."

"FUCK! Right, OK, I'm on my way."

I ended the call and began frantically packing away my things. I trudged through the sand in the direction of the stairs that led up to the main road, but suddenly realised I had no money for a taxi since I'd spent the only ten euros I'd brought on a drink and some fresh fruit.

Without hesitation, I picked up my phone, hoping and praying he'd answer.

"Anthony? Thank God. Where are you?"

"I'm just in the airport waiting to board. What's up? You sound a bit flustered. Are you OK?"

Tears began streaming down my cheeks. "It's Dad . . . He's had a, a heart attack. I . . . I don't know what to do . . ."

"OK, calm down, where are you?"

"I'm at the beach. I need to go the hospital but I've got no taxi money."

"OK, stay there. I'll come and pick you up."

It had been three years since Dad's first heart attack, a time which I'd tried my best to forget, hiding it away in the little box in my brain titled 'Shit Memories' never to be reopened. But getting the phone call from Mum and finding out that Dad had suffered another one brought it all flooding back, like the box had burst open spreading its ugly contents all over my brain like a tumour.

"Do you want me to come in with you?" asked Anthony, as we stood outside Dad's room in the hospital, the potent smell of antiseptic making me nauseous.

"It's OK, you should get to the airport. See if you can make the next flight."

"Nah, there probably won't be one until the morning now. I'll hang out here for a bit . . . If that's OK, like?"

I smiled appreciatively, and slowly opened the door.

I gasped at the sight of Dad's weak and motionless body in the bed, and the myriad of tubes coming out of his arms like he was a puppet. His face was void of any colour, making the dark circles under his eyes look practically charcoal. *He's going to be OK, he's going to be OK*, I chanted in my head whilst swallowing back the tears.

Mum, who was sat next to him holding one of his hands, looked up and smiled weakly. Her eyes were red and her face splotchy, like she'd been hovering over a hot pan. "Is OK, Isme. He will be OK."

Slowly, I walked over to the other side of the bed and placed a hand over his. His skin felt lukewarm and leathery. I watched his chest slowly rise and fall, and listened to the familiar beep of the heart monitor machine. Suddenly, I felt a rush of something familiar and uninviting, like déjà vu of a nightmare, except this nightmare I'd actually witnessed before. My heart began to quicken, the air around me suddenly feeling thick and dense. The overwhelming sense of needing to escape overtook me, and I bolted for the door.

"Isme, are you OK?"

I looked up at Anthony, tears beginning to fill my eyes. He wrapped his broad arms around me and I slumped into his embrace.

*

Thankfully, aside from a few lifestyle adjustments to get his blood pressure back down to a less critical level, including regular exercise and trying to reduce his stress levels, Dad was going to be OK.

So why wasn't I relieved?

Once the initial shock had subsided, closely overtaken by angst and worry, there was another feeling niggling away inside like an unwelcome parasite – and that was guilt. Dad had collapsed a few days after I'd caught him red-handed in the bathroom on the phone. Was I to blame? Mum and Maria put the cause down to the stress from the debt situation – a situation which I could prevent by finding someone Greek to marry. So, I guess no matter how I looked at it, I was to blame.

Neil had been bombarding me with messages and calls ever since, making sure I was OK and offering to make Dad some green juices recommended by The British Heart Foundation.

In an attempt to make him feel useful, I asked him to bring me and Mum a tahini-drenched chicken souvlaki one night, which I appreciated was a big deal not only for a vegan but also for someone who regards any fast food as a gateway to coronary blockage. He drew the line at getting me some halloumi fries though.

"He's a good boy, Isme," said Mum after he'd done a UNICEF style drop-off at reception – apparently hospitals give him terrible anxiety. "He make very good husband."

But we both knew that it wasn't just that he could make a good husband. It was that, ultimately, he could save us all.

*

EMAIL
From: Christina Paxos
To: Ismeena Eliades
Re: Maroni village mini triathlon

Dear Isme,

We hope preparations for the Maroni village mini triathlon are going well, and you are looking forward to taking part!

Just a reminder that the race starts at 9 a.m. prompt, and you should be at the start line at least fifteen minutes before.

Good luck!
Christina

I hadn't given much thought to the triathlon since Dad's heart attack, but when it *had* crossed my mind, a rush of dread would ripple through me and I'd push it firmly to the back. I'd been stupid to think two weeks was enough time to train, and completely delirious if I thought two days was sufficient. But as I read Christina's email, an image popped into my head of Dad lying helpless in the hospital bed, and I knew I had to give it a try. After all, what was there to lose, aside from my last breath?

I made my way through the village and to the start line on the small stretch of sand by the harbour, pushing through the throng of locals who had come out to either support or take part. There seemed to be a mix of ages amongst the competitors, ranging from the young sprightly types to geriatrics, which gave me *some* level of confidence, but then I spotted Nico and remembered not to be fooled by the Greek elders.

"Isme, it is so good to see you again." Nico patted me on the back with the force of someone twice his size, taking my breath away. "This is my daughter, Thalia. She has come to see me win." He winked.

"*Ochi*, papa, you are so modest!" They shared a smile, and a lump formed in my throat as I thought about Dad and how I'd give anything to have him here with me, looking as fit and healthy as Nico.

"Are you alone?" asked Nico, as if reading my mind.

"No, my family are on their way," I said, which was a lie. I hadn't told them I was taking part as they would only worry, and I couldn't risk Mum questioning the quality of the moussaka.

"Isme, you made it." Neil appeared wearing a black one-piece swimsuit that accentuated his pecks and crotch, and I felt myself blush. "I thought you might back out at the last minute . . . you know, with everything that's been going on," he added, once he noticed my stern expression.

"She is Greek, Neil, and you know us Greeks are not quitters. Isn't that right, Isme?"

"You bet, Nico!" I said, as convincingly as I could.

But as we reached the sand and I noticed the lighthouse, which looked a lot further away than I remembered, my insides churned, and I felt a sudden urge to flee.

Maybe I was a quitter after all.

*

Maddy: "Well at least you gave it a go, babe, that's all that matters."

Me: "I didn't even make it to the lighthouse, Maddy!"

Maddy: "Yeah, well. Swimming is hard! I can't even do one length and I feel like I'm gonna puke. And anyway, I bet you don't feel half as bad as Neil, losing out to someone almost twice his age! I would have loved to see the look on his face."

Me: "Ha, it was quite funny, like! I just feel like a big failure, Mad. That money would have really helped Mum and Dad out. Now I'm back to square one."

Maddy: "Babe, these things have a way of working out. You'll see."

Me: "I hope so, Mad, I really hope so."

*

"I blame the moussaka, the vegan option was far too stodgy.

I mean, how do they expect you to get through all that potato?" scoffed Neil, as we strolled along the beach.

It had been two days since the mini triathlon, and we were still dissecting his defeat.

"At least you still completed it. I didn't even make it past the first round!"

"Don't be so hard on yourself, Isme. You've had a lot on your plate lately." We reached a small cove in the corner of the beach and Neil halted, looking around. "Yep, I think this is the perfect spot."

He wasn't wrong. It was like a mini haven set back from the main beach, surrounded by raised, smooth white rocks and shrubbery which looked practically emerald under the light of the sun.

Neil retrieved a checked picnic blanket from his rucksack and lay it down on the sand, followed by two plastic champagne flutes, some strawberries and a bottle of Nosecco. I would have preferred the real stuff, but would be glad of a clear head the following morning.

It was our last day together in Cyprus before he flew home, and whilst I still hadn't made up my mind about whether to carry on seeing him post-holiday, I couldn't resist the possibility of a little farewell foreplay. I'd even worn a floaty summer dress for easy access, so had to hide my disappointment when he'd suggested a beach picnic amongst the general public.

"To us," said Neil, holding up his flute.

"Yes, to, er, us!" I clinked my flute against his and took a swig, which tasted more like the real thing than I thought. Fizzy with a hint of pear.

"You know, you're the first girl who hasn't run a mile when I've told them about my pre-marital celibacy."

"Really? Wow." I tried my best to act surprised, but I was far from it. I'd been ready to do a runner myself when he'd made the shock revelation, and it was only thanks to his quick thinking with his hands that I didn't. "Some people are all about the sex." I tutted and rolled my eyes up at the sky. God, I deserved an Oscar.

"Exactly! And what's wrong with waiting until marriage? And the wait wouldn't be long for people who meet at our age. I know a few from the Church who've met and been married within the year." Neil winked and I grimaced. At least I now knew where he stood on hasty engagements.

I lay on my back with my arms propped up, mesmerised by the waves as they crashed back and forth, their sound like rhythmic percussion. The sun was setting in the distance, it's golden rays reflecting off the water and stretching far and wide.

"I'm going to miss this," I sighed, as I thought about the meagre sunsets at home, which you're lucky to see behind the dense cloud that occupies the sky on the daily.

Neil lay down next to me on his side, his head propped up on his hand. "And I'm going to miss *you*," he said, as he started making circles with his finger across my chest. "So, can we see each other again when we get home?"

Neil was looking at me expectantly. *Did* I want to see him

again? Or was it more a case of *having* to, now that the triathlon winnings were out of reach? There *was* still the job promotion, but Mum and Dad had already made it clear that the extra money I'd earn wouldn't really help.

Unable to muster up any words, I grabbed his neck and pushed his lips onto mine.

"Woah, Neil, we can't! Not here," I laughed, as he reached a hand under my top.

"There's no one here! Plus, why do you think I chose this little corner?" I felt a rush of unnerving excitement at the prospect of a little al fresco action. I quickly scanned the area, but all seemed quiet.

"Anyway, you haven't answered my question," whispered Neil into my ear, which made my skin tingle. Slowly, he began running a hand up my leg, my heart beating gradually faster as it neared the top of my thigh.

Lost in a cloud of lust, I found myself panting, "Yes, yes," as his hands reached inside my knickers.

*

"Give over, woman, if you plump them up any more I'll be bent over."

"*Ochi*, Stephen, the doctor say you must keep upright." Mum persisted to plump Dad's back cushions up, her bulky frame getting in the way of his view of the television.

"I just want to watch *Homes Under the Hammer* in peace." Dad sighed, staring up at the ceiling, as if hoping it contained a portal that would take him back to a time when he was fully fit and healthy.

I sat in the chair beside the hospital bed as we waited for the doctor to come and give his verdict on whether Dad was fit to fly home, smiling quietly to myself. It was nice to hear, and see, that he was almost back to himself, especially given that just over a week ago you wouldn't have given a quid for him.

A week on, and whilst he was still quite jaded, largely as a result of the medication they had him on, and his complexion still on the pasty side, he looked loads better – less *Walking Dead* and more *The Vampire Diaries*.

Finally, the doctor on duty arrived – who, with his goatee and stern expression, reminded me a bit of Doctor Strange, albeit an unkempt and less fit version. Throw on a cape though, and I might just be persuaded.

"Have you been under any undue stress recently, Mr Eliades?" he asked, peering over his rimless glasses.

"You could say that, Doctor. The crypt over there is keeping me awake at night with his snoring." He attempted a laugh, which manifested into a full-blown coughing fit. Mum ran to his aid with a glass of water and put it to his lips.

"I'm not a bleedin' baby, Elana!" Dad snatched the cup from her, spilling some of the contents on himself as he did so.

"Well, you are acting like one, Stephen Eliades," huffed Mum as she stormed off to the far side of the room whilst Doctor Strange watched on with a bemused expression, tapping his foot and checking his watch.

With the pair of them sulking like Theo and Tomaso after being told they can't have sweets, I cleared my throat and stood up to take my position as the family spokesperson, explaining about the con man running off with their savings and forcing them to sell the house.

"Well, that certainly explains why your blood pressure has been through the roof," said Doctor Strange once I'd finished, as he started jotting some notes down on his clipboard. "I'm going to prescribe you some tablets, but you should also be doing things to help. In particular, finding ways to manage your stress levels."

He handed Dad a leaflet on 'hobbies for the heart', before signing off his fit-to-fly form and rushing out.

"Well, isn't that great, we can all finally go home!" I said cheerily, digging my phone out of my back pocket to ring the airline who, after a lengthy telephone conversation when we were due to fly home a week ago, had agreed to allow us to move our flights.

Mum started gathering Dad's belongings and shoving them ever so forcefully into a holdall, while Dad sat scanning the leaflet.

"You're not gonna believe what the first thing they suggest to do is," he said, shaking his head.

"Erm, join a gym? Go on a hike?"

"Go on bleedin' holiday!"

I think our laughter could have been heard all the way down in the morgue.

*

"Due to some minor mechanical issues which we are working hard to resolve, we will unfortunately have to remain on the tarmac for at least an hour, possibly two."

"You've *got* to be kidding me." I threw my head back against the headrest and sighed at the announcement over the PA system, my patience already wearing thin from the sound of Mum's heavy snores beside me. She suddenly jerked in her sleep and elbowed me in the arm, which made me squeal. A week on from the triathlon and my arms still felt like I'd done ten rounds with Mike Tyson.

I looked over at Dad for some solace, but he'd plugged his earphones into the armrest to listen to the radio, so was completely oblivious.

In need of a distraction, I switched my phone on and turned aeroplane mode off ready for some mindless Instagram scrolling, when some messages pinged through moments later.

> **Neil:** It's only been a week since our night on the beach but feels like three! Can't wait to see you again once you're back in Liverpool. Have a safe flight x

> **Isme:** Thanks. See you on the other side x

After hitting send, I stared aimlessly out of the aeroplane window, noticing a pigeon perched on top of the terminal building. I wondered why it would choose to spend its day sitting there, watching people take off to all corners of the world, when it could do just that itself. I imagined having wings. Where would I go right now? What would I do?

I remembered Mum telling me about an island in Greece where people 'forget to die' – they sleep late, get up late, take frequent naps, wear no watches and live off the land. It had sounded like such a boring and dull existence. But now, with thoughts turning to getting home and trying to resolve the Eliades Greek debt crisis, it felt like it would be the perfect escape.

I thought back to the flight out only a couple of months earlier, and the excitement I'd felt about the prospect of starting a new chapter of my life. Little did I know that new chapter would be more messed up than the first.

A snore of epic proportion from Mum brought me back to the present. I gave her a gentle nudge and she sleepily repositioned herself so that she was resting her head on Dad's shoulder, who was now sound asleep himself, catching flies with his open mouth. As I watched them, all cuddled up and snoozing so peacefully, I felt a warmth in my chest, and couldn't help but smile to myself.

As easy as it would be to flee from everyone and everything, just like that pigeon, I belonged here. And with Maria busy with her own problems, all they had was me – and I was determined to make things better for them.

PART THREE

Wonders never Greece . . .

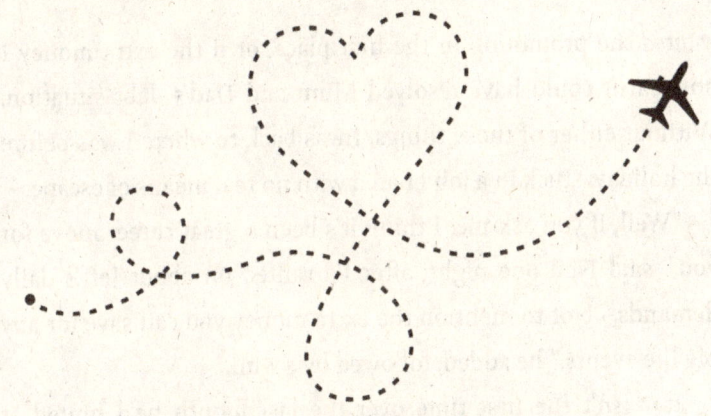

SEPTEMBER

ONE MONTH LATER, AND THE ONLY THING I'D MADE better was my waistline, thanks to my kitchen vibrator and Neil's weekly green juice recipes, although I'd always still choose my *own* green juice of midori and soda given the chance.

For the first few weeks after being home, all my focus had been on Dad's recovery and getting back into work, which had been busy, to say the least, after getting the promotion – I now had to account for every hour of my time by filling in a timesheet, which meant no more solitaire or sneaky under-the-desk Facebook scrolling.

Unluckily for me, my days were now jam-packed with transcribing and proofreading legal documents, amongst many other things, so I hardly had the time to even *look* at my phone most days. It was exhausting, but wouldn't be so bad if I had actually *wanted* the promotion in the first place, or if the extra money I now earnt could have resolved Mum and Dad's debt situation. Without either of those things, I was back to where I was before the holiday: stuck in a job I hated with no real means of escape.

"Well, if you ask me, I think it's been a great career move for you," said Neil one night, after I'd ranted on about Jeff's daily demands. "Not to mention the extra money you can save for any big life events," he added, followed by a wink.

It wasn't the first time over the last month he'd hinted at marriage, which I wasn't sure was down to a real desire to get hitched, or more a desperate need to get his end away. God knows I'd almost shouted out 'I do' a few times when we'd been in the throes of passion, and whilst it *was* still fun doing everything *but* sex, I couldn't help but wonder when it might grow tiresome. And, as the saying goes: when the fun stops, stop.

Neil was nothing like anyone I'd ever dated before. Whether that was a good thing was yet to be decided, but for the time being I was enjoying having someone to Netflix and chill with and have around the flat. That is, apart from the time he decided to delete all my pre-recorded episodes of *Celebs Go Dating* and replace them with a programme about the environmental impact large scale factory farming has on our planet.

Or the night I came home from a hectic day at work ready to raid my beloved emergency sugar snack drawer, only to find that all the original contents had been replaced with what can only be described as rabbit food – baldy rice cakes, kale chips, dried banana chips and sesame sticks.

One can be forgiven, though, when they're the key to resolving the family's financial crisis.

*

"They're not bad them, Freckiades. Not bad at all," said Anthony, peering over the thirty baby shower themed cupcakes I'd made for a friend of Sandra's. "I still don't know why you gave up on doing this full time."

I sighed. If only it was that easy.

I'd been reluctant at first, when Sandra had asked me to make the cakes. With work being so hectic, I was struggling to muster up the energy to do any baking in the little spare time I had, and even when I did, it was like my brain would fog over and I'd forget a critical step or ingredient, like eggs in a ravani cake or honey in baklava. But I was determined not to completely lose sight of my baking foundations, and after stocking up on some Red Bull I eventually agreed.

After hours spent Googling images of baby shower cupcakes, some of which looked well beyond my capabilities (I mean, how was I supposed to make a baby's head peering out from a blood splattered vadge?), I decided to keep it simple. I made a selection of baby themed toppings using fondant icing, including tiny pink and blue feet, dummies and teddy bears, and rested them on top of swirls of blue and pink buttercream.

The idea of trying to sculpt these tiny shapes initially filled me with dread, especially after Peppa Pig-gate, but once I started rolling the sticky, sweet icing in my hands, the process felt almost therapeutic, with the stress of work lifting with every baby themed topping I managed to mould. It also helped that I wasn't battling thirty-degree heat this time, so with the kitchen window slightly ajar allowing the autumn chill to waft through, the icing stayed firm beneath my hands.

"So, how's steg head?" asked Anthony, as we settled on the sofa with a beer.

"He's fine. And you know, it wouldn't do you any harm to call him by his real name," I scoffed.

"OK, sorry. How's Neeee— STEG HEAD! Sorry, I can't do it." I threw a cushion in his direction which hit him on the head, making us both chuckle.

Since getting back from Cyprus, things seemed to have resumed back to normal between us, with no more weird dreams or cookie-dough play-fights. It was still unclear how we'd ended up in such a strange phase of our friendship, but whatever it was, I was glad we'd moved past it. There *were* some days when my mind would wander back to earlier in the year and that dream, but I'd quickly shake it off and try and imagine it was Neil standing by my bed and not Anthony. Their faces always seemed to blend into one though when I did, which was confusing.

"What are you doing later? Fancy going out?"

"Can't. I've told Neil I'll go and meet his mum."

"OK. How about tomorrow?"

"Got the work party with Nei—"

"Neil, yep. Got it." Anthony picked at a corner of the beer label that had come loose, and a wave of guilt washed over me. Admittedly, we hadn't spent as much time together over the last month as we normally would, with my time already stretched between Dad, work and Neil. But this was Anthony – he had to fit in too.

"I'm free Sunday. Maybe we could go and see that dinosaur exhibition."

Anthony's eyes lit up. "Can we re-enact the 'Welcome to Jurassic Park' scene, for old times' sake?"

I smiled. "Only if I can be Alan and wear the cowboy hat."

*

Neil's mum lived on the north side of the city where, in Neil's words, as he made a point of saying to me on the drive there, 'people are more down to earth', adding that they still have just as much money as those living in the southern suburbs. I resisted the urge to tell him to stick his North vs South Liverpool dig where the sun doesn't shine.

We pulled up outside a house in a quiet little cul-de-sac that reminded me a bit of Brookside Close, with its semi-circle of modern detached houses, and the overwhelming sense that all the occupants were watching our every move from behind their curtains. Large oak trees lined the streets like guards on duty, their amber autumn-kissed leaves already shedding and carpeting the ground.

As we stepped out of the car, the door to number four burst open.

Facially, Neil's mum was probably in her mid-fifties but dressed like she was ready for World War Two rationing. She was wearing a pleated grey skirt and white cashmere cardigan, despite it being an unusually warm September day, and her short brown hair was tied back in a low bun.

"Oh, my darling boy, it's so nice to see you." I got a whiff of lavender and biscuits as she wrapped her arms around Neil and planted two wet kisses on his cheeks. She then turned her attention to me.

"This must be the lovely Isme I've been hearing all about!"

"Mum, this is Isme. Isme, this is the other special woman in my life."

"Oh, hi, Mrs—"

"Joan, you can call me Joan, love. Now come in, I've just put the kettle on and the banana loaf is almost ready, although I hear you're an avid baker, Isme, so I hope it's up to your standard!"

"Ha, don't be silly, I'm sure it's delicious."

I gave my shoes a quick wipe on the door mat before following Joan inside, not paying too much attention to the 'Jesus Loves You' that was written across it. A bit of holy décor was to be expected from the woman who'd taught her son to believe that sex before marriage was a sin.

But there's 'a bit', and then there was the living room, which was like a scene from *The Da Vinci Code*, swarming with mini statues of religious figures and holy crosses, with the walls covered in biblical paintings. The place even smelt like a church, thanks to the scattering of incense sticks burning away. I felt an overwhelming urge to recite the Hail Mary.

*

"Oh my God, Neil, you didn't tell me you were a plump kid!" I laughed, as Joan handed me another picture from the pile of old family photos. His face was barely recognisable, his familiar features hidden behind puffy red cheeks and four chins.

"Do we really have to do this, Mum?" he huffed as he poured more tea from the teapot, which was housing a ceramic cross on the top of the lid. I had to stop myself from doing the sign of the cross as he poured.

"Oh, stop being a spoilsport, will you!" Joan handed me another picture. "This was from when he won the doughnut-eating competition at Butlins."

I burst out laughing at the picture of the little chubby seven-year-old holding up a doughnut-shaped medal and grinning at the camera like he'd just won an Olympic gold.

"Oh, is this your dad?" I picked up a picture that had slipped from the pile onto the floor, which looked like it was taken in the late eighties from the *Wham!* style oversized black suit jacket, white shirt and mullet bouffant the man in the picture was sporting.

Joan snatched the picture out my hand and shoved it to the back of the pile like it was a piece of hot coal. "Yeah, that's him, all right. That's the last picture I've got of him before he left us for some floozy down the pub." I felt my face redden like a beetroot.

"I'm sorry, I didn't know. Neil's never spoken about it."

"Well, telling someone you were abandoned as a baby, leaving you to feel worthless for the rest of your life, isn't exactly a conversation I'm eager to have, Isme."

An awkward silence descended across the room. I took a long sip of my tea as Joan continued shuffling through pictures. I tried to catch Neil's gaze, but he was staring at the floor with a glum expression.

"Oh look! A picture of me in my wedding dress!" cried Joan, breaking the silence. "It was still the best day of my life, despite the outcome." She handed me the picture, and I couldn't help but smile at the gleaming twenty-something Joan standing proudly in a full-length white lace gown and puffed-up sleeves. "Do *you* want to get married, Isme?"

Neil averted his gaze from the floor, and was now glaring in my direction.

I cleared my throat. "I mean, yeah. I do want to get married someday, definitely."

Neil's frown slowly turned into a smile, eventually resembling a similar grin to the seven-year-old doughnut-eating champion from the picture.

*

The annual Mulligan's 'late' summer party at The Pig's Head was an event which usually ended with me (and Maddy, when she still worked there) shit-faced and scoffing a greasy kebab in a nearby takeaway by midnight. But with Neil at my side this year, closely monitoring my alcohol intake, and Maddy only briefly making an appearance having received a 'special' invite from Jeff, the night took a rather different turn.

"You must be Isme's better half!" said Jeff, who made a beeline for us as soon as we arrived, shaking Neil's hand with so much force his body shook with it. "I'm 'The Boss', for my sins, HA HA HA!" His guffaw vibrated in my chest.

"It's so nice to meet you, Jeff," said Neil enthusiastically. "I hope this one's been behaving herself." He wrapped his arm around me and pulled me into him. It was like parents' evening all over again.

"She can be a bit unruly sometimes, but I keep her in check. HA HA HA!"

"HA HA HA!" We'd only been there five minutes and Neil had already mastered the fake work laugh.

"I've got to say, Neil, that is a fantastic shirt. I've got a similar one myself." Neil's face beamed with delight. I'd been with him when he picked it out of the sale at TK Maxx a few days earlier, and it had clearly been dug up from the depths of the summer stock, with its vibrant paisley swirls of pink, red and white.

"Well it *is* supposed to be a summer party, Isme," he'd protested when I'd questioned its suitability, given that the current average temperature was around twelve degrees and the autumnal night chill had firmly set in. But I told myself that at least there was no chance of us getting run over on our walk to the party in the dark.

As the mutual appreciation society continued, I peered around for Maddy among the sea of faces, but she was nowhere to be seen. It wasn't unusual for her to be late though, and she was most likely still at home applying her third face.

"What a great man," said Neil, once Jeff had left to greet some more guests. "I wish I had a boss like that."

"Pah! You can have him," I scoffed, as we made our way over to the buffet table.

"Oh, come on. He's not that bad, surely?"

"Yeah well, you don't work for him, Neil."

The truth was, getting the promotion and working directly for Jeff (much to Sue's delight, who practically whooped for joy when she realised she no longer had to put up with my CBA work ethic) was like switching from a Ford Fiesta to an F1 racing car. My desk was constantly piled high with legal papers to organise or invoices to process, and no sooner had I burned through them, he was there, refilling the pile without so much as a 'please' or a 'thank you'. Then there was his constant daily demands for refreshments – the man drank more coffee than Neil, and *that* was saying something.

I never thought I'd hear myself say it, but I longed for Sue and her micro-managing ways.

"Wow, they really know how to put on a spread," scoffed Neil, as he cast a disgusted look over the contents of the buffet, which was like something from a kid's birthday party – lots of beige and E numbers. "And not one vegan option in sight."

"Stop your moaning, there's some nuts over there." I indicated to the sad-looking bowl of peanuts. Neil gave me a scornful look as I began piling my plate with a selection of sandwiches and sausage rolls. I was quite partial to a good old-fashioned party spread, plus there was no room for fussiness when you hadn't eaten since breakfast.

"That's all going to play havoc with your insides tomorrow, Isme. Just saying."

"Yeah well, that's tomorrow's problem," I scoffed, shoving an egg mayonnaise sandwich into my gob, and grabbing another off my plate.

"I thought I might find you by the food, Isme."

I jolted at the sound of Zara's voice, almost choking on my

sandwich. She was wearing a white bandeau mini dress, her hair and make-up annoyingly flawless. She eyed up my plate of food with the same level of disgust that Neil had just seconds before.

I hadn't seen much of Zara since coming back to the office, which had suited me fine. The pre-Cyprus Isme would have given anything to lock her in a room and have it out with her about getting me suspended, but with everything that had happened since, I was over it. I still wouldn't mind giving her a slap right across the chopper, though.

"God help your stomach after all that," she smirked, flicking a lock of her long brown hair from her shoulders.

"That's what I said!" cried Neil, sidling up next to me. "My gym instructor at Nuffield's would have a hernia if he saw me eating any of that."

Zara's eyes widened as she caught sight of Neil, scanning him from head to toe like she was sizing up her meat at the butchers. "Oh, do you go to the one down the road from here?"

"Yeah."

"Me too! What a small world. We'll have to do a class together sometime. I'm Zara, by the way. And you are?"

"Sorry, it's Neil. I'm with Isme." The way he said 'with' made it sound like he was my carer.

"Interesting," smirked Zara, as she looked from me back to Neil again. I'd seen that look before, when I'd first brought Anthony to one of our work nights out, and it made me uneasy. "Well, it's nice to meet you, Neil. I'm sure I'll see you again. LOVE the shirt, by the way." With that, she turned on her stilettos and glided away.

"What a lovely girl," said Neil, once Zara had pissed off. "So have you two been friends long then?"

"Long enough," I muttered while poking at my food, having lost my appetite. "And I wouldn't call us friends. More, work acquaintances." And she's an absolute bitch who almost stole my best friend and got me suspended from work, I was tempted to add.

"Babe, there you are. I've been looking everywhere for you. And don't even ask," Maddy said, sensing my amusement as I caught sight of what can only be described as two peacocks on her eyes. "They didn't have my usual lashes in, so it was either these or go bald, which just wasn't an option."

"So do you regularly use the fur of dead animals for personal vanity?"

I gawped at Neil. "Neil, what the hell—"

"Those eyelashes, presumably they're made from mink?"

Maddy looked completely baffled. "Er, I've never really thought about it."

"Most are these days," Neil continued, "unless you opt for ethical ones. You know they're bred and slaughtered on fur farms around the world for their fur. It really is animal cruelty at its worst."

Maddy sloped off to the loo shortly after. When she hadn't reappeared after twenty minutes, I opened up my phone.

Isme: Where are you? I've just bought a round

Maddy: Sorry babe, I've left. I had to take

those eyelashes off, they were doing me tits in,
and couldn't stay looking like I had alopecia

Isme: I hope Neil didn't offend you with what he said
He's just a bit anal when it comes to animal rights 🙈

Maddy: I'm donating to RSPCA as we speak

*

Annoyingly, Neil had been right about the egg sandwiches, especially when mixed with vodka, so I found myself agreeing to go the gym with him in a bid to burn off the bloat.

It was fairly quiet when we got there, the smell of bleach still lingering in the air and burning the back of my throat from the previous night's clean down. Apparently, it's best to exercise first thing of a morning because it speeds up your metabolism, or some other shite like that.

"We'll start easy," said Neil, ushering me to the rowing machines and fiddling with the screen to set the resistance. "Just a nice gentle row to get that heart rate going."

"The rowing machine? Really?" I scoffed, plonking myself down onto the seat and securing my feet in the foot straps. "I'd burn more fat doing the dishes."

"Yeah, if you ever did any dishes. Now stop complaining and get going. I'll be on an exercise bike if you need me."

Five minutes later, I was eating my words and pissing with sweat. I looked over at Neil to signal for help, but he was too busy talking to a petite blonde on the bike next to him, who was wearing skin-tight leggings and matching crop top, revealing a toned torso.

Eventually, Neil came striding over from the exercise bike, not one bead of sweat on his brow. I tried to speak, but all that came out were heavy rasps of breath.

"Why don't you take five minutes out and follow me over to the stepper once you're ready?"

I nodded, although I had no intention of doing anything else, not unless I fancied joining Dad in the heart attack club.

I snuck off to the water machine, downing two cups in record speed, which wasn't hard considering the size of the cups they put in those things. I was just pouring myself a third cup when a familiar voice from behind me said, "Well, I never! Freckiades in a gym. I've seen it all now."

"You can talk," I laughed, as I turned to face Anthony. "You always said you would rather suck Ann Widdecombe's big toe than join a gym."

"Yeah, well. I can change my mind, can't I?" Anthony took a swig from his water bottle. "I've even just subscribed to *Men's Health*." I almost choked on my water.

"What brings *you* here, Anthony? You get lost on your way to KFC?" Neil sidled up to me, placing an arm around my shoulders and giving me a gentle but firm squeeze.

"Woah, Neil, that's a bit harsh."

"It's OK, Isme, I can take a joke. Clearly, you can too – after all, you take *him* everywhere with you."

"Now come on, children, let's not fight." I laughed in a bid to lighten the mood, but Anthony and Neil stood motionless, their chests puffed out like two gorillas about to battle for dominance.

Thankfully, Toned Torso came over to get some water out of the machine, breaking up our dysfunctional threesome.

*

"Honestly, Maria, you wanted to see the pair of them. It was like watching two wrestlers about to get in the ring."

"Ha! I would pay to see *that* fight." Maria scooped a finger into the dregs of the tzatziki and licked it off. "It'd be like watching Ant Man take on The Hulk."

"*Ochi*, Maria, please! Did your mama not teach you any manners? *O thee mou.*" Mum began clearing the plates from dinner, which had consisted of a small roast chicken, salad and half a pitta bread each.

"Well, maybe if you fed us properly I wouldn't still be hungry," scoffed Maria. She grabbed a piece of pizza off Theo's plate, who was too engrossed in his iPad to notice.

"Theo, Mummy's just—"

"SHHHHHH! I'll buy you a toy, Tomaso."

He grinned, and turned his attention back to YouTube.

"Come on now, Maria, your mum is doing her best," said Dad, getting to his feet.

"Yes, everything will be OK once we sell thee house." They exchanged a weary smile, before Mum scurried off to the kitchen.

"You OK, Dad?" I asked, as he rubbed at his chest. I hoped another heart attack was not on the cards. I still hadn't got over the last one.

"Yeah, just heartburn, love." With that, he shuffled off to the kitchen.

"Seriously though, Isme, what are you going to do about Anthony and Neil?"

"What do you mean?"

"Well, first Maddy, now Anthony. Don't you think it's a massive red flag, the fact that he doesn't get on with your mates? At least George, for all his faults, can have a laugh with my friends."

I sighed. I knew Maria was right, but seeing how the stress of their financial situation was still weighing heavily on Mum and Dad, I had to at least see where things could go.

Plus, the foreplay wasn't bad either.

*

After Neil and Maddy's awkward first meeting at the work summer party, I arranged for us all to meet again at a local shisha cafe in a bid for them to get along. An unusual choice, I know, but where do you take a non-alcoholic drinking vegan and gluten-allergic?

But my image of the three of us walking out arm-in-arm at the end, laughing and joking, with the *Friends* theme tune playing in the background, were dashed when Maddy turned up looking like Pat Butcher in the biggest fur coat.

"What, it's Baltic out there!" she said, sensing my anguish, before turning to Neil. "It's fake, babe."

I sank into my chair, hoping it would absorb me like quicksand. To be fair, it was a particularly cool September day, so a fur coat was not *entirely* out of place – just not when you're sat with an animal rights activist.

Neil's face had turned so red I thought he might spontaneously combust. She unravelled the mound of furry material from her shoulders and placed it on the back of her chair.

"That's part of the problem you see, Maddy. By you wearing the fake stuff, it keeps the *real* animal fur coats in fashion. People's ignorance is the root cause of the problem in today's society."

Maddy looked non-plussed. She took a deep dreg on the shisha pipe that smelt of minty toothpaste, and blew a big puff of smoke in Neil's direction.

"So, babe, have you thought any more about doing the cake stuff full time yet?"

I sighed. "No, I haven't had a chance. Work's been hectic – you know, since getting the promotion and that. I'm not getting time to bake *anything* at the moment, never mind take any orders."

"How *is* work going since the promotion?"

Absolutely shit. I only went for it in the first place because I thought it would help Mum and Dad out with their debts, but it turned out it wouldn't even cover a month's credit card payment. So here I am, still stuck in a career I never wanted to be in with a boss that makes David Brent look like Steven Bartlett.

That's what I *wanted* to say, but instead I took a deep dreg on the pipe and said, "Yeah, it's sound."

"Well, you know what they say, babe. It's never too late to focus on your dreams."

"She's only just been promoted," scoffed Neil, "why would she throw all that away for some little cake business? We're not exactly talking Pattiserie Valerie."

Maddy put down the pipe and fluffed up her fake fur. "It's her dream job. How can you be like that about it?"

"In the same way as you are about animal cruelty, I suppose. Oh, and while we're on the subject, I see you're still contributing to the many minks' lives that are lost each year with those eyelashes?"

Maddy pushed back her chair with so much force she hit the table behind and knocked over their pipe, which hit another, then another, like shisha dominoes. "Sorry, Isme, but I've had enough."

"Take no notice of him, Mad. He's like Piers Morgan, he doesn't know when to shut the fuck up . . ." But Maddy was already forcing her arms through her coat, bits of fake fur flying everywhere as she did.

"If you must know, Leonardo DiCaprio, these are ethical eyelashes that I had imported from America after you had a go at me last time! You can shove your sarcastic comment up your arse." With that, she stormed out of the cafe, knocking another table and three more pipes as she went.

I glared at Neil, waiting for some sort of apology or admittance that he was in the wrong, but he just huffed and said, "I suppose we're paying for her share of the bill, then."

*

Isme: *Picture of someone hugging a tree with Neil's head superimposed onto it*

Maddy: 😄 Seriously though, babe, what do you see in the lad?

Isme: He's good with his hands?!

Maddy: Do you remember that episode of
Friends, where Ross makes a list about
Rachel's pros and cons?

Isme: Yeah?

Maddy: I think you could do with a list, babe

Positives
1. *Has some amount of Greek blood,
   so could unlock the inheritance
   money if we get hitched.*
2. *Fit bod.*
3. *Face that's pleasant to look at.*
4. *Good with his hands.*

Negatives:
1. *Vegan.*
2. *Wall wanker.*
3. *Spends far too much time in the gym.*
4. *Drinks a worrying amount of coffee.*
5. *Takes himself a bit too seriously.*
6. *Doesn't drink.*
7. *Doesn't get on with my friends.*

I sent the list to Maddy in the hope that she would provide me with some words of wisdom.

> **Maddy:** 7 points to 4. I think that says it all,
> doesn't it, babe?
> Also, what's a wall wanker? Is it some kind of fetish?

I let out a gusty sigh. I'd been trying to convince myself that dating Neil wasn't just about the inheritance money and had been hopeful that, over time, I'd like him more and more until eventually developing The Feels, making any forthcoming engagement proposal easy to accept. But the list confirmed what I'd been feeling in my gut: Neil carried more red flags than a lifeguard on a stormy day. Yes, no Neil meant no inheritance money, but could I *really* carry on dating him in the hope that he'd change?

I think I already knew the answer.

*

> **Isme:** Can you come round to the flat later?
> We need to talk

> **Neil:** Great, I'd like to talk to you too.
> I'll be round at 7

I glared at my phone, my mind racing. Was I about to be the dumpee rather than the dumper?

"Do you mind if I talk first?" said Neil, as we sat down on the sofa. He was wearing a tight, fitted T-shirt, which accentuated his pecks perfectly. If he'd worn it intentionally to entice me in, then it was working.

7 to 4, Isme. 7 to 4, I chanted internally.

"Erm, well—"

"Great." Neil shifted his position on the sofa so he was facing me, and took my hands in his.

"I really like how things are going between us, Isme. I've spent so many years alone whilst I recovered from my alcohol addiction, wondering if I'd ever meet someone again." Neil paused and stared down at his hands. Was that . . . ? Oh please, don't let it be . . . a tear?

"I never thought I'd love again, and then I met you by the pool in Cyprus and everything changed. I guess what I'm trying to say is . . . I think, or, I know. I mean, I, I . . . I think I'm falling in love with you."

His words hung in the air for a moment, hovering over us like an unwelcome guest. My heart pounded against my chest, and for a moment I couldn't catch my breath.

"That's, erm, wow. I didn't expect you to say that. Goodness, is it just me or is it hot in here?" I grabbed a copy of *Take a Break* from the coffee table and frantically began fanning my face. How the hell was I supposed to call it off now?

"I also just wanted to say . . ." Oh God, there was more? Cue more frantic fanning. "You know my situation when it comes to marriage, but I just want to make it clear. I'm ready to get married . . . no pressure, of course!" he added, when he saw the look of sheer panic on my face. "I'll wait for as long as you need. When you're ready, just say the word."

Suddenly, my phone came to life with an incoming call from Mum, which was a welcome relief from the heavy love and marriage chat.

Mum: "Isme, *koumera*, I have some great news! We got an offer on the house and it has been accepted!"

Me: "Oh, wow. That's, erm, great!"

Mum: "I know. It's really great. Here is your papa."

Dad: "Hi Isme, love. It's great, isn't it."

Me: "Yeah, it's . . . great!"

I'd known it was coming – after all, Mum and Dad live in one of the most sought-after areas in Liverpool. Yet that didn't stop the flood of sadness that rushed through me hearing the news. And despite Mum and Dad's best efforts to sound chirpy, I could tell from the overuse of the word 'great' that they felt it too – it was as if repeating the word might make them believe it themselves.

"So, what did you want to talk to me about, Isme?" asked Neil, once the call ended.

I hesitated for a moment, fiddling with a loose strand on one of the sofa cushions as my insides churned in turmoil. I'd been so convinced that I was ready to call things off with Neil after making the list, despite the fact it would mean going back to the drawing board in terms of helping Mum and Dad out of their financial mess. And whilst I'd known it wouldn't be long before any offers came through on the house, I'd naïvely hoped I'd have more time to find an alternative solution (or husband).

That feeling of guilt I'd felt in the hospital in Cyprus, right after Dad had the heart attack, came flooding back like a nasty bout of diarrhoea – gut-wrenching and uncomfortable. All I could think was: *You can resolve this, Isme, you can make this all go away.*

Eventually I found myself saying, "Don't worry, it was nothing."

*

EMAIL
To: Luke Jones
From: Ismeena Eliades
Re: Will stuff

Hi Luke,

How's the family?

I heard you might know a thing or two about Wills.

So, I have a friend who's got this family Will, and it says that she's entitled to £25k, but only when she marries someone who is Greek.

Just wondering, do you know if there's any way you can release the money once you're engaged, or would you have to wait until the wedding?

Asking for a friend, like I said.

Thanks,
Isme

To: Ismeena Eliades
From: Luke Jones
Re: Will stuff
Hi Isme,

I'm getting divorced, but thanks for asking. No idea about Wills. Your best bet is Zara.

When you ask her, tell her if she ever wants to get together for old times' sake, she knows where I am.

Thanks,
Luke

I leant back in my chair and sighed. The last thing I wanted to do was go asking Zara for help. She'd see right through me, and I couldn't trust that she wouldn't go blabbing to everyone in Greek church.

But with inheritance specialists scarce at Mulligan's since Carol, who overstated the figures on a client's probate forms to the tune of hundreds of thousands of pounds, gaining her a five-year ban from The Law Society and the nickname Count-up Carol, my options were limited.

*

Me: "Hello, Maria? Can you hear me? . . . MARIA! ARE YOU

THERE? . . . MAAARRRIIAAA!!"

Maria: "ISME, I'M IN A BAR, I CAN'T HEAR YOU!"

Me: "Well, go outside then will you for fuck's sake, it's about Dad."

Maria: "WHAT?"

Me: "IT'S DAD!! THEY THINK HE'S HAD ANOTHER HEART ATTACK, YOU NEED TO COME TO THE HOSPITAL NOW."

Maria: "ISME, I CAN'T HEAR YOU. JUST SEND ME A TEXT, OK?"

*

It turned out to be a mild angina attack which, according to the doctors, was not in itself life-threatening. But it *was* a warning sign that Dad could be at risk of another heart attack unless he sorted his blood pressure out.

"Another holiday, then?" I joked, as I drove him home from the hospital.

He gave a half-hearted smile, whilst staring aimlessly out the car window. "When will this nightmare end?" He sighed, rubbing at his eyes. "I'm honestly not sure how much more I can take, Iz."

I didn't notice his tears until we pulled up at some traffic lights. My heart sank, my own eyes beginning to well up at the sight of Dad's. The last time I'd seen him cry was when they lost the restaurant, and it pained me just as much as it had back then.

"I'm going to make things better for you, Dad. I promise," I said, squeezing his leg.

It was clearer than ever then what I had to do.

Isme: The word

Neil: I understand 😊

*

I'd often wondered what it would feel like to be engaged, aside from the new piece of metal occupying your left hand, and whether it would make me feel instantaneously different, more grown up, perhaps?

I observed my reflection in the mirror this morning, expecting to see something different, some kind of symbol of my newfound maturity – a new wrinkle perhaps, or strand of grey hair. But all that was staring back at me was a dishevelled, heavy-eyed mess that had spent most of the night lying awake wondering whether I'd made the right decision. One thing that certainly *was* different though was my left hand.

I'd never been a fan of wearing rings, and had spent most of the morning rubbing my thumb along the underneath of it and taking it off and on – a subtle eighteen carat, white gold, diamond ring. It didn't exactly scream 'wow' when Neil first opened the box, but it was nice enough.

"Surprise!" Neil had exclaimed as the taxi pulled up outside the West Tower, a forty-storey tall skyscraper which is home to one of Liverpool's most swanky restaurants on the thirty-fourth floor.

"We're not abseiling down it, are we?" I asked, looking up at the majestic building, which made me go a bit dizzy.

"Ha! Not today. Now come on, let's get you in." Neil wrapped an arm around my shoulders and ushered me inside the building, and to the lifts.

There's no going back now, Isme, I thought, as the doors to the lift slowly closed on us and we began to ascend. I watched as the numbers on the screen creeped up and up, my tummy bubbling each time they did. An unexpected image of Anthony popped into my head, and I suddenly longed to be with him in the safety of his bedroom watching repeat episodes of *Schitt's Creek*.

After what felt like for ever, we finally reached floor thirty-four, and as the doors to the lift opened, we were greeted by the pleasing savoury aroma wafting through from the kitchen and an overly smiley hostess. She took our coats and ushered us to our table, right by the window, the view almost taking my breath away. The late afternoon sky was a burnt orange, casting a warm glow over the city's skyline, highlighting its iconic buildings.

I could have sat there looking out all night, especially with the gentle sound of instrumental music playing in the background. When I did peel my eyes away, Neil was already out of his seat and kneeling down next to me, holding a small black box. I had no idea how long he'd been there but was very conscious of the silence that had descended across the restaurant, and the many eyes on us.

"Isme, will you do me the honour of becoming my wife?"

A million thoughts whizzed through my head at that moment. *Couldn't he at least have waited until we'd ordered our food? ... Please don't let there be anyone in here that I know . . . I wonder if anyone will notice if I just slowly slide under the table? . . .* But at the very forefront of my thoughts was Dad lying helpless in the hospital bed after the heart attack, his arms bruised and bloodied from all the needles and tubes they'd had to poke and prod him with.

"This is the part where you say yes," Neil whispered impatiently.

Before I knew it, I found myself saying, "Oh, er, yeah, go on ... I mean, yes! Yes, I'll marry you."

*

> **Isme:** Hey, I've tried calling you loads but it keeps going straight to voicemail

> **Anthony:** Sorry, yeah. I'm on that conference with work and the reception is crap
> What's up?

> **Isme:** Nothing, really. Just wanted to talk to you

> **Anthony:** Well I'm back tomorrow, so I'll see you at your dad's hospital discharge celebration thing

*

I knew as soon as we pulled up outside Mum and Dad's and saw the many cars lined up along the road and banners on the door, that telling them about the engagement was not going to go as planned. What I'd thought was going to be an intimate family gathering for Dad coming out of hospital had transcended into a full-blown party.

Mum had invited everyone from church including Father Demetrios, who looked like he was ready to break out into a rap in his very snazzy gold-trimmed black vestment and oversized gold cross and chain. She'd even invited the old fella that stands outside church during Sunday mass and keeps an eye on your car in return for a few quid. We never used him, I think Dad would have paid him to *make* our tin on wheels disappear.

"You could have told me all these people were coming," I said to Mum, smiling through gritted teeth, once we were inside and had endured all initial pleasantries. Most of these consisted of the same round of awkward questions: "When you getting married?" "When you have thee kids?" "When you have more kids?"

"I want it to be a surprise for your papa," she said, her eyes already taking on an alcohol-induced glaze. She was holding a tray of ouzo which, if it wasn't for Neil standing next to me staring at it and looking as tense as Donald Trump's lawyer, I would have downed the lot.

"Why you look so miserable, Isme?" she said, squeezing a cheek which made my jaw throb. "You have thee lovely Neil here, you have nothing to be sad about. Now go, get a drink. Ah Zorba's dance! Higher, Maria, higher!"

Mum formed a circle with a few of her GWAGS and they started shuffling from side to side to the rhythm of the *bouzouki*, people's dull chatter turning to claps and cheers.

I could have throttled her for not giving me the heads up on the party, but it *was* nice to see her enjoying herself after months of stress and worry. Dad, on the other hand, looked just as pleased as I was at the unexpected soiree when I found him in the corner of the room attempting to camouflage himself behind a yucca plant.

Maria was standing next to him holding a large glass of wine, which looked like it belonged to the BFG. George had been left at home to look after the twins, which was a welcome relief – the last thing I needed was that idiot and his inevitable sarcastic comments about my hasty engagement.

"I'm glad there's so many people here to hear the news," whispered Neil, as we picked at some food from the buffet, which largely consisted of Costco sandwich platters and crisps.

I smiled wearily at the familiar, and some not so familiar, sea of faces, trying to reassure myself that it was all going to be fine, as I chewed half my nails off. But when I caught sight of Sandra coming through to the front room, followed by a clean-shaven and smartly dressed Anthony, my heart sank.

Anthony smiled over in my direction, and I responded with a pathetic little half wave. I needed to get to him before the announcement, but just as I started to make my way over, Neil pulled me back.

"CLINK, CLINK, CLINK. Could I command everyone's attention, please."

The whole room descended into silence. I couldn't look at Anthony. My heart was beating so fast inside my chest I thought it might pop out.

"Sorry, I know this may seem a little strange, especially as most of you won't know who I am, well, not yet anyway. I'm Neil, Isme's better half. I haven't known the Eliades family long, four months to be exact – but in that short space of time they've really welcomed me into the family which, for someone who grew up without much family around, well, it . . . it really means a lot."

His voice trailed off and, to my horror, he looked like he was going to cry. I looked over at Mum, who was clutching at her chest and wiping away tears with a tissue, like she was watching Barack Obama's inaugural address.

"Anyway, I just wanted to say thank you and how happy we all are that Stephen is back on the mend." Neil lifted up his glass of lemonade. "To Stephen! Or, should I say, Father-in-Law."

Dad's eyebrows dropped halfway down his face as he looked from Neil to me. The only response I could muster came in the form of a nervous grin.

"Yep, that's right." Neil turned to face the room again, then said in a booming voice, "Me and Isme are engaged!"

I jerked as the whole room erupted into a chorus of cheers and claps. The next ten minutes became a blur of bear hugs, words of congratulations and showing of the ring, which was welcomed with lots of 'oooh's and 'aaaaah's.

Mum was bouncing around so much I was worried she might spontaneously combust, whilst Dad hugged me gently and said, "So long as you're happy, love." It was a question more than a statement.

I caught sight of Anthony, who was gawping at Neil, his jaw trailing the floor.

Maria, who had resumed the same spot next to Dad through-out the whole thing, her facial expression unwavering from mystified, sidled up to me and whispered, "I think you've made a mistake."

Those words stayed with me the rest of the night, especially when, after the immediate post-announcement chaos had quietened down, I went to find Anthony to explain that I *had* tried to tell him first, only to be told by Sandra that he'd already left.

*

"Go on then, let's see the ring."

I slid my hand across the pub table. Anthony leant forward to get a closer look.

"I always thought you wanted a gold ring with an emerald stone?"

I sighed. "Yeah, well, beggars can't be choosers when you're getting a family hand-me-down. It was his nan's, apparently." I fiddled with the ring, twisting it from side to side, wondering when I might get used to wearing it.

"Bet that's saved him a few bob then, jammy bastard."

"Ha, yeah I know."

Anthony ran his hands around the rim of his beer glass, seemingly deep in thought. There was something off about his demeanour, almost melancholy.

"You OK?"

"Yeah, sorry. Just tired, with work and stuff." Anthony forced a smile. "I'm happy for you, really I am."

"Buuuuut . . . ?"

"Nothing, it's just . . ." Anthony chewed his upper lip. "Are you sure about this? About Neil?"

I looked into the familiar brown eyes of my best friend, the one person who knew me inside and out and who I could always rely on to be brutally honest if I was doing something stupid. I wanted to tell him that no, I absolutely wasn't sure. In fact, I'd never been this unsure about anything since making my *X-Factor* final vote and choosing Matt Cardle instead of One Direction, and had spent the last week since saying yes with a gut-wrenching feeling in the pit of my stomach telling me it's a big, fat, ugly mistake.

But I forced myself to think about Mum and Dad and how it was going to save the family home, and the feeling eased. Still uncomfortable but manageable, like a mild bout of trapped wind.

Thankfully, my phone rang before I could answer. It was Neil.

Neil: "Hey, I'm just at the shop. Do you want me to pick up some ingredients for a tofu salad for tea tonight?"

Me: "Erm, yeah. Sounds delightful."

Anthony pretended to bork, which made me giggle.

Neil: "What's so funny?"

Me: "Sorry, nothing. So, about this salad?"

"Another drink?" whispered Anthony, but loud enough for Neil to hear.

Neil: "Is that Anthony?"

Me: "Yeah, I've just met him for a quick drink on my lunch."

The line suddenly went dead, and I wondered whether Neil had buttoned me.

Me: "Neil, are you still there?"

Neil: "Yeah, I'm here. You know what, I might go to the gym later instead. I'll call you tomorrow."

*

Mum: Isme, we need to talk about the party 🎉 🎉

Isme: What party?

Mum: The engagement party, koumera!
We need to organise

Isme: I'm not having an engagement party.
No chance, sorry

Mum: Is tradition, Isme. You know that
You remember Maria's, when everybody
was throwing money at them while her
and George did the Syrtos dance?

Isme: So, what date were you thinking?

*

After getting inundated by Mum on WhatsApp with pictures of various venues for the engagement party which she deemed suitable – not because of their ability to cater for the ridiculous number of people she was inviting or their good drink selection, but because they were all Greek restaurants owned by people she knew from the church (God forbid we hold an Eliades family gathering anywhere else) – we settled on Stavros's restaurant.

"Three shots of ouzo for my favourite customers!" said Stavros, placing the shot glasses on the table. "And for giving me the honour of hosting your engagement party, which was a lovely surprise." He winked at Mum, who not-so-subtly winked back – she can't quite close her eye so just ends up looking like she's had a stroke.

They couldn't be any less obvious and had clearly agreed on it weeks ago.

Mum and Maria downed their ouzo shots without a second thought, as I opted for a sip of my soda water instead. Maria eyed my full shot glass suspiciously.

"Hang on a minute, you're drinking soda water, and you're not touching your ouzo?" Her eyes diverted down to my stomach area. "Iz, you're not, are you?"

Mum's eyes almost popped out of her head when she realised what Maria was getting at. "ISMEENA ELIADES, IF YOU HAVE BABY BEFORE MARRIAGE I SWEAR BY THE PATRON SAINT OF IRENE—"

"Will you two chill, I am NOT pregnant." Far from it, I wanted to add, but TMI. "I'm trying to be more aware of what I'm putting into my body, that's all. Speaking of which, Mum, will you ask Stavros if he can do a vegan option for the buffet?"

Mum and Maria looked at each other for a moment then burst into a fit of giggles.

"I'm being serious, you two. A lot of people are turning to veganism these days. It's good for the mind *and* the body."

"Who the fuck are you and what have you done with my sister?" said Maria, wiping her wet eyes with a napkin.

"I told you, I'm just trying to make better life choices."

"Isme, being vegan is not life choice," scoffed Mum, reaching over for my ouzo, "is an autoimmune condition." She lifted up the shot glass. "*Yamas.*"

*

Isme: Mum, have you sorted what you're going to cook for Neil later when we come round with Joan for dinner?

Mum: Yes yes Isme, is all sorted 👍

Isme: And you're absolutely sure it's going to be vegan-friendly?

Mum: Ochi, Isme, stop worrying!
I make something very special for Neil.
He is going to love it 😊

"Is that . . . what I think it is?" said Neil with pursed lips as he caught sight of the dining table, which was so crammed with food I wondered when the rest of the disciples were coming. Taking centre stage was a whole roasted salmon, head and eyes still intact.

"Yes! Isme tell me you don't eat meat, so I make you some fish. Is very good quality too," said Mum, grinning and winking in my direction.

Joan and Neil burst out laughing, much to Mum's confusion. I *had* explained to her on many occasions that vegans also don't eat fish, but she refused to believe me. The concept of someone not eating any kind of living creature to her is like telling the Pope there's no such thing as God.

"Oh, so you aren't joking," said Neil once the laughter subsided and he noticed Mum's confused expression.

"You no like?"

"It's not that I don't like it, Elana, I choose not to eat it. They're two very different things."

"It's OK, Neil, I'm sure there's something here you can eat," said Joan cheerily, peering around the table. "There's bread, and salad and—"

"Let's just eat, shall we, before everything goes cold," said Dad impatiently, plonking himself into a chair and sticking his spoon into the Greek lamb stew, the savoury smell of it making my mouth water. But just as Dad was about to tuck in, Joan took one of my hands in hers and insisted we say Grace.

Mum, who looked a bit put out by the unexpected takeover of her dinner party, forced a smile and said, "Greek Orthodox don usually say prayers before meals, Joan, unless thee priest here."

"Oh, I see," said Joan, retaining her grip on my hand. "It's only that Neil and I have always said Grace before our meals, regardless of where we are, so if you wouldn't mind . . ." Joan signalled to Mum's hands, and, after a lengthy pause, Mum reluctantly took it and closed her eyes.

"So, have you thought about where you might have the ceremony?" asked Joan, once Grace was over and we started tucking into the food. "You know I can put a good word in with Father Paul at our local church – he baptised Neil, so I'm sure he'd be delighted to hear that he'll be marrying him as well."

Mum held her forkful of lamb stew in mid-air and slowly turned her head to look at Joan. "Isme is Greek Orthodox, Joan, so she get married in thee Greek church."

Joan shook her head. "I'm afraid that's just not going to be possible, Elana. Father Paul will insist on them getting married in the Catholic church."

I slunk down into my chair. There was only one way this battle of the religions was going to go. I looked over at Neil to give him a what-the-fuck-do-we-do-here look, but he was busy removing any bits of feta from his plate of salad.

"Isme, no get married in an English Catholic church," cried Mum, her voice going up an octave. She was wafting her cutlery in the air, which I feared might soon become a weapon. "She is Greek Orthodox, so she get married in thee Greek church."

Joan tutted loudly. "Neil is Catholic, so why should he be the one to conform to *your* religious beliefs?"

"He is Greek too, no? So why he baptised Catholic? It make no sense?"

Joan slammed her cutlery down on her plate, which made us all jump. When she spoke, her voice was low and gravely. "He is only Greek by blood, his father's blood, and that man ruined our lives. When he left . . ." Joan's voice trailed off and she dabbed at her eyes with a tissue, although I couldn't see any visible tears. I was starting to doubt the sincerity of these outbursts whenever Neil's father was mentioned.

Neil, who finally seemed to be aware of what was going on, placed a hand over Joan's, stood up and cleared his throat.

"Look, I've been giving all of this some thought, because I knew it was going to be an issue. At the end of the day, we have to be respectful of both religions, so with this in mind I took it upon myself to meet with Father Demetrious and Father Paul."

I sat bolt upright. "Er, when were you going to speak to me about this?"

"You've been busy with work, and I didn't want to bother you with it all."

"Bother me with it? Neil, it is my wedding as well, you know."

"She has got a point, lad. You should have spoken to Isme first." I smiled gratefully at Dad. "If there's one thing I've learnt after all these years of being married it's that—"

"Just let him finish, Stephen," said Mum, wafting a hand in the air.

"Thank you, Elana," sighed Neil. "Anyway, after a lengthy discussion, I'm pleased to say they've both given their blessing to us having two ceremonies – one in the Greek church and the other in the Catholic church."

Mum clapped her hands and Joan did the sign of the cross. Dad and I slumped back into our seats like two stroppy teenagers.

The mood in the room soon lifted and polite conversation continued. I sat quietly back and reflected on the fact that I'd been unsure if I'd wanted one wedding, yet somehow, I'd just ended up with two.

*

Agnes: Hullo! Long time no see! How are ya?

Isme: *sends photo of engagement ring*

Agnes: 💍 FUCK OFF! Is that an engagement ring?!

Isme: I'm afraid so 😩

Agnes: NO FUCKING WAY! Who's the lucky fella?
Is it that Anthony one you were always talking about?

Isme: Ha! No, it's someone I met in Cyprus on a
baking course. His name's Neil

Agnes: Right, we need to celebrate.
Clear your diary tomorrow.
Aggy is coming to town! 🎉 🍷

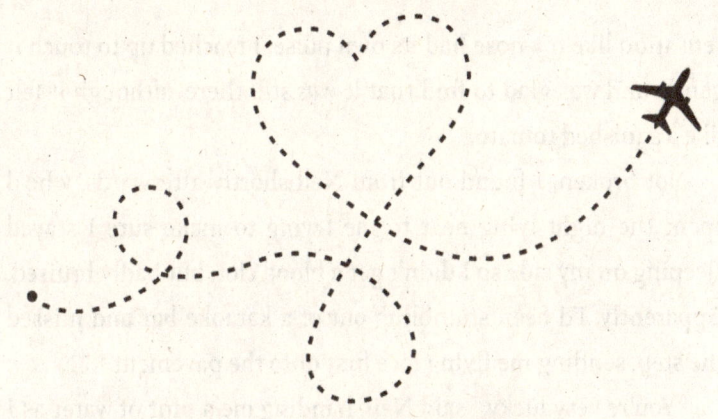

OCTOBER

I'D HAD MY LION'S SHARE OF MORNING-AFTER-THE-
night-before flaps. Mostly it's like playing a game of Cluedo,
trying to piece together the night, knowing in my gut that
somewhere along the way I'd made a tit of myself; running
through the streets with a traffic cone on my head, or pressing
my chest up against the kebab shop window in the hope they'd
give me a free chicken shish because I'd run out of cash (both true
stories, unfortunately).

But waking up this morning after my night out with Agnes and
finding splatters of blood on my white cami top was a first. The
very sight of it sent me into a wave of panic, a million questions
running through my thumping head. Was it *my* blood? If not,
whose blood was it?

I broke into a cold sweat. That's when I felt it, a throbbing sensation like my nose had its own pulse. I reached up to touch it gently and was glad to find that it *was* still there, although it felt like a squished tomato.

Not broken, I found out from Neil shortly afterwards, who'd spent the night lying next to me trying to make sure I stayed sleeping on my side so I didn't get a blood clot, but badly bruised. Apparently, I'd been stumbling out of a karaoke bar and missed the step, sending me flying face first onto the pavement.

"You're very lucky," said Neil, handing me a pint of water as I lay in bed, which I took off him gratefully with trembling hands. "It could have been a lot worse. You could have had concussion and ended up in a coma."

I took a sip of the water, which lingered at the back of my throat threatening to come back up.

"I remember the very last time I had a drink before I went into rehab," he said, sitting down on the edge of the bed. "I'd been out on an all-day drinking session with some friends, but we all got split up as the day went on and I somehow ended up on my own. Rather than take myself home and admit defeat, I stumbled into some old man's pub and found myself downing shots of whisky at the bar like water." He paused, picking on some loose skin on the palm of one of his hands. I felt bad for inadvertently making him relive what was clearly a painful memory. "Anyway, they had to kick me out, but when I stood up to leave, I lost my footing and ended up smacking my head against the bar. I ended up in hospital for a week with concussion. That's when I knew enough was enough."

"I'm not an alcoholic, Neil," I said defensively.

He placed a hand over mine. "I'm not suggesting you are. I'm just saying I know the signs, and it's a slippery slope." He stood up. "I'll go and make us some coffee. Come out when you're ready."

I closed my eyes and sighed, gently rubbing at my sore nose. Maybe laying off the booze for a bit wouldn't be such a bad thing, at least not until the engagement party.

"Ag? I didn't realise you were here?" I stumbled into the living room to find Agnes sitting on the sofa next to Neil, holding her head in her hands while Neil rubbed her back. She looked up at the sound of my voice, her face looking just as rough as mine, minus the squished nose and scratches.

"Is everything OK?" I said, looking from Neil to Agnes and back again.

"Aye, just a bit of the morning-after-the-night-before blues, ha!" Agnes dabbed at her wet eyes with a tissue and stood up. "Shit, Iz, ye look like shite!"

I smiled sheepishly. "You want a coffee?"

"Nah, I were just leaving. I'll be in Liverpool for the week, Izzy lass, so I'll see you before I leave, OK?"

I nodded.

"I'll walk you out, Agnes." I watched as Neil ushered Agnes out, one arm around her waist and the other holding her arm like he was taking an OAP to the shops. They stopped at the door talking in hushed tones, then Neil handed her a small piece of paper, which Ag took from him gratefully.

"What was all that about?" I asked once she'd gone.

Neil let out a heavy sigh. "Just another one who needed to see the light."

I shrugged my shoulders and stumbled back to bed, unable to process what had just happened but convinced it was the hangover fog playing tricks on me.

*

"An alcoholic, Agnes, really?"

"Aye, known for ages, like. Just been in denial."

"Shit." I took a long, drawn-out sip of my coffee as I tried digesting Agnes's words. It was her last day in Liverpool before heading back to Glasgow and she'd asked me to meet her in Starbucks, to which I'd replied, "Since when did Starbucks get an alcohol licence?!"

Little did I know.

"It's called a functioning alcoholic, apparently. At least, that's what Neil told me." Agnes circled the rim of her coffee cup and stared into it with a strained look. "You know, if it wasn't for me talking to that laddie of yours the morning after our night out last week and him making me realise I had a drinking problem, I reckon I'd be in an early grave from liver failure."

A sudden wave of guilt washed over me. Surely, as her friend, I should have been the one to realise how I'd never actually seen her *without* a drink in her hand. I had always wondered why her cheeks were permanently flushed.

"I'm so sorry, Ag. I should have realised."

"What ye sorry for?! It's my own fecking fault." Agnes placed a hand over mine and leant forward in her chair. "Ye got a good one there, Iz. Don't lose him now, will ye. Team Neisme all the way!'

I smiled. It was a welcome relief having someone actually sing his praises for a change.

As I wandered home afterwards, I thought back to the pros and cons list I'd made a month ago, making a mental note to add onto the pros list 'saved my friend's life'.

Surely that trumps all the cons?

*

I hadn't seen Joan since the meal at Mum's, and would have kept it that way for as long as I could get away with to avoid any more questions about the wedding. But my time was up: it was her birthday and Neil had summoned me to her house after work.

Neil was running late from work – or running from work, I couldn't quite remember – leaving me to work my way through some 'small' talk while we waited for him.

"So, Isme, have you decided on buffet options for the engagement party yet?"

"Yeah, nearly. Just got to agree some prices with Stavros."

Lie number one. The truth was, Mum was adamant she wanted to be in charge of the food options, but flat-out refused to cater for the vegans, or bunny huggers as Dad called them. So I just needed to come up with a way of throwing some vegan-friendly options in there without her knowing.

"And what about the wedding; how are the plans coming along there?"

I took a sip of my tea to drench my dry throat before answering. "Erm yeah, I've started a spreadsheet listing out all the things we need to sort and how much they're going to cost."

Lie number two. I'd Googled 'wedding checklist' after watching an episode of *Don't Tell the Bride* one night, resulting in a mini panic attack at the realisation that there was a ridiculous amount of shit that needed sorting for a wedding, and it was all going to cost a bomb. I'd been too scared to open my laptop again since.

"Oh, Isme, you're so sensible," said Joan, placing a hand over mine. "Neil told me about talking you out of a career in baking – that must have been hard, but Neil is right. You really can't afford a drop in income now."

I smiled through gritted teeth. "Well, I'm not going to give up on it completely, it's just not the right time."

"Happy birthday, Mum!" Neil came bursting into the living room, handing Joan a bunch of brightly coloured lilies and kissed her gently on the top of her head. Joan took them from him gratefully, her face beaming.

"Oh, son, these are absolutely beautiful!" she said, sticking her nose in the middle of them and taking a whiff. "They must have cost a fortune."

"Nothing less than you deserve."

Their little exchange gave me a bit of a warm fuzzy feeling inside, and I couldn't help but smile.

'Our' present turned out to be a spa day at a swanky hotel in town for three people, which was a pleasant surprise. OK, third-wheeling with your boyfriend and his mum wasn't exactly ideal, but who could resist those lovely warm, soft dressing gowns they give you that feel like you're wearing a cloud, not to mention a relaxing head, neck and shoulder massage?

My joy was short-lived though, when Neil revealed he'd bought it for me, Joan and Mum so we could 'get to know each other a bit more and talk weddings and stuff'.

I saw a hint of disappointment in Joan's face, and I couldn't blame her. I'd done a spa day with Mum once before and it was about as relaxing as a root canal at the dentist. This is the woman whose idea of relaxing is clearing out the garage or defrosting the freezer.

*

"Why couldn't she just type it up and email it over?" I asked Dad, when he turned up to the flat with a list of buffet options for the party from Mum that, unsurprisingly, had no mention of any vegan-friendly choices. I wouldn't get any sympathy off Dad though – he's more carnivorous than a lion. "Or you, now you're a whizz on the computer after that course you did."

Dad's cheeks flushed pink, and he muttered something about forgetting half the stuff they taught him after the heart attack, whilst clutching at his chest – he could still get a bit breathless from time to time, which the doctor assured him was perfectly normal.

"Do you want to stay for tea, Dad? Neil's out picking something up, there'll be plenty to go around." It was a risky move, having Dad and Neil together in such close proximity, but I had to at least *try* and make them get along.

Dad hesitated, but then said, "Yeah I suppose I could stay for a bit."

"What's this we're having then?" asked Dad, peering over

Neil's shoulder once he arrived home and started placing the takeaway boxes on the dining table.

"Goan style tofu curry with kitchari, with a side of squash and cabbage sabzi," declared Neil proudly. "Or, in your case, Stephen, anti-heart attack food, haha!"

Dad glared down at the food like he'd been presented with a plate of dog food. "To-what-now?"

"Tofu, Stephen, also known as bean curd," said Neil, his tone a little impatient. "It's used a lot in vegan recipes as a meat substitute. So much better for you. You, of all people, should know this. Didn't the doctors in the hospital give you any diet advice?"

Dad placed his knife and fork down firmly, but gently. "Yes, they did, thank you, Neil. But they didn't say anything about eating bean turd."

"It's curd," muttered Neil through gritted teeth, his nostrils flaring. "Bean *curd*."

Thankfully a call came through on Dad's phone, breaking up the awkward tofu stand-off, and he left shortly after, blaming a panicked Mum on the other end of the line. Apparently he'd forgotten to take his blood pressure medication.

"That's odd, I'm sure I saw the name Carol pop up on the screen when it was ringing," said Neil after he was gone and we were tidying up the plates.

"Nah, you must have got it wrong," I said, scooping Dad's uneaten plate of curry into the bin, ignoring the heavy sigh from Neil as I did. "Why would he lie about who was ringing? Plus, he doesn't know anyone called Carol."

Neil shrugged his shoulders. "Just telling you what I saw."

As Neil disappeared into the bathroom, I grabbed my phone.

Isme: Do you know anyone called Carol?

Maria: Carol Vordemon? Carol Burnett?

Isme: No, like actual people, stupid arse

Maria: Last time I checked they were
actual people, stupid arse

Isme: OK, let me rephrase. Have you ever
heard Dad talk about anyone called Carol?

Maria: Nope, don't think so.
Only when he's watching Countdown

I plonked myself down onto the sofa and sighed as I thought back to the night before Dad's heart attack in Cyprus, when I'd caught him on the phone in the bathroom. Any suspicions I'd had about Dad having an affair had been put to the back of my mind with everything that had happened since that night, yet here they were, rearing their ugly head again.

*

Agnes: Looking forward to a catch-up with team
Neisme later! The coffees are on me x

Neil bailed on me at the eleventh hour, something to do with a hold up at work. I tended to go a bit brain dead when he talked shop – I'd always thought quantity surveyors just walked around newly constructed buildings wearing a hard hat and high-vis jacket, ticking off boxes on a clipboard, but apparently there's a lot more to it than that.

"Just let Aggy know I'm really sorry and I'll catch up with her soon, OK? I really need to get to the bottom of these unexplained outgoings." If he was as thorough with his own finances as he was with his work projects, then I was never letting him see my online banking. It looked like something off *The Matrix*, except the numbers were mostly negative.

Luckily for him, Agnes thinks the sun shines out of his arse, so she didn't seem too put out by his absence. She must have told me at least three times in the first ten minutes how much of a 'good laddie' he was.

Agnes looked . . . well, almost unrecognisable. There was a glow to her complexion, and her short black hair, which I only ever remember seeing tied up in a bun, sat loose on her shoulders, glistening from the rays of sun that filtered through the window of the cafe.

"You look great, Ag! Positively glowing." I leant in towards her and whispered, "You're not up the duff, are ya?"

Agnes nearly choked on her latte. "Aye, right! There's more chance o' me climbin Ben Nevis in nuthin but ma pants!"

I chuckled. Drunk or sober, the girl was a howl.

As she filled me in on her 'journey to sobriety', which included

a lot of 'fooks' in between sentences I struggled to understand –
I always need an hour or two to warm up to her broad Scottish
accent after seeing her again – I couldn't help but feel a moment
of appreciation for Neil and his alcoholic-dar. I was about to
send him an averagely soppy text when Agnes revealed that, as
a surprise, he'd arranged for us to go and visit a bridal shop so I
could try on some dresses.

I began furiously typing.

> **Isme:** I hope you've managed to get to the bottom
> of those outgoings, you lying bugger

> **Neil:** 😁😁😁

The bridal shop was a short walk from the coffee shop, and
one that I've passed many a time on my lunch break and vowed
never to step foot in. It's like the TK Maxx of bridal shops, with
big ugly sale signs plastered all over the shop front, and inside,
endless rows of big clunky dresses squeezed onto rails, making
the place smell musty.

"I honestly don't know where to start," I muttered as I stood
staring at the sea of dresses, like a mountain climber about to
tackle Everest. Agnes looked just as bewildered, and together we
stood there like two aliens entering a new world.

"Are you Isme?" We both jolted at the sound of a woman's
voice from behind and turned round to find the source – a woman
with short blonde hair and a sour expression.

"Aye, this is she," Agnes said, when I struggled to find my voice.

"OK, come with me. Your fiancé has already picked a dress out for you."

"He's WHAT?" My jaw almost fell to the floor. I turned to Agnes for some solidarity of Neil's exercise of control, but she was almost in tears at the gesture. I had no choice but to follow the shop lady to the back of the room to the changing room.

"Give me a shout when you've got it on," said the woman, before pulling the curtain across.

The dress was hung up in a clothes bag, and I knew within the first few pulls of the zip that it wasn't the dress for me. For starters, it was silky and fitted, two things that should be avoided at all costs for a woman of my shape. Then there were the straps, two pieces of flimsy string that would have a tough job keeping my double Ds intact. I'd never given much thought to what I wanted my wedding dress to look like, but I knew this wasn't it.

Reluctantly, I took off my clothes and placed the nightie-dress over my head, the material sticking to my clammy skin like glue. Unsurprisingly, it got stuck at my hip area and I tried squeezing it down with all my might, trying not to rip it in the process – the last thing I needed was to have to fork out my entire month's wages on the thing – but it wouldn't budge.

"Everything OK in there?" came the voice of the shop lady outside.

"Yeah, I'm just struggling to get it on . . ."

"That's strange, we've never had a problem with other girls trying it on. If anything, it's always a bit big."

You've never had a Greek woman with good childbearing hips try it on, I wanted to shout, but she didn't look the type for banter.

Instead, I changed back into my clothes, thanked her for her time and got out of there quicker than you can say 'I do'.

*

"So, what did you think?" asked Neil, back at the flat later on.

"Not really my style. More suited to a stick-thin model."

"Come on, I'm sure it looked great."

"Neil, I couldn't even get the thing over my arse!"

"Well, you keep saying you need to start eating better and exercising more. So, maybe this is the motivation you need."

I eyed him suspiciously. Had he purposefully picked out that dress to force me into losing weight?

"Anyway, Agnes told me to give you this," I said, handing him the dark green envelope that Agnes had given me earlier on. "She said it was for the both of us as a thank you to you *and* an engagement present."

I watched with anticipation as he opened it at an annoyingly slow speed, pulling out what appeared to be a postcard. On the front was an idyllic picture of a castle set back from a clear blue lake, surrounded by immaculate green lawns and trees, standing tall over the castle like protective guards. He turned it over to find a note from Agnes which read: 'I hope you love Loch Lomond as much as I do x', followed by details of a hotel paid for us to spend a night.

"How lovely is that!" I gasped, taking the postcard from Neil's hands to have a closer look. I could feel the excitement building as I pictured us lazing around on a picnic blanket on the grass outside the castle, bees buzzing around us, the late autumn sun beaming down as we watched the boats gliding past and . . .

"Oh my God! This place has the *best* watersports facility, like, the best in the UK! We could go scuba diving and jet skiing! I need to ring Aggy and thank her!"

I stared in disbelief as Neil hot-footed it off the sofa and into the kitchen to grab his phone, my vision of a relaxing romantic getaway now feeling about as probable as Aggy's naked mountain climb.

*

Isme: Maria, where are you? Are you OK?
Maria, where the hell are you? George is here and we're both worried sick

Maria: What, he's at your flat?

Isme: Yeah, he came round hoping you were here after you didn't go home last night. He's in a right state

Maria: Serves him right, the useless shit
Tell him I'm fine and I'll be home soon

"Thank God for that," sighed George, as I relayed Maria's messages to him. He walked over from the kitchen, where he'd been annoyingly pacing up and down since arriving, and slouched himself down onto the one-seater sofa. "Did she say where she'd been?"

I shook my head.

We sat in silence for a bit, which felt weird. We'd always been able to fill any moments of hush, usually by me tearing a strip out of George for his poor husband skills, or him making sly comments about my lifestyle. Without the desire for either of those things, we had nothing else to say to each other. For once, though, we were in agreement over something, and that was that Maria was bang out of order for not going home the night before.

"I've been trying, Isme, honestly I have," said George, as if reading my mind. "I've been doing more around the house and have been having the twins more to give her a break. Don't laugh, but I've even been taking salsa lessons on the sly because she's always said she'd love a man who could dance."

I couldn't hold back the smirk on my face at the thought of George giving it the bifters to 'Livin La Vida Loca'.

"I'm trying everything, but it's like nothing is good enough for her. It's like—" his voice broke off, and his eyes started to well up, "it's like she's given up on us."

He buried his head in his hands and his shoulders started to shake.

"Look, I'll try and talk to her, OK?" I said, handing him a tissue and saving any awkwardness of a hug. "I can't promise anything, like, but I'll try."

He blew his nose loudly into the tissue. "Thanks, Isme. I really appreciate it."

After he left, I called Maria. As much as I didn't want to get involved in their marital affairs, a promise was a promise.

"So, where were you then?"

"I just went out with some mates, had one too many shots and ended up crashing on one of their sofas. No biggie."

"Yeah, OK, but maybe next time just let your husband know you're OK?"

"Since when did you start taking George's side?"

"I'm not taking any side. I'm just saying it doesn't do any harm to let him know you're staying out."

"OK, Mum. Can I go now, please?"

After the call ended, I stared out of the flat window wondering how I seemed to have become the sensible Sally/marriage councillor of the Eliades family. It was only six months ago that *I* would have been the one downing shots and making terrible decisions, while Maria looked on with consternation.

It felt like that film *Freaky Friday* and me and Maria had swapped lives (internally pushing away any thoughts of shagging George), and soon enough everything would revert back to the way it was. Whether that was something I wanted to happen, I wasn't quite sure. I had a lot of respect for the present-day Isme. She was fit(ish), healthy(ish), worked hard(ish), and could say things like, 'Have you got a vegan menu?' without feeling like a complete tit.

Whether I *liked* her was another question altogether.

*

Isme: Do you want me to have the twins

at the weekend? Give you and George a
chance to talk and sort your shit out

Maria: Is the Pope a Catholic?
What time can I drop them off?

Neil wasn't thrilled about our weekend of responsibilities. He'd
only met the twins once, and it had ended with them shouting
"POO-POO HEAD!" and blowing wet raspberries in his face.
I told him that *will* happen when you kneel down to their level
and tried to engage in small talk.

I couldn't say I was jumping for joy myself, even though it *was*
me who'd offered, especially after another oppressively manic
week in work. But I had to think of the bigger picture: Theo and
Tomaso seeing their mum and dad like this, not to mention how
Mum would cope if Maria and George's marriage broke down – she
prides herself on the fact that Greeks have the lowest divorce rate
in Europe and likes to occasionally remind me and Maria of this.

I would have thought Neil of all people would understand,
though, given how he was brought up in a broken home.

"But I wanted us to go to Loch Lomond this weekend," he
whined after I broke the news. "We need to use the voucher by the
end of the month, plus most of the watersports will be finishing
soon for the winter season."

I smirked. Now that *was* a shame. "Look, if it was *your* sister's
marriage on the brink, wouldn't you want to do anything to help?"

He sighed, folding his arms like a stroppy teenager. "I just don't see why we have to sacrifice our weekend. Plus, the kids need some stability now more than ever, and I can't see how palming them off is going to help the situation. As for their marriage being on the rocks, haven't they heard of marriage counselling?"

I didn't bother getting into Mum's views on marriage counselling. We didn't have all night.

*

I hadn't even had time to have a wee when I got home from work and Maria was already banging on the door like a debt collector. She flung the twins and their rucksacks inside, reeled off some instructions and scarpered, shouting "FREEDOM!" and waving her arms in the air as she went.

No sooner had I shut the door then the twins had already discarded their coats and shoes, and were treating the sofa like a climbing frame. "Right, who's hungry? I've got your favourite, turkey dinosaurs and chips, then for afters—"

Theo stopped mid-climb. "We don't like turkey dinosaurs any more."

"Since when?" They both shrugged their shoulders and then continued their climb-a-thon. "Oh, er, right, OK. How about pizza, then? You do still like pizza, right?"

They looked at each other as if telepathically discussing whether pizza was a good enough option, before nodding in agreement.

I clapped my hands. "OK, great! Then after tea I've got us some yoghurts and then we'll watch a film—"

"Are they the Peppa Pig ones you gave us last time?" This from Tomaso.

"No, they didn't have those ones in the supermarket," I said, my palms beginning to sweat under the pressure of these two demanding little humans. "They're just the supermarket's own brand..."

"But they're the *only* ones we like." Tomaso stomped his foot on the sofa to emphasise his point.

I sighed. It had only been five minutes and I already wanted to give them back. Not wanting the weekend to get off on the wrong foot, I rang Neil and asked him to pick some of said yoghurts up on his way over.

"I'm so sorry, Isme, I was just about to call you. I'm not going to make it tonight after all. Something's come up with work and—"

"You're kidding, aren't you, Neil? You promised you'd help me put them to bed. Can't you get out of it?"

"I really wish I could, but I can't. I'll be round in the morning as early as possible though, to give you a hand . . . promise."

He hung up, leaving me staring at the phone wondering, with increasingly sweaty armpits, how I was going to break the news to the problem children that they would just have to make do with my no-frills yoghurts.

Isme: SOS
Babysitting the twins and need Peppa Pig yoghurts
or fear they might murder me in my sleep

Anthony: Sorry Isme, I was just on my way out

"UNCLE ISME, UNCLE ISME, THEO HAS DONE A POO-POO IN HIS PANTS!"

> **Isme:** Could you at least come over and give
> me a hand? Pleeeeeaaaassseee!

*

"Do you think it's possible to get an IV drip of wine?" I said to Anthony, who arrived just as I'd finished dealing with the poo carnage, which left me with PTSD. Trying to pull Theo's underpants off without getting a trail of poo juice down his legs was bad enough, but then trying to scoop it out was just plain wrong.

"You've only had them for a few hours!" laughed Anthony, as he prepared the pizzas for tea. "How come steg he— sorry, *Neil* hasn't come to help?"

I sighed. "Don't ask."

The twins ate most of the pizza and, after some initial sniff tests and more telepathic discussions, ate my own-brand yoghurts with minimal fuss. But with their messy table manners and never-ending questions, having dinner with them was about as enjoyable as waxing my bikini line.

"Where are we sleeping tonight?" asked Theo, wiping his tomato-splodged mouth with the back of his hand.

"In my bed, I'm going to sleep on the couch."

"With Anthony?" Theo smirked, and I felt the heat rise to my cheeks.

"No, I'm not staying, Theo. There isn't enough room."

I smiled at Anthony, grateful for his input with question time.

"Why is your flat so small?" said Tomaso, licking the pizza grease from his fingers.

"Because I couldn't afford anything bigger, now can we just eat our pizza—"

"Why?"

I closed my eyes and sighed. "Because, Tomaso, I've got a rubbish job. Now, let's finish eating so we can watch a film, eh? Or it might get too late." Thankfully my bribery worked, and they began shovelling their last few slices of pizza into their tiny mouths.

"Where are we going tomorrow?" asked Theo, revealing a mouth full of mushed up pizza, which turned my stomach.

I began clearing away the plates. "The park!" I said with as much excitement as I could muster.

"Why?"

BECAUSE WE JUST FUCKING ARE OK? NOW HURRY UP AND EAT YOUR PIZZA SO I CAN PUT YOU TO BED. I said this in my head of course, whilst smiling through gritted teeth and actually saying, "Because it will be fun!"

"We only sleep in our PJ Masks bedding," said Theo, wrinkling his nose, once we'd brushed their teeth and got them into their pyjamas, which in itself was like *Challenge Anneka.*

"Ah well, you see, this is magic bedding!" said Anthony, with animated eyes. "It turns into PJ Masks bedding, but only once you're asleep."

Theo and Tomaso looked from Anthony to me with puzzled expressions, and for a moment I thought he'd been rumbled. Then

Tomaso shouted, "I'm getting in first!" and climbed under the covers, closely followed by Theo.

I gave Anthony a congratulatory nod for his prompt improvisation before positioning myself on the bed on one side of the twins, Anthony on the other. Unexpectedly, they snuggled into us and rested their heads on our shoulders, sending a wave of warmth through my chest. I glanced over at Anthony, who looked just as touched, and we shared a smile.

Two hours later, after reading some book about a wonky donkey that had the four of us in stitches – although surprisingly didn't seem as funny after reading it four times over – three trips to the toilet, and umpteen requests for a snack, the twins finally closed their eyes and gave in to sleep.

As did me and Anthony.

*

"UNCLE ISME, UNCLE ISME, WAKE UP, WE'RE HUNGRY. WHAT'S FOR BREAKFAST?"

The sound of the twins shouting the odds jolted me from my sleep. I looked at the clock – 5.45 a.m. Were they messing? It was still the middle of the night. Also, why was I still fully clothed on top of the covers on the bed and not on the couch? A grumble from the other side of the bed confirmed my fears.

"SHIT, ANTHONY, WE MUST HAVE FALLEN ASLEEP." I hot-footed it off the bed, thoughts of Neil bursting in and getting the wrong impression sending a wave of panic through me.

"I know, I haven't slept that well in ages!" Anthony stretched out his arms and legs lazily.

"Ah, that's nice . . . now up, come on. You're gonna have to go."

"Why?"

"Because, because . . . it's late, and I've got stuff to do, and, and—"

"Oh, I see." Anthony hoisted himself up from the bed. He looked hurt, and I couldn't help feeling guilty. Anthony had stayed over in the flat loads of times before, so why should it be different now?

"You can stay and have some breakfast first though . . . if you want, like." I just had to hope that Neil's definition of 'early' was after eight a.m.

The four of us sat at the dining room table with our Cheerios, and it wasn't long before the Spanish inquisition started.

"I thought you weren't sleeping over?" said Tomaso, squinting his eyes at Anthony.

"I wasn't, but I fell asleep."

"Why?"

"Because Auntie Isme's bed is so comfortable." Anthony winked in my direction and heat rose to my cheeks.

"Why does your hair look like that?" said Theo, glaring up at my tangled mane.

"Because I haven't brushed it yet."

"Why?"

"Because it's reeeeally early in the morning. Anthony, have you finished those Cheerios yet?"

"When are we going to the park?"

I sighed impatiently. "Once we're ready, Theo, and Neil is here."

"WE DON'T WANT STINKY NEIL TO TAKE US, WE WANT

ANTHONY," cried Tomaso, stamping his foot on the floor, closely followed by Theo with "OH PLEASE, UNCLE ISME. PLEASE, PLEASE!"

Right on cue, I heard the key in the door and my heart sank. I jumped up from my seat, causing my half-eaten bowl of Cheerios to spill onto the table.

"MILK!" It was the only thing in my line of sight – that and Neil's sour expression as he caught sight of Anthony. "We needed milk for breakfast and Anthony was in the area so offered to bring some round."

But from Anthony's crumpled T-shirt and messy hair, it didn't take a genius to work out he'd stayed the night.

Neil frowned. "In the area at this time on a Saturday morning? Why didn't you just ask me?"

"Well, because you were bringing the yoghurts and—"

"YAY, PEPPA YOGHURTS!" Saved by the twins and their excitement for branded yoghurts. They jumped off their seats and bounded over to Neil, grabbing the plastic shopping bag out of his hands.

"What are these?" asked Theo, as he pulled two pots out of the bag with a mixture of confusion and disappointment on his little face.

"These aren't Peppa yoghurts! Where are our Peppa yoghurts?" huffed Tomaso.

"They're almond milk yoghurts," said Neil enthusiastically. "They're so much better for you than the Peppa ones and will make you so much bigger and stronger." He emphasized the 'stronger' part by tensing his biceps.

"What an idiot," muttered Anthony under his breath, scooping up another spoonful of cereal and shoving it into his mouth.

"What did you say?" said Neil through gritted teeth. He puffed out his chest, his eyes firmly resting on Anthony.

"I *said*, what an idi—"

"I think it's time you left," I interjected, sternly. Anthony looked at me and shook his head, but he deserved it. He was being an arse.

"Fine," said Anthony, standing to his feet. "I'll just go and get my shoes . . . out the bedroom."

"Uncle Anthony said the bed is so comfortable," declared Theo, banging the last nail well and truly into my coffin.

*

Isme: Hey, just wondering when you're picking the kids up, just so I can make sure they're ready
No rush though!
OK, got them ready just in case you haven't seen my message and are on your way over ☺
I know I said no rush, like, but if you could just give me some sort of indication of when you're coming that would be great
Fucking hell Maria, are you coming to take these kids off me or what?

Maria: Sorry, Isme. I don't think I'm going to make it until teatime

Isme: What the hell am I supposed to do with them all day? It's raining and I've already exhausted all my pre-recorded episodes of Peppa Pig

Maria: There's always soft play 😬

I'd only ever been to a soft-play centre once, when Maria dragged me there, and I was still haunted by that sweaty feet smell and the sound of crazed Fruit Shoot-fuelled kids bouncing off the walls. This visit was no different.

I spent most of the afternoon on all fours chasing the twins through the many twists and turns of the soft-play maze – which is perfectly designed for little bodies to climb through and *not* my busty frame.

I had asked Neil to come, but he was still mad at me after finding out Anthony stayed the night (I think he was more peeved that he'd caught us using full fat cow's milk though).

During a moment of calm at the soft play, bribing the twins with some cookies and Fruit Shoots in return for some time out, I rang Maddy.

"What's Neil's problem? You and Anthony have been friends for donkeys."

I sighed. "Yeah, I know. I guess he feels threatened."

"Why, though? It's not like anything has ever happened between you and Anthony, or will ever happen. Right?"

"God, no, pah! Can you imagine?" I cleared my throat.

"Look, I didn't really want to have to tell you this, but I seen Zara in town the other week and she said she's met Neil for a coffee a few times after the gym."

I paused for a moment as I digested Maddy's words. Was I surprised? A little. Did it bother me? Probably not as much as it should. "Yeah, well, they go to the same gym so they're bound to see each other from time to time."

"That's not what it sounded like to me, you know. Zara was quite adamant it's always prearranged."

"She's a liar, Maddy. She'll say anything to get one up on me."

The line suddenly went quiet. "Why are you protecting him, Isme?"

"I'M NOT!" I hadn't realised how high my voice had gone until I saw the twins gawping at me like I had three heads. "Why are you trying to make him look bad, Maddy? Is it because he had a go at you about your eyelashes and fur coat?"

"Oh, you think I'm lying just to get back at him?"

"I dunno, are you?"

"Wow, babe."

With that the line went dead.

*

Isme: Trying to find out if I can get the money
before the wedding
Do you think Dad could persuade the bank
to hold off on the sale until we know? 🙏

Mum: Isme, your papa still not know about

the Will and I prefer not to tell him yet 😖
I don't want it to cause him stress and raise
his blood pressure again

Isme: He's going to find out soon enough,
Mum. OK, well you might just need to find other
ways of stalling the sale

Mum: OK, Isme. I tell them the house burned
down 😊

Isme: Er, preferably something more
believable, Mum?

Mum: 👍 👍 👍

*

With things progressing quickly with Mum and Dad's house sale, I went in search of Zara. The last thing I wanted to do was ask for her help, but it was getting desperate.

I found her in the copier room. When she caught sight of me, she took a big exhale of breath and ran her fingers through her shiny locks.

"Isme, if this is about that Will thing you were asking Luke about, I haven't had a chance to look. Been really busy, in work *and* out."

I smiled as warmly as I could, although I imagined it looked more like a snarl.

"On first glance, though, it doesn't look like anything can be done. You'll have to wait until the wedding before the money can be released, although I'm not sure marrying Neil will get you it. It says you have to marry someone Greek, and isn't Neil only like a quarter? That's what he told me, anyway."

My insides churned as the realisation of not being able to get the inheritance money until we got married hit me, although it *had* been a long shot to think it was a possibility. Having to wait meant we'd need to tie the knot pretty quickly to have any chance of saving the house from being sold, and I'd naïvely hoped that time would be on my side.

Zara picked up her photocopying and began sashaying out the room. "Was there something else, Isme?"

"Actually, yeah. I wanted to ask why you're going round telling everyone you're having regular coffee dates with my fiancé?"

Zara casually shrugged her shoulders.

"Is it true, then?"

"We go the same gym; we like the same things. Like healthy food and looking after ourselves." Zara scanned me up and down as she said this, and I felt the blood rush to my face. I wanted nothing more than to chin her one right in her smug grid, but I couldn't give her the satisfaction.

The photocopier took a slight beating from my left foot after she left, instead.

*

It had been three days since Maria had relieved me of my auntie duties and my body was still aching from the hell that was soft play. So, when Neil rang and told me he'd booked the spa day I was thrilled – a day of pampering was just what the doctor ordered.

"I think it'll be good for us to have some space as well, after the whole Anthony-staying-over thing."

I sighed. "Are you really still annoyed about that, Neil? I don't know how many times I have to tell you, we're just friends. Anyway, have you had any sleepovers with Zara?"

Neil hesitated for a moment. "What do you mean?"

"Maddy said the two of you have been having coffee together after the gym."

Neil cleared his throat. "Yeah, we bump into each other in the gym and have met up for a coffee once or twice afterwards. It's no big deal. Maddy is just trying to make it sound like something it isn't, you know she doesn't like me and is just trying to create tension between us."

"Yeah, but—"

"Anyway, about the spa. I've called your mum and told her it's booked. She said something about making you all some Greek pie and salad for lunch, but I told her she didn't need to bother. Mum's already said she's making some vegan cheese butties."

And so, the Greek vs English battle continued.

*

The spa website read: 'Press the pause button and join us for a relaxing day that will leave you feeling refreshed and renewed'. What they should have added on the end was: 'Unless you're going with your manic Greek mother and very-much-English mother-in-law who don't see eye to eye on your upcoming nuptials, in which case you may find it more relaxing to stay at home and stick pins in your eyes.'

We met in the dimly lit reception area of the spa, which smelt like lavender and was so peacefully quiet you could hear a pin drop. That was until Mum bounced in like a bull in a china shop, moaning about the size of the car parking spaces – "*Who they think I am, Lewis Hamilton?*". She only drives a Toyota Yaris, but with her poor level of spacial awareness on the road it might as well be a Range Rover.

Mum and Joan seemed genuinely pleased to see each other, although that could have just been a front for my benefit. Joan complimented Mum on her flowery blouse, while Mum paid homage to Joan's brown strappy sandals – God knows why, they looked like something straight out of Bethlehem.

After getting changed, we were ushered into three separate rooms for our treatments, mine a forty-five-minute back massage. The thought of having to bare my naked torso to a stranger initially filled me with dread, with Neil's voice playing over in my head about shifting some pounds. But once they got to work it wasn't long before I was in a state of pure relaxation.

I felt like I was floating on a cloud afterwards and glided out to the pool area, but I soon came back down to Earth with a bang when I spotted Mum and Joan. They were in the jacuzzi having what I hoped was a civilised conversation, but their flushed faces and Mum's arm movements, which tended to become quite erratic when she's trying to get a point across, told me otherwise.

"I don't understand why we can't have my church choir sing at both ceremonies," Joan was saying. "What am I supposed to tell Father Paul?"

"What you want me to do, Joan, change thee traditions of thee Greek Orthodox Church just so your little choir can sing a few hymns?"

Joan let out a gasp. "I'll have you know they are not just some little choir, Elana. Their legacy goes back many years. They sang at my mum's wedding, and her mum's wedding and—"

Mum waved her hands in the air dismissively, but as she did, one of them made contact with the water, causing a big splash to hit Joan slap bang in the face.

"Oh my God, I'm so sorry, Joan," said Mum, covering her mouth with her hands. "I really didn't mean to— AAHHH!"

Joan had retaliated, completely drenching Mum's face and hair, and before I knew it, water was splashing everywhere and they were having a full-scale water fight.

I should have bounced over and demanded they break it up, but it was like one of those videos on YouTube of someone squeezing slime between their fingers – you don't know why, but you just can't stop watching it. In the end, one of the pool attendants politely asked them to stop.

Needless to say, we didn't stay much longer after that.

*

I called round to Mum and Dad's, timing it so that Mum was out at her Zumba class. I needed to get Mum to apologise to Joan for splash-gate, which I promised Neil I'd do, and who better to help me than the man with the most experience breaking through the stone wall that is Elana Eliades.

The living room blinds were closed, and low voices and shuffling could be heard from inside when I got to the door. I thought that maybe Mum hadn't gone to Zumba after all. Could him and Mum be . . .? Where they . . .? Thankfully, the car wasn't there though, putting those distressing thoughts to bed.

So if Mum wasn't there, then who was?

I thought back to the recent Carol conundrum when Dad had stayed for tea at the flat, which was just one of a long line of mysteries and strange behaviours from him this entire year. Any previous opportunities to confront him had been overshadowed by his deteriorating health, but now he was on the mend it was time for answers. Without any further thought, I grabbed the spare key that Mum always leaves under one of the wheelie bins, turned the key in the door and burst into the house like the police on a raid.

"Isme, what the bleedin' hell are you doing here?" Dad, who thankfully was fully clothed, jumped up from the armchair, his face startled. Although from the two mugs on the coffee table – one of them Mum's favourite 'I'm not rude, I'm just Greek' – all that seemed to have gone down so far was a bit of tea drinking.

Opposite him on the other chair sat a woman around Dad's age with short brown hair and a warm smile, who looked oddly familiar, although I was pretty certain I hadn't met her before. I had a good mind to wipe that smile clean off her face.

My heart was pounding so much I could hear it thumping in my ears. "I could ask you the same thing! Who's this?"

Dad rubbed at the back of his neck. "Oh, well, er, I can explain, you see, erm . . ."

"I'm Carol, his nutritionist, I was assigned by the hospital after his heart attack. And you must be Isme – I've heard so much about you." She stood up and reached out a hand and I hesitated, unsure whether to shake it or slap it away. With no evident signs of inappropriate behaviour, I opted for the shake.

"Right, well, we're done here, Stephen," said Carol, straightening out her black pencil skirt, which she wore with black tights and clumpy black flats, and putting on her beige mac – she looked more like a social worker than someone qualified to advise people on their diets. "You're doing great, keep up the good work. It was nice to meet you, Isme."

"Dad, what's going on?" I said once she'd left, my blood still boiling. "If you expect me to believe all that nutritionist crap then you really don't know me at all."

Dad sank down into his chair and let out a sigh. After a pause, he said, "OK, OK. She's not my nutritionist."

I slumped myself down on the sofa and rubbed at my thumping head. "Oh god, Dad, an affair? Really? Mum's going to be devastated, not to mention absolutely raging—"

His eyes widened. "WHAT? Don't be so bleedin' daft, Isme. I'm not having an affair. Jesus, is that really what you thought?"

"What else was I meant to think? All those outings with your so-called 'computer friends' and the way you've been so edgy whenever your phone goes off. Then I find you sneaking around behind closed blinds with some woman while Mum is out! I mean, come on, Dad."

"OK, fair enough, I can see how that looks," he said sheepishly. "But I promise you, Iz, I'm not having an affair. You know I adore your mum, and I also value my life."

"If you're not having an affair with her then who is she?"

He leant towards me and placed a hand on my leg. "I want to tell you, love, really I do, but I just can't. Not right now, anyway. I need to figure a few things out myself first and then I'll tell you all, I promise. You need to trust me, OK?"

I looked into his pleading eyes, and despite everything pointing in the direction of him playing away, I couldn't help but believe him. But what could be so important to him to keep it from his whole family?

"Iz, do you trust me?" said Dad, breaking me from my thoughts.

I sighed. "Yes, I do. But you best tell us all soon – you know Mum doesn't like secrets. Remember how much she kicked off when you ate the last piece of that cheesecake and blamed the twins?"

*

Maria: Have you got any wine?

Isme: Yeah, I might have a bottle stashed away somewhere. Why, you on the lend again?

Maria: Fancy sharing it with me tonight?
Could do with a chat

Isme: Yeah of course, come round. You can have

307

the bottle all to yourself though, I'm still trying to
stick to the Schloer after my piss up with Agnes

Maria: Oh shit, yeah. I forgot about the baby

Isme: 👆

I lasted five minutes on the Schloer before I caved and had a glass of the good stuff. I needed it to calm my nerves from all the revelations that were pouring out of Maria's mouth.

"George is trying really hard to make the marriage work. You know, he even started taking dance lessons to try and impress me, the daft sod. I told him he's gonna need to do more than a few shitty salsa steps to make up for being a crappy husband all these years, and even then, I'm not sure I want it to work. I'm not sure I even love him any more, Iz."

It was hardly surprising to hear she wasn't happy with George, but to say she wasn't sure if she loved him was unexpected. I'd always thought of them as a bit like the Jim and Barbara Royle of the Greek world, and no matter how much George did her tits in with his lazy, selfish ways, she still couldn't help but love him.

"Oddly, we do still have quite a lot of sex, usually after we've had a big fight. And I've got to say, Iz, he might be useless round the house, but he doesn't half make up for it in the bedroom."

That answered my last question.

"A job has come up as a hair stylist for a TV company. I'd love to go for it, but I just don't know if I'm good enough. Ask me what the daily programme schedule is for CBeebies, and I can reel it off no problem, but when it comes to anything outside of being a mum, I feel pretty inadequate. It sounds a bit dramatic, but I feel like I've lost my identity."

Even though I had no juveniles of my own, I got it. I'd seen through Maria how these little people come along and consume your life, making anything you did/liked to do before pale into insignificance. But I told her she was mad not to at least give it a go.

"You know, I nearly kissed someone when I was out a few weeks ago. He approached me on the dancefloor and didn't say anything, just put his arm around my waist and we started swaying to the music. For the first time in a long time, it was just me, Maria Eliades. Not Mum, not wife, and someone actually wanted *me*, just for me. My God, it felt good to be wanted like that."

This one sent me reaching for the second bottle of wine. Yeah, OK, she didn't kiss the lad, but to come that close sent so many alarm bells ringing in my head. Thankfully, Neil turned up before I got round to opening the wine, and I shoved it back in the fridge before he saw.

"What's going on here?" Neil stood frozen to the spot as he caught sight of the empty bottle and glasses, his face reddening. "I thought you were going to try and lay off the booze after your night out with Agnes?"

I went to speak, but my dry mouth wouldn't let me.

"Sorry, Neil, my bad," said Maria, sensing my unease. "I made her do it." She went to stand up but lost her balance and somehow ended up prised between the sofa and the coffee table. The pair of us collapsed into hysterics – I couldn't help it – while Neil watched on with pursed lips.

"Don't you think you should be getting back to George and the twins?" he said, through gritted teeth. "I'm sure there's a lot you need to talk about."

Maria stood up, stumble-free this time, and grabbed her coat. "You're absolutely right, we have got a lot to talk about." She turned to face me, placing one of her hands on my shoulder. "Thanks for tonight, Iz, it was much needed."

"Don't mention it. Look, I'll help out with the twins as much as I can while you and George sort your shit out, OK?" I ignored Neil's purposeful cough.

"Could you pick them up from pre-school on Tuesday? I've got the chance to do a cash-only job on the side, and every little bit of money counts."

"Why doesn't she just have them move in here?" scoffed Neil once Maria had left.

*

I'd been driving home from work a few days later when a phone call came through from Mum. Had Dad finally revealed the truth about Carol?

"So, I speak to Joan. I feel bad after the spa . . . even though I didn't start it."

I breathed a sigh of relief. "That's great! So you apologised, then?"

Mum hesitated before answering. "Not exactly."

"Ohhhh-kaaaay. Then what?"

"I tell her she can't bring her choir to thee Greek wedding, but they can do some songs at thee engagement party instead."

I had to stop myself from slamming on the brakes. "YOU SAID WHAT?"

"Calm down, Isme, it'll jus bee a few hymns at thee start while everyone is arriving."

"Mother, it's a party, not Sunday mass! When was the last time you got down to 'Here I am Lord' on the dancefloor?"

To be fair, 'Gloria' was a proper tune, but I wasn't going to admit that – it's one thing belting it out in church, but it hardly sets the mood for a party.

I told her she was going to have to go back to Joan and tell her it's off, but she'd already been rehearsing.

My only hope was that the whole choir came down with a bad case of laryngitis before the party . . . or that the music charts are taken over by hymns. Look at that Military Wives choir, it *is* possible.

*

Neil: Are you in? I need to come and see you

Isme: Yeah, just give me an hour. Still trying to
tidy up after having the twins round

Neil: It's OK. I won't be staying long

"I won't even ask," said Neil when he spotted the mess in the flat, which included a perfectly round yellow wee stain on the carpet, splashes of milk on the dining table and scatterings of Maltesers all over the floor. He took a seat on one of the dining room chairs, wiping away the cluster of Cheerios first, and signalled to one of the other chairs for me to do the same.

"Look, I'll get right to the point," he said, running his fingers through his hair. "I know about the Will."

I swallowed hard. "What about it?"

"That you need to marry someone Greek to get your inheritance, and how I'm conveniently Greek?"

"And who told you that?" I scoffed. "Oh, let me guess, was it Zara?"

Neil reddened. "It doesn't matter who told me—"

"It bloody well does, Neil! What exactly *is* going on with you two?"

Neil hesitated, fiddling with a rogue Cheerio. "OK, it *was* Zara," he said, flicking the Cheerio to the other end of the table, "but I've already told you, nothing is going on between us. I just regularly bump into her in the gym, and we get talking."

I eyed him suspiciously, looking for any sign he was lying, but he seemed relatively composed, maybe even a little melancholy.

"Look, just answer me one thing, Isme," he said, his voice beginning to break. "Are you only marrying me to get hold of that money?"

I hesitated for a moment before answering, the doubts I'd had about Neil and our relationship before we got engaged resurfacing, bringing new red flags with them (not getting on with Dad, zero paternal instincts, doesn't understand my relationship with Anthony. Do I need to go on?). The question was whether I was *actually* enjoying being in a relationship with Neil, or if I was just trying to convince myself that I was to justify the engagement and, ultimately, the release of the inheritance money. I honestly wasn't sure of the answer.

"Of course I'm not," I eventually said, my voice a little high-pitched, "and anyway, you're only, like, an eighth Greek, so it doesn't count. If you don't believe me, ask Zara!"

Neil slumped back into the chair and did a praying gesture with his hands up to the ceiling. "Well, now that's sorted, I'll put the kettle on."

He began telling me all about a recent work trip, but I wasn't listening. All I could think of was the Cheerio on the other end of the table that was now free from Neil's clutches. I've never longed to be a piece of cereal so much.

*

Isme: Do you want to come with me to take
the twins trick or treating next week?
It is kind of your fault because Maria's
doing your mum's hair colour
Oh and they have specifically asked/
begged for you

Anthony: Will Neil be there?

Isme: No

Anthony: Then yeah

We decided to take the twins trick or treating round by Anthony's – living in an apartment block mostly full of students you were more likely to get a handful of weed than Haribos, although both *can* make you hyper. There were quite a few young families living around by theirs as well, so I knew we wouldn't feel out of place.

It was a chilly autumn night and there was a sprinkling of mist in the air, making the oak tree-lined street look like a scene from a scary movie. What *wasn't* scary were the twins, who'd dressed up as Mario and Luigi from *Super Mario Bros* and looked about as threatening as chihuahuas in tutus. They did look cute in their little dungarees and stick-on moustaches, though.

"Uncle Anthony, we made you some cookies!" cried Theo, handing the Tupperware box of pumpkin-shaped ginger biscuits that we'd made earlier to him.

"That's so kind, thank you." Anthony ruffled the top of Theo's head. "Did Uncle Isme help you?"

"Hmmm, a little," said Tomaso, with a cheeky grin.

"So have you still been baking a bit, then?" asked Anthony, as we started to make our way along the road.

"Not really, I can't seem to find the time. These cookies are the first thing I've made since I did those baby shower cakes for your mum's friend, and that was only because I convinced Jeff to let me finish early if I made the time back the next day."

"That's a shame. I know how much you love your baking."

I let out a heavy sigh. "I know. Hopefully I'll be able to pick it back up again at some point."

We came to the first Halloween-decorated house, which had a giant spider's web leading up to one of the upstairs windows, and a giant pretend black spider perched on top. "TRICK OR TREAT!" shouted the twins to the owners as they came to the door. They handed Theo and Tomaso a lollipop each, which they grabbed excitedly before running off.

"I haven't heard from you since the night I stayed over," said Anthony, as we moved along the road to the next house. "Has Neil put his foot down on who you can be friends with?"

"What? No, don't be stupid. And even if he did, I'd take no notice."

"So, why were you so embarrassed that I'd stayed over, then? We've done it a million times before."

I kicked at a conker on the ground. "Yeah, I know, but things are different now, I suppose."

"I see." Anthony turned away and I knew in that moment there'd been a tidal shift in our friendship. We were no longer young, free and single Anthony and Isme, who could do anything we wanted and answer to no one.

The trick or treating was cut short after half an hour when Tomaso knocked over someone's garden gnome, shattering it into pieces, followed by Theo almost pissing his pants. He shot through the door of Anthony's house when we arrived, almost knocking Sandra over in the process.

"Oh, I didn't think you and Maria would be done this early," I said, following Sandra into the house. She looked at me with a puzzled expression. "You know, to do your hair colour?"

"She never agreed to do my hair, Isme. Said she'd get into too much trouble with work if they found out."

I rubbed at my head. "That's weird, she definitely said she was doing your hair. That's why she asked me to take the twins trick or treating."

I thought back to our conversation last week about her supposed near-miss with a lad on a night out – was that a lie, too, and she was currently having a second helping? Right on cue, my phone beeped with a message from Maria.

"You OK?" asked Anthony. "I know it's Halloween, like, but you've gone a bit pale."

"I just need to—" I stumbled over to the sofa and slumped down.

"What is it, Isme?" Unable to speak, I handed the phone over to Anthony and he read Maria's message out loud.

"Iz, I'm so sorry to do this to you but I need to go away for a bit. I'll explain everything when I get back, I promise, but can you please look after the twins for me? You're the only one I trust. Please don't hate me." Anthony shook his head. "She can't just up sticks and leave you with two kids, just like that! Why can't they stay with George?"

I let out a heavy sigh. "Because they'd probably end up in social care after a day, from neglect."

The panic was rising inside at the level of responsibility that had just been put on my shoulders, and before I knew it I was crying. "Fuck, Anthony, what am I going to do?"

Anthony rushed over to my side and placed a comforting arm around me.

"Look, it'll be OK. I'll come and help as much as I can. You won't be on your own, I promise."

I rested my head on his shoulder and we sat in silence watching the twins who, completely oblivious to the drama, had resorted to whipping each other with their stick-on moustaches.

"And look, if all else fails, we'll get you a taser gun."

Somehow, in the middle of my panic, I managed a smile.

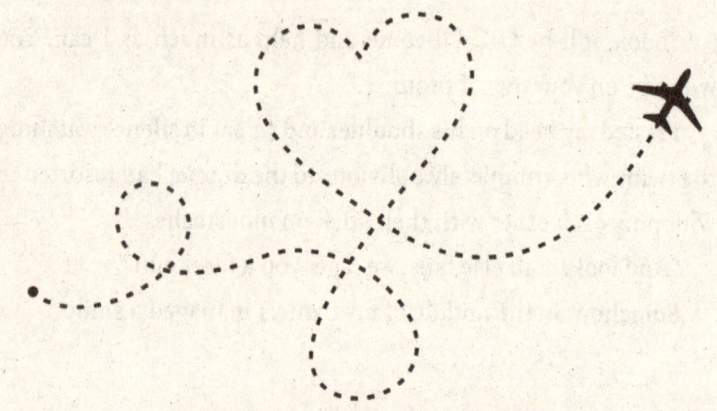

NOVEMBER

AFTER DROPPING THE TWINS OFF AT PRE-SCHOOL, and calling Jeff to let him know I had to take an emergency day's leave – "So long as it's just one day, Isme, you know I can't stand Sue's coffee" – I decided to call round to George's to get some answers to the many questions that had been swimming round my brain all night. Like, did he know Maria was gonna go AWOL? And, more importantly, why had I been lumbered with the kids?

"Wow, you look like shit." George stood at the door. His eyes were puffy, and his hair looked like it hadn't seen a comb in weeks. "Jesus, when did you last have a shower?"

He stumbled back into the house and slumped onto the sofa. I took a seat opposite, wiping away the debris of questionable crumbs first and opening a window to allow the stale smell of mouldy food and sour body odour to escape. Maria had only been gone a day. I daren't imagine the state of the place after a week.

"What's going on?"

George stared down at his hands and picked at some broken skin. "She's left me, Isme. The love of my life has . . . has left me." His voice broke off and he started to cry, loud ear-deafening sobs that made my insides vibrate.

"Did she say why? Or where she was going?"

George wiped his nose on the sleeve of his dressing gown. "Just that she wasn't happy any more and was going to stay with a friend down in London." George broke off and looked heavenward. "WHY, GOD? WHY WOULD SHE DO THIS TO ME?" This was followed by more bawling.

"You need to get a grip of yourself, George. If not for yourself then do it for the kids, will you. Do you think they want to see their dad like this?"

George looked taken aback by my hostility. Fearing another bout of the waterworks was on the way, I threw an empty beer can in his direction.

"I know you're right. I just can't live without her, Isme."

"Well, you need to try, at least for now. For starters, sort this shit-hole out, because when Maria does come back, she won't want to see you or the place like this. You need to show her that you can look after yourself, *prove* to her that you're still the man she married."

Without warning, George leapt up from the couch and pulled me in for a hug, which was awkward and oppressing, and left a potent smell of stale sweat on my top after he pulled away.

"Thank you. I know we've never exactly seen eye to eye, but I've always thought of you like my little sister. A bit of an annoying one, like, but a sister all the same."

I have him a gentle nudge.

Who would have thought it, me and George being nice to each other? This year had been full of surprises.

*

Agnes: Hullo, me little Scouse pal,
how was Loch Lomond?!

Isme: We haven't been yet, Ag, can't seem
to find the time at the moment

Agnes: That's weird. The hotel have sent
me an email just now asking me to fill out
a questionnaire about the stay.
Let me ring them and make sure some
fecker hasn't used the voucher.
Izzy, I've just spoken to them, and they said
someone by the name of Neil stayed last weekend.

I stared at my phone in complete disbelief. The teeny tiny hint of relief that I'd bypassed a weekend of dreaded watersports aside, what right did Neil have just upping sticks and going on his own when it was *our* engagement present . . . and not discussing it with me first?

I asked him to meet me and the twins at the local park, without mentioning my conversation with Agnes – I wanted to put him on the spot and watch him squirm in his meggings. It was my turn to squirm first though, when he turned up with a box of kids' organic oat bars, which were met with just as much disgust from the twins as the almond yoghurts.

"Any word from Maria?" he asked, planting a kiss on my cheek and taking a seat on the bench next to me. I folded my arms tightly around my chest to gain some warmth from the bitterly cold breeze.

I sighed. "Just a few messages asking if the twins were OK."

Neil shook his head. "I still can't believe she's dumped the twins on you like this. What sort of mother does that?"

"She's a good mother, Neil," I said sternly, loosening the woolly scarf from around my neck, which was starting to itch against my heating skin. "She's just going through a bit of a mid-life crisis or something – and if going away for a bit sorts her head out, then I'm all for it."

"She could have at least asked you first though," he snorted. "Surely a good mother would at least do that."

We sat in silence for a bit, with only the faint sound of cheers and claps in the distance from a kids' football match, and stomping from the twins who were running up a slide. Thankfully, no one else had braved the bitter November morning, so there were no disapproving mums to deal with.

"I was wondering whether we should look at booking Loch Lomond next weekend?" I said, not turning my gaze from the twins. "I could leave the twins with George, I'm sure he'd be able to manage *one* night on his own."

Neil wriggled in his seat. "I thought you, er, didn't want to go?"

"I never said that. I just wasn't keen on the watersports, but I'll give them a go if it'll make you happy."

Neil rubbed at the back of his neck. "OK, well, er, let me sort something out . . . OW, WHAT WAS THAT FOR?"

"I can't believe you went without me!" I cried, jumping up from the bench and swallowing down the pain coming from my hand where I'd given him a dig. "Why would you do that without at least speaking to me first?"

"Woah, Isme, calm down. Jeez." Neil rubbed at his arm, although I doubted my weak blow had caused much pain against his hardened biceps. "You've been so preoccupied with the twins lately. Then I found out about the Will and needed to get away to clear my head." I didn't like his defensive tone, and his attempt at passing the blame.

"Don't you think *I* want to get away, Neil? Did you even consider that?" I was really shouting now. "I've got parents who are one mortgage payment away from being homeless, a sister who is so unhappy it breaks my heart, and have been lumbered with the responsibility of keeping two little human beings alive!"

"It's not my fault your sister is incapable of looking after her children."

"You know what, I can't be arsed with this. Come on, you two, we're going."

The twins, who had been watching the heated exchange with

gaping mouths, ran to my side and followed me out the park.

"Why were you shouting at angry muscle man?" said Tomaso, once we were out of earshot.

"Because he's a big selfish shi— I mean, poo-poo pants."

We walked in silence for a bit, until Theo said, "I think we should change his name to angry muscle poo-poo pants man."

I smiled. "Perfect."

*

Day three of playing Mum, and I was over it. It was like running on a constant treadmill every day, from the moment they woke up at the crack of dawn demanding breakfast before they'd even properly opened their tiny little peep holes, to when I tucked them into bed at night and they asked me what's for breakfast the next day.

Then there was also trying to juggle work in between, with a boss who, with no children of his own, had no concept of flexibility for working parents. He almost broke into a cold sweat when I'd asked him if I could temporarily change my working hours to fit around pre-school drop-off and pick-up times, but after a brief consultation with HR agreed, *"So long as you can still meet your daily work demands, even if it means picking up the slack at the weekends."* How fucking generous.

When I *hadn't* been running round after the twins picking up their shit, I was picking up actual shit – I saw what I thought was a chocolate magic star on the floor last night during my nightly twins tornado tidy up, only to find on closer inspection that it was a little tiny ollie.

I reached the end of my tether this afternoon though, when I left the room for all of three minutes to go the loo and came out to find the twins in my bedroom, rummaging through my underwear drawer.

"What's this?" asked Tomaso, waving my vibrator in the air like a sword. It was given to me as a joke one year for the work's Secret Santa, and had been a good friend to me ever since.

"Mummy's got one of these," said Theo, taking it from Tomaso to give it a closer inspection. "She said she uses it to go to her happy place."

"Right, come on you two, out," I said, snatching the vibrator from Theo and launching it back in the drawer before my ears bled from any more shocking revelations about my sister.

"Are these for your nose?" I turned round to find Tomaso in the process of shoving a tampon up one of his nostrils.

"NO, THEY ARE NOT!" I shouted, retrieving it from his nose. "Now, OUT." I pointed in the direction of the door, and the twins sulkily did as they were told.

I sat on the edge of the bed and buried my face in my hands, mentally willing Maria to come back soon before I had some sort of Britney Spears type breakdown and shaved my own head. I almost jumped out my skin when my phone pinged a few seconds later – had my telepathic thoughts worked?

> **Anthony:** I'm in the area. Want me
> to come and help with the kids?
> I could bring us some food?

*

"ANTHONY, ANTHONY!" The twins bolted to the door when he arrived, throwing themselves into his arms.

"Have you two been misbehaving for your Auntie Isme?" They nodded their heads like butter wouldn't melt. "Do you know what happens to kids who misbehave?"

After a pause, Tomaso said, "They don't get any presents off Santa?"

Anthony laughed. "Well, yeah, there is that. But they also get ... TICKLED!"

I watched as Anthony proceeded to play a game of chase and tickle with them around the flat, whilst they screamed and chuckled, and something inside my chest fluttered. He'd always been a natural with kids, and it was no different with the twins, but now that I was playing Mum, it made me appreciate it even more. I suddenly imagined that the twins were *our* kids, and how grateful I'd feel having Anthony as their dad.

Suddenly, the game came to an abrupt end when the tickling became a bit too much for Theo's weak bladder, and I was brought firmly back to the present.

"I wish I would have thought of that," I said to Anthony as he emerged from the bedroom later on after putting the twins to bed, which he insisted on doing so I could have a rest.

"What's that, then?"

"Tickling, throwing them about, chasing them around pretending to be a dinosaur. It would have saved me a fortune on all those crappy kids magazines that get launched for the toys."

"Don't be hard on yourself. I'm sure you're doing your best. Especially when you're trying to hold down a full-time job."

I smiled at him gratefully. "I honestly don't how people do it, Anthony. It's so bloody knackering."

Anthony nodded and grabbed his coat. "Anyway, I best be off. I wouldn't want Neil getting the wrong impression again."

I wanted to ask him to stay, to tell him all about Neil and Loch Lomond and how I didn't care what Neil thought, but the words just wouldn't reach my mouth.

*

Neil: Isme, when are you going to talk to me?
How many times do I have to say I'm sorry?

Isme: Well, I'm still annoyed, so I'd keep going

Neil: Let me come round tonight and make us all
dinner. I could do us a Quorn bolognese? I bet
the twins won't even know it's not meat!

Isme: I gave them Tesco's own brand chicken
dippers the other day and they wouldn't eat them.
Believe me, they'll know
Look, I think it's best if we keep our distance for
a bit, at least until the twins go back home

Neil: Are you breaking up with me?

326

Isme: No. I just think a bit of a break will
do us both good

Neil: I disagree, but if that's what you want.
By the way, I noticed the 'Under Offer' sign on
your Mum and Dad's house has been taken off.
You might want to find out what's going on

I immediately picked up the phone and called the house.

"Dad, what's all this about the house not being under offer any more?"

"Sorry, love, we were going to ring you. We got a call a few days ago to say the people who had put the offer in had to withdraw it."

"Did you find out why?"

"Nope, the buggers aren't legally obliged to tell us."

"So what now, then? Presumably it goes back on the market?"

"Yeah, that's right, love, although the market has slowed down a bit recently with it coming up to the festive season, so I can't see us getting another offer until the new year."

I had to stop myself from letting out a whoop down the phone, so did it to the empty flat once the call ended instead. The house sale being temporarily on hold meant I could breathe a little in terms of planning the wedding, although I would have to forgive Neil first or there would be no wedding at all. I *would* forgive him, but for now I was enjoying seeing Anthony whenever I wanted without him breathing down my neck. Not having to stomach a bowl of blag Bolognese was just an added bonus.

Isme: Do you want to come and watch the
fireworks with me and the twins at the flat?
If you haven't got any plans, like

Anthony: Have you got permission off Neil?

Isme: Come on, don't be an arse

Anthony: Yes, I'd love to

Anthony came round just after six, giving me enough time to change out of my dreary grey work dress and run a brush through my tangled hair. I was just about to leave the bedroom when I spotted a red lipstick on top of my bedside table that the twins must have found buried deep in one of the drawers during their rampage. Without much thought, I smothered it onto my lips.

"Freckiades, you look, er, different," said Anthony, as I opened the door. He handed me a bottle of red wine, which I took off him gratefully. I didn't think much of his comment until I spotted my reflection in the bathroom mirror a bit later and realised that in my blind lipstick application haste, I had ended up looking like The Joker.

After eating some hot dogs, we waited at the window of the flat, which had a decent view of the River Mersey where the annual fireworks display was about to start. It was a clear night, the sky aglow with the bright lights of the city. In the distance, crowds of people were gathering by the water's edge, the waves glistening like silver threads against the light of the moon. The window was slightly ajar, allowing the scent of bonfires and gunpowder to creep in.

"I wonder if Mummy will be watching the fireworks too," said Tomaso, which tugged at my chest. In my 'woe is me' state from having to play Mum, I hadn't stopped to think of the effect Maria's absence was having on the twins.

Sensing my anguish, Anthony reached across and placed a comforting hand on one of my shoulders that felt warm and familiar. I smiled at him gratefully.

"When will Mummy be ba— WOAH!"

Saved by the fireworks. We all watched in awe as the sky was lit up by a dazzling display of colourful fireworks, some shooting straight up before exploding, others shattering into thousands of sparks, the loud booms and cackles echoing through the flat.

I peered over at Anthony and watched as each flash of light from the fireworks bounced off his face, highlighting his deep-set brown eyes and rugged features. I didn't realise I'd been staring for that long until Tomaso tugged at my arm and said, "Have they finished?"

In need of some distraction from my weird 'Anthony appreciation' moment, I sought refuge in the kitchen to make us all a hot chocolate to go with the shortbread biscuits I'd made earlier – one positive of working school hours was having some time after pick-up to bake. Plus, it occupied the twins for a good solid fifteen minutes before they inevitably got bored and started pretend sword fighting with their wooden spoons, leaving the kitchen to look like the inside of a microwave after a heating explosion.

But the mess was worth it to see the joy on their faces as they tucked into the finished product. It gave me the same satisfied feeling as when I used to sell cakes at my trade stall and get positive reviews from customers, and it was a feeling I'd never grow tired of.

I was closely followed into the kitchen by the twins, who were insistent on helping with the hot chocolate. As I watched them laughing with each other about the marshmallows looking like little snowmen as they carefully placed them into their mugs, I felt an overwhelming rush of love for these two little human beings and scooped them up for a cuddle. They were surprisingly receptive to my rare moment of affection, until it went on a bit too long and Theo started crying because his 'little marshmallow men were melting'.

*

"You're more of a natural than you think, you know," said Anthony, pouring us each a wine once we'd put the twins to bed.

"Ha! I don't know about that," I said, plonking myself on the sofa. "I'm winging it every day."

"Honestly, you are. I was watching you make the hot chocolate with them. You were so patient." He paused to take a sip of his wine. "You'll make a good mum one day, Freckiades."

My cheeks burned from the unexpected compliment – I'd criticized myself every day since the twins came to stay, whether it be for shouting at them too much or not playing with them enough.

"When do you think Maria *will* come back?" asked Anthony, taking a seat next to me.

I sighed. "I honestly don't know."

"But surely George will have to take over at some point?"

"Maybe, but Maria specifically asked me to, and for good reason. You wanted to see the kip of him when I went round the other day, Anthony. How can he look after them properly when he can't even look after himself?"

We both took a sip of our wine whilst silently reflecting on the situation with Maria which, if I thought too much about it, was pretty messed up, so I tried not to. I had to crack on for the twins' sake and hope that once Maria came back, she would be in a much better place.

"I've been meaning to ask you," I said, keen to change the subject. "That night when you stayed over, you said you were on your way out. Where were you meant to be going?"

Anthony fiddled with the stem of the wine glass. "Remember that indie band I've always loved, but could never seem to get tickets for their shows because they would sell out so quickly?"

I laughed. "How could I forget! You loved them so much you grew your hair long and wore skinny black jeans that were so tight they cut off the circulation in your legs, just so you could look like the lead singer!"

Anthony cleared his throat. "Yeah. Well, they were doing a final tour around the UK before going their separate ways, and me mate got us VIP all-access tickets to the very last show in London."

Goosebumps slid along the back of my neck as I absorbed Anthony's words. "What? And you gave them up to come and help *me*?"

Anthony shrugged sheepishly. "Ah, it was nothing."

I stared at him in disbelief. "But you shouldn't have . . . I can't believe you—"

Time seemed to stand still for a moment as we stared into each other's eyes, and before I knew what I was doing, and without any regard for the consequences, I found myself reaching for his face and pulling it towards me. Anthony looked startled at first, but then his face softened and he began to move in closer. This was it, the end of our friendship as we both knew it, but I didn't care. All I wanted in that moment was to feel his warm lips on mine, to run my hands through his thick dark hair, to, to . . .

"UNCLE ISME, UNCLE ISME! I'M SCARED, I'M SCARED!" We jolted from the sound of Theo's cries and I bolted to the bedroom, where a firework had been set off so close by it illuminated the room and echoed off the walls.

I lay next to Theo and stroked his head to calm him down, my heart pounding from what had just taken place in the living room. Had I *really* just almost kissed my best friend? Not only that, had I *really* just almost cheated on Neil without a second thought?

A wave of guilt washed over me as I thought about Neil and his recent (admittedly weak) attempts to win me back. I had to speak to Anthony, to tell him it was a silly moment of madness and hope that we could just laugh it off. As soon as I heard Theo's soft snores I snuck out the room, but he was nowhere to be seen. Then I noticed my phone that I'd left on the coffee table, lighting up with a message notification.

Anthony: Sorry Iz, I had to go.
Thank you for a lovely night

I sat on the edge of the sofa staring at the door and willing Anthony to come back, but he never did.

*

Anthony: Can I come round tonight?

Isme: Yeah, of course
I'm making lasagne, if you want some

Anthony: It's OK, I'll come round a bit later once the kids are asleep

As soon as I opened the door, Anthony barged past me with a sombre look on his face.

"Everything OK?" I asked, following him through to the living room, although it was clear from the way he was pacing up and down that it wasn't.

"I need to ask you something, Isme, and you need to be completely honest with me."

"Of course, anything."

Anthony cleared his throat. "Last night, when we nearly . . . you know. If we hadn't been disturbed by Theo and went through with it, what would have happened after that? Would you have called off the engagement and that?"

I rested my wobbly legs on the arm of the sofa as I pondered his question. In the heat of the moment, I hadn't given any thought to beyond the kiss. Even worse, cheating on Neil had been more of an afterthought.

"I'm not sure. I hadn't really thought about it—"

"OK, well, I'm asking you now," he said, moving closer to me so I could smell the sweet tones of his aftershave. "Will you call off the engagement?"

So many thoughts swirled through my head at that point, it was hard to follow them – like the money we'd spent on the imminent engagement party that we couldn't afford to lose, Mum and Dad and how close we were to resolving their money worries, and ultimately how much I wanted to grab Anthony's face and pull him to me.

"I, I . . ."

Anthony shook his head. "Thought not," he said before storming out of the flat, slamming the door behind him.

*

Could I *really* risk calling off the engagement to Neil in the hope that me and Anthony worked out? We'd never crossed the romantic boundary before – what if we got the major ick factor, which would then make it too awkward to even be friends any more?

If we *did* work out, then Anthony is Greek so we could still unlock the inheritance money, but would need to get married pretty sharpish to have any hope of saving the house. Would Anthony be down with that?

Cue another pros and cons list.

Call off the engagement

Pros:

1. I don't have to go through the embarrassment of watching Joan's church choir drain the life out of the engagement party.

2. I can stop pretending to like vegan food.

3. I can drink wine without being made to feel like I'm one sip away from having a drinking problem.

4. Dad will be made up.

5. I'll still have Anthony in my life.

Cons:

1. If I'm not married by the time I'm thirty-five then I lose the inheritance

money, which only gives me a year to get married.

2. We'll lose the money we've already paid out on the engagement party.

3. I'll carry the stigma of having a failed engagement around for a bit and will probably get some pitiful looks off people in the Greek Church.

4. Mum won't be happy.

I could feel my stomach knotting as I read over the list. *'I'll still have Anthony in my life.'* Everything else I had written blurred into insignificance. I had to have Anthony in my life, no matter what.

*

Isme: Will you come round tonight?
There's something really important
I need to say to you

Anthony: I think your silence said enough
the other night, don't you?

Isme: Please, Anthony

Anthony: OK

I was sitting in work on my lunch break, jotting down some notes about what I wanted to say to him – I didn't want to end up fumbling my words and looking like a complete tit – when a Facebook notification came up on my phone telling me that Zara had posted a new picture.

"So what?" I muttered to myself and carried on writing, but something was niggling at me. Intrigue, maybe? Hope that it was a picture of her not looking her best that she hadn't meant to post, possibly? I clicked onto it, and threw my phone down like it was hot coal when the picture appeared.

It was a selfie of her and Anthony, both looking a bit worse for wear. Anthony was pulling a tongue at the camera while Zara planted a kiss on his cheek. I tried convincing myself that it could have been taken ages ago, well before *my* 'thing' with Anthony started, but then I spotted the caption: 'Bonfire night with this one'. The night we nearly kissed.

I sat staring out the window in a daze as I tried to process everything, my heart thumping against my chest. There was me assuming he'd left the flat the way he had because he was confused about my intentions – when it was actually because he was desperate to go and see Zara. Did they have a right old laugh at my expense?

"I can't believe she tried to kiss you!" I could hear Zara saying, throwing her head back and cackling like a witch.

"Ha, I know! And her breath smelt of hot dog," I imagined Anthony scoffing back.

I thought back to earlier in the year when he'd told me he

had no intention of pursuing anything with her after they'd kissed, and how he'd promised there would be no more secrets between us. My stomach lurched at the thought that he had been lying this whole time, and just when I thought I knew him better than ever.

I took some much-needed deep breaths before unlocking my phone and opening up my message chat with Anthony.

> **Isme:** No need to come round tonight after all
> And by the way, the answer is no, I won't call
> off the engagement

It was the right thing to do. It had to be.

So why did my heart feel like it was about to shatter into a million pieces?

*

For the first time in the whole two weeks that the twins had been staying with me, I woke up before them after a restless night, my brain a scrambled mess of Anthony and Zara. Whenever I did manage to doze off, they'd invade my dreams, their mocking faces swirling around my head, slowly morphing into big scary clown faces, and I'd jolt from my sleep.

I tiptoed to the kitchen, excited at the prospect of having a cuppa in peace, when I heard a gentle tap on the front door. My immediate thought was that it was Neil – it was only a matter of time before he came on the warpath demanding to know where he stood.

The last person I expected to see standing there when I opened the door was Maria.

She looked different, in a good way. Her hair, which she'd normally throw up in a messy bun, looked luscious and shiny as it sat loosely around her shoulders, and there was a glow to her complexion you only get from having sufficient kip. Standing next to her with my greasy mane which, as Theo had kindly pointed out the night before, smelt like the bin, dull skin and three-day-old pyjamas that were riddled with questionable smudges, we were like a before-and-after poster for a parenting magazine.

I'd thought a lot lately about what I'd do when Maria turned up. Would I slap her in the face, like in the movies, and call her every name under the sun? But here she was, standing in front of me with a very apologetic look on her face, and all I wanted to do was hug her. So, I did.

"Isme, I am so sorry for leaving the way I did," said Maria, wiping at her wet eyes. "I honestly can't thank you enough for looking after my boys for me."

I wanted to tell her it was fine and that I'd quite enjoyed it (most of the time), but there *was* still a part of me that was pissed off she'd left me in the lurch the way she had, so I wasn't going to give her an easy ride.

"You've got a lot of explaining to do." We walked inside.

Maria took in a deep breath. "Have you ever felt so trapped it's like the walls are literally closing in on you, and if you don't escape right there and then they're going to crush you to death?"

I nodded. It sounded all too familiar.

"That's what I've felt like these last few months, trapped in my own life, every day a monotonous repetition of the one before. The morning I left, I was carrying out my usual juggling routine to get us all out the house on time while George slept away another hangover, when Tomaso dropped his bowl of milk and cereal on the floor. It happens all the time, and I usually just sigh and tell him he needs to be more careful, but that morning something inside me flipped." Maria's voice broke off and she looked on the verge of tears as she struggled to relive the memory. I placed a comforting hand on her lap to encourage her to carry on.

"I roared at him so loud he cried and hid under the table, and instead of feeling guilty, which I normally would do, I felt glad that he was scared. What sort of a mother does that make me?"

"A bloody normal one," I scoffed. "If there's one thing I've learnt over these last few weeks, it's that these little people know how to push our buttons, and it would take a certain person not to lose their shit every once in a while."

Maria smiled gratefully and proceeded to tell me how, in a panic, she bought an open return train ticket to London and arranged to go and stay with a friend from hairdressing school.

"I should have asked you first, but my head was up my arse. I needed to escape to get my head together and didn't want anyone trying to talk me out of it."

"Did you? Get your head together, I mean."

"Yeah, I think I did. You see, I realised what I've been doing wrong all this time. I've been *allowing* George to take me for granted, and getting increasingly more annoyed and resentful about it, snapping at him over the stupidest things, and taking my frustrations out on the twins, when I should have just told him how I felt."

"What now then?" I asked, after a pause.

"The last few weeks has made me realise that I'm bloody lucky. I'm lucky to have two gorgeous boys who, although they are a handful at the best of times, are also loving and gentle and kind. I'm lucky to have a husband who, despite his bone idleness, loves me and is making every effort to make our marriage work. I know I said to you a few weeks ago that I wasn't sure if I loved him any more, but my head was cabbaged. I love him like a migraine, but he's my migraine and I can't imagine ever being with anyone else."

After Maria and the twins left, a range of emotions washed over me – happiness that Maria had sorted her head out and was going to make things work with George, relief that I was no longer responsible for the life of two little human beings, excited at the prospect of having a poo in peace. But ultimately, I felt sad. Moaning aside, the twins had become part of the furniture – partly because there were remnants of them *on* the furniture – and, as I looked around the empty flat, I wanted nothing more than to have them back.

With loneliness getting the better of me, I picked up my phone and dialled Neil's number.

*

It had been two days since the twins left and, despite loving the peace, I would find myself getting choked up at the smallest reminders that they'd been there, like when I found one of their PJ Masks action figures in the bed.

"They're not dead." Neil had sneered as he sat next to me on the sofa reading a bridal magazine. Joan had bought me it months ago but I always seemed to find excuses not to read it. "I'm sure you'll see them again soon, when Maria inevitably decides she needs another holiday."

I let out a heavy sigh. "It wasn't a holiday, Neil, more a retreat for the mind and soul. Anyway, whatever you want to call it, it's done her the world of good and that's all that matters."

Neil muttered something under his breath about me being naïve, which I chose to ignore. He'd done his fair share of grovelling recently, so it was only a matter of time before he reverted back to being an arse.

"Did you know that the tradition of a wedding cake comes from Ancient Rome?" said Neil, reading from the magazine. "Apparently, revellers broke a loaf of bread over a bride's head for fertility's sake."

"Really?" I said, while Googling recipes for a carrot cake that someone had asked me to make in work for their mum's birthday. Having the twins around had reignited the little baking fire in my belly and, despite being back on my normal working hours, I was determined to try and keep the fire alive, even if it meant sacrificing some evenings, or part of my weekends, to deal with any orders.

Neil closed the magazine abruptly. "When are you going to take this wedding seriously, Isme?" I hadn't realised he'd been peering over at my phone.

"I am! Look, I'm researching wedding cake flavours," I said, waving the phone in his face. "Carrot cake is up there as being one of the most popular."

I think he bought it because his face softened into a smile, and he carried on perusing the magazine, even tearing out some of the pages he deemed useful, which sounded deafening in the quietness of the flat. I longed for the twins and their rowdiness.

*

Mum: Isme, will you help your mama
with something this week?

Isme: You're not going to ask me to wax
your legs again, are you?
It still gives me nightmares

Mum: No Isme, is special project

I burst into a fit of laughter when Mum picked me up for our 'special project' and I caught sight of her in the driving seat. She was dressed all in black, in a top and leggings, topped off with one of Dad's ribbed woolly hats.

"Oh my god, Mum, we're not robbing a bank, are we? I know times are hard, like, but—"

"Shush, Isme, we not rob a bank."

I relaxed into the passenger seat. "OK, where to then, captain?"

"You find out soon."

'Soon' turned out to be an hour, the first fifteen minutes of which were spent with Mum faffing around with the wing mirror and trying to figure out first gear. For the other forty-five, I had to listen to Mum recite the entire Nana Mouskouri album and watch as she changed gears with the brute force of The Hulk. By the time we pulled up, I was in desperate need of a wee, and new eardrums.

"Where are we?" I asked, squinting through the car windows, which were starting to steam up against the heavy downpour that had started outside. From what I *could* see, we were positioned on the edge of a small cul-de-sac in an area I didn't recognise. Thankfully, there didn't seem to be any banks in sight.

"Mum, what's going— Oh, you've GOT to be kidding me?"

Mum had pulled out a pair of binoculars and was peering through them in the direction of the far corner house. I felt like I was on an episode of Agatha Christie's *Miss Marple*.

"SSSSHHH, Isme. Jus wait."

I threw my head back against the headrest and waited for whatever it was that was about to happen – hopefully Ant and Dec popping out of the bushes and revealing I was part of a prank for *Saturday Night Takeaway*. After a couple of minutes, I spotted a familiar figure walking up the path of the house Mum had been spying on.

"Is that . . . Dad?"

Mum put down her binoculars and sighed.

"Mum, what's going on? Why are we following Dad?"

"Your papa, he say he go to a spin class in thee gym every Thursday, but I find out it finish months ago. I started to follow him and this is where he comes."

We watched as Dad knocked on the front door and a small plump lady answered it.

"Wait, that's Carol!"

Mum gasped. "WHAT? YOU KNOW HER?"

"Yeah, it's Dad's nutritionist, well kind of, you see—"

SLAM!

Mum bailed out of the car before I could explain, battling through the rain like a woman possessed to get to Dad. I followed closely behind, just making out Mum's bulky frame through the rain that was blurring my vision.

"STEPHEN ELIADES, WHAT IN *HADES* IS GOING ON!"

Dad jolted at the sound of Mum's voice, and almost stumbled backwards into the house. "Elana? Love? Is that you?"

"No, Stephen, it is the Lord Jesus Christ himself. Of course it is me!"

"What are you, um, doing here?"

"I ask you thee same question, Stephen!" shouted Mum, waving her arms in the air uncontrollably. "Who is this, this floozy?" Mum looked at Carol like she'd just caught the trail wind of a very smelly fart.

"Why don't you come in," said Carol calmly, maintaining her composure despite the floozy insult. "I'll get you some towels to dry yourselves off."

"I don want your, your towels," spat Mum, barging inside. "I want an explanation."

We walked through the brightly lit hall and into the front room, where the enticing smell of home cooking filled the air –

cooking oil, coupled with hints of cinnamon and mint. It smelt familiarly like one of Mum's Greek lamb stews, and I wondered how inappropriate it would be to ask for a plate.

"Please, sit." Carol signalled for Mum and me to sit on one of the beige leather sofas, that looked about as tired and dated as I felt. As I looked around, that seemed to be the general theme – brown, patterned carpets that wouldn't look out of place in a 1970s showroom, an old Panasonic TV that looked just as ancient as Mum and Dad's, and a glass cabinet in the corner containing a jumble of crystal glasses, ceramic jugs and vintage serving plates.

I kindly obliged, whilst Mum opted to stand, folding her arms across her chest and staring stony-faced at Dad, as she waited for an explanation – I hadn't seen her that angry since the Papadopouloses were axed from *Eastenders*.

Dad cleared his throat. "Elana, Isme, I want you to meet my sister, Carol."

I felt my mouth slowly fall open as I tried to take in Dad's words.

"Wait . . . what? But you don't have a sister? Nan and Grandad didn't have any other kids?"

"No, Carol is from my biological parents' side." That's when it all started to make sense. "I've always been interested in knowing who my real family were," Dad continued, "and even started looking a few years ago but it just led me to a dead end, and I lost all hope. The whole process left me feeling disheartened and upset, so I never tried again. I also felt bad on your nan and grandad because I didn't want them to think they weren't enough for me, so I never told them. In fact, I didn't want any of you to think that, so I kept it from all of you. But in the end, it turned out I didn't need to look, because they found me! They've been looking for me for years apparently, and it's only thanks to a linked connection on Facebook that Carol found me."

Dad looked over at Carol and they shared a smile. It seemed that, despite the many years they'd missed together, a close bond had already formed, and I couldn't help but smile too. Mum, on the other hand, still wore the face of someone ready to kill.

When she did speak, her voice was deep and gravelly. "Why lie, Stephen? I am your wife, why would you lie to me about this?"

"Because I honestly didn't believe it was really them, love, and I needed to find out for myself first. Then, when I did meet them, all that kicked off with the failed investment, so it just didn't feel like the right time."

There was a pause while we all waited for Mum to make her next move.

"You shouldn't have lied to me, Stephen. I can never trust you again. Isme, *ela*. We leave." With that, Mum darted out of the house.

Hell hath no fury like a Greek woman scorned.

*

I called Dad to make sure Mum hadn't done anything too hasty, like 'put a spade too 'is head' or kicked him out – I loved the bones of him, but couldn't have him staying in the flat, especially with Neil back on the scene. There'd be more tension and testosterone than a bull fight.

I was also keen for him to know that I was pleased he'd met his real family, and to reassure him I had no deep-rooted insecurities about him binning us all off for them.

"Thanks love, it really does mean a lot. I just wish your mum would see it like that."

"She'll come round eventually, I'm sure. You know she doesn't like being lied to."

"I know, I just thought I was doing the right thing by not telling her with everything else that's been going on. Carol's son, Andrew, is getting married next month, and I'd really like your mum to come with me. I'd like you all to come. It would mean so much to me."

"She prides herself on honesty and expects the same from everyone around her, and now you've broken that trust. You may just need to give her some time."

*

Mum: Isme, don't forget, you and Neil come to church today

Isme: What's it for again?

Mum: Father Demetrious is going to do a blessing for you and Neil. Then he come back to the house for dinner and to go over some final things for the party

Isme: Bloody hell, how many more free dinners is the man gonna squeeze out of us?

Mum: Isme, don't be so rude, he is man of the cloth

Isme: Man of the free meals, more like

Father Demetrius ended up bypassing the meal. Something about not feeling too good, although my guess was that he was still reeling from Neil sabotaging his Holy Communion when he asked if there was an alcohol-free option.

I was disappointed; without Father there, Mum wouldn't have to put on her happy families face and pretend that everything was OK, and Dad wouldn't have to pretend to like Neil. Cue awkward meal for four.

"Could you pass me the potatoes please, love."

Mum looked at Dad like he'd just announced a worldwide shortage of coriander. She muttered something under her breath and handed me the bowl of spuds to pass to him.

The sound of cutlery on plates was deafening against the silence that followed. I needed to say something, and fast. Luckily, Dad got in there first.

"I was speaking to Sandra before. Anthony's been moping round like a wet weekend the last few weeks. Any idea why?"

I shrugged my shoulders, but inside I was reeling. Was I the cause of his misery? Was he regretting choosing Zara over me? The thought made my belly flutter, and I quickly forced myself to remember that, regardless of whether he was regretting it or not, he'd lied. Would I ever be able to trust him again?

"You don't seem to knock about with him any more, do you?"

Dad went on. "How come?"

I cleared my throat, that was becoming increasingly drier. "No reason really, we've just grown apart a bit I suppose and—"

"And she's got me now," interrupted Neil.

"I don't think it's a trade-off, Neil—"

"And I'm Greek too," Neil went on, "so we can still get the inheritance money. Two birds, one stone, and that."

Dad looked puzzled. "What do you mean?"

"The Will? That Elana's mother left?" I nudged Neil's leg under the table, but he carried on regardless. "You know what it says about Isme having to marry someone Greek or she doesn't get the money?"

Dad looked over at Mum, who was doing her best to hide behind her fork.

"Elana, you told me your mother left all her money to charity?"

"She did! Well, some of it."

"So, let me get this straight," said Dad, his tone deepening, "you've been giving me a hard time for not telling you about meeting my real family, when all along you've been keeping *this* from *me*?"

A flush swept across Mum's cheeks, and for the first time in her life, she didn't know what to say.

"You're unbelievable," said Dad, slamming his knife and fork down on the plate and storming out of the room. Mum hesitated for a moment, as if internally battling with herself whether, for once in her life, she could admit that she was in the wrong. She followed after him.

"What the hell was that about?" I said to Neil once they were gone.

"What? I thought he knew?"

"Don't lie, you know I told you Mum had been keeping it from him. Bloody hell, Neil, you've opened up a right can of worms there."

Neil let out an exaggerated sigh. "What is it about this family and all the secrets? I feel like I'm marrying into the Mitchell family."

Insult aside, he had a point.

*

Maria: Happy engagement party eve! I've left you
a box of pampering goodies outside the flat

The box turned out to be more like a treasure chest full to the brim with weird and wonderful beauty products that I hadn't the faintest what to do with, like a paper mask that looked like something off *Halloween* and some fake eyelashes that stick on with magnets.

I'd just finished applying an unusual blue substance to my face that smelt like Play-Doh when I heard a knock at the door. I hoped it wouldn't be Neil; I'd reeled off some crap to him about it being bad luck in Greek culture to see each other the night before the engagement party so I could have the night to myself.

"Bleedin' hell, Iz, what's that all over your face? You look like one of those smurfs." It was Dad with, thankfully, no overnight bags in site.

"You won't be laughing when I've got the skin of a ten-year-old," I scoffed, closing the door behind him.

"Yeah, and a houseful of mushrooms."

I tried to laugh but the mask was restricting my facial muscles. Now I knew what it was like for Jackie Stallone.

"What are you doing here, anyway?" I said, putting the kettle on. "Is it about what happened at dinner on Sunday?"

Dad started picking at his fingernails. "Kind of, yeah."

I sighed. "Look, Dad, I've been telling Mum for ages to tell you about the Will, I don't know why she didn't—"

"I haven't come here to have a moan about your mum, love. I mean, I am still quite miffed about it, but at the end of the day I was keeping a big secret too, so in a way we're both as bad as each other."

I leant against the kitchen counter and folded my arms. "What is it, then?"

Dad cleared his throat. "I know why you're marrying Neil, love, and you can't do it. I won't let you."

I swallowed down the lump that had formed in my throat. "I . . . don't know what you mean."

"Come on, I wasn't born yesterday. You marry him, you get that money, and you give it to me and your mum, so we don't have to sell the house. Am I right?"

"It's not just about the Will, Dad," I said defensively, handing him his tea. "I do like Neil, too. He's a good lad."

Dad almost spilt his tea. "Is he? OK, well answer me this, then. If the Will didn't exist, would you still be marrying him?"

I stared down at the floor, unable to meet his gaze. "Probably, yeah," I mumbled.

"I don't believe you, Iz, I'm sorry. You're not yourself when you're around him, love, you always seem, I dunno, on edge or something. Like you're waiting for him to say or do something that's going to piss someone off."

I let out a nervous laugh. I wanted to tell him he was wrong, to convince him that I wasn't just marrying Neil for the inheritance money, but I couldn't find the words.

Sensing my internal conflict, Dad put down his mug and sidled up next to me against the kitchen counter. "All I've ever wanted for you, hoped for you, is that you meet someone who makes you happy. Someone who brings out the best in you and keeps that fire in your belly, that I've always loved about you, alight." He gently prodded my stomach. "He's not that person for you, Iz, I know he's not. And from the look on your face, you know it too."

I stared into my mug, hoping that if I looked hard enough I might be able to suppress the tears that were beginning to fill my eyes. He was right, of course he was, but I couldn't admit it. There had to be a point to the last six months, otherwise what was it all for?

"Look, Dad, I know you mean well, but honestly, I'm happy with Neil!" I tried forcing a smile, but the mask had turned to stone. "Now, come on, be off with you, I need to wash this mask off before my face peels off with it!"

Turns out, I didn't need to wash the mask off, the tears that came after Dad left took care of that.

*

"Isme, how come you're not changed? Come on, we're going to be late!" Neil came barging through the door like the white rabbit from *Alice in Wonderland*, frantically tapping his watch.

"Sorry, it's Maria's fault. She bought me these magnetic eyelash thingies which, it turns out, you need a degree or something to use." Thankfully, after a YouTube tutorial, I'd managed to get them on.

"So long as they're not made from real mink, Isme. You know how I feel about those. Speaking of animal cruelty, is Maddy coming tonight?"

I sighed. "No, I don't think so."

The truth was, I hadn't spoken to her since our heated discussion last month, when she'd told me about Neil and Zara meeting for coffee, and had been too stubborn to try and make amends since. But I missed her more and more as the weeks went on, and in the midst of my eyelash panic, I'd called her for advice, and couldn't help feeling deflated when she didn't answer. Was it too little, too late?

I rushed off to the bedroom to change into my party frock – a black and white cutwork embroidered mini dress from Karen Millen that I'd scooped up in the sales months ago. With the colder, darker nights firmly set in, it ideally wasn't the best time of year to be flashing my bare legs. Then there was Mum, who deemed tights a wardrobe must whatever the season, who would have a hernia when she saw me. But for the first time in a long time, I felt good in something, so I'd decided it would be worth the lecture (and hyperthermia).

"Shit, Agnes is ringing," I said as I went to throw my phone into my clutch bag, but Neil grabbed it out of my hand before I got the chance.

"There's no time, come on! We've got to go." He began escorting me out of the flat and into the lift like a security guard. Once the lift doors were closed, he grabbed my waist and pulled me towards him. "You look great, Isme." He lifted my chin up and leant in for a kiss. His lips felt warm and soft, but all I could think about was the conversation with Dad the night before, his words repeating over and over in my head. *He's not the person for you, Iz.*

"Are you OK?" asked Neil, pulling away and sensing my reluctance.

I smiled, weakly. "Yes, I'm fine! Just pre-party nerves. Now, come on. Let's go."

A handful of people were at the restaurant once we arrived, including Father Demetrios, who was already invading the buffet, and Joan and her 'choir', which consisted of another woman sporting the same hideous sandals as Joan, and two grey-haired men who looked one breath away from heart failure. ABBA, eat your heart out.

Mum was also there, barking out orders to the staff like she owned the place, and so was Dad, who looked on from the other side of the room with a look of distaste. Clearly, they still weren't on speaking terms. I waved over to Dad, and he smiled awkwardly.

"Isme, you look . . . too skinny," said Mum, as she came bouncing over from the bar. "You need to eat something. *Ela*, come, have some buffet."

Before I could protest, Mum dragged me over to the food and began filling up a plastic plate with all my favourite Greek food, that would normally have me licking my lips. But my stomach was bubbling and the sight of it was making me nauseous.

"Elana, I assume the vegan options are still to be brought out?" said Neil, eyeing the buffet suspiciously.

"No, they are already there, see!" She pointed to two sad-looking bowls at the end of the table containing various nuts and seeds.

Neil rolled his eyes. "Isme, will you please explain to your mum, once again, that vegans eat more than nuts."

I sighed. It was going to be a long night.

*

By eight o'clock the place was filling up, and my facial muscles were aching from all the forced laughs and small talk. During a brief moment of peace, and whilst Neil was busy having a guffawing match with Jeff, I looked around the room at the familiar, and not so familiar, sea of faces. There was a real sense of merriment in the air as they laughed and clinked glasses, but I felt detached from it all, like I was watching through a lens. I felt like a gatecrasher at my own party, and longed for the comfort of a friend – but with no Maddy or Anthony to turn to, I was lost.

Suddenly, the music stopped and Joan and her cronies took to the stage. Everyone began clapping excitedly, ready to get down to some live music.

"This little light of mine,
I'm gonna let it shine.

This little light of mine,
I'm gonna let it shine.
This little light of mine,
I'm gonna let it shine, let it shine, let it shine, let it shine . . ."

Excitement quickly turned to confusion, as people exchanged what-the-fuck glances with one another and stood gawping up at the stage. Then there was Neil, who was singing along and clapping away like a groupie. I decided it was time for a stronger drink, and headed to the bar.

"Is one of those for me?" came a familiar voice from behind me, as I handed my cash over to the bar attendant for the two much-needed jägerbombs.

The sight of Anthony made my heart pound, and for a split second I almost forgot what had happened a week ago and wanted nothing more than to just grab his face and pull him to me. Then the photo of him and Zara popped into my head and my whole body tensed.

"What's with *Songs of Praise* over there?" he laughed.

"If you've just come here to take the piss, Anthony, then I'd prefer it if you left."

"Sorry, no, I'm just a bit nervous, I guess." Anthony put his hands in his pockets and stared down at his feet. "Look, Iz, there's something I really need to say to you."

I folded my arms across my chest in an attempt to maintain my angry demeanour, but inside I was mush. "Well, go on."

Anthony cleared his throat. "You can't marry Neil."

"Oh yeah, and why is that?"

"Because I'm in love with you."

Time seemed to stand still for a moment as his words hung in the air. My heart hammered against my chest, willing me to accept Anthony's declaration of love and just snog his face off. The very thought of it set a flurry of butterflies off in my tummy. But then my head interjected, reminding me that he went running to Zara the night we almost kissed, and then I felt an overwhelming urge to throw my drink in his face.

"Are you in love with Zara too?"

Anthony frowned. "Wait, what?"

"I know you were with her the night we nearly . . . you know."

"Who told you—"

"Isme, there you are!" Neil suddenly appeared, planting a heavy kiss on my cheek. He put his arm around me like a cat marking its territory. "Anthony, I didn't realise you were coming."

"He was just leaving."

Anthony hesitated for a moment, as if waiting to see if I would change my mind. Eventually, he turned and walked away, his shoulders hunched over like a disobedient kid who'd just been told to go on the naughty step. The pain in my chest was too much to bear, and I bolted to the toilets.

I leant forward against the toilet sink to steady my wobbly legs, my pulse still racing. 'Because I'm in love with you.' Anthony's words replayed over and over in my head, as if trying to reassure me that, yes, my best friend of thirty years, who I had realised I had feelings for, had finally said the words I'd been longing to hear. The butterflies in my stomach suddenly came to life again, until quickly turning to dust at the thought of Anthony's betrayal. Why did he have to go and fuck it all up? Why?

I looked up at my reflection in the mirror and hardly recognised the girl staring back at me. Her usual ample cheeks had sunk inwards, and the creases at the side of her eyes were more prominent than they were six months ago.

I wasn't myself. I hadn't *felt* myself for a long time, but had been too wrapped up in Neil and the engagement to really take note.

I closed my eyes and all I could see was Anthony standing in front of me, his eyes wide and hopeful. I wanted nothing more than for him to come bursting through the toilet doors and to wrap his arms around me. He'd make me feel myself again, but was his declaration of love enough to bury all the lies and deceit?

"Isme, there y'ar! I've been trying to call you all day." Agnes suddenly appeared in the toilets, a look of concern etched across her face once she caught sight of me. "Are you OK? Ye look like you've seen a ghost."

I splashed some water on my clammy hands. "Yeah fine, sorry. Neil's had my phone." I noticed she was still wearing her coat, like she wasn't planning on staying. "Come on, let's go and enjoy the party." I went to open the door, but Agnes grabbed my arm.

"Look, there's something you really need to know before you go back out there, Iz."

"Oh no, has Neil joined his mum up on stage?!" I was trying to lighten the mood, but could tell from her pained expression that it was something more serious.

A group of young excitable youths came bounding through the toilet door, giggling and singing at the top of their lungs. "*Gloria! Gloria! In excelsis Deo. Gloria! Gloria! In excelsis Deo!*"

Agnes mouthed something to me, but I couldn't catch it over the high-pitched singing.

"WHAT DID YOU SAY?" I shouted, as we made our way out of the toilets and back out to the party.

"I SAID, NEIL DIDN'T GO TO LOCH LOMOND ALONE, HE TOOK SOMEONE WITH HIM."

The song finished and the room erupted into claps and cheers. Someone at the back of the room shouted, "Show us yer tits!" and a flushed-faced Joan and her cronies scurried off the stage.

I scrunched my face at Agnes. "Nah. He couldn't have."

"It's true, Iz. The hotel rang to say someone left some expensive face cream in the hotel room. La Mer or something."

I immediately recognised the name, because I used to go on to Zara about how she could justify spending so much on a cream. That's when I spotted her, standing in the middle of the dancefloor, her face beaming up at Neil, who had now taken to the stage.

"I want to start by saying sorry for anyone who's vegan," he announced to the room. "There's been a bit of a . . . a mis-understanding with the buffet, shall we say."

Neil started to reel off his speech, but I didn't catch a word. I was honed in on Zara like a bull to a rag. Neil must have said something remotely funny because she threw her head back and laughed, and something inside me clicked.

"ONE MAN NEVER HAS BEEN ENOUGH FOR YOU, HAS IT?" I shouted, as I stormed over in her direction. The whole room went deathly silent.

Zara looked around innocently, as if I was talking to someone else.

"First Anthony, now Neil! You really are something, Zara."

"Isme, what's going on." Neil had come off the stage and tried to grip my hand.

"Don't touch me, you piece of shit! I know you took her to Loch Lomond."

"What, no I nev—"

I shushed him with my hand.

"I honestly don't know what you're talking about, Isme." Zara was doing her best to look innocent and shocked, but there was a hint of a smirk on her pretty little face, which sent a ripple of fury through me. Before I knew what I was doing, and without any regard for the consequences, I drew my fist back ready to attack, but was stopped by someone grabbing me from behind and pushing me out of the room.

"IT'S OVER, YOU GOBSHITE," I shouted back at Neil, while everyone watched on with a mixture of shock and bemusement on their faces. "THIS JOKE OF AN ENGAGEMENT, IT'S OVER!"

The brisk November air hit me as I got outside, and I started to shake uncontrollably. Dad wrapped his arms around me, and I sobbed, big, drunken, heavy sobs that made my body shake and soaked his shirt.

"It's OK, love, it's all over now," he whispered in my ear. I felt like a little girl again being comforted after a fall.

As my sobs subsided and I could no longer feel the cold, my whole body started to relax, and an overwhelming feeling of relief washed over me.

I was free.

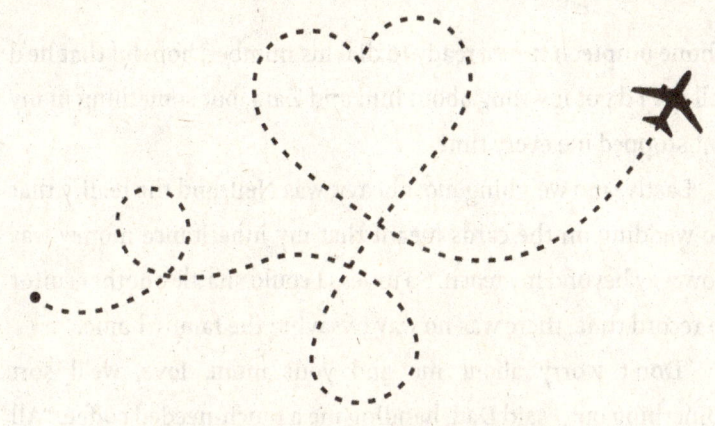

DECEMBER

IT WAS THE MORNING AFTER THE NIGHT BEFORE, and I was struggling to lift my head off the pillow, which wasn't to do with any hangover; I'd sobered up good and proper once it all kicked off with Zara and Neil. I just felt . . . heavy. Like I was finally free of the biggest ball-ache that had been occupying my life for the last six months, but there were still a million and one other things weighing me down. I mean, where do I start?

Firstly, there was Mum, who'd want to string me up for causing such a scene in front of her lot. I'd had visions of her making me do a *Game of Thrones* style walk through the streets of Liverpool, chanting 'shame' while all the Greeks threw piss and rotten vegetables at me.

Then there was Anthony, whose words had continued replaying in my head all night like a song stuck on repeat. I'd picked up my phone umpteen times, ready to dial his number, hopeful that he'd tell me I'd got it wrong about him and Zara, but something in my gut stopped me every time.

Lastly, and weighing most heavy, was Neil, and the reality that no wedding on the cards meant that my inheritance money was now way beyond my reach. So unless I could snaffle another suitor in record time, there was no way of saving the family home.

"Don't worry about me and your mum, love, we'll sort something out," said Dad, handing me a much-needed coffee. "All that matters to us is that you're happy."

"I doubt Mum will see it that way," I scoffed.

Dad placed a hand on my shoulder. "Leave your mum to me. You just get your head together and come round once you're ready."

After Dad left, I picked up my phone, which I soon regretted. Fourteen missed calls, two voicemails and ten text messages, most of which seemed to be from Neil. I'd expected him to show up at the flat, although it wouldn't have surprised me if he had when I'd been asleep and Dad had taken great delight in turning him away. The thought made me smile.

I jolted as my phone started buzzing in my hand – Neil, again. Without hesitation, I pressed the decline button and switched it off for the rest of the day.

Ignorance is bliss.

*

It had been two days since the engagement party and I still hadn't changed out of my pyjamas. The flat resembled the same mess from George after Maria had left, with empty pizza boxes and cans sprawled across the coffee table, the kitchen sink piled high with dirty dishes.

I'd briefly turned my phone on, only to quickly turn it back off again as the text and voicemail messages came through from a very angry Neil who, in his words, couldn't understand why I had reacted the way I did and blamed the number of drinks I had.

I launched my phone across the floor and rubbed at my sleep-ridden eyes. I felt angry. Angry at Anthony, for telling me he loved me when it was too little, too late. Angry at Neil, for going behind my back with Zara and making me look like an idiot. But ultimately, I was angry with myself for putting up with him for as long as I did, allowing him to change who I was and come between my friendships with Maddy and Anthony.

I needed to start to put things right, starting with Maddy. I turned my phone on to send her a suitably apologetic message, when one pinged through from Joan.

> **Joan:** Isme, I don't know what's going on with
> you and Neil, but he really didn't take that
> Zara girl to Loch Lomond
> I can prove it
> Will you meet with me so I can explain?

Joan having proof that Neil didn't take Zara to Loch Lomond wouldn't change my mind about him and the engagement, but I needed some sort of closure (and an excuse to have a shower), so something told me to go and find out.

I arranged to meet her in a Costa in town, and she was already sat at a table when I arrived, cradling a mug and sipping the contents like she was having the cup of wine at Holy Communion. She tilted her head slightly when she saw me, with a look of concern on her face. Or was it pity?

"Thank you for meeting me."

I sat down and she pushed a cup of what looked like green tea across the table, which I eyed suspiciously. Was her niceness a front and she was going to poison me to death for publicly shaming her beloved son?

"It's herbal tea. Neil tells me you like it."

I forced a smile and, under Joan's watchful eyes, took a sip. It tasted like grass, which was exactly what I told Neil every time he'd tried to convince me to drink it.

We sat in silence for a bit, which was deafening amongst the chitter-chatter of other customers and loud, screaming noise coming from the coffee machine. 'Last Christmas' was coming from the speakers, and it suddenly dawned on me that, with everything that had been going on, I hadn't realised that the festive season had crept up.

"So, that was quite a show you put on, on Saturday!" Joan said.

I tightened my grip around my mug. "It wasn't a 'show', Joan. I was really upset."

"Sorry, forgive me. I didn't mean it like that." She did.

"What is it you wanted to tell me?"

"Ah, yes." Joan reached into her handbag and pulled out a small tub of La Mer face cream, which I glared at inquisitively. "It's mine. *I* left it at the hotel, not Zara."

I couldn't help the laughter that burst out of my mouth. "Come off it, Joan. No offence, but you don't exactly strike me as the type of person who spends over two-hundred pounds on a face cream."

"You're right, I'm not. I won it on an Easter raffle."

I eyed her suspiciously for any sign of fabrication, but she appeared relaxed, her eyes not losing contact with mine. If she *was* lying, she was doing a bloody good job of it.

"Look, you don't have to believe me," she said, sensing my doubt, "but does this look like the face of a sixty-two-year-old?" To be fair I had always quite admired her smooth complexion, but I'd always put it down to her good honest Catholic lifestyle.

"There you have it. It was me who went to Loch Lomond with Neil, not Zara. Now, I think you owe my son an apology, don't you?"

I let out a heavy sigh. "Look, Joan, this doesn't change anything—"

"Hello, Isme."

I jolted at the sound of Neil's voice from behind me. He walked round to where Joan was sat and placed a hand on her shoulder, which she covered with one of her own. It was like some weird mother-and-son mob set-up, minus the heavy armoury and general feeling of threat.

"What are you doing here?" I asked, although I already knew the answer from the smirk on Joan's face. She stood up from her chair and signalled for Neil to take it.

"I'll leave you two to it. I'm sure you've got a lot to talk about."

"I'll get us a drink first." I watched Neil stride up to the counter, his toned frame accentuated by the tight joggers and sweatshirt he was wearing. I thought back to six months ago when we'd first met, and how flustered I'd felt at the very sight of him. Little did I know that the man behind the 'body' would be such a tit, and the only internal sensations I now felt were the kind you get when you've had an Imodium (Damn that green tea).

"Now you've got proof that I didn't take Zara to Loch Lomond," said Neil, once he returned with our drinks. "I'm not happy with how you acted on Saturday, but I can forgive you and move past it so we can get things back on track with this wedding."

I almost choked on my coffee. His cock-sure attitude that we could just pick off where we left off was laughable. "It's off, Neil. The engagement . . . us. It's over. We're just too different, you and me. Surely you can see that too?"

He stared into his cup, and for a moment I thought he might be about to turn on the waterworks.

"You can't call it off," he said, his face hardening. "You need me, remember? Otherwise, how else are you going to get that money?"

"That's not important right now."

Neil folded his arms across his chest and sniggered. "Don't tell me, your mum and dad have found some other poor abiding soul to bail them out of their financial mess?"

"Don't bring them into this," I said, pointing a finger in his direction. "This is about you and me, no one else."

"But it's not, Isme, is it. Your family are always around with one problem after another, and trying to thrust their Greek traditions at us. Don't you ever feel suffocated by them all?"

I shrugged my shoulders. "Sometimes, yeah, but who doesn't feel like that at times with their family?"

Neil stood up from his chair. "Well, you know what? You've done me a favour, because now I won't have to pretend that I like them any more."

"YEAH, AND I WON'T HAVE TO PRETEND THAT I LIKE YOU AND YOUR JESUS-SANDAL-WEARING MOTHER!" I didn't realise how loud I'd shouted until I noticed that the room had gone deathly silent, all eyes on us.

Neil stood frozen to the spot, his wide gaze firmly on mine. We stayed like that for several seconds, like a Mexican stand-off, with no chance of a retreat from my side. No one talked shit about my family and got away with it.

Neil caved. He downed his coffee (because imagine if he didn't get his money's worth), mumbled something about expecting the ring back 'in due course', and stormed out.

I couldn't help myself. I pulled the hideous piece of tin out my purse, where it'd been housed any time I wasn't with Neil, followed him out of the coffee shop and threw it at him. "THERE, IT'S ALL YOURS. GIVE IT BACK TO YOUR MUM, YOU TIGHT ARSE!"

*

Isme: On a scale of 1-10 how mad is Mum still?

Dad: I'd say she's a firm 8. Love, Dad 🤍 🐝

Isme: 🙈

Dad: Look, love, the longer you leave it
the worse it's going to be
Why don't you just come round later?
Love, Dad 👽

Isme: I think I'd rather meet her somewhere in
public. At least then I'll have witnesses

I asked Mum/asked Dad to ask Mum, to meet me for lunch in The Boat Club in the city centre – it's the only non-Greek restaurant she's willing to go to because she's a big fan of their margaritas and hanging kebabs.

I arrived early to make sure there was a margarita for her, ready and waiting. It was a Christmas special version, with white cranberry juice and cinnamon which would be right up her street, although I knew it was going to take more than a bevvy to win her over.

I took a sip of my own to calm my nerves, which tasted like Christmas in a glass – spicy-sweet with an earthy undertone. As I looked around the restaurant at the twinkling festive lights and hanging mistletoe, I couldn't help but feel a tinge of excitement at the thought of Christmas, and the love and togetherness it usually brings.

But then I thought of Anthony, and the prospect of spending our first festive period in thirty years apart, and my heart ached.

It had longed for him every day over the last week since the engagement party; every time I pictured him standing in front of me, pouring his heart out. I wanted so badly to forgive him for running off to Zara the night we nearly kissed, and to explore a new romantic side to our friendship. But the trust we'd built in our thirty-year friendship was severely fractured, and I feared it was beyond repair.

It was half an hour later before Mum arrived, by which time my margarita was long gone and I'd started considering drinking hers. She plonked herself in the chair opposite, whipped off her chunky-knit scarf and folded her arms like she was about to conduct an interview.

With an apologetic smile, I pushed the margarita across the table and waited with bated breath for her to say something, but she didn't. Instead, she picked up her glass and took a sip, with about as much speed as a sloth. The suspense was all too much.

"Look, Mum, I—"

Mum shushed me with her hand. "Isme, I talk first."

I braced myself for the onslaught. She took another long, drawn-out sip of her drink. If she was trying to build up the tension and make me feel more nervous than I already was, then she was doing a bloody good job of it.

"I knew from the moment I see those . . . those silly man pants that Neil is no good for you," she said. "I knew he was no good for you and I see that you were not happy, but I let you carry on with him because I want you to settle down like Maria and have thee babies and, and . . ."

"And you wanted the inheritance money."

Mum dropped her chin to her chest, unable to meet my gaze. I placed a hand over hers.

"It's OK, Mum. You never asked me to marry Neil. That was my decision. I just couldn't stand the thought of you and Dad being turfed out of the house, and would do anything to protect you from that happening."

Mum looked up, a smile spreading across her face. "You are a good person, Isme. And I know I don't say enough but I am very proud of you."

A flush swept across my face at the unexpected praise. I could feel a celebratory round of margaritas on the cards . . .

"OUCH! WHAT WAS THAT FOR?" I rubbed at the side of my head where Mum's hand had made contact.

"I cannot believe you embarrass me like that in front of all those people, Isme! Not to mention Father Demetrious, who say he never heard such filthy words come out the mouth of Greek Orthodox woman . . ."

I could have kissed the face off the waiter when he came to take our order ten minutes later, and Mum stopped for breath.

*

It was my first weekend post-Neil – no wedding talk to avoid, no exercise to be forced upon me, no bland plant-based meals to pretend that I liked. I should have been jumping for joy around the flat with 'Free Woman' by Lady Gaga on full blast. So why did I feel more trapped and alone than ever?

I thought back to the list I'd made just before the engagement party, and how not having Anthony in my life was a sacrifice I'd been unwilling to make. Yet here I was, no engagement and no Anthony. How had things gone so badly wrong, so quickly?

In desperate need of distraction, some mindless entertainment where I could switch off from my crappy life – and, well, probably deal with some actual crap – I dialled Maria's number.

"What, you're asking me if the twins can come over and stay?"

"Yeah, what's wrong with that?"

Maria burst into laughter. "Oh nothing, only that it's normally the other way round and you usually come up with some weird and wonderful excuse like, what was it that time? Oh yeah, you needed to defrost the freezer!"

"I did need to defrost the freezer! It was an emergency. I couldn't fit my frozen battered cod in."

"Ha, whatever! I'll drop them off straight from pre-school."

I sighed with relief when she put the phone down; distraction aside, I'd missed the little buggers.

With things back on track with Maria and George, they'd been doing more as a family – taking the twins on fun days out at the weekends and going on little mini-breaks. I was happy that things were working out, but admittedly there was a little part of me that missed being so involved in the twins' lives, and I couldn't help but feel a bit put out. I forgot all of this, of course, when Maria dropped them off a few hours later and they came bursting into the flat, making a beeline straight for the sofa, seemingly confusing it with a bouncy castle.

"Is Anthony coming?" asked Tomaso, mid-jump.

"No, not today, sorry."

"Why?"

"Because he's busy."

"Why?"

"Oi, will you behave. Auntie Isme said he's not coming, and that's the end of it."

I smiled gratefully at Maria and hoped she hadn't noticed my face, which had turned the colour of crimson.

"Look, I don't know what's going on with you two," she whispered, out of earshot of the twins, "but surely it can't be that bad to waste away a whole lifetime of friendship."

I sighed heavily. "It's a long story, Maria, and not one I'm going to get into right now."

Maria held up her hands. "OK, fair enough. All I'll say is that if there's one thing the last few months have taught me, it's that it's not what we have in life but *who* we have that matters."

Maria's words hung in the air for the rest of the night, and as I read the twins their bedtime story, involving a lonely Christmas carrot who finds love on a magical train journey, I found myself staring longingly over at the empty space on the other side of the bed.

"When will your carrot be back?" whispered Theo, as if reading my mind.

I held him a little tighter and sighed. "I don't know, little man. I honestly don't know."

*

I called round to Mum and Dad's to see where things were up

to on the house hunt. With the engagement called off, and no inheritance money imminent, all I could do now was try and help them find somewhere remotely decent to live.

The first thing I noticed when I pulled up was that the 'For Sale' sign was no longer occupying the front garden like an oppressive relative.

"Where's the sign gone?" I asked as I followed them into the kitchen, trying to ignore the fact that they were both in their dressing gowns in the middle of the day, and whilst I was glad that they seemed to have kissed and made up, I didn't want a front-row seat to the reconciliation.

"Sorry, love, we were going to call round and see you later to tell you the news." They exchanged a smile.

"Come on, what? What is it?"

"We don't need to sell the house any more, love," said Dad, his face beaming. "Carol has some family money from when our parents died that I'm owed, which she kept away for me all these years. It's one of the reasons she was so eager to find me."

I shook my head in disbelief. "Wait, what?"

"Is true, Isme! Is enough to settle our debts with thee bank, and they have already agreed to take thee house off the market. We're staying put!"

"OH MY GOD, THIS IS GREAT!" I threw myself at Mum and Dad, almost winding them in the process, and quickly pulled away as I remembered what had possibly occurred before I arrived.

*

It was my first day back in work after the disaster that was the engagement party, and I arrived super early to try and minimise the embarrassment of doing the walk of shame through a busy office. I slid quietly into my seat, crouching down as best I could to take advantage of the desk dividers.

"I thought you might want this back," sneered Zara, slamming a brown envelope down on my desk. "The Will. You know, the one that says you have to marry someone Greek to get your inheritance money. You know, THE SOLE REASON YOU WERE MARRYING NEIL IN THE FIRST PLACE. I MEAN, TALK ABOUT SHALLOW." A chorus of gasps spread across the room.

I hesitated as I contemplated my next move. Did I a) punch her one right in the kipper which, although would feel extremely rewarding, could cost me my job, or b) just smile politely, thank her for giving it back to me and carry on with my work.

Every sly comment she'd ever made about my weight, the many times she'd belittled me in front of other people, the wedge she'd created between me and Anthony . . . It was all building up to this point, rushing through my body and down to my fists, that were now tightly clenched and ready for battle.

But despite the satisfaction I'd get from seeing her flawless face hit the deck, I opted for b). She *wanted* a reaction from me, she *wanted* to see my arse get fired, so I wasn't going to give her the satisfaction.

"Good luck finding your next victim," she muttered before sashaying back to her desk, purposefully dropping something on the floor as she did. It was a pen, and as I picked it up to study it more closely, I recognised the name written across it as being the hotel Agnes had booked for me and Neil in Loch Lomond.

The realisation that Neil did take Zara to Loch Lomond should have filled me with blinding rage, especially as it now seemed that Joan was in on it as well with the whole face cream cover-up. Of course it wasn't Joan's cream. Neil must have asked her to lie to cover his back, which she would do without a second thought for her beloved son. What *would* Father Paul think about her sin? Tut, tut.

But instead of confronting Zara and unleashing a tirade of angry expletives, I found myself laughing uncontrollably and, once I started, I just couldn't seem to stop. In the end, I had to rush to the toilet for fear that I might start leaking.

*

"Happy birthday to me,
I'm no longer thirty-three,
Happy birthday dear me,
My head's the size of a pea."

I remember when birthdays used to be fun, and when absolutely no emphasis was put on the number but rather on how long I could milk the birthday celebrations for. I also had the added bonus of having a birthday close to Christmas, so December was usually a delicious cocktail of Christmas *and* birthday festivities, not to mention double the presents.

Yet here I was, in the shower, making up a song about turning thirty-four, my only planned celebration an Indian takeaway at Mum's, where she'd probably spend the whole time trying to convince me to go on Tinder.

As if my pathetic birthday celebrations weren't bad enough,

turning thirty-four also signified the fact that it was my last year to get hitched before I could get my hands on that £25k. I might as well kiss goodbye to that now.

"Cheer up, Isme, at least your tits still defy gravity, and you don't need to wear Tena lady," said Maria over dinner, in an attempt (I think) to cheer me up. "Tomaso, will you stop throwing that poppadom around. It's not a frisbee."

"Come on, you two, behave." George wrapped an arm around Maria's shoulders and kissed her on the side of the head. She looked up at him and smiled, and I couldn't help but feel a pang of jealousy.

"Who is this Tena lady?" said Mum, waving her empty fork in the air – she still liked to hold one when she was doing her Christmas lent, so she didn't feel left out.

"You know, those things you wear to stop you from pissing yourself," laughed Maria.

"Ah, I never need them, I have strong, how you say, faginal muscles."

I almost choked on my onion bhaji.

Dad cleared his throat. "Look, love, you should focus on all the good things you've got going for you, like the fact you've got a well-paid job, good family, good friends."

"Here, here," said George, holding up his bottle of beer. "You've got a lot going for you, Iz, don't ever forget that." I waited for some form of piss-take follow up but it never came. We exchanged a smile, which was witnessed closely by Maria, who muttered, "Well, fuck me," and the three of us burst into laughter.

"Speaking of friends, Anthony was round here earlier," said

Dad, leaning over and scooping up a spoonful of madras. My stomach fluttered at the sound of his name. Despite everything that had happened, had he found it in himself to drop me off a birthday card? "He needed to borrow the foot pump for the air on his tyres."

I felt myself deflate like the air out of his tyres.

*

> **Isme:** Are you free later to come round to the flat?
> I'd really like to see you
>
> **Maddy:** Will Neil be there?
>
> **Isme:** Absolutely not.
>
> **Maddy:** I'll be round at 7

I had a well-rehearsed speech planned, filled with apologies and philosophical quotes that would be right up her street, but it wasn't needed. Maddy bounced into the flat, shoved a bottle of wine into my hands and said, "Babe, let's just forget everything that happened and move on. Life's too short for petty fall-outs."

I'm not one for hugging it out, but in that moment I felt overwhelmingly grateful to have my mate back, and I couldn't help but wrap my arms around her and give her a good squeeze.

"Is this the Will?" asked Maddy, a couple of glasses in. She picked the brown envelope up from the coffee table, which was now a makeshift coaster.

"Yeah. I don't know why I haven't burnt the bastard yet, for all the shit it's caused me."

Maddy smiled to herself. "That reminds me of this client meeting I was in once, taking notes. Apparently, the client's mum changed her Will to leave everything to a local dog's home after they had a falling out, and he was absolutely fuming!"

"Ha! I can imagine."

"Anyway, turned out he needn't have worried because the Will was invalid anyway. The old bag forgot to get it signed by two witnesses, so the family contested it and everything got distributed as per the first Will."

I laughed. Whilst I may have a bit of a mental block/disinterest when it comes to matters of law, one thing I had picked up somewhere along the way was that a Will has to be signed by two witnesses to be valid.

"Who signed your *yiayia's* Will?"

"Some family friend and her daughter, who was one of Mum's school friends when they lived over in Cyprus."

Maddy took the Will out of the envelope and started scanning the words. "So, if she was a friend of your mum's, that must have made her what, eighteen? Nineteen?"

"Yeah, I think so. Why?"

"Just checking. A witness has to be over the age of eighteen when they sign it, you see."

I took the Will off Maddy and checked the date again: 14th August 1987, two months after Mum's eighteenth birthday. But what about her friend? Curiosity getting the better of me, I typed a message to Mum and bolted up from my seat like a dog hearing the word 'walkies' when her reply came through a few minutes later.

"I don't fucking believe it."

"Shit, Isme, what?"

Unable to find any words, I handed Maddy the phone and showed her Mum's message.

> **Mum:** 20th August. I always remember because that was the date we fled Cyprus

*

EMAIL

From: john@wills-direct.com

To: Ismeena Eliades

Re: Will enquiry

Dear Ismeena,

Thank you for your recent enquiry.

We have reviewed the Will you have sent us and can confirm that it is, indeed, invalid as one of the witnesses who signed the Will was under the age of eighteen at the time of signing.

You have advised that your *yiayia* had a previous (valid) Will which excluded the term regarding the beneficiaries marrying someone of Greek heritage before accessing their inheritance.

We can therefore apply to the court for the estate to be redistributed in accordance with the old Will, which would essentially mean you would be able to access your share without the need for marriage.

Please note that this will have no bearing on the inheritance already accessed by your sister.

I will be in touch again once I have made the application to the court. In the meantime, if you have any queries, please let me know.

Regards,
John

I was right on the phone to Mum to tell her I'd be round after work with some 'big news', to which she replied, "Oh God, Isme, please don tell me you are having a baby and don know who father is?"

"Sit," I instructed Mum and Dad, signalling in the direction of the dining table. Once in position, I pushed the email across the table and waited for their reaction that I'd been imagining in my head all afternoon – Mum would gasp and clutch her chest as she fought back the tears, whilst Dad would applaud me on my discovery.

What I got was the pair of them squinting at the piece of paper like it'd been written by The Borrowers, before scurrying off to get their glasses.

"Hang on, after all this, the Will wasn't even valid?" said Dad, after an excruciating number of minutes reading.

"WHA?" Mum snatched Dad's glasses out of his hand and started scanning the page hurriedly.

I smiled smugly. "Yep, *Yiayia* must have been in a rush to get it signed before they fled Cyprus, so either the solicitor thought they'd be able to get away with it or it was a genuine oversight."

Mum, a few seconds behind, piped up from behind the paper. "So what this mean? I don understand?"

"It *means*, Mother, that we can contest its validity and, if successful, the terms of her previous Will stand, i.e. that I don't need to marry a Greek man by the time I'm thirty-five. So we can get the £25k and share the money as a family!"

Dad sighed. "This money, it's yours, Isme. Not ours."

"But I want to help you out. It's all I've wanted to do ever since you told me about the money you lost."

"I know, love, and that's really kind of you, but we're doing OK now after getting that windfall off Carol. It's yours, and there's no chance we'd take it from you."

I sat back in my chair and let the realisation sink in that I could shortly have twenty-five thousand pounds in my bank account. Twenty-five big ones. The most money I'd ever had in there was three thousand when my student loan got paid in, and I got so excited, it was spent within a month, mostly on vodka and doner kebabs.

"You could use it to start up that cake business you've been dreaming about doing for years," said Dad. "It would certainly be enough to get you all set up."

I sighed. "It's not as easy as that, Dad. For starters, I signed a three-year contract with Mulligan's when I got the promotion."

Mum, who had been sitting silently throughout most of my conversation with Dad, sat forward in her seat and placed a hand over mine. "Un-sign it. You never been happy in that place, Isme. This is your chance to do something else, something you love! You should take it."

I smiled gratefully. It was a surprising turn of events, Mum encouraging me to follow my dreams and not the money, but a pleasant surprise all the same.

"What would you tell your friends at church *then*?" I teased.

"I tell them, I tell them my daughter is going to be thee next Paul Hollywood of Liverpool!"

I grimaced awkwardly. "Well, Paul is a wool from Wallasey. Can I be Mary instead?"

"OK, I tell them my daughter is going to be thee next Mary Berry of Liverpool then!"

I smiled. "Much better."

*

Dad: Hi Isme, it's your Dad. Don't forget we're round at Carol's for tea later to meet the rest of the family Love, Dad 😊🛡️

Isme: Don't worry, I haven't forgotten, although

I'm a bit nervous 😰

Dad: Don't be daft love, there's nothing to be
nervous about
Love, Dad 🧑‍🦳 🐾

Isme: What if they don't like me?? Or you end up
liking them more than me??

Dad: They're going to love you, just the way I do 😌
Love, Dad 🫶 🐾

Carol greeted me at the door, pulling me in for a hug. She smelt like someone who had spent all morning cooking in the kitchen, which reminded me of Mum – familiar and homely. I felt myself relax. "I can't wait for you to meet everyone!"

I took a deep breath and followed Carol through to the front room, which was busier than the number ten bus at rush hour. I waved over at Mum, who was standing with Dad by the glass cabinet, and she smiled back meekly. She seemed to be, dare I say it, quiet and reserved – two words I'd never associate with Elana Eliades.

The same couldn't unfortunately be said for the twins, who were attempting a game of tag, weaving in and out of people's legs, almost knocking them over in the process. Refreshingly, it was George who kept a watchful eye on them and towed them back in line every now and then, allowing Maria to sip on her wine and chat to some family members.

"Isme, hi, I've heard so much about you already."

Andrew, Carol's son, was nothing like I'd envisaged. After hearing he was a keen businessman, I expected him to look a bit like a Wall Street banker, all suited and booted shouting down his phone to one of his minions. But actual real-life Andrew was quite the opposite – a bit like Mark Zuckerberg in his non-descript navy T-shirt, dark blue denim jeans and grey Nikes, except he also had a beard and glasses. His fiancée, Julia, seemed just as unassuming.

"Congratulations on the wedding! You must be so excited."

"Well, that's if this one doesn't change her mind beforehand and leaves me standing at the altar!" Julia gave him a gentle nudge and Andrew kissed her on the top of her head.

"Are you able to make it?" asked Julia, in an almost pleading way. "I know it's on New Year's Eve, and you've probably got other plans, but we'd really love it if you could."

"Of course! I'd never turn down a party, it's my middle name!"

"Then you're especially going to like the Jäegermeister ice bar we'll have set up," said Andrew, with a wink.

The sight of the spread Carol had put on almost took my breath away; it was like that scene from *Hook* with Robin Williams, where he imagines all the food being there and then the table is jam-packed with all his favourite food. I looked over at Mum, expecting her to look put out at being upstaged on the Greek feast front, but she looked suitably impressed, and I even heard her asking Carol how she managed to get her hummus so smooth (it's all in the blend, apparently).

Sitting there, tucking into the delicious food, reminded me of so many nights at home growing up, the sound of cutlery hitting plates amongst the endless stream of conversation and occasional bursts of laughter. I felt like I had done back then: at home, like I'd known everyone much longer than a couple of hours.

I looked over at Dad who was chatting to Carol, his face beaming. He caught my gaze and smiled over in my direction. I knew in that moment that it wasn't a case of them *or* us, but them *and* us.

*

Cake business set up to-do list:

1. Come up with a name. 'Isme's Cakes' – too boring. 'Greek Delights' – sounds like a backstreet massage parlour. 'Creamy Creations' – sounds a bit perverse.

2. Buy equipment.

3. Open business bank account.

4. Set up Facebook and Instagram pages.

It was the last weekend before Christmas and I still needed to finish my Christmas shopping, but instead spent most of it putting more thought into the cake business, or the feasibility of it, jotting down a to-do list and even putting a spreadsheet together of my predictions for income and expenses in the first twelve months.

The conclusion? It wasn't going to make me even half of what I earned at Mulligan's, at least not in the first year anyway, but I had to be hopeful that if I could stretch out the £25k for as long as possible then I *could* make it work. I mean, Alan Sugar started out without a bean, selling electricals from a van, and look at him now. A miserable fucker, I know, but absolutely minted all the same.

As I made my way up in the rickety lift to the office on Monday morning, my mind was still racing with thoughts of the business. I was so deep in thought I didn't notice somebody sitting in one of the reception chairs as I walked through, but it wasn't long before the smell of chip fat hit my nostrils.

"Carlos, what are *you* doing here?" I peered around to make sure no one else was there – the last thing I needed was the office to think that Carlos was some kind of pathetic rebound.

"Isme, long time no see." He went to kiss me on the cheek, which I dodged before pushing him into the nearest available meeting room.

"Look, if you're here to try and get with me again because you heard I'm not engaged any more, then you can do one."

Carlos looked a little taken aback. "No, Isme. I come for some advice. I am going to buy a house and your mama say you can help me with all the legal stuff."

"Oh." I felt a flush creep across my cheeks. "I know nothing about buying a house, Carlos. It's a conveyancer you need. I can put you in touch with—"

He wasn't listening – someone had caught his attention from outside the room. I followed his gaze to find Zara striding through reception, laughing and joking with one of her cronies. She looked over and her face turned crimson when she caught sight of Carlos. He made to stand but she scurried away like a mouse escaping the clutches of a cat.

"Do you two know each other?"

"Yeah, we know each other very well," smirked Carlos.

I almost choked on my own spit. "Ha! Yeah, right."

He looked away into the distance and clutched his chest as if he was about to recite a poem by Shakespeare. "I will never forget the date, fifth of November, bonfire night. The night all my dreams came true – and there weren't just fireworks going off outside, if you know what I mean!"

With my mind racing, I grabbed my phone from my bag, opening up Zara's profile on Facebook and the picture she had posted of her and Anthony. That's when I realised – it was a repost from the year before when the three of us had been in the pub, and you could just make out some of my hair on the other side of Anthony where she'd cropped me out.

I slumped down into my seat and put my head in my hands. In the words of Bradley Cooper in the opening scene of *The Hangover*, 'we fucked up'.

And by we, I mean me.

*

'I'm also just a girl, standing in front of a boy, asking him to love her.'

Terrible idea watching *Notting Hill*, one of my all-time favourite romantic comedies. I was sobbing uncontrollably by the end of it, especially the scene where she goes into the shop and declares her love for him. It just made me think about Anthony at the party, and how much it must have taken him to open his heart up to me like that, only for me to slam it down on the floor and stamp all over it. "God, you're such a tit, Isme," I declared to the empty flat after the film finished, and wiped my wet face with a tissue.

I'd spent the last three weeks since the engagement party convincing myself that rejecting Anthony's declaration of love was the right thing to do and that, over time, I'd get over my feelings for him, and soon it would all be nothing more than a distant memory. I'd been so blinded by the thought that he'd gone to see Zara the night we nearly kissed, which helped me to lock away my feelings for him behind the wall of anger and upset I'd felt. But now I knew it wasn't true, the wall had come tumbling down and all I wanted to do was tell him how I felt – which was that I was so in love with him it hurt.

I'd contemplated going round to his house and making a Julia Roberts style speech on his doorstep, but the fear of rejection pulled me back every time. What if he'd changed his mind about his feelings since the party? Or worse, what if he'd moved on already?

The thought of either made my chest hurt. What the fuck was I going to do?

*

Isme: Happy Christmas

It was hardly a declaration of love, more an olive branch, but it was a start. Anthony replied a few minutes later.

It may have only been three simple words, but it meant so much more.

"ISME, ARE YOU AWAKE? COME ON, WE DO THEE PRESENTS NOW."

I jolted at the sound of Mum's foghorn voice coming from the bottom of the stairs.

The succulent smell of pork roasting in the oven perfumed the air as I made my way down and into the living room, where Mum and Dad were waiting by the brightly lit fake Christmas tree. It had witnessed many an Eliades chaotic Christmas, hence its tired-looking branches and lopsidedness.

"Happy Christmas, *koumera*!" said Mum, wrapping me up in a hug. She smelt of cinnamon and baked bread, which made my stomach growl.

"Happy Christmas, love." The lights on the tree reflected off Dad's face, highlighting his gleaming eyes and ruddy cheeks, and his hefty frame filled his pyjamas perfectly. It was quite a contrast to the weak, fragile man that lay in the hospital bed only five months earlier, and I couldn't help but smile to myself.

I handed Mum and Dad my gifts first, with Dad smiling gratefully at the Fitbit I bought him until asking what it was. (It *was* a risky purchase considering how much of a technophobe he was. I remember trying to show him how to use an iPod – it was like trying to teach a baby Pythagoras's theorem.)

Mum tore through her wrapping paper like a drug addict

opening their latest stash, exclaimed how lovely the scarf was that I picked for her without making any attempt to try it on, and then thrust a red gift bag into my hands.

"Happy Christmas, *agape-mou*." Mum watched eagerly as I lifted a rectangular-shaped box out of the bag and started tearing off the paper. Whatever it was, I hoped to God I liked it, or I was going to have to pull out the big guns on the present poker-face game.

"Ah, Mum, it's lovely!" I exclaimed, running my hand over the smooth rose-gold whisk and my initials that she'd had engraved on the handle.

"For when you start your new business," said Mum, gleaming.

I suddenly felt overcome with emotion. I made to stand to give Mum a thankful hug, but she stopped me in my tracks.

"Wait, there's more in the bag!"

Intrigued, I sat back down and reached into the bag to find a smaller rectangular box. A set of rose gold measuring cups to match the whisk, perhaps? Or some metric spoons?

"PREGNACARE VITAMINS? Mum, I haven't even got a fella!"

"Ah yes, but the lady in the shop say you can start taking them now, you know, to get everything ready."

I stared at Mum, then Dad, and back again, waiting for the punchline, but Dad just shrugged his shoulders and Mum started to clear up the wrapping paper, confirming the end of present time.

*

"Aw, Maria, they're beautiful!" I gasped, admiring the silver clover-shaped earrings in their box.

"They're made of moonstone, which is the stone of new

beginnings. I just thought they were quite fitting."

I swallowed down the lump that had formed in my throat. I knew she was referring to the baking business, but it didn't stop me from thinking about Anthony. "That's really thoughtful, thank you."

"It was my idea." George winked, and Maria gave him a gentle shove.

"Uncle Isme, are these for us?" asked Theo, indicating to the remaining two wrapped presents under the tree.

"They are indeed. Merry Christmas, my two little bezzies." I managed to give them a quick squeeze before they began tearing off the wrapping paper like crazed animals.

"OUR OWN BAKING SETS!" cried Tomaso, holding up the box. "Look, Theo, our own baking sets!"

"WOW!" Theo began tearing open the box and emptied the contents all over the living room carpet for a closer inspection.

"Well, I know how much you enjoyed baking with me at the flat, so I thought you might like your own tools and stuff . . . You can leave it all at the flat for when you're staying over at mine and we'll do it together," I quickly added for Maria's benefit, who smiled appreciatively.

"Thank you, Uncle Isme!" The twins came bounding over to me and threw their tiny arms around my neck, and a warmth filled my chest.

Mum soon declared that Christmas dinner was ready, and we all made our way into the dining room.

"Let's hope we're not on rations today," whispered Maria, but she couldn't have been more wrong. The dining table was a wonderful sight of crispy roasted potatoes, homemade christopsomo bread, lahanodolades (cabbage rolls filled with minced meat and rice), Greek salad with pomengrate and, in the middle, a traditional roast pork seasoned with rosemary and thyme.

"Bleedin' ell, Elana, when are the rest of Liverpool coming?" laughed Dad, taking his seat at one end of the table, with Mum at the opposite end. She stayed stood up while we all sat down, and clinked her glass. The room descended into silence.

"I just want to say, it has been a tough year for me and your papa. But we wouldn't have got through it without our . . ." Her voice broke off and tears began filling her eyes. ". . . Our family."

Dad cleared his throat and stood up, holding his glass of beer in the air. "*Yamas!*"

"*Yamas!*" We all repeated in unison, taking a sip of our drinks before tucking into the food.

*

Andrew and Julia's wedding was being held in a hotel a short walk from the flat, although it felt much longer trudging through the frost-covered streets in my block-heeled boots, trying not to go arse over tit.

It was taking place in one of the hotels largest rooms on the ground floor, with floor-to-ceiling windows that led out to the waterfront, and grand high ceilings, which had been decorated with illuminated drapes and pretty flowers for the occasion.

The décor itself was minimalist but classy – tall candelabras with draping crystals and round flower bouquets in the middle of every other table, white chair covers with cream chiffon drapes tied into a neat bow at the back. Most impressive, though, was the ice bar in the far corner of the room that was serving up shots of Jäegermeister, amongst other things.

The bar was calling out to me like a mothership, and after greeting the bride and groom, who looked so blissfully happy I got a pang of the green-eye, I headed over. But I'd no sooner had my first sip when Carol came bouncing over with Mum, like two excitable kids, demanding I join them on the dancefloor for the *Tsamiko* dance – a traditional Greek dance involving everyone forming a semi-circle on the dancefloor and shuffling from side to side while the person on the end does some acrobatic style high leaps.

I'd never been able to get the hang of it and always seemed to end up in the unfortunate position of being wedged between the two sweatiest, hairiest men. I'd always managed to get through it though by making sure I was suitably well-oiled beforehand, but tonight I didn't have that luxury.

I ended up next to Andrew, who was going to be the designated acrobatic, meaning I had to support his weight as he did his thing. Easy enough. But as the *bouzouki* band started playing, and the circle started moving, something from the edge of the dancefloor caught my eye.

Was it . . . ? Could it be . . . ?

Completely distracted, I shuffled my feet one too many to the right whilst everyone else went left, causing me to pierce my four-inch heels into Andrew's foot. He cried out in pain, hopping from one foot to the other, causing him to lose his balance and fall into me. The effect was like a game of dominoes, and the whole circle ended up in a heap on the floor.

"Bloody hell, Freckiades, you really know how to make a scene, don't you?" laughed Anthony, wiping away tears from his face.

"I, I thought you weren't coming?"

I hadn't expected him to say yes when I'd sent him a message inviting him to come as my plus-one a few days earlier – after some persuasion from Maria – but it still hadn't hurt any less when he replied saying he already had plans. Yet here he was, standing right in front of me in his smart navy suit, looking every inch my Greek knight in shining armour that I'd been waiting for all year.

"I wasn't, but someone told me you were doing the *Tsamiko* and I thought, I can't miss that. Remember my uncle's wedding when you kicked so hard your shoe fell off and hit someone right in the kipper?"

"How could I forget? The poor woman ended up needing stitches!"

We laughed at the memory, and for a moment it felt like the old uncomplicated us, the events of the last year nothing but a bad dream.

I took a deep breath, ready to have a conversation I'd been having with him in my head since finding out that he wasn't with Zara the night we nearly kissed. But as I looked up, Anthony appeared distracted by something over my shoulder. I turned round to find the Eliades clan gawping at us like we were performing seals.

"Shall we?" I said, pointing in the direction of the door that led outside to the waterfront.

It was a bitter December night, one that didn't warrant wearing a dress with no tights. We stood by the water, the waves glistening like silvery threads against the light of the moon. I didn't realise I was shivering until Anthony took off his suit jacket and placed it around my shoulders, his integrated body heat thawing me. It was such a simple gesture, yet it felt like the most intimate thing in the world, and I became very aware of my heartbeat, which was thumping hard against my chest.

I couldn't wait any longer. I needed him to know how I felt.

"Anthony, I'm sorry. I jumped to conclusions about you and Zara even though nothing was going on, you told me you loved me, and I pushed you away and, and—"

"Woah, calm down! You'll upset those peacocks on your eyes... They look great, by the way. *You* look great."

I smiled sheepishly, whilst making a mental note to thank Maddy for giving me one of her Scouseovers. I'd been apprehensive, especially when she pulled out the eyelashes that looked so big I feared I could take off. But I was pleased with the end result – understated and classy.

"What made you think something was going on with me and Zara?"

I explained about the picture Zara posted on Facebook the night we nearly kissed, and how I'd assumed that's why he'd left the way he did. "I thought you'd ran off to tell her I tried to kiss you, and that the two of you were having a right old laugh behind my back."

"Wow. Well that explains your messages about not calling off the engagement. It was a jab to the heart reading that message, Isme. I'm not gonna lie."

I stared out at the water, unable to meet Anthony's gaze. "I'm sorry, Anthony. I was angry and hurt, and wanted to hurt you too." I took a deep breath as I summoned up the courage for what I was about to ask. "Everything you said at the party, did you mean it? Do you still mean it?"

Anthony hesitated for a moment, and my insides churned at the thought of facing yet another rejection. Of course he'd moved on – I was stupid and naïve to think otherwise. I swallowed down the lump that had formed in my throat.

"I meant it. I've been in love with you ever since I can remember, but was too young and stupid to do anything about it. Then you got with that tosser Neil, and everything changed."

His words sent a tingle through my body, as the realisation of his hidden love hit me. I suddenly became very aware of my wobbly legs, and steadied myself against the safety railing. "Why didn't you tell me sooner how you felt?"

Anthony put his hands in his pockets and kicked at a small stone on the floor. "I dunno. Fear of rejection, I suppose. We've been mates for so long, I just couldn't stand the thought of putting our friendship at risk and losing you completely."

I nodded. It sounded all too familiar.

"Would it have changed anything? If I had told you sooner, like?"

"It would have changed everything, Anthony. For starters,

I would have binned Neil off in a heartbeat if I'd known how you felt."

Anthony eyes widened. He took his hands out of his pockets and held them in mine. They felt warm and soft, like a cosy blanket. "Really?"

"Really."

The doors to the wedding reception suddenly burst open and all the wedding guests descended outside for what I presumed was a fire drill, until I heard someone shout "Fireworks!" and the sky came to life.

As we stood watching the dazzling display, I looked over at Anthony, just like I had on that night in the flat when we'd watched the fireworks with the twins from the flat window. Only this time I could touch the outlines of his face and not worry whether he might flinch, and he could pull me to him and press his soft warm lips down onto mine, without the twins gawping at us and making disgusted noises . . .

"Eugh, get a room!"

The sound of Maria's voice was like a distant car horn. Nothing could take me away from this moment, from the feel of Anthony's body pressed against mine as our lips interlocked. It was surreal yet familiar, like I'd spent the whole year wandering aimlessly through life and had finally made it home.

Then, a chorus of claps and whoops came from behind us. Reluctantly, I pulled away from Anthony to find Mum, Dad, Maria and George standing there with beaming smiles on their faces.

"I told you those vitamins were a good idea, Stephen," said

Mum, and we all burst into laughter, aside from Anthony who watched on in bewilderment.

Neil was right: my family *were* always there with their little problems and Greek traditions. But I wouldn't have it any other way.

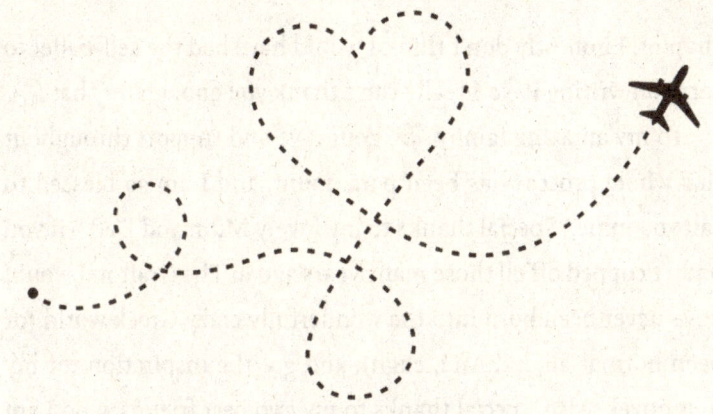

ACKNOWLEDGMENTS

First and foremost, thank you to the wonderful team at UCLan Publishing for putting their faith in the book and helping shape it into the finished (better!) version it is today. In particular, thank you to Hazel Holmes for taking it on and allowing me to be part of UCLan's launch into women's fiction. It really is an honour. Also massive thanks to my wonderful editor, Jasmine Dove – I am so grateful for all your constructive feedback and invaluable suggestions at every stage of the editing process, and for your patience for all the times I forgot to italicise certain Greek words!

To my agent, Clare Coombes of the Liverpool Literary Agency. Thank you for believing in me and my writing, and in the book when it was nothing more than a few pages of random scribbles all those six years ago! If you hadn't encouraged me to write that first chapter, I honestly don't think I would have had the self-belief to carry on writing it, so I really can't thank you enough for that 🫶.

To my amazing family 🤍. Your love and support throughout this whole process has been paramount, and I am so blessed to call you mine. Special thanks to my lovely Mum and Dad – if you hadn't copped off all those many years ago in The Grafton I would have never been born into the wonderfully crazy Greek world (or been born at all, ha! And, eugh), and got the inspiration for my first novel. Also, special thanks to my two best friends, who I am lucky enough to also call my sisters, Jayne and Helen, for giving me their feedback in the early stages of writing the book which, in summary, was 'cut down on the swear words!' 😂

Thank you to my two beautiful children, Rosie and Theo, who haven't complained (much) when I've been permanently glued to my laptop. It's been hard being so distracted and not being able to fully explain to you why (or expecting you to understand) but I hope one day you'll appreciate that if you want something, you've got to work for it, even if it means passing on a few games of marble rush or some bum-wiping (Theo). And if I can write a book through having baby number two and a global pandemic, then you can do anything! The world is yours my *agape mous*.

To all my lovely friends. Thank you for your continued support throughout this crazy journey, and for letting me have a good old moan when I've needed it (and I've needed it a lot!). I'm so glad you can all finally read it after the many times you've tried to coax the story out of me (and whether you're in it!), but save your thoughts and opinions for the book club please.

Thank you to my amazing husband, Paul. Six years ago I was about to finish my maternity leave and go back to a job I disliked, when all I wanted to do was 'walk dogs and write books'. Thanks to you, I was able to quit my job and focus on my writing (with a bit of dog-walking thrown in too!) and doubt I would have started writing the book if it wasn't for you creating the opportunity for me to do so (or at least I'd probably still be writing the first draft now!), so for that I will be eternally grateful. And for the many nights you've had to occupy yourself with hours of playing computer games, you're welcome.

Finally, a massive thanks to you, the reader. It means so much that you've decided to give my book a chance, and I truly hope you've enjoyed reading it and spending time with the crazy Eliades clan. *Yamas!* 🍻

If you liked this, you'll love . . .

Zoë Richards

Garden of her Heart

Can Holly's heart heal, and life blossom at the Pinewoods Retreat?

'A heartwarming, uplifting debut. The perfect holiday read.'
Neil Alexander

young love

suzanne ewart

'A beautifully written and relatable story of heartache, heartbreak, and the hope of young love.'
NetGalley Review